# THE AVON

### *Four years old and better than ever!*

We're celebrating our fourth anniversary...and thanks to you, our loyal readers, "The Avon Romance" is stronger and more exciting than ever! You've been telling us what you're looking for in top-quality historical romance—and we've been delivering it, month after wonderful month.

Since 1982, Avon has been launching new writers of exceptional promise—writers to follow in the matchless tradition of such Avon superstars as Kathleen E. Woodiwiss, Johanna Lindsey, Shirlee Busbee and Laurie McBain. Distinguished by a ribbon motif on the front cover, these books were quickly discovered by romance readers everywhere and dubbed "the ribbon books."

Every month "The Avon Romance" has continued to deliver the best in historical romance. Sensual, fast-paced stories by new writers (and some favorite repeats like Linda Ladd!) guarantee reading *without* the predictable characters and plots of formula romances.

"The Avon Romance"—our promise of superior, unforgettable historical romance. Thanks for making us such a dazzling success!

# SILVERSWEPT
## LINDA LADD

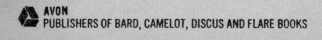

AVON
PUBLISHERS OF BARD, CAMELOT, DISCUS AND FLARE BOOKS

AVON BOOKS
A division of
The Hearst Corporation
1790 Broadway
New York, New York 10019

Copyright © 1987 by Linda Ladd
Published by arrangement with the author
Library of Congress Catalog Card Number: 86-91003
ISBN: 0-380-75204-2

First Avon Printing: May 1987

# Prologue

*Cornwall, England*
*April 5, 1811*

From Alysson Tyler's position atop a craggy
boulder, she could hear the riotous roar of the mighty
Atlantic surf pounding the cliffs behind her, but she
paid it little heed, intent upon fastening Mathilde's best
woolen shawl at an effective angle around her slender
shoulders. When it was tied just right, she straightened
the worn brown muslin skirt she wore, then pushed her
long hair over her shoulders. Her hair was her one
pride, and in truth, there were few who could disagree
that the rich, softly curling tresses that hung well below
her waist were not most beautiful. She threaded her
fingers through the honey-colored strands that glinted
with golden lights when touched by the sun. Although
she usually wore it braided into a long queue down her
back, today she was Juliet Capulet, and she wanted it
loose and shining for her Romeo.

"For pity's sake, Aly, I'm a tired of standin' here
waitin'! What are you doin' up there anyway?"

Alysson glanced down at the eleven-year-old boy
who stood complaining on the ground below her perch.

"I am preparing myself for my soliloquy, of course.
All actresses have to forget who they are and become
their part, and besides, this is the first time Juliet and
Romeo are alone together."

"Well, hurry up. Mama's cooking the rabbit I caught
yesterday, and I'm a hungry!"

1

Alysson ignored the last, turning clear green eyes to the far horizon where the barren hills were just becoming green. She knew the play by heart, every line of every part, but she stood motionless for another moment. Her fine-boned profile was tilted to an elegant angle that accentuated her delicate features as she thought about the words she was about to recite.

How would it feel to fall in love with your father's enemy? she pondered, pursing her full pink lips. Her answer came without hesitation. She would love her father's enemy just for being such. She hated her father more than any living creature on earth. Teeth clenching at the mere thought of Daniel Tyler, she shook her thoughts away, concentrating again on the coming scene. After another moment, she leaned gracefully over a flat rock before her, pretending it was a balustrade. Young Frederick scowled up at her.

"'Ay me!'" she breathed, setting her face in melancholy lines, then waited for Freddie to speak his part. But he only shifted his bare feet in the dust, frowning down at the small book he held.

"Go ahead, Freddie, say your lines."

"Hold on to yourself, I lost my place again!"

Alysson sighed, exasperated with him.

"'O, speak again, bright angel!'" she prompted him impatiently. "And do what I told you with your hat!"

Freddie pulled off his cap, revealing an unruly thatch of tan hair, then started off haltingly, the hat held awkwardly over his heart in the way Alysson had taught him.

"'O, speak again, bright angel!'" he began, his freckled face intent, his tone of voice leaving no doubt that he had been badgered into speaking the lines at all, "'for thou art as glorious as this night—'"

"'*To* this night,' Freddie!"

"'To this night, being over me—'"

"'O'er my head.'"

Freddie glared up at her then, his fists on his hips.

"I don't wanna do this anymore, Aly. I don't even know what I'm asayin'."

"You're talking about me, silly, about your true love, Juliet. Surely you can imagine how it feels to be in love with a girl!"

"No I can't," Freddie defended himself quickly. "And neither can you, I wager. You ain't had a beau either, and you're almost grown-up."

It was a sore point with Alysson, because she was almost eighteen, but she couldn't deny it since there were only a handful of men around, and most of them were farmers with wives and broods.

"You just have to read books like I do and think how it must feel, that's all. It's a feeling up here in your mind." She tapped her temple with one slender forefinger, but Freddie didn't look particularly impressed.

"Aw, criminy, Aly, I don't even like girls. They giggle and act dumb all the time—except for you," he added quickly, not ready to offend his best friend. "Anyway, we've been doin' this old play all day, and we should be gettin' back home. Your mama's gonna wake up and she'll be all upset if you ain't there."

"Oh, all right," Alysson answered, turning to climb down the rocks to where he stood.

He was right about her mother. Even though Mama had been better lately, sometimes lucid for hours, she did get agitated and worried if Alysson wasn't there to soothe her. The darker times when she sank into her private world of the past were still frequent but not as lengthy. Just the other night Mama had laughed aloud when Alysson had mimicked the shrill voice and pinched-nose expression of hateful old Parson Clements of the Anglican Church. Alysson smiled at the memory.

She pulled her hair over her shoulder when she reached Freddie, braiding it with quick, deft fingers, then handed Freddie her prized scarlet ribbon to tie it for her. The ribbon had been a gift from a traveling peddler in return for a hot meal, and Alysson treasured it.

"Give me the book, Freddie, so you won't lose it," she said as he finished tying the bow, and he complied gladly. Alysson stuffed it in her skirt pocket as they began to make their way down a rocky ravine to the stone cottage in which they lived with their mothers. Frederick's mother, Mathilde, was from the Hesse-Darmstadt region of Germany and was their only servant, but Alysson considered both Mathilde and her son as part of her family. She loved them more than she had ever loved the man who had sired her.

"How about us playin' pirates down at the caves after you take your mother on her walk," Freddie suggested, brown eyes alight with his newest idea.

"I'm too old for that."

"No you're not, and besides, that's not fair. I play Romeo and that little elf—what's his name—when you want me to, but when I want you to do something you always say you're too old!"

"His name is Puck," Alysson said, but seeing the disappointment on her young friend's face, she relented. "Oh, all right, I will, but it will have to be later."

"They say there's treasure buried around here, you know," Freddie called back as he ran ahead and sent a rock hurling out over the rocky hill. "From when the storms drove the Great Armada of Spain into the cliffs. Maybe we'll find it someday and become as rich as kings! Then I could buy my own ship and we'd be real pirates!"

Alysson smiled at the way Freddie's eyes had grown round with excitement. "You could take Mama and me to America to find Adam Sinclair. She would be happy again if she were with him—he was her one true love, you know. And I would become a famous actress."

"You will anyway, Aly. You're already better than those players who came through at Christmastide. None of them could mimic the voices of other people like you can, and even they applauded when you made your voice come from somewhere else."

Alysson felt a warm glow of pleasure at his compliments. She was proud of her gift for mimicry and throwing her voice. She had discovered it when she was barely eight years old, the day her grandfather Laurence had roared with laughter when she made her dog talk like their prim little butler.

Pain clouded her face. It was only the year after that he had died and Alysson's father had sent them away from their beautiful London house to live alone here in the country. She shook off such memories, not liking to think about them, as they came upon a succession of flat red rocks. She stopped there and looked down at the cottage below with its steep-pitched thatch roof and the curling plume of gray smoke rising from the kitchen chimney. She raised her gaze to the vast view of Cornwall, and her eyes sharpened as a black carriage rolled into sight on the serpentine dirt road from the village of Penzance. She froze; her heart plummeted to her toes.

"Oh, no, Freddie, he's coming!"

Freddie looked up fearfully and fixed his eyes on the coach, traveling at a high rate of speed toward the lane to their farmhouse.

"You've got to stop him, Freddie! So I can get to Mama first. Put something in the road so his driver will have to get out and move it! And shut the gate!"

Freddie was already off, scrambling and sliding on his backside down a steep hill that led to the road, and Alysson ran in the opposite direction, leaping from boulder to boulder until she reached the point where the cliffs began to level into barren fields of tan grasses. Able to run faster now, her feet flew over the well-worn path, and all the while she berated herself for wandering so far from the house. If only she had known he was coming! Then they could have gotten her mother away from the cottage and well hidden! He hadn't come in over a year now, and she had grown complacent about his visits.

A low stone wall traversed the eastern edge of the small copse, the crumbling rocks nearly covered with weeds, and Alysson leapt it at a run, frightening Minerva where she grazed nearby. The old brood mare jerked away, then trotted off indignantly, but Alysson wasted no thoughts on the horse as she darted through the trees to their front garden, where Mathilde somehow managed to coax wild flowers and vegetables from the rocky ground.

Always fleet of foot and agile, Alysson burst through the wood-slatted gate, which squealed on rusty hinges before banging shut behind her. She bounded up the pebbled path then into the kitchen door, startling Mathilde where she stood before a black kettle suspended over the brick hearth. The sturdy German woman jerked around, her long wooden spoon in hand. Her wide, smooth face was ruddy and flushed from hovering so near the bubbling stew, but she recovered her shock as Alysson ran past her, thundering up the crude steps that led to the second-floor bedchambers.

"What ye be thinkin' ta do, *Fräulein?*" Mathilde began, shaking her head with its braided crown of gray hair. Her English was heavily accented, and she finished by a warning shake of the utensil in her fist. "Yer mudder still be asleepin'! Do ye wanta be wakin' her with yer racket?"

"He's coming, Mathilde! Freddie's gone to latch the carriage gate!"

The stern expression on Mathilde's face fled abruptly, and she paled, dropping the spoon to the table. Without a word, she rushed toward the front parlor to set the bolt, well rehearsed in the precautions taken when the master decided to visit his wife.

Alysson took the rest of the steep stairs two at a time, swinging around the newel post on the upstairs landing, the rickety banister wobbling precariously as she let it go. She ran down the narrow, low-ceilinged hallway to her mother's bedchamber door. Panting hard from her run, she drew up for an instant to catch her breath. Please, Lord, let her be in her right mind, please, Alysson prayed silently. She must not frighten Mama, or she would begin to scream; then they would never get her to a hiding place. Forcing a bright smile, she turned the door handle and peeked inside.

"Mama? Are you awake?"

The frail and wasted shell of a woman lying in the bed started slightly at the sound of Alysson's low voice, then pushed herself up on one elbow to stare at Alysson out of faded blue eyes.

"Who are you?"

The question was hesitant, and Alysson groaned in dismay, glancing toward the casement windows which had been opened for the warm spring weather. Was that the rattle of his carriage she heard? She moved forward quickly, a thread of urgency roughening her voice despite her attempt to hide her anxiety.

"Mama, it's me, Alysson, your daughter. You know that. We go on walks together every day. Remember, we fed a carrot to Minerva yesterday, just before it rained."

Judith Hampstead Tyler's eyes narrowed, and she tilted her head, twisting a long strand of graying blond hair around her finger as she tried to remember the slim young girl before her. She frowned slightly, slender fingers trembling as she pressed them against her wrinkled cheeks.

"My daughter? Are you really?"

"Yes, Mama, of course I am, but we must hurry now," Alysson murmured in the crooning voice that she and Mathilde had learned to use when Mama was frightened. She took hold of her mother's thin arm and helped Judith from the bed. She kept her voice low and gentle as she guided one thin arm into the sleeve of a faded silk robe.

"All the wild flowers are blooming now, Mama, the gorse is all yellow and bright. We'll pick some if you like, but we must hurry."

Judith giggled, the high-pitched sound that only the mad could make, and Alysson gasped, trying to stifle it with her palm.

"Sssh, Mama, please," she whispered as they made their way into the dusky corridor. They stopped in their tracks as a feared masculine voice bellowed Judith's name from somewhere below. Judith's whole body went rigid, and Alysson tried to support her mother's weight when she suddenly went limp. Alysson looked around frantically as booted feet clomped with heavy tread upon the steps, and Judith sank to her knees and whimpered, her eyes dark with fear.

Daniel Tyler appeared on the stairs before Alysson could move, first his head with its slicked-back dark brown hair, then his powerful shoulders encased in an expensive navy blue cape. He turned his head and Alysson shivered as his steely blue-gray eyes trapped her where she stood. His face was long and thin, and though not particularly ugly, it was offensive to look upon—a face perpetually flushed, reflecting a life of debauchery, and cold eyes, lacking any semblance of compassion. He smiled at them, an evil, malignant show of teeth, and Alysson's eyes dropped to the short black riding crop he gripped tightly in one strong, black-gloved hand. He slapped it threateningly against his thigh, in a way that Alysson knew very well, and her stomach twisted with terror and great, loathing hatred.

Daniel climbed the last two steps, his eyes never leaving his daughter's. "You weren't so clever this time, girl, were you now? My dear little Judith will have to enjoy my husbandly attentions after all."

A low moan came from deep inside Judith's throat, a terrible, pathetic trapped sound, as Daniel Tyler crossed his arms over his chest, his whip held idly in his right hand. He laughed softly as his wife hid her face in the folds of her daughter's skirt. When he took a step toward them, Alysson moved protectively in front of her mother.

"I won't let you beat her, Papa," she said, her own voice trembling so much that her words wavered together. Judith's hands clutched tighter at the back of Alysson's skirt.

Daniel stopped, his lips curving in an amused twist, and his words came low and oil smooth. "Do you defy me, Alysson?"

Alysson could not speak, remembering other times he had used that tone, and she had to exert a conscious effort not to sprint away from him. He still grinned at her, and Alysson gasped when he moved so quickly that she couldn't dodge. Hurting hands clamped over her arm, twisting it cruelly behind her back before he gave her a hard shove. She grunted with pain as her shoulder hit the wall, and she crumpled to her knees as her father loomed over her, the whip raised above his head.

She tried to elude the blow as it whistled downward but could not, and it landed against her back with a biting explosion of pain. She screamed in agony and tried to scrabble away as he raised it again, but his arm froze in midair as Judith jumped to her feet from where she had cringed near the banister. Shrieking words of insane hatred, she flew at her husband, clawing at his face.

Daniel dropped the whip as her long nails raked down the side of his face, drawing blood, then he bellowed an enraged curse, drawing back one meaty fist and sending it against Judith's fragile cheekbone. The immense blow sent Judith flying backward into the railing, and Alysson screamed in absolute horror as the balustrade cracked and gave way, hurtling her mother to the floor below.

Alysson ran to the top of the steps, moaning as she saw her mother sprawled lifelessly on the kitchen flagstones, her head at an impossible angle. A sob caught in Alysson's throat as she ran down the steps to kneel at her mother's side.

Blood trickled in an obscene crimson path from the corner of Judith's mouth, and Alysson began to weep as she gently lifted a thin, limp hand and held it against her cheek.

Daniel Tyler moved down the steps to stand just behind his daughter. His words were indifferent.

"If the bitch is dead, get her out of here."

Judith Hampstead Tyler was buried the next afternoon. The lovely spring weather that had visited the countryside fled, as if consoling those who mourned her death, and rain threatened with swift-moving gray clouds that hung over the landscape until pushed out to sea by howling, moaning winds. The willow tree near the front windows of the cottage was tossed and shaken by gusts, flinging spattering rain to run in forking rivulets down the oval casement windows. In the small parlor, a plain wooden box had been placed upon a long trestle table that had been dragged in from the kitchen.

Alysson sat with Mathilde and Frederick on a short bench in front of the coffin, and Daniel Tyler surveyed the three contemptuously as he retrieved his small gold snuffbox from his coat pocket. He opened the lid and pinched a bit of the tobacco between his thumb and forefinger. He pushed it into his nostril, breathing deeply to draw the potent substance into his thin, aristocratic nose. After the sneeze that followed, he leaned back in the shabby wing chair and folded his hands over his stomach. He wished the damned parson would be done with the ridiculous mumble-jumble that he was spewing forth in his irritating nasal voice. Judith's death had indeed been fortuitous, though he had not intended to kill her. But it worked well with his plans, the only nuisance being that he was forced to stay an extra day to see her put into the ground. Pressing matters awaited him in London, especially now that Donovan MacBride was in England, trying to block the wedding.

His eyes hardened as he watched Alysson wipe her tears with a lacy white handkerchief while the old German woman tried to comfort her. The little chit legally bore his name, but he had never known for sure if she was his. His teeth came together as the bitter memory punctured his mind like so many steel spikes. Twenty years had gone by since Judith Hampstead had humiliated him by running off with another man while she was betrothed to him—with a nobody, a penniless actor from the American colonies. He had never allowed her to forget the embarrassment she had caused him.

He had never really loved her anyway, of course. Their engagement had been arranged by Judith's father, Laurence Hampstead, and it was the Tyler name and title that Laurence had wanted, and the respectability and prestige that went with it. Daniel himself had been more than willing to marry into the wealthy merchant family. Judith's dowry alone had replenished his dwindling coffers. Laurence Hampstead had been enraged when his carefully drawn plans were thwarted by Judith's elopement, and it had been he who had hired men to bring her back. Their marriage had been performed the same day she returned, and when Judith had become pregnant at once, Daniel was never quite sure if she carried her lover's seed or his own. It galled him to this day that he had not been able to force the name of the man out of Judith, not even after Laurence Hampstead had died ten years ago and left both Judith and Alysson in his complete control, as well as the vast Hampstead fortune. It gradually had grown to the point where he couldn't stand the sight of her, and he had sent her here to Cornwall where he wouldn't have to abide her or her brat. But now she was dead, and it would be easier for him to force Alysson to marry the American.

He stared at his daughter a moment, objectively assessing her appearance. She had inherited her mother's hair, a rich red-gold that gleamed even now beneath the black woolen veil she wore. She was a beauty, as Judith had been before she began to age and lose her mind. Alysson's eyes were particularly lovely, as green as emeralds, breathtaking against her smooth white skin. He smiled. Donovan MacBride had tried for over a year to get out of the marriage contract he had signed years ago in a business deal with Laurence Hampstead, but perhaps when MacBride saw Alysson with his own eyes he might change his mind.

Daniel sat up as the parson finally ended his droning eulogy and stepped forward to pat Alysson's arm. Daniel signaled with a jerk of his head, and the two grave diggers he had hired clumped from the back of the room in their shabby homespun coats and mud-caked boots. They picked up the casket, both men casting compassionate glances at the beautiful girl weeping so pitiably. He stood as they passed him, swirling his heavy wool cape over his shoulders.

Outside, a fine steady drizzle drenched the ground, making it difficult to walk, and Daniel kept his regard on Alysson's trim figure as they walked slowly through the soggy yard to the gravesite on a hill behind the cottage. He had never paid much attention to her in her childhood years, and it mattered little to her since her grandfather Hampstead had fawned over her every word and action. It was Laurence's love for the girl that had prompted him to secure her future with the American, that and the lucrative business contract that went along with it. Laurence Hampstead had not been a man who neglected his business interests.

Daniel had spent those years working with the anti-American factions in Parliament. He had hated the upstart Americans with their talk of freedom and equality even before Judith had run away with one of them, and he was still ready to do anything in his power to see the United States brought back into the British harness. Now Alysson had become a very important, if unwitting, pawn to accomplish just that, and her beauty would be an extra enticement to persuade MacBride to honor the agreement. He really had no choice, anyway; he had been legally bound to Alysson since he had penned his name beneath Laurence Hampstead's signature.

Daniel chuckled to himself, pulling his cape tighter at the throat as wind drove stinging gusts to strike his face. He hadn't been able to believe his good fortune the day Laurence Hampstead's solicitors had presented him with the betrothal agreement between MacBride and Alysson. He had recognized the name at once. His informants in America knew MacBride well and had even heard rumors that he was involved in American espionage. If so, all the better, and if not, MacBride was still a prominent New York patriot and businessman. But even more important to Daniel and his agents, MacBride had high connections in the American Congress and even with President Madison himself. With Alysson married into such a household, Daniel's agents in New York would have legitimate social connections to the inner circle of American politics. With war about to erupt between England and America, he wanted Alysson there and married to MacBride, and he would see it done, by god, no matter what he had to do to accomplish it.

Alysson watched with hollow eyes as the coffin was lowered into the rectangular black hole to settle at the bottom, the ropes slapping against the wooden sides as they were pulled out again. Poor Mama, she thought with aching heart. Perhaps she was at peace at last. That's what Mathilde had said. She blinked back a fresh wave of tears, her fingers groping for the dainty cross of intricately wrought silver filigree where it hung around her neck. Adam Sinclair had given the necklace to her mother before Alysson had been born, and Judith had never taken it off, not until yesterday when Mathilde had removed it to prepare her body for burial. Now it was all Alysson had left of her mother.

A clod of dirt hit the top of the casket with a dull, final thud, and Alysson watched silently as the two men built a mound of red mud shovelful by shovelful. She felt Mathilde's arm around her shoulders, urging her to her feet, and she stood, moving to the grave to lay upon it the small bouquet of wild daisies that Freddie had picked early that morning. She turned to leave, but cruel fingers settled in a painful grip on her arm.

"Prepare yourself to come to London with me, girl," her father's detested voice said close to her ear. "You are to be wed there."

Alysson jerked away from his touch, her face twisted with hatred. Daniel flinched at the look in her green eyes.

"Never," she said through gritted teeth. "I will never marry and let myself be beaten and abused by a man as you did to Mother."

Daniel's initial surprise at her defiance turned to pure rage, and he swung the back of his hand at her face. Alysson groaned and fell sideways against her mother's grave, tasting the metallic tang of blood as it welled from her split lip.

"You'll do as I say, girl, or you'll end up in a hole like your whoring mother."

Mathilde began to cry as he strode away with long angry strides, then knelt by Alysson, dabbing gently at the blood oozing from the cut at the corner of her mouth.

"I won't do it," Alysson murmured, her small chin rising with a determination that rose from the very core of her soul. "Never. I would *rather* be dead than do his bidding."

# Chapter 1

The dainty ivory and ormolu clock on the mantel ticked softly, the only sound in the spacious bed-chamber with its white canopy bed and lace-draped windows. It was the very room Alysson had occupied as a child before she was abruptly uprooted and trans-planted to the wilds of the Cornish coast, and during the month that she had been back in London, she had slept there again, painfully reliving the happy days be-fore her grandfather had died.

Now, as she stood motionless beside her chamber door, she had but one purpose in mind. Turning the polished brass handle ever so slowly, she peeked out into the marble-tiled hallway. The footman who had been instructed to guard her room sat in his place, his straight-backed velvet chair propped against the wall beside the door. He idly flipped a penny off his thumb and tried to catch it atop his other wrist as Alysson silently closed the door and slid the bolt into place.

The time had come to make her escape. After days of pretending to have resigned herself to the forthcom-ing marriage, she would flee her father's house forever. She moved quickly across the mauve and royal blue oriental carpet to where a tall lancet window opened out over the rear lawns. Twin pale blue satin settees flanked the window, and she stepped up on the cush-ions of one to reach the high window latch. The win-dow swung easily outward, a warm May breeze fanning the loose tendrils around Alysson's face as she leaned out over the sheer three-story drop to the ground.

Dusk was settling silently over the gardens and walkways of the Tyler ancestral mansion, but the cobbled drives were deserted since the servant staff were supping in their dining hall in the south wing. Daniel Tyler was busy in his study off the entry foyer with his solicitor, no doubt seeing to the final embellishments on the wedding between her and the unknown Donovan MacBride. This very night she had been scheduled to meet the bridegroom at his home, so it was imperative for her to be off the estate and lost in the crowded streets of London before anyone found out her escape plans.

Alysson's soft lips curved into a bitter smile as she envisioned the look on her father's face when he found her gone. The imagined visage also brought a shudder undulating down her back, and eager to be away, she picked up the small bag she had packed. She looked around again, then dropped it, watching as it fell into a box hedge growing against the first-floor windows. She let fall her heavy black cape next, then, without hesitation, she pulled the back of her dark blue silk skirt up between her legs and tucked it into the front of her bodice. That done, she climbed with the utmost self-confidence out upon the high window ledge.

She was not afraid of the drop yawning menacingly beneath her. She and Freddie had climbed down cliffs higher than that to reach the ocean caves, where the sea had thundered with magnificent echoes. She allowed herself a pang of regret at the thought of Freddie and Mathilde, wondering if they had made it safely to the village of Standington, where Mathilde's kin lived, after Alysson's father had callously cast them out of the farmhouse. She hoped they fared well, but now she couldn't let herself worry about anything but her escape.

Leaning around, she grasped the sturdy vines covering the outside wall, pulling down to test them with her weight. The glossy green leaves of the ivy held firm, inexorably tangled after a hundred years of steady growth on the facade of the red-brick house. She held on tightly, finding a foothold, then carefully began her descent, avoiding the windows. Three feet from the ground she let go, landing in a squatting position behind a fragrant oleander bush. She waited an instant, listening. There was no sound other than the trilling of songbirds in search of a night roost, and she struggled to part the hedge in order to retrieve her bag. Once she had it, the first wave of elation shot through her.

She was out of the house! She pulled on the cape and her heart sped wildly as she tiptoed along the side of the house behind the bushes. Like a dark wraith, she crossed a pebbled path and melted into another hedgerow that led to the rear wall of the estate where the rose gardens were laid out.

Long ago, when she had been five years old, she had discovered a crumbling portion of the high outer wall while playing hide-and-seek with her mother. It was well hidden by trees and a trellis of climbing roses, and she headed there now, knowing full well she could not escape down the carriage road or even through the rear servant's gate without being seen.

The scent of roses perfumed the air as she moved past beds filled with huge red roses from China, then others with delicate blossoms of white and pink, all blooming profusely. Behind a rare apricot-tinted bush, she found her road to freedom. The bricks were in disrepair just as she remembered, and she agilely climbed the low-hanging branches of a huge oak tree, bag in hand, then carefully pulled her skirts and cape over the black spikes mortared into the top of the wall before she climbed down the other side.

Outside the confines of the Tyler demesne, carriages rolled by with a loud clattering of metal wheels and clopping hooves, and Alysson's heart lifted as she stood in the shadows looking at them go by. She wasted no more time, however, hurrying across the narrow street, avoiding the black-clad lamplighter who was affixing flame to the corner lamppost. As she put distance between herself and her prison, few of the other pedestrians paid heed to the slender, heavily cloaked figure, most of them intent on reaching their own homes and hearth fires before it grew late.

Nearly four blocks away, she drew to a stop near a corner intersection. Across the way, a long line of hansom cabs sat along the curbing, the drivers congregated in the yellow circle of a street lamp. She hesitated there, trying to make up her mind. If she hired one of them, and her father found out, he could force her destination out of the driver. The thought shook her. She couldn't risk that.

Her next consideration was finding her way on foot to the Crownover Theater, but she was not ignorant of the dangers for a woman alone in the streets and alleyways of London. Her gaze alighted on a wagon being unloaded on the opposite corner, and she deliberated a moment longer as she watched several young servants lift down a metal-rimmed barrel of wine then roll it up an angled platform to the door of a tavern. She made her decision quickly as she was wont to do, then walked unhurriedly across the street toward the working men, dodging a smart landau rattling its way down the dark street.

The driver of the wagon slouched indolently against the tall front wheel of his wagon, hands resting upon his fat paunch, and he eyed Alysson with interest as she stopped before him.

"Do you know the way to the Crownover Theater in Southwark?" she asked him, and he shifted his booted feet, standing upright. He scratched at his groin as he peered askance at the young girl with coppery braids swinging over her ears.

"I reckon I do, missy, but wut do a purty little gull like ye want to go there fer?"

"That, my good sir, is none of your affair," Alysson answered coldly, and the man's eyes widened in surprise before he let out a harsh guffaw.

"Ye be a saucy bit o' a wench, ain't ye?"

"I have a piece of gold to pay for your trouble, but I can hire yonder hack if my money does not interest you."

She gestured at the high-seated carriages across the street, but the man's small dark eyes riveted greedily on the shiny coin, one of the ten gold pieces that Alysson had taken from her father's desk drawer. He reached for it, intending to test its authenticity between his teeth, but Alysson pulled back her hand before he could touch it.

"After we arrive at the Crownover, if you please," she said, one finely arched brow lifted, and the driver muttered a few unintelligible remarks before he agreed.

"Then be gittin' in the back wid ye afore me change me mind," he said with a grunt. Alysson smiled as she swung up into the bed of the dusty wagon. She had dealt with peddlers and tinkers in Cornwall and learned to haggle with the best of them. She leaned back into the corner behind the driver's seat and raised her hood as the man called out gruffly to the huge horse. The wagon lurched, then began its rumbling journey through the dark, twisting streets of London.

It was hard for her to believe that she had really

managed to escape. For the first time in her life she was completely on her own. It was a little frightening, not having her mother or Mathilde or Freddie with her, but the important thing was to get away from Daniel Tyler and the man he intended her to marry. She reached down into the deep pocket of her skirt and retrieved a piece of parchment. The paper was old and yellowed, with well-worn creases where it had been opened and refolded for years by Alysson's mother. She carefully spread the playbill on her lap and strained to see the printed words in the dim light from the driver's lamp, though she knew them by heart.

It was an advertisement for the Crownover Theater dated the fifth day of March, 1790. Twenty-one years ago it had heralded the accomplishments of a London Shakespearean troupe performing *The Taming of the Shrew*, but it was the list of bit players at the bottom that Alysson sought. Adam Sinclair. Her mother's true and only love. Her mother had told Alysson how she had met the young American actor. It was by pure chance, when the wind had blown Judith's bonnet from her carriage and he had retrieved it for her. He had begged her to meet him in a coffeehouse, and although Judith had been engaged to Alysson's father, she had gone with him. Afterward, she had attended every matinee in which Adam Sinclair performed his small part.

Alysson folded the parchment and leaned her head back against the rough planks of the wagon. They had eloped, but Alysson's grandfather had found his daughter and forcibly brought her back. She had never seen Adam Sinclair again. It was so sad, Alysson thought. But now that she was alone in the world, she meant to find Adam Sinclair. He was an actor, and that alone was a kindred link between them.

All her life, Alysson had dreamed of performing on the stage, ever since an early age when she realized she had a talent for memorization and mimicry. And now she would try to obtain work at the Crownover Theater. Any kind of work, either as a maid or as one who cared for the wardrobe, until she was given a chance to prove herself. When she had enough money saved, she would buy passage to America, where she would look for Adam Sinclair, if he were still alive.

She slid the advertisement back into her pocket as the horse slowed. She stood and handed the gold coin to the driver, then looked at the white pillared building looming beside them, as she climbed from the back of the wagon. It was dark now but apparently too early for theater patrons to arrive for the evening's performance, and Alysson moved through a large archway supported by Corinthian columns to a long covered portico with four sets of arched doors. Huge lamps had been lit at intervals along the front, each with a sketch beneath it advertising the current play.

Alysson stopped before one of them, staring at the likeness of an elegant woman in the dress of Desdemona. "The acclaimed American actress, Madame Rosalie Handel, on her Grand European Tour," she read. How many times had Alysson imagined her own name on such a playbill? Not as Alysson Tyler, but as Silver Sinclair. She liked the sound of the name she had chosen to use for her stage life. It was a name people would remember. She never wanted to use the name Tyler again.

She stared at the woman in the picture. The fact that Madame Handel was an American was a stroke of good luck. Perhaps she would even know of Adam Sinclair. Alysson deemed that highly unlikely, but nevertheless she scanned the names of the players beneath the picture. Adam Sinclair's name was not there, as she had known it would not be.

Alysson turned as a hansom cab came to a stop just

behind her, and she watched as a tall, slender man who looked to be in his early thirties stepped out, an ivory cane in his hand. Giggling came from within the carriage, and Alysson continued to watch as he handed out a pretty young woman with bouncing auburn curls. She was tall and slim and giggled again as she fell against her escort. Alysson realized then that the girl had had too much to drink. The man frowned at the girl, holding her elbow as he paid the driver. He led her beneath the portico, and they stopped near Alysson when the girl lost one of her slippers. The man spoke then, clearly impatient with the tipsy condition of his companion.

"I can't think what possessed you to go to a party on the night of a performance! Look at you, you're foxed, and Rosalie's going to be furious! She'll probably change her mind about taking you with us!"

"Oh, pooh, Edgar," she returned, stopping as a hiccup interrupted her words. "I cannot help, zis, *chéri.* Champagne is my weakness, and Milty kept filling my glass to the very top."

Her speech had a slight French accent, and Alysson took note of it, silently mimicking the pronunciation of her words. The girl dissolved into new giggles, and the man rapped his cane angrily on the tiled floor.

"Don't mention Milton to me! My brother is a disgrace, and Rosalie's going to be as angry with him as she is with you! You know good and well that you were supposed to do a private party tonight, and there's been no one to replace you since Jenny eloped with that Spaniard in Madrid. And it's for a good friend of Rosalie's at that!"

"But, *chéri,* I am quite capable of performing," she insisted, weaving precariously on her feet until Edgar had to get a firm grip on her arm.

"You're going to find yourself back in Paris, or left

here without a friend to your name, if you don't sober up in time to play that part, and that's less than an hour from now!" His voice grew exasperated. "Are you even listening to me, Odette?"

Odette smiled up at him in a slow and sensuous way, then ran the palm of her hand up beneath the lapel of his coat. Her voice was low, her eyes sultry, as she worked her feminine wiles on the angry man.

"But you will help me, *oui, chéri?*"

With that, Alysson realized that a very unexpected opportunity was suddenly within her grasp, and she took a step toward the couple.

"Please pardon my intrusion, but I couldn't help overhearing part of your conversation."

She smiled, as both Edgar and Odette turned to look at her. Edgar was still frowning in annoyance, but Odette smiled widely at Alysson, her small lace-trimmed bonnet tipped askew over one ear.

"My name is Silver Sinclair," Alysson told them, "and I think perhaps I could be some help to you. I am an actress in search of employment. That is why I am here tonight, to see Madame Handel."

Edgar's eyes sharpened, looking her up and down quite openly, and Odette clapped her hands in delight.

"Ah, my guardian angel! How sweet of you, *ma petite*. You can take my place this night, and Rosalie will not be so angry with me, *oui?*"

Edgar ignored Odette's prattle. His eyes moved over a very beautiful, but exceedingly youthful face. "Have you acted before, Miss Sinclair?"

"Oh, yes," Alysson answered without hesitation. "I have played roles in nearly every one of Shakespeare's tragedies."

It was true, she rationalized to herself. She and Freddie had done them for her mother and Mathilde.

"Here in London?"

"No, sir, but I have performed often for a select audience in the countryside. I am most eager to join a theatrical company here in the city to improve my skills."

Alysson held her breath as Edgar looked at Odette's flushed face and vacuous smile, and when she giggled again and pressed a kiss to his cheek, he frowned, looking back to Alysson.

"Well, Miss Sinclair, it appears you are in luck tonight. Come along, and we'll see if Rosalie will consider you for the part."

Alysson eagerly followed them through the nearest double doors, then across a high-ceilinged lobby resplendent in red velvet wall coverings and gold-edged carved moldings. A small hallway led down one side of the theater to the stage dressing rooms. Edgar stopped before one of them and knocked. A low-pitched female voice answered from within, and Edgar took a deep breath, then ushered the two young women through the portal.

Madame Rosalie Handel sat before a large, gilt-framed mirror, and Alysson stared in awe as the accomplished actress half turned on her stool to look at them. She was very beautiful, and although older, perhaps nearing fifty, her face was relatively unlined. Her dark red hair was streaked with gray and woven into intricately coiled curls and ringlets. Her face was heavily made up for the night's performance, and there was a distinctive black beauty mark on her right cheek. Alysson had never seen a real stage actress, and she thought Rosalie Handel looked magnificent in the flowing yellow silk robes of Desdemona. She watched the older woman turn large brown eyes lined with black kohl on Odette.

"Odette? Why aren't you ready to leave? You're to be there by seven o'clock."

Odette sobered somewhat on hearing the smooth, soft voice, the tone of which, however, demanded an immediate explanation.

"Ah, madame, I am afraid I drank the champagne too long..."

Realization dawned in Rosalie Handel's face as Odette's voice slurred, and she rose with an imperious rustle of yellow silk.

"How could you do this to me, Odette! You know he asked specifically for you! I can't send you there like this!"

Edgar broke in, his tone conciliatory. "Now, Rosalie, love, it's not as bad as you think. It's all Milton's fault, anyway, and Odette's as contrite as she can be, and I have already found a stand-in for her."

Alysson stood watching everyone with great interest, and a glance told her that Odette's expression was anything but contrite. Alysson smiled as Edgar gestured toward her.

"Here she is, Rosalie, Miss Silver Sinclair."

Rosalie's eyes swept over Alysson dispassionately, as if ready to dismiss her, but Alysson did not give her the chance.

"How do you do, Madame Handel? It is a great privilege to meet an actress as famous as you."

Surprise flashed across the older woman's face, then she smiled graciously, acknowledging Alysson's compliment.

"That is very kind of you, my dear. You must forgive me my distress, but Odette's benefactor this night is a special friend of mine and the performance is of great importance to him."

"I am most willing to take Miss Odette's place," Alysson offered hurriedly, "and if it is a French woman he requires, I am fortunate to have a gift for mimicry, and I can speak as Odette does, as I am doing now. It is most convincing, *oui?*"

It was indeed most convincing, and the three others stared at her, amazed at how she had changed in the course of a sentence from flawless English to a faintly French-tinged accent. Alysson ended with a dazzling smile, and Rosalie Handel studied the young girl standing before her with renewed interest. She was astonishingly beautiful, more so than Odette, and Odette's beauty was the main reason she had been selected to play the part.

"Very impressive, Miss Sinclair, but I am not sure that such an accent will be necessary, or, for that matter, much acting at all. It is a private party of sorts where you will be masquerading as someone else, and for reasons of his own, my friend wishes to remain anonymous. He has sent a coach to take you to his residence." While she spoke, she had been scrutinizing the large green eyes and heavy red-blond braids, and suddenly she was quite eager for Silver Sinclair to take Odette's place. "I can assure you that my friend is a perfect gentleman, and you will be quite safe there with him."

"I only wish an opportunity to prove my acting ability to you, Madame Handel, in the hope that I might find a place in your company."

Rosalie smiled. "I can assure you, dear, that if my friend is satisfied with your work tonight, I will be more than happy to hold an audition for you."

"I promise that you won't be sorry for giving me this chance, Madame Handel," Alysson said with shining eyes, but Rosalie had already turned back to Odette.

"All right, Odette. Sit down there before you fall down." As Odette gigglingly obeyed, Rosalie gave Edgar crisp instructions. "Order coffee for Odette, then take Miss Sinclair down to the back stage door. The carriage should be waiting there for her. Then come back and get Odette back to the hotel. My god, I'm on in thirty minutes!"

Edgar ushered Alysson out quickly, giving her a wink.

"She's really an angel, but she's got a reputation for being as strict as a mother superior," he murmured softly to Alysson, then called out to a young boy who was hurrying past them. "Billy! Run and fetch Odette some coffee. She's in Rosalie's dressing room."

The very handsome youngster changed directions at once, and Edgar took Alysson's arm and led her quickly down another hallway.

"Do your best tonight, love, because Rosalie is choosing a few of us to return with her to New York. She's been on tour here alone, but she's forming her own theatrical company."

"She's from New York?" Alysson asked as they passed a pair of men carrying a rack of medieval-looking clothing.

"No, I believe she's from Boston, but she intends to work in a theater in New York."

"Has she ever mentioned an actor named Adam Sinclair?" Alysson inquired hopefully as they reached the heavy stage door where an old man with gray hair sat on duty to repulse overeager fans.

"No, not that I recall. Is he a relative of yours?" he asked absently, remembering her name.

"No, I was just wondering. He is a friend of my mother's, and I took his name as a stage name."

"Sorry, love, but I've never heard of him," he said brusquely as he pushed open the outside door.

Alysson followed him down the steps to where a well-polished black coach stood waiting. A huge Negro driver rose from where he had been sitting on the lowered step, and Alysson stared at him curiously, never having seen a black man before. Othello, she thought to herself, the valiant Moor.

"Miss Sinclair, this is Jethro. He will drive you to the man's house, then wait there for you. Good luck, my dear."

Edgar was gone then, leaving them standing there together, and Alysson stared up at Jethro, who towered over her, at least six feet tall. He grinned shyly under her open scrutiny, his teeth enormous and white against his ebony skin.

"I have never seen anyone with black skin," she told him honestly, and he nodded slightly.

"Yassum."

Alysson listened with interest to his slow drawl. "You would make a magnificent Othello, Jethro. Are you a Moor as he was?"

Jethro grinned uncertainly. "I don' know no Otheldo, ma'am. I is from Charleston town in de Carolinas. Masta brought me here to drive dis carriage fo' him."

Alysson found him fascinating, his looks, his speech. "Your hair is very different from mine, isn't it? Would you mind if I touched it?"

A shocked look appeared on the wide-featured black face above her, and he looked distinctly uncomfortable.

"No, ma'am, I reckon not, if you wants ta."

To his acute embarrassment, the lovely young lady did just that, then smiled up at him. "Thank you, Jethro."

"Is yo ready ta go now, ma'am?"

Alysson nodded, still thinking about his accent as he helped her inside the carriage.

She settled back in the soft red velvet squabs and smiled.

"Yassum," she tried out slowly. "I is from Charleston town in de Carolinas."

Her rendition of Jethro's Southern drawl was nearly

perfect, and a great excitement assailed her. Already
she had seen things and met people she had never seen
before. Her years in Cornwall had been lonely and solitary, with few opportunities to study other people and
how they spoke and acted. There was a whole world
waiting for her to discover, she thought, smiling again,
as she stared out the window at the houses they were
passing, their candlelit windows bright in the darkness.

This was her chance to truly become an actress, to
learn and listen and live! It was a chance brought by a
twist of fate, one she would surely never get again, not
in a hundred years. She had to do well tonight, had to
convince Rosalie of her talent. It was strange and a
little frightening to have no idea of her destination or of
the role she was to play, but she supposed that was the
way of an actor's life and she would grow used to such
things. But how much better it would have been if
Odette had been scheduled to play a real part on the
stage of the Crownover Theater—one of the parts that
Alysson had dreamed about, Ophelia or Portia or Cordelia or Juliet. She already knew most of them by
heart, and she could have worn one of the splendid
costumes she had seen at the theater. But that would
come later, she reminded herself. Now she must concentrate on the job at hand, and do it so well that Rosalie's friend would recommend her to Rosalie in glowing
terms. Then she might even be chosen to accompany
her to America. Even if she wasn't, she could work
hard until she earned enough to pay her own passage to
the United States. Everything was working out admir-
ably well, better than she could ever have imagined.

Alysson leaned forward and peered out at the passing
buildings as the coach rocked along the busy streets,
then sat back after a moment, realizing it was unlikely
she would see anything familiar. She hardly remembered anything about London, except for the fairs along

the Thames where she had gone with her grandfather. Just the two of them had gone, eating spicy cakes together and watching the Punch and Judy shows. She smiled at the memory, but her thoughts fled moments later as the coach slowed.

Outside her window, a large town house appeared, its windows ablaze, and Alysson watched as a servant ran down the steep flight of front steps and opened a tall, wrought-iron carriage gate. Jethro drove his horses through and down a narrow drive to a bricked rear courtyard. The landau drew to a stop, and the carriage swayed as Jethro stepped to the pavement to open the door for her.

Alysson climbed out, looking up at the back of the house where a man stood at the top of the steps, holding a candle.

"I be awaitin' fo' yo, ma'am," Jethro said, removing his hat. "Mr. Stephens dere, he gonna show yo de way now."

Alysson thanked him, lifting her skirts to climb the wide stair to where the other servant awaited her.

"This way, miss," Mr. Stephens said brusquely, but it was not until they were inside a narrow corridor beside the kitchen that she got a good look at him.

He was short, not much above Alysson's own height, and she immediately assumed he was the butler of the house from his immaculate attire of black frockcoat and trousers and a stiff white collar. He was quite fat around the middle but his features were pleasant, his hazel eyes calm and intelligent. He wore a short, manicured mustache, and his mien and mannerisms were very formal and precise.

"You are tardy, Miss Larousse. Please follow me, as time is of the essence."

Alysson started to correct him as to her identity, then changed her mind, trailing after him as he entered the

kitchen and crossed alongside spotless white counters
upon a shiny wooden floor to a back servant's stairway.
Upstairs, the corridor was wide and lavishly decorated,
with handsome chairs and tables lining the walls below
oil-darkened pastoral landscapes that Alysson longed to
stop and admire. The fastidious butler did not show any
inclination to let her, however, and Alysson had to
hurry to catch up to him, thinking that whoever Rosalie's friend was, he was very rich. Stephens finally
stopped before a door at the far end of the corridor.

"You will find your costume inside. The master will
join you shortly."

He opened the door, standing back politely as she
walked past him. He pulled the door shut behind her,
and Alysson stopped and looked around the spacious
bedchamber. It was done in obviously masculine tastes
of midnight blues and deep wine reds. Her gaze halted
on a huge mahogany bed with a massive carved headboard.

A wave of apprehension swept her as her eyes examined the rest of the room, the tall armoire of dark wood,
a matching pair of wing chairs in wine velvet that
graced either side of a black marble fireplace. A fire
burned a cheerful welcome, the snapping and crackling
of the flames loud in the silent chamber. She saw no
costume at first, but a Chinese silk screen with black
lacquered frame was positioned in one corner near the
bed. She walked across to it, running her fingertips admiringly over the scarlet silk embroidered with silver
pagodas stitched at the base of blue cloud-ringed
mountains.

Stepping around it, she found a flowing black satin
nightgown hanging on a hook. She lifted the smooth
fabric, never having felt anything quite so soft. She had
never worn anything remotely resembling the expensive garment, and she smiled to think of her plain,

high-necked linen nightdresses. They seemed very childish indeed next to such wicked-looking apparel. She found herself torn, a trifle frightened to think of wearing it in the presence of a man, despite Rosalie's assurances of his honor, but on the other hand eager to slip into it and luxuriate in the feel of the lustrous satin against her bare skin.

She lifted down the hanger. Rosalie had assured her that her friend was a gentleman, so why should she worry? Rosalie would certainly not have sent Odette into a potentially dangerous situation. With that thought firmly in mind, she unfastened the buttons down the front of her dress. She slipped out of it, and pulled the black gown over her head, frowning as it settled into place. The black silk was cut to drape in a low v both in front and back, and the white chemise Alysson wore showed quite clearly over her breasts. She obviously could not wear it that way.

She bit her lip, reluctant to take off any more of her clothes. Why, she would be practically naked without her chemise! She tried to tuck the undergarment where it wouldn't show, then frowned and gave up on it. She would have to take it off. She did and was completely scandalized at her appearance in the mirror on the wall behind her. She stared at the white flesh of her breasts barely covered by the clinging gown, then up at her face to find a blush rising into her cheeks at the mere thought of some strange man, and perhaps even others, seeing her in such a way.

Her gaze lit upon the thick braids looped over her ears, and a sudden burst of inspiration brought a relieved smile to her face. Her hair was very long and thick. Down and unpinned, it would cover her shoulders completely, as well as the revealing bodice of the gown. She began to unbraid her hair, her eyes still upon her reflected image. Such a gown indicated that she would be playing a very worldly, sophisticated woman, a woman like Rosalie Handel. She carefully set her face into the cool, aloof expression of the tall, flame-haired actress, preparing herself mentally for the masquerade to come.

# Chapter 2

Donovan MacBride left his place before the hearth to pace restlessly across his study. He stopped before an elegant rosewood liquor cabinet and picked up a small lead crystal decanter of whiskey. His leaden jaw was set in tight angry lines, and he frowned darkly as he threw back his head and downed the drink in one deep draught. He refilled the tumbler, absently stroking his forefinger over a small star-shaped scar just beneath his right eye. He downed the second drink in the same impatient manner. Black eyes roamed the quiet room from the ceiling to floor, book-lined walls to the large oak desk with papers strewn carelessly upon its polished surface.

Damn, if he didn't feel helpless, he thought furiously. Daniel Tyler was probably already on his way, his daughter in tow. If he was, it wasn't because Donovan hadn't done everything in his power to block the bloody marriage contract. If he hadn't agreed to the blasted clause in the first place, he wouldn't be in such a damnable mess.

Anger shot through Donovan again, and his long, tanned fingers tightened, threatening the fragile glass he held. He wanted to hurl it into the blazing logs, but he didn't. Instead, he intentionally relaxed his grip and set the tumbler almost gently atop the table before him. Donovan MacBride was not, and had never been, one to lose control of his temper. He kept his emotions tightly in check, and he prided himself on the fact that few ever knew what he was thinking. Much of his success in his business dealings relied on such self-control, and it was imperative in his intelligence work.

He recrossed the room and gazed down into the crackling flames for a long moment, bracing an elbow on the carved mantelpiece. He had run out of options concerning the unwanted marriage to the Tyler girl, and worse than that, he had run out of time. He had been barely twenty-four when he had signed the agreement with Laurence Hampstead, eleven long years ago, and at the time, a vague betrothal to Hampstead's seven-year-old granddaughter had seemed a minor sacrifice to cinch a contract that would triple the fortunes of the MacBride family within a year of the signing. He had needed the money then, but he had expected that it would be easy enough to buy his way out of the betrothal when the time came. He had seen Laurence Hampstead for the doting grandfather he had been, and when he had died the year after they had become partners, Donovan had thought little more of it, assuming the marriage would be forgotten. And it had been, until Lord Daniel Tyler had come into the picture. Damn the man!

Donovan absently rubbed at the scar on his cheekbone again, then ran his fingers over his bearded cheek to stroke his jaw. His eyes grew hard. Lord Tyler had begun pressuring him to honor the marriage clause a little over a year ago, and Donovan knew full well why he had. Tyler never bothered to hide his politics. He was the most blatantly anti-American member of Parliament, and Donovan's London agents believed he was involved in British espionage as well. If that were true, what better way for Tyler to infiltrate New York than to ensconce his own daughter in Donovan's house?

Over my dead body, he vowed inwardly, both fists clenching. He had never wanted a wife, and especially not some simpering British girl with a treacherous father. He knew next to nothing about the girl herself, and the secrecy surrounding her whereabouts for the last ten years was suspect in itself. So much so, in fact, that Donovan had hired investigators to discover more about her. They had come up with very little, only that her mother had died years ago, which coincided with Daniel Tyler's story, and that the girl had been educated in an Italian convent. No one in London had seen the girl in years, and Donovan was beginning to wonder if it really was Laurence Hampstead's granddaughter he was about to meet. There was something strange about all of it, and the fact that Tyler had fought Donovan tooth and nail when Donovan had resorted to legal channels to dissolve the contract made it even more suspicious. He had haggled with Tyler's English solicitors for months, and when that had failed, he had offered the bastard enough money to ransom the Regent himself. Tyler had turned him down flat.

Donovan clenched his jaw. The tension between America and England had heightened in the last year as Napoleon's fight with England disrupted neutral American shipping. War was inevitable. Within the year, if Donovan's intelligence bore out, and he had prepared for that eventuality during this last trip to London, methodically severing his ties in London, both commercial and private, and if his last effort to discourage the marriage failed, he would return to New York alone and let Tyler do what he could from London to force his daughter down Donovan's throat.

He straightened at a soft rapping on the door, turning as his personal valet entered behind him.

"The young lady has arrived, sir."

"Thank you. You do remember what you are to say to Lord Tyler when he arrives?"

"Yes, sir, I am to bring him directly to your bedchamber."

"Very good, and remember, they are not to be announced. Just show them in."

"Yes, sir, I quite understand."

Donovan lowered his gaze to the dancing flames again, not particularly proud of the dishonorable scheme he was about to perpetrate against Tyler's daughter, but he had little choice. The man had forced his hand by insisting on the wedding. No man, not even one like Tyler, would subject his own daughter to marriage with Donovan, if what he planned went off as intended. Even if Daniel Tyler held firm, there was no doubt Alysson Tyler herself would refuse him. He grinned suddenly. The more he considered it, the more he thought the plan just might be bold enough to work, and now the time was drawing near to find out. Tyler and his daughter were due within the hour.

More confident now, Donovan quit the library and mounted the curving staircase to the upstairs hall. He strode quickly down to his bedchamber, his footfalls muffled by the thick carpet. He rapped a knuckle on the door panel, then went in.

Alysson jumped, then whirled around at the sound of the door closing. She stared in silence at the big man beside the door, her heart hammering inside her breast. He seemed absolutely huge, even taller than Jethro, probably four or five inches over six feet, and his shoulders appeared enormous in the black silk waistcoat and loose-fitting white shirt he wore.

She swallowed hard as he came toward her, his eyes jet-black and unreadable as they took in her hair and face before traveling downward over her body in a way that made her want to back away from him.

"Who the hell are you?"

The dark eyes burned into hers in the most compelling way, arousing the uncanny sensation that he could see deep inside of her, that he would know if she told him lies. He seemed absolutely satanic standing there with his close-cropped black beard and even blacker hair that swept back over his temples in loose waves. He was very handsome in an ominous way, with fine features, deeply browned by the sun. She struggled to get hold of herself as a massive frown brought dark brows down over narrowed eyes.

"My name is Silver... Silver Sinclair," she began, hating herself for stuttering. He would never take her for a worldly woman if she acted so nervous! "Rosalie sent me," she added.

Donovan stared at the girl standing before him, unable to take his eyes off her exquisitely beautiful face. She had seemed all hair at first glance, shiny golden tresses rippling well below her waist, but now, on closer inspection, she seemed sheer perfection with her flawless white and pink skin, delicate features and soft lips, and absolutely huge green eyes, the color of sun-warmed emeralds. She was undoubtedly the most beautiful creature that he had ever seen, and she was young, very young. He spoke, his eyes never leaving her face.

"Where's Odette?"

Alysson tried to meet his penetrating gaze as steadily as she could. She had assumed her role now and she would play it to the best of her ability.

"She came home from a party quite foxed, so Rosalie hired me to take her place."

"You're English?"

He seemed displeased that she might be, and Alysson forced a smile.

"Only if you wish me to be," she said in her normal voice, then turned her next words into Odette's French-accented English. "I can be French if zou wish, or perhaps a Fräulein vould be more to your liking."

The last was Mathilde's husky voice to perfection, and she watched in triumph as the man grinned, his strong white teeth contrasting sharply with his dark skin and beard.

"You'll do as you are, English, if you can act as well as you do accents."

Alysson watched uneasily as he turned slightly, his fingers unfastening the buttons on his black silk waistcoat. He shrugged out of it and tossed it on a nearby chair. His legs were long and hard-muscled, encased in black trousers and glossy black boots, and as he turned Alysson saw a small, pearl-handled pistol tucked into a holster at the small of his back. He glanced at her as he took off his belt and slid it beneath one of the pillows.

"Do you know why you're here, English?"

She shook her head, wondering why he continued to call her that, and in such a mocking way.

"No, Rosalie didn't tell me."

He gave her a sardonic grin, and his black eyes held hers until she could not look away.

"You're going to pretend to be my lover tonight," he said, tipping his head toward the bed as he finished unbuttoning his shirt, revealing a dark tangle of hair on his tanned chest. He pulled the shirttail out of his waistband until it hung free. "Over there, on the bed."

His last words shocked her; he could easily read her feelings in those extraordinary green eyes of hers.

"You can handle it, can't you?"

Alysson recovered her composure quickly.

"I am an actress," she told him, meeting his challenging eyes. "I can be anything I want to be."

"Shall we, then?" Donovan said, sweeping his arm toward the bed. "My guests should be here soon."

Alysson hesitated as he moved to the bed and pulled back the velvet coverlet with one sharp jerk. Suddenly Alysson was very aware that she was alone in a strange house with a strange man who expected her to climb into his bed with him. Never in her life had she imagined herself in such a predicament, and now she had only Rosalie Handel's word that the big, handsome, virile-looking man staring at her so mockingly was a gentleman who would not take advantage of her.

"Do you really think it necessary for us to be in the bed? Surely the fact that I am here in your bedroom, dressed like this, would be enough."

The shadow of a smile hovered at one corner of his mouth as he sat down and leaned back against the headboard.

"It's necessary. I mean to make my point in a way that will be hard to forget."

Alysson hesitated a moment longer, then walked around to the opposite side of the bed. She sat down gingerly on the edge, facing away from him.

Donovan looked at her prim posture, then grinned. "Is that the best you can do?"

Alysson looked around at him. "What would you have me do?"

"My women don't usually keep one foot on the floor when we're in bed together. For god's sake, come over here. They'll be here soon."

The last was nothing less than a peremptory command, and Alysson crawled across to sit on her heels nearer to him, but not too close.

"That's better," he said softly, reaching out to grasp a handful of her hair. He caressed the silky texture between his thumb and fingers.

"You have beautiful hair, English, so soft and fine, like spun gold."

His voice had lowered and roughened slightly, and a shiver of something akin to fear raced down Alysson's spine as he wound the thick strand around his fingers, drawing her closer with a gentle tug.

"Can you tell me what is about to happen?" she asked nervously as he sat up, propping one palm behind her on the bed, his dark, handsome face very close to her own.

"No."

Alysson sat stiffly, her eyes on the door, wishing whoever was coming would hurry up and come. Every nerve in her body was attuned to the overpowering masculine presence so very close to her.

"I hired you to act as my lover; surely you can be more convincing than this," Donovan said, pulling back the luxurious fall of red-gold hair to tuck it behind her ear. His eyes dropped admiringly from her delicate profile to the white flesh swelling so temptingly beneath the black satin bodice.

He was so close that Alysson could not breathe, so close that she could pick up the scent of tobacco and the light essence of some kind of manly cologne. Her heart began to pound as he touched her cheek with his fingertips, drawing her face around so that she had to meet his eyes. Her lips parted breathlessly at the burning intensity she saw in them, and an unfamiliar, all-encompassing excitement took hold of her. He was going to kiss her, somehow she knew it, but she could not bring herself to pull back. Was this the way it felt to be touched by a man? This weak giddiness and hot, flushed feeling?

His face was very close above her own now, and he smiled a slow knowing smile that bespoke arrogant male self-confidence, but Alysson was beyond the point of caring as his lips came down to touch hers, as gentle and undemanding as the touch of a feather. She relaxed and felt his arm come up to brace her shoulders. So this is what it is like, she thought in wonder, this is what it is like to be kissed. Her eyelids fluttered closed as his mouth pressed harder upon her lips, molding them to his, gently but insistently. She moved her own lips as he was doing, then started slightly as his strong fingers came up to cup her fragile jaw, and his tongue explored the sweetness of her mouth. She pulled away breathlessly, and his hand dropped away.

Donovan smiled at the heated blush rising in her cheeks and the heaving of her breasts, wondering if she was really as innocent as her reactions indicated. Where on earth had Rosalie found her? She lay relaxed against him, her head in the crook of his arm, and he brushed the soft tendrils off her brow, then ran one finger over the elegant curve of her cheek.

"Show me what a good actress you are, English. Make me believe you are mine to have."

His lips caressed her ear as he whispered the words of challenge, and before Alysson could move, he had twisted until he lay half atop her. His hard chest pressed her deeper into the silken pillows, and a weak moan escaped her as warm male lips took complete possession of her mouth. His kisses were more intense this time, no longer gentle as if he tasted her, but hungry, ravaging kisses that melted her will, then her bones. Her senses began to reel as his tongue parted her lips, and she was not prepared for the electrifying currents that reached to the deepest parts of her body, making her want to arch herself up against him. Without understanding why, she slid her hands over his broad shoulders and felt them tense beneath her palms. Could her touch affect him the way his did her?

Alysson gasped as his mouth left hers and moved to the soft flesh of her shoulder, and she realized from deep within the swirling mists of her awakening passion that he had slid the straps down her arms, baring her shoulders and breasts. His dark head moved lower, his lips at the base of her throat where a pulse throbbed out of control, then still lower to the silky curve of her breast.

Donovan heard her muffled protest as he swept her gown to her waist, but he captured her wrists beside her head as his lips tasted her sweetly fragrant flesh, reacting to her with a passion that half shocked him.

"Please," Alysson managed as his hard body pressed intimately against her naked thighs.

His lips moved against hers in a husky whisper. "Please what, English? Shall I stop? Or do you want me as much as I want you?"

The sound of the door opening brought them both back to awareness, and Donovan rolled to his back, taking a trembling Alysson with him. He pulled up her gown to shield her nakedness when he saw Stephens and two other men in the doorway. Lord Daniel Tyler's face drained of color as his eyes met Donovan's, then slid over to the small girl held tightly in Donovan's arms.

Donovan gave a satisfied smile, his eyes leaving Tyler, and then, for the first time, he realized that Alysson Tyler was not with him. Instead, there was a heavyset constable in blue uniform, staring with open-mouthed astonishment at the entwined couple on the bed. Donovan looked back at Lord Tyler, and the horrified expression on his face indicated that his daughter's presence would not be necessary. Donovan wanted to laugh as Tyler struggled to speak. His words came at last, hoarse and strangled.

"My god! Alysson?"

Alysson? Donovan thought in confusion, then looked down as Silver Sinclair stiffened in his arms.

"Father..." Alysson breathed in absolute horror.

"Father?" Donovan repeated dumbly, then realization hit him like a pitcher of ice water flung into his face. Before Daniel Tyler could reach the bed, Donovan was out of it, gun in hand.

"I'll relieve ye of the little gun, mate, unless yer hankering fer a hole in yer heart."

The fat constable cocked his flintlock pistol and pushed it into Donovan's back. Donovan whirled on him, black eyes full of fury, and the peace officer stepped back uncertainly but held the gun directed on the muscular brown chest, if slightly unsteadily. Donovan considered taking the gun away from him, then remembered the girl on the bed directly behind him; she could be hit if the constable fired. So with great reluctance, he gave up his gun, turning cold eyes on Daniel Tyler.

"You'll not get away with ruining my daughter like this, MacBride," Daniel said fiercely, his face livid with anger. "Seducing her here in your bed without the sanctity of wedding vows! By god, I'll see that you do right by her, and I'll see it done this very night! No court in the land will let you leave the country after this! You'll rot in prison if you don't marry my Alysson!" His voice became shriller. "Constable Riggins is my witness that you had your way with her! Look at her, half naked, she is!"

The constable looked at her, but Donovan stared at Tyler, just beginning to understand the gravity of his predicament. Tyler had somehow turned everything around in order to compromise him into marrying his daughter. And she had been in on it from the beginning! He turned to look at the girl cowering in the bed. Alysson's stomach lurched with sick fear as Donovan MacBride's black eyes bored into her with cold, lethal contempt.

Three quarters of an hour later, Donovan stood ramrod straight, his back to the fire. He was fully dressed again, his face set in inflexible lines. Lord Tyler sat in a deeply cushioned gold brocade chair be-

side the bed, with the constable close behind him, gun
still trained on Donovan. Tyler met Donovan's cold regard with a mocking, self-satisfied smile. A muscle
twitched spasmodically in the lean contours of Donovan's cheek. As he turned his eyes to the girl, he fought
his desire to jerk the bastard up by his lapels and send a
fist into his leering face.

She sat on the edge of the bed now, looking suitably
upset and frightened. Yet another of her brilliant performances, he thought, rage roiling around inside him,
fighting to be released. How could he have been so
stupid? And how could Tyler have found out Donovan's plan to trick him with Odette? Someone had to
have betrayed him. But who? Only a few trusted
friends knew about his plan: his brother, Brace, and
Stephens, of course. And Rosalie and Edgar and
Odette. It had to be the French woman; she was the
only one not a part of his spy network.

The fury boiled higher, churning, intensifying by degrees as they waited for Stephens to return with the
justice of the peace. Heavy, foreboding tension hung
over the quiet room like a cloud of lead, and the girl
never looked up, not at him, not at her father. She did
well to be afraid, he thought, his jaw growing harder.

Daniel Tyler rose quickly as Stephens entered the
room with a tall, gray-haired man. He took Alysson's
elbow tightly and pulled her to her feet, and still she
kept her eyes on the floor as he led her to the center of
the room, her fingers clutching the bodice of the black
satin gown together over her breasts.

Constable Riggins waved Donovan forward with his
gun, and Donovan gave him a look of cold distaste
as he took his place beside Alysson. While the justice
of the peace read the vows, his eyes traveled from
the bride to the groom with unconcealed curiosity. The
girl's voice was barely audible as she repeated the

words, and Donovan said them with bland indifference that belied the absolute fury grinding away inside him. What a stupid fool he had been! Taken in by her beauty and her innocent looks. Taken in by her soft perfumed flesh and lovely lying lips! He held himself stiffly, not daring to touch her for fear of wrapping his fingers around her long white throat. The thought of being legally tied to such a woman sickened him.

Daniel Tyler grinned as the ceremony drew to a finish, well satisfied with the outcome of a night he had feared to be a disaster. He had no idea how Alysson had come to be writhing in Donovan MacBride's bed at such a fortuitous time, but he was not a man who questioned good luck. He had been sure all was lost when she had fled his house, and he had been coming to tell MacBride of her disappearance when he had found them together. It was only good that he had reported her missing to the watch and brought along the constable to prove it. He chuckled to himself. Now, after a very long wait, he had MacBride exactly where he wanted him.

"I'll have your clothes packed and sent to you here, daughter. I'll bid you farewell now."

Alysson didn't look up or answer, and Daniel shrugged, glad to finally wash his hands of her.

Alysson sank weakly onto the bed as Donovan MacBride and the constable followed Daniel Tyler from the room. Alone for the first time since the unthinkable had come to pass, she could not prevent her emotions from slipping behind the wall of iron restraint she had erected around them. She dropped her face into her palms and sobbed aloud. How could such a horrible thing have happened? How, how? How could her father have known that she was there? Or had he known? She had seen the stunned expression on his face when he had first recognized her. He had not known, she realized

suddenly, and it was clear that Donovan MacBride
hadn't, either. But now he did, and he thought she had
been the one to deceive him.

Ripples of fear raced down her spine, rattling already
quivering nerves as she remembered the look on his
face when he realized who she was. Hatred, disgust;
cold, bitter, awful. And all because of some hideous,
unbelievable twist of fate that had brought them together in the wrong place at the wrong time.

She sat up, dropping her hands away from her face
as another terrible thought came to her. It had been
Alysson herself who Donovan MacBride had intended
should find him in bed with Odette! How much did he
despise her to go to such extreme lengths to stop their
marriage? Or was it her father he despised? Whichever,
his rage was now twice as violent and directed at her
for tricking him into a marriage he did not want.

Alysson's teeth caught at her lower lip, green eyes
enormous with fright. She was his wife now, his property to use and abuse as her father did to her mother.
He was big and frightening, even without the intense
hatred he now held for her. Would she be beaten merci-
lessly like her mother?

Heart-squeezing panic rose inside, and she jumped
up and ran to the window, wanting to flee his wrath, to
hide anywhere before he could return. It was a straight
drop to the bricked carriage road below, but this time
there were no vines to give her a means of escape. She
leaned her head against the cool glass, clasping her
hands together to stop their shaking. She had to think,
think of a way out of this. She had to make him listen
to the truth. Moving away from the window, she leaned
against the wall, trying desperately to compose a reasonable explanation, one he would be able to believe.
But the truth sounded more bizarre than what he had

thought had happened! He would never believe her! Never! She could hardly believe it herself!

She began to pace the floor, wringing her hands, trying to sort through her tangled, frightened thoughts, but any semblance of calm she attained fled forever when the door opened. She froze, watching with heaving chest as Donovan MacBride closed the door and leaned back against it. Black eyes burned into her, devil eyes, eyes that tied knots of fear in her stomach. Where he stood, the candlelight glinted off the fine planes of his face, carving hollows around his eyes and mouth. He looked like a devil, ready to claim another soul.

"What is this? My precious wife isn't awaiting my pleasure in our wedding bed?" His words were low, lethal, coiling around her like a deadly serpent. Alysson shivered as he continued in cold, controlled contempt. "You were eager earlier, before you sprang your nasty little trap. It's time you finished what you started."

"Please, please, listen to me." She swallowed convulsively as he took a step toward her, wearing a smile that could chill the sun. "It's not what you think, I swear. I can explain if you'll . . ."

She cried out as he reached out suddenly, his fingers grasping the front of her gown. One violent downward jerk ripped it from top to bottom, and Alysson backed away in terror, holding the remnants of it across her breasts.

"Get in that bed, damn you."

His voice was low, almost conversational, making it all the more threatening, and Alysson obeyed, scrambling quickly beneath the coverlet. She stared fearfully at him as he stopped at the foot of the bed, one hand grasping the thick bedpost, the other rubbing at the scar near his eye.

"You're not going to like being my wife, English,

because I'm going to make sure you don't," he said softly.

Alysson blanched at his words, wetting parched lips as he unbuttoned his vest and flung it to the floor. He stripped off his shirt with one angry motion, wadding it into a ball before he hurled it onto the chair beside the bed. His black eyes never left her face. When his fingers went to his belt buckle, Alysson began to speak with urgency.

"I know how it looked to you," she began, stopping as Donovan gave a low, unamused laugh. "But I don't want to be married to you any more than you want it! I swear it! I even ran away from my father because I wanted to be free of him!"

Donovan ignored her, muscles knotting in his arms as he put a knee on the bed and grabbed her by the shoulders. He jerked her to her knees, bringing his face up close to hers.

"You're lying again, girl, and I don't like liars."

"I had no idea Rosalie was sending me here to you! I didn't even know your name! Ask her if you don't believe me!"

Donovan's words were ground out from between clenched teeth. "Do you honestly think I would believe anything you have to say? I sure as the devil don't know *how* you came to be here tonight, but I know exactly why. And believe me, you'll rue the day you became my wife until the day you die."

His last threat brought alive Alysson's anger, pushing aside some of her fear. She tried desperately to jerk away from his painful grip on her arms.

"I already rue this day, more than you ever will, and I can prove it!"

Her sudden defiance surprised Donovan, because she had seemed quite terrified only moments before. But he couldn't forget that she had already proved herself to be a consummate actress. He thrust her away in disgust, and Alysson fell back into the pillows. Donovan glared down at her, hands on his hips.

"Then, by all means, prove it."

Alysson pressed herself as far away from him as she could, holding the sheet in front of her. She rubbed her arm where he had held her so brutally.

"I am not sure," she said slowly, "but I do not think that we had time to . . . to consummate our vows before my father came."

Donovan's harsh expression turned to incredulity, then he gave a short bark of laughter that ended abruptly.

"Just how stupid do you think I am? Don't play the innocent with me now, not after the way you writhed and clutched me to your luscious little body, not an hour ago. You know damned well nothing happened between us, despite what your father told the authorities."

A hot, dark flush rose beneath Alysson's delicate skin as she remembered in vivid detail her wanton reaction to his kisses.

"I am most willing to have an annulment from you," she said hastily as he leaned toward her again. "I'll sign anything you wish, I'll agree to anything you wish, to be released from this marriage!"

Her desperate words gave Donovan pause, but he stared suspiciously down at her face, angry that he was still racked with desire at the sight of her half-clad body, even now, when he was gripped with rage. But it was true that the marriage had not been consummated. Once in New York, away from Lord Tyler's political influence, it would be easy for Donovan to obtain an annulment, especially if the girl did not contest it.

"Are you saying that you'd be willing to relinquish any claim to my name?" he asked with heavy skepticism, and Alysson nodded without hesitation, encouraged by his guarded show of interest.

"Yes, I swear, and your property. I'll do anything you ask. All I want is to go with you to America where my father can't find me. After that, you'll never see me again, I swear it upon my mother's grave."

Donovan didn't trust her, not for one short minute, but he couldn't think of any ulterior motive she might be contemplating. She had nothing to gain with such an offer, none that he could envision, but that didn't mean she didn't have some other trick in mind. She had proved herself very clever.

"You would be willing to sign a legal document to that effect?" he asked, black eyes searching her face for subterfuge, and Alysson nodded again, breathing easier as he moved a few steps away from the bed while he considered. She released her held breath as he picked up his shirt and shrugged it on. He looked back at her as he buttoned it.

"I'll have such a document drawn up, but you'll sign it *before* we set sail. And before witnesses of *my* choosing."

"I'll do whatever you say, whenever you say."

Alysson's heart stood still as their eyes locked for another long moment, his dark ones distrustful.

"I give you fair warning, English, you had better mean what you say."

Alysson nodded mutely, watching as he strode to the door. He turned back to look at her one last time.

"I intend to sail for New York in the next few days, and until that time, you will stay here, alone, in this room. You are not to speak to anyone or see anyone, including your father, is that clear?"

She nodded again beneath his narrow-eyed stare, then collapsed backward on the bed as he let himself out of the room. She heard a key turn in the lock, and all the bravado she had shown him melted away like sugar in the rain. Heavy despair settled over her heart as warm tears welled and flowed in delayed reaction to all that had happened. She wept hard, racking sobs for a long time, and it was well into the night when her tears subsided enough for her to drift wearily into a troubled, nightmare-ridden sleep.

# Chapter 3

The *Halcyone,* the newest addition to the MacBride merchant fleet, lay close along a dockside stone quay. A sleek-lined frigate with only three ocean crossings to her credit, her reputation already had been heralded throughout elite London circles as the foremost passenger transport of the times. The likes of her elegant staterooms and spacious dining and gaming parlors had never been seen before by those civilians forced to travel seas made dangerous by the strife between England and France. The *Halcyone*'s passenger docket for her return voyage to America had been filled within a fortnight of her arrival in England several months earlier.

Not least among the *Halcyone*'s attractions was the presence of her handsome captain, a man whose reputation for expert navigation barely outshone his repute for charming the fair ladies. Many a young lady whiled away her hours convincing her father of the benefits of an ocean voyage after having met Captain Brace MacBride.

On a bright, sunny afternoon in late May, Brace MacBride stood with palms braced on the quarter rail of his ship as he surveyed with critical eye the preparation for disembarkation. They would sail on the evening tide, and Brace was eager to hoist the top gallants and leave England behind. He had been ashore much too long, for weeks, and he longed for the roll of the ocean swells beneath his feet. Ever since he had signed on at age sixteen as a cabin boy with one of Donovan's merchant captains, he had been enamored of the sea and its mysteries. Now nearing thirty, he owned his own ship, and he was well content to leave the responsibility of the vast MacBride empire in Donovan's capable hands.

He scanned the decks, where boarding passengers milled around the scrubbed decks of his ship. The last few days he had stayed aboard, supervising the loading of their merchant cargo, as well as the furnishings from their London house. Donovan had indeed pulled up roots in England as he had sworn to do. Brace searched the deck for his older brother. He found him near the gangport with their good friend Rosalie Handel. Donovan's hands were clasped behind his back, and he wore the same look of cold displeasure that he had worn for the entire last week.

Brace shook his head. Donovan had landed himself in a hell of a mess with Lord Tyler and his daughter. If it were not such a serious problem, the whole thing would be rather amusing, since Donovan was usually in complete control of his life. Donovan, however, did not find it amusing, and he had questioned Rosalie about the new French girl she had hired from a Paris brothel. Brace had to agree with his brother that it was very hard to believe it had all been some bizarre coincidence as the Tyler girl would have Donovan believe. But Rosalie had worked as an agent for them since the beginning, when the War Department had approached Donovan for his part in intelligence work. For five years, she had given them information, and several months ago, when she had met them in Madrid, she had had invaluable knowledge of Napoleon himself. It was hard to believe she could betray them, but as Donovan had pointed out, it had been her suggestion to Donovan to use Odette to discourage the Tyler girl. The fact that Donovan had been desperate enough to try it in the first place had surprised Brace, for his brother was not one to rely on such methods. He usually won in his business deals because he was smarter than those he dealt with.

Brace stared at Donovan where he stood listening to Rosalie. Never had he seen Donovan so enraged as he had been since he had been forced to marry. In the years since the war of rebellion with England, Donovan had been an outspoken opponent of the British and their arrogance in dealing with Americans, and now he found himself married to the daughter of an English earl, a man he had despised from their first meeting.

The rattling of a carriage against the uneven cobblestones of the wharf caught Brace's attention, and he turned his eyes away from Donovan as a coach jounced to a stop on the quay below him. His eyes sharpened with interest, wondering if Donovan's notorious English bride had arrived at last. He watched intently as the driver climbed down and opened the door.

A moment later, a woman paused in the opening as if reluctant to step out, and he watched as she was assisted to the ground. Even from his place on the quarterdeck, he could see that she was lovely, her golden hair glinting in the sunlight. Brace cast a glance in Donovan's direction and was surprised to find his brother only a few steps away.

"The convincing little bitch has arrived" were his first words to Brace, and Brace looked at the harsh set of Donovan's mouth, then back to the woman he denounced.

"That she may be, brother, but a beautiful one, if my eyes do not deceive me."

Donovan made an unpleasant sound. "Don't be taken in by her beauty, or her green eyes and blond hair. She may look the part of an angel, but it's a black widow she really is."

Brace wondered at his brother's detailed list of the girl's attributes, thinking it sounded as if Donovan were not as immune to the lady's charms as he declared himself to be. Below them, the hired coach rolled away, leaving the small woman alone on the quay with the red morocco trunk that her father had sent. Brace glanced at Donovan.

"Aren't you going to send someone to help her?"

Donovan's jaw grew hard as two young men near the gangplank became aware of Alysson's plight and moved toward the lovely lady in blue with the utmost haste. Donovan spoke between clenched teeth.

"As you can see, she is most adept at enticing men to do her bidding."

Brace thought she had hardly done much to entice the two overzealous dandies, but he remained quiet as Donovan moved away. He looked back to the girl, who was being subjected to a gallant session of bowing and hand-kissing. He thought she looked uncomfortable with the two young men paying her such elaborate court, and Brace's gentlemanly instincts came to the fore, despite Donovan's inclination to let the lady fend for herself.

He started toward the gangplank, and as he drew near to the quay, the two rakes were arguing in flowery language over who should have the honor of toting her trunk, and more importantly, who would have the greater pleasure of escorting the lovely lady herself.

"Pardon me, madame," Brace said, and slanted green eyes, greener than the sea, came up to meet his gaze. Though Brace was no stranger to beautiful women, his breath caught. His brother's wife, whether guilty or not, was nothing less than exquisite to look upon. "Please allow me to introduce myself. I am your husband's brother, Brace MacBride, captain of the *Halcyone*. At your service, madame."

Alysson stared incredulously up at the tall man with shaggy blond hair and glinting blue-gray eyes. "But you can't be."

Brace's smile widened, and he quirked a brow in a manner reminiscent of his older brother. "I can't? Why is that?"

Alysson had to smile at his engaging grin. "You are just so different, is all. You look nothing like . . ."

Brace answered as her voice trailed away without naming Donovan. "I was fortunate enough to inherit the fair features and disposition of my mother." He paused, his eyes taking on a devilish gleam. "While, alas, poor Donovan was left to possess our father's black hair and eyes, and ofttimes dire moods to match."

Alysson's lips parted in surprise, but Brace only smiled, then turned to the two young men still haggling over her trunk.

"Good of you, chaps, to come to the rescue of this fair lady. Kindly follow us with that, if you will. Milady?" He grinned down at Alysson as he proffered her his crooked arm.

Alysson put her fingers on the smooth blue fabric of his uniform, already liking Captain Brace MacBride a far cry better than she did his older brother. He escorted her up the gangplank, leaving two disappointed would-be suitors to wrestle aboard her heavy trunk. As they reached the ship's main deck, Alysson gave him a grateful smile, and Brace set admiring eyes on the deep dimples that framed her small white teeth. Her green eyes moved past him, and her expression faltered uncertainly. Brace turned to find Donovan presenting her with a deadly glare that would surely wither the hardiest rose from its stem. No wonder the girl's eyes had lost their light.

"Come this way," Donovan said in clipped tones, eyeing her in cold distaste. "You, too," he added to Brace, annoyed at his brother's attempts to pamper her. He moved away, barely glancing at the two fools with the trunk, who were smiling at Alysson as she thanked them for their help. Jagged anger scraped together like a fractured bone as he walked with long strides to the door below the quarterdeck. He would soon find out if she meant what she had said about signing a document of annulment, or if that was another of her lies, because he meant to have her signature dried and witnessed before they raised a single sail.

Alysson looked around in curiosity as she followed Donovan across the deck and through a doorway. She had never been aboard a ship before, not even a small boat, and she was most impressed by the wall panels of cream-colored silk and the finely crafted glass lamps that lit the carpeted companionway down which he led her. It was little different than being in a fine home, she decided, just smaller and more compact, as they came upon two ladies conversing in the corridor. Both were dressed in the latest fashion, with high-waisted gowns: one of pastel pink, the other of daffodil yellow. Both wore high-crowned bonnets to match their dresses. Donovan stopped, politely bidding them a good day, and the ladies' fawning remarks made no secret that they found him to be most attractive. As Brace Mac-Bride came up behind Alysson, they greeted him with equal enthusiasm. As for Alysson, she was scrutinized by two pairs of envious eyes as she proceeded along with the tall and handsome MacBride brothers.

Not long after, in a different hallway, Donovan opened a door, and stared indifferently at Alysson as she preceded him into the cabin. Inside, she found a large, beautifully decorated stateroom with elegant furnishings. On the wall across from her, four round portholes draped in plush gold velvet were set above a comfortable sitting area where couches of green-striped satin were built into the wall. On her close right, a large desk was at right angles to a corner liquor cabinet. The two men relaxing in chairs in front of the desk rose upon sight of her.

Donovan left Brace to close the door and moved behind the desk. Alysson sat down in a black leather desk chair that Donovan indicated with a wave of his hand as he greeted the other men. Alysson had to steel herself not to shudder as he put those burning black eyes on her.

"This is my personal secretary, Mr. Lionel Roam," he said, looking at a slender young man with small wire-rimmed spectacles perched on a thin nose. He gave Alysson a nervous-looking smile. "And this is the first officer of the ship, Lieutenant Robert Statler."

The officer, a middle-aged man with lively blue eyes and a thick black beard peppered with gray, gave a smart bow from the waist.

"How do you do?" Alysson murmured to them, feeling self-conscious and ill at ease in the presence of four men she hardly knew. As they returned courteous responses, Donovan reached in front of her, slid open the top drawer of the desk, and removed a crisp sheet of fine white parchment covered with small, precise handwriting.

"These gentlemen have kindly consented to act as witness to your signature on this document, as has my brother. Neither Mr. Roam nor Lieutenant Statler know what is written herein, since I penned it myself. Brace, of course, I have taken into my confidence."

He laid the document in front of her, pushing into her reach a heavy silver inkwell and quill pen.

"You may take the time to peruse it, if you think it necessary, then affix your signature near the bottom where I have indicated."

Alysson was well aware that four pair of masculine eyes followed her every movement as she bent over the paper. Despite her nervousness and desire to be done with the distasteful business, she read every line slowly and with great care. Donovan MacBride's hatred was not something she could take lightly, and she didn't trust him any more than he trusted her. He could very well have included some incriminating remark that, once her signature was upon it, would see her thrown in jail where he would be rid of her forever.

To her relief, however, she found that though the terms were couched in eloquent language, the facts were stated in a simple, straightforward manner. It said in effect that she had no claim now or in the future to the MacBride name or holdings. It further gave her unqualified consent to a speedy annulment once they arrived on American shores. She read the last clause through, then frowned and read it again. Furthermore, it stated, Donovan MacBride had been coerced into marriage by the trickery and deceit of Alysson Tyler. By trickery and deceit! The incriminating words ate into her mind like acid, and she raised determined green eyes to meet the black ones contemplating her.

"I cannot sign this agreement unless the last words in this line are deleted," she said firmly, placing her slender forefinger on the offending text.

The eyes of the three witnesses swung to her, surprised at her quietly voiced objection, then just as quickly swiveled back to Donovan to gauge his reaction.

Donovan's face revealed nothing as he leaned over her, glancing at the words she found unacceptable. He straightened.

"You are in no position to make demands of me, madame," he said coldly.

Alysson's fragile chin came up a bare notch. She would not be bullied into signing her name to a lie.

"I believe, sir, that you have far more to lose if you do not delete those words than I will lose by not signing this paper."

Her calm defiance first shocked Brace where he sat watching, then he hid a smile behind his hand. It was a rare occasion indeed when Donovan was bested over a contractual point, and he knew, as he was sure Donovan did, that Alysson Tyler was right.

A muscle flexed and held in Donovan's bearded cheek, but he took the pen from Alysson and scratched out the disputed phrase. Once done, Alysson picked up the quill without hesitation and carefully wrote her name at the bottom.

Donovan took the parchment out of her hand before she had barely lifted the quill. He examined her signature scrawled in a rather childish hand, half expecting her to have used Silver Sinclair, or one of the other aliases she no doubt had. He sprinkled sand over the wet ink, then shook it off, folding the parchment until only the bottom half was left uncovered for the witnesses's signatures.

Everyone watched silently as Lionel Roam signed his name in a scholarly slant, followed by Lieutenant Statler's hasty signature. Brace MacBride signed last, carelessly scrawling his name, then giving Alysson a conspiratorial grin as he dropped the quill on the desktop. Donovan frowned darkly at his brother's friendly overture to Alysson, but she felt distinctly better because of it. Donovan ignored her as he melted hot wax on the fold, then sealed it with his gold signet ring.

"Thank you very much, gentlemen," he said, shaking hands with each as they arose. He waited until the door closed after his secretary and Lieutenant Statler, then looked at Alysson.

"I prefer that no one know about what transpired between the two of us in London. I intend to let it be known around the ship that you are a friend of our family who is traveling under my protection. Unfortunately, it will be necessary for you to make the crossing here in our stateroom with my brother and me since all the other cabins are booked."

Alysson's eyes widened in alarm; she was completely unnerved by the thought of living in such close quarters with Donovan MacBride for over a month. A long shiver rippled over her skin as a vivid picture of the two of them entwined on the bed in Donovan's town house intruded in her mind.

Donovan's smile was brittle, as if he could read her mind. "I assure you that you will not be molested by me. There is a draped bunk across the cabin from my own, and I have had a screen set up in front of it."

Alysson looked across the room and found the black and scarlet Chinese screen that had been removed from the bedroom in the town house that very morning.

"No one will disturb you here," Donovan continued. "And after witnessing the way you flaunted yourself in front of those two fools on the docks, I think it best to keep an eye on you." His voice was cruel. "I don't intend to put myself in a position of being falsely accused of a paternity suit from your casual shipboard dalliances."

Alysson lowered her eyes, a wave of embarrassed color rising to darken her cheeks. Even when she heard the door close after Donovan, she couldn't bring herself to meet Brace MacBride's eyes.

"Believe it or not, Miss Tyler, my brother is a perfect gentleman most of the time. That remark was unpardonable."

Alysson looked at him, grateful for the sympathy in his eyes. "I can understand how he feels. He believes my father and I tricked him into marrying me. If I thought such a thing about someone, I also would despise the two I thought had compromised me."

Her understanding of Donovan's boorishness surprised Brace. He searched the slanted green eyes. "And is that true?"

"No, but I cannot expect you to trust me any more than he. I can only wait until the annulment is com-

plete, then be on my way. That should prove that I am
sincere."

Brace smiled. "And that will be the day that my
brother owes you a sincere apology for his rudeness
this day. You and I both know that you did nothing to
encourage those men on the quay."

"Thank you, Captain." Alysson smiled up at him. At
least he was willing to give her the benefit of the doubt,
which was more than his brother was willing to do.

"Now, madame, if you will be so good as to pardon
me, my duties await me topdecks."

He bowed, and after he had left, Alysson looked
around at her elegant surroundings, relieved that Brace
would be along on the voyage to soften the piercing
hatred in Donovan MacBride's black eyes.

She turned at a light rap on the door. Stephens bus-
tled inside, giving Alysson a businesslike nod before he
turned to direct a burly seaman following him with
Alysson's trunk. The man carried it across to the lacquered screen as directed, but his eyes remained appreciatively on Alysson. He lowered the chest with one
muscular forearm, smiling at the pretty blond lady until
a disapproving stare from George Stephens reminded
him to be on his way.

"Mr. MacBride has instructed me to see that you are
made comfortable during the voyage, Miss Tyler. If
there is anything you want or need, I will be more than
pleased to see to it for you."

Alysson smiled at the fastidious little man, having
gotten to know him somewhat during the last week at
the MacBride town house. Although he was always terribly formal with her, he had been kind. Early in her
stay there, she had detected the barest hint of the King's
English beneath his clipped Americanized speech.

"Thank you, Mr. Stephens," she said, smiling.
"Could you be of English birth, by any chance?"

"Aye, miss, but I prefer to think of myself as a true American, and it pleases me prodigiously that Mr. Donovan thinks of me that way as well."

Disdain for his English heritage was obvious, and Alysson could not help but wonder if all Americans held the British in such contempt. She contemplated this as Stephens moved to her trunk and lifted the top. Curiosity about the MacBride family prompted her next remark.

"It sounds as if you have been with Mr. MacBride for a very long time, Mr. Stephens."

Stephens nodded as he transferred a folded blouse to a built-in chest of drawers behind the silk screen.

"Yes, miss, for sixteen years now. Mr. Donovan took me in when I was sold into indenture to pay my father's gambling debts."

Alysson couldn't hide her surprise. "He must have been very young then."

"Aye, he was not yet twenty, but he had had the responsibility for his whole family even before that."

"His father must have died very young."

Stephens glanced up at her. "The redcoats hanged his father, miss, during the revolt."

Alysson stared at Stephens as he went on with his unpacking, wondering if that were part of the reason Donovan MacBride detested the English, but she didn't want to ask Stephens any more questions for fear he would repeat them to Donovan.

When Stephens had finished his task, he came toward her again.

"I share a small cabin next door with Mr. MacBride's personal secretary," he told her. "Should you have need of my services, there is a bellpull there near the lamp. 'Twill ring a bell beside my bed."

"Thank you, Stephens, but I do intend to see to myself as much as possible. I'll try not to bother you over-much."

Stephens looked visibly startled. "I assure you that is my job, and I will be honored to serve you as my master's guest, Miss Tyler. If you'll excuse me now, I will see to Mr. Donovan's things."

Alysson nodded and looked around the room, wondering what to do with herself now, and as for that, what to do with herself for the long weeks of the voyage. After a few minutes, Stephens noticed her listless contemplation of the empty cabin and offered a suggestion.

"The ship is about to be winched to midstream, miss. Perhaps it would interest you to go topdecks and observe our disembarkation?"

Alysson smiled, welcoming his suggestion. "That does sound nice. I have never sailed before, you know."

"Yes, miss."

Stephens busied himself on the other side of the stateroom, where Donovan and Brace had draped bunks and dressing areas, and Alysson left quietly. There was no one in the companionway outside her door, and when she came up into the fresh air, she realized that the thirty or so passengers were congregated at the railings to watch Captain MacBride weigh anchor.

Most were on the main or quarterdeck, and Alysson immediately picked out the tall, statuesque figure of Rosalie Handel, surrounded by her entourage of actors. She hesitated, wondering if she should join them, then decided against the idea, afraid they would hold her responsible for Donovan MacBride's anger.

Instead, she made her way up the steps to the forecastle deck, where she chose a solitary spot near an immense figurehead that leaned out over the water. She recognized the female figure at once as Halcyone from the Greek myth, and she admired the carving with its flowing wooden robes molding the body as if the sea-wind already swept over it.

The ship began to move as longboats towed her to center stream, and Alysson looked behind her as Captain MacBride called orders. His crew moved to their tasks, and sails were hoisted with a rattle of booms and yards. The brisk wind caught the great sheets of canvas with a whooshing sound, filling the topgallants, and the *Halcyone* began to move in the current of the Thames River.

Alysson stood alone beside the figurehead, the wind at her back, blowing her hair over her cheeks. She breathed deeply, feeling very alone. Her dream of going to America was coming true, but how very different were her feelings from what she had expected. She felt empty inside, and loneliness lay like a heavy stone upon her heart. She was without her mother and Mathilde and Freddie, with no friends, no money, no one around with whom to talk, but only a man who looked upon her with black eyes full of loathing. How could she take joy in such as that? She shivered, pulling her white silk shawl closer around her shoulders.

It was the beginning of a new life, and she should face it with more courage, she told herself. She was going to America, and she would never see her father again. That in itself was reason to rejoice.

She closed her eyes tightly as the ship skimmed along the wide river, past anchored sloops and brigs bearing the flags of faraway places, past river estates nearly hidden in their great deer parks, and others with river gardens and pavilions at the river's edge where the rich held their great parties and balls. A curious ache touched her heart for she was truly leaving her homeland forever. She never wanted to return, but what awaited her on the other side of the ocean?

*"Bonjour, ma petite,* is this not exciting?"

Alysson recognized the French accent at once and turned to find Odette Larousse close beside her, her dark curls blowing every which way. Odette gave her a bright smile.

"I came here to thank you for taking my place as you did. Rosalie was quite cross with me over it, and if it had not been for Edgar's talking to her, I am afraid she would have left me here in London. I could not bear that, since I want to go to America very much, even though I miss the gay life of Paris and all my friends. Your real name is Alysson, *oui?"*

"Yes, Alysson Tyler," Alysson began, smiling as Odette chattered on before she could say more.

"We look like the wooden woman there, do we not? Though why she holds the bird's nest, I cannot say," Odette said, reaching up to pat her hair, while the wind whipped her skirts, molding them to her legs until she did, indeed, look like the masthead.

"She is Halcyone from the Greek myths. They believed that she was so heartbroken when her husband, Ceyx, drowned in the Aegean Sea that the gods took pity on her. They turned both of them into birds they called halcyons. After they build their nests upon the surface of the ocean, the waters were supposed to grow calm and the winds grow quiet."

Odette stared at her. "I surely hope the sea is calm for us, for even the channel crossing from France made my stomach heave and twist."

Alysson laughed. "It is only a legend, but I think we will be quite safe in Captain MacBride's hands."

Odette closed her eyes in a show of ecstasy.

*"Ooh la-la,* is he not *magnifique?* I would put myself in his hands quite eagerly, would you not? And his brother, so dark and tall and handsome! And those

eyes, so black and like fire! I would welcome his hands on me!"

Her words sent an embarrassed flush climbing Alysson's neck as she remembered a night when those very hands caressed her bare flesh. She was glad when Odette took hold of her arm.

"But come, Alysson, I nearly did forget. Rosalie wishes to speak with you, and I will introduce you to the others with us."

Alysson let herself be drawn along, down the steps to the main deck, where two men stood together at the rail. Odette stopped beside them.

"Here she is. This is Alysson. You have already met Edgar, but this is Edgar's brother, Milton. They are twins, as your eyes will tell you."

"How do you do," Alysson said, and the one named Milton swooped low over her hand, pressing it to his lips while his brother shook his head and rolled his eyes upward.

"My sweet little flower," said Milton, "it is my pleasure to meet you."

"You can tell them apart by sniffing their breaths," Odette informed her, behind her hand, but loud enough for them both to hear. She laughed. "Milty loves the wine."

They were identical in countenance, Alysson had to agree, tall and slender with the same full mustache and brown bushy hair. Even the eyes were the same dark blue with laugh lines at the corners. She did note, however, that Milton's skin was of a much darker hue.

"I am sure I will be able to tell you apart by your darker skin," she said to Milton, looking around in surprise as they all laughed at her.

"Not after a week has gone by," Odette explained. "That is a stain on his face. He played Othello last week, and it has not yet worn away."

Alysson laughed with them as Rosalie came up, dressed elegantly in an olive-green velvet skirt and jacket with a froth of white lace at her throat and cuffs. A young boy was with her, and Alysson remembered thinking him handsome when she had seen him at the Crownover Theater.

"So there you are, Miss Tyler," Rosalie said in her low, husky voice. "Mr. MacBride told me you would be aboard with us."

Alysson thought she saw something in Rosalie's brown eyes as Rosalie gestured to the boy with her, but she could not be sure.

"This is Billy Brock, one of my newest members. I have great hopes for him, once we rid him of his atrocious cockney accent."

"Me 'oner, miss," Billy said, smiling shyly at Alysson. He was really quite pretty for a boy with his big blue eyes and curly blond hair. His face was still smooth and unbearded, with a natural flush in his cheeks, and Alysson guessed his age to be around fifteen or sixteen. Alysson turned away from him as Rosalie spoke brusquely to the others.

"Run along now, all of you, and see to your unpacking, because I have need to speak to Miss Tyler alone."

The others bid Alysson good-bye and moved away, except for Milton, who lingered to kiss her hand again. After he had gone, she looked warily at the elegant red-haired woman. She knew Rosalie Handel was a good friend of Donovan MacBride, and she would no doubt think Alysson as guilty as he did. Despite her thoughts, the bluntness of Rosalie's next words came as a shock.

"I am not one to mince words, Miss Tyler. I know all about your compromised marriage to Donovan Mac-Bride, and I would like to know if you used me to trick him as he says you did."

Alysson's face went white, and she wondered just how much Donovan had told Rosalie about that terrible night.

"Then I will be frank as well. I did not trick him. I want no marriage with him, and I have already signed an annulment agreement to that effect. In truth, I am eager to arrive in New York and be away from him."

Rosalie stared down into almond-shaped green eyes. She wondered if the girl spoke the truth. There weren't many women who would let a man like Donovan Mac-Bride get away once she'd gotten him to the altar, but Donovan certainly didn't believe a word she said. He was still furious with her and believed her to be a spy for her father. She certainly looked innnocent right now, very young and vulnerable, but Donovan had insisted the girl was a born actress, and if she *had* fooled Donovan MacBride with an act, she had to be extremely good. Donovan MacBride was nobody's fool. She was intrigued enough to want to see Alysson Tyler perform.

"Whether I believe you or not is of very little matter," she said, searching Alysson's face. "But I did promise you an audition, and since I am expected to put on a play for the passengers, I might be able to use you."

She watched a look of pure delight overtake Alysson Tyler's face. "Oh, Madame Handel, I would work very hard if you'd give me such a chance, and I would take any part you wished."

"It will only be a temporary thing, of course, but if you prove yourself capable, we will talk further."

Alysson nodded eagerly, and Rosalie went on. "I feel it only fair to warn you, Miss Tyler, that I am very strict with the members of my company. Odette broke one of my rules by going out on the day of a performance, and her action caused us all a great deal of trouble."

"Especially me," Alysson said quickly, and Rosalie hid a smile at Alysson's grim expression. The girl had no doubt tasted a generous dose of Donovan's anger, and Rosalie knew from experience that could be most troubling.

"Donovan informed me that you are to be known during the voyage as a friend of his family and will be using his stateroom."

She stopped, thinking the girl looked less than thrilled about the living arrangements on the voyage. "There is no room for you in our quarters, but if you wish, you could take your meals at our table in the dining hall."

"Oh, yes, thank you, I would like that very much."

Rosalie smiled slightly as Alysson thanked her again, then rushed off, looking very much like a little girl invited to her first birthday party. She glanced at the quarterdeck and found Donovan's black eyes on Alysson where she hurried toward the quarterdeck doors. Her gaze narrowed speculatively at seeing the massive frown on his face. He usually hid his feelings well, but he stared at the girl with an intensity she had rarely seen in him. Good or bad, she decided, Donovan MacBride felt quite strongly about Alysson Tyler's presence aboard. Rosalie could not help but wonder what his true feelings were.

# Chapter 4

The passenger dining hall of the *Halcyone* was small but ornate, with hanging crystal chandeliers and velvet-edged panels displaying paintings that depicted life in America. The tables were draped with fine white damask and lit by two-branched silver candelabras, and it was at a table for six that Alysson sat with her new-found friends on the evening of departure. Rosalie sat at the head of the table between Edgar and Billy Brock, and Alysson had been seated at the other end with Odette and Milton on either side of her. After all had been served, Rosalie looked down the table at Alysson.

"Edgar and I have decided to do *Romeo and Juliet* for the passengers, and if your audition goes well, Alysson, we intend to cast you as Juliet."

Alysson stared at her in disbelief, then smiled widely as a thrill of pleasure shot through her. "That would be wonderful, Madame Handel. I know the lines by heart."

All eyes turned to her in surprise.

"Indeed?" Rosalie said, and Alysson nodded eagerly.

"It is my favorite of all the plays, and I have read it often. Memorization comes easily for me."

"It would be nice if it did for everyone here," Rosalie answered, giving a pointed look at Odette, who blushed under the mild criticism. "But we shall see if you will get the part tomorrow." She looked around at the others. "Since there are so few of us, we'll have to play several roles each. Billy here will be Romeo, I suppose, and he'll also have to play the parts of various Montague or Capulet young men in the street scenes. Odette, you will be Juliet's mother, and I will be the nurse. Edgar, I think you would do best as Friar Laurence, and Milton, you'll be Mercutio, I think."

Alysson listened with rapt attention as they discussed the coming production, hardly able to believe she might actually become part of a stage company. She looked at Billy, who had said little, wondering if he was a good actor. Though he had been quiet, she had noted the severity of his cockney accent, and he was very young and very shy. While she looked at him, he glanced up, then colored when she smiled at him. Odette and Milton were speaking in low tones, and the subject of their discourse stole her attention away from Rosalie's conversation with Edgar about costumes.

"I think Mr. MacBride is the most divine man ever created," Odette was whispering. "Look at him over there, with those black eyes. Do you know him well enough to introduce us, Milty? You are from New York, *oui?*"

Alysson followed their gazes across the room to the captain's table, where the two MacBride men sat with a couple. She was surprised when the man she didn't know met her eyes, then lifted his wineglass in a salute to her. She nodded slightly, wondering who he was.

"I know of him, of course. Everybody in New York does," Milton answered Odette, refilling his goblet with wine for the fourth time. "The MacBrides are one of the richest families in the city, so we don't exactly run in the same social circles."

"So Donovan MacBride belongs to the *crème de la crème* of New York, eh?" Odette said, a speculative gleam in her eye. "I wonder if he is married."

Alysson choked on her wine, and both Odette and Milton turned concerned eyes to her.

"Are you all right, *chérie?*"

"Yes, yes," Alysson assured them quickly, taking a bite of her biscuit, but Odette was not finished with the subject she found more than fascinating.

"I saw him once in Paris at Mademoiselle Rochet's house. He was a frequent visitor there before the war made it difficult for Americans. She entertained him herself when he was in town."

"Was she a relative of his, then?" Alysson asked innocently, and Milton laughed aloud, causing heads to turn at the nearby tables.

"They had relations, you might say," he ventured, draining his glass.

"You hush," Odette chided him with a frown. "Alysson does not know about such things yet. She is *une jeune fille* and *innocente.*" She looked at Alysson and lowered her voice. "Mademoiselle Rochet is a famous courtesan in Paris. She had many men who came to visit her, but he was her favorite. I worked there with her until she lost favor with Bonaparte and was banished to the countryside."

"A courtesan?"

Milton grinned again. "A very expensive prostitute, Aly, love, kept only by men who can afford her."

Alysson was a bit scandalized, but she tried not to show it. "And you mean Mr. MacBride kept her that way?"

"Oh, no, they say he will not be tied to one woman."

"And it is said in New York that he has two passions —women and horses," Milton added. "And it is rumored he rides both equally well."

Alysson blushed, and Odette was quick to discern the reasons. She frowned at Milton.

"You have embarrassed her with your silly talk."

"No, I'm not embarrassed," Alysson said, but she was, for reasons neither of them understood. "I think it's most interesting, since I will be forced to share the same stateroom with him."

Odette's eyes grew round, and Milton leaned back in his chair, grinning.

"You best watch yourself then, girl, for Brace MacBride's reputation with women almost equals his brother's, although his mistresses have to contend with his love of the sea and this ship."

*"Mon Dieu,* I cannot believe you actually are to live with both those *magnifique* men," Odette breathed. "The gods surely favor you! But why do you stay with them?"

"My father insisted," Alysson said on a dry note. "But I assure you they have no interest in me. I have my own bed with a privacy screen around it."

"But sharing a cabin with Donovan MacBride for the whole crossing! *C'est formidable!* If I could only have such good fortune!"

"I'd change places with you right now if I could," Alysson said, and Odette stared at her as if she had lost her mind.

Milton nodded with approval. "You're right to feel that way. Odette said herself he had many women, and one of them is the biggest scandal in New York. Her name is Marina Kinski, and she's a Russian countess. The gossips say he fought a duel over her in Venice and killed her husband, then she followed him to New York when he left her there. Now they are lovers, and he bought her a magnificent house of her own, but he still squires around the more socially acceptable women, for appearances' sake."

Alysson found that none of Milton's remarks shocked her. Donovan MacBride had certainly tried to seduce her at their first meeting, and he would have probably seduced Odette, if she had been able to go to his house. Alysson felt nothing but pity for any woman unfortunate enough to become his lover. Wanting to change the subject, she lifted her wineglass and directed a question to Milton.

"Have you and Edgar been actors for a long time?"

"Since we were twenty, about ten years now. He's the one with the brains, and as you now know, I like wine and the company of beautiful women, like the two of you." He raised his glass toward his companions.

"*Oui,* and you got me drunk and in trouble with Rosalie when I listened to your flowery words, so do not listen to him, Alysson."

Milton laughed good-naturedly. "Ah, but we had a hell of a good time before Edgar came and dragged you off, didn't we, love?"

His smile was so charming that Alysson had to smile. "Have you acted in New York, Milton?"

"Yes, we did *As You Like It* there a year ago."

Alysson got to the question she really wanted to ask him. "I heard once that there was a very good actor there at one time named Adam Sinclair. Have you ever heard of him?"

She thought at first he had by the expression in his eyes, but then he shook his head. "No, never heard of him. Is he a friend of yours?"

Alysson was saved a response as Odette clutched her arm, whispering excitedly.

"Look, Donovan MacBride is heading straight for us. What could he want?"

Alysson tensed all over as Donovan approached. She tried to act nonchalant while all the time her stomach rolled with apprehension. What if he ridiculed her or said something that would be impossible to explain to Odette and the others?

She waited expectantly as he paused beside Rosalie's chair and made a few polite remarks to the others at the table. He did look superb in his dark evening attire, she had to admit, but she stiffened when black eyes found her.

"I was hoping you would lend me the company of Miss Tyler for a moment or two, Rosalie. My dinner companions would like to meet her."

Alysson glanced quickly at the couple seated at the table with Brace, wondering why they would be interested in her.

"Of course, Mr. MacBride. We are just finishing anyway." Donovan held her chair as Rosalie stood, still speaking to the others. "The rest of you should go ahead and retire, because I intend to have the audition first thing after breakfast. Alysson, my dear, I'll see you then."

"You are too lucky," Odette whispered as she put down her napkin and stood. She moved away on Milton's arm, leaving a reluctant Alysson behind.

Donovan drew back her chair with the utmost politeness, but when he spoke to her, his tone held none of the cordiality with which he had addressed Rosalie.

"Mr. Atkinson is my business associate, and since you saw fit to give him such a blatant invitation to sample your charms, he has insisted on meeting you."

"I did not! He raised his glass to me, and I only—"

"Shut up." He cut her off sharply. "Just say hello, then make your excuses and go below."

For the first time since she had met Donovan MacBride, Alysson was incensed. A great tide of resentment rushed from deep inside her to prick at her pride. She was suddenly quite tired of his hatefulness, his cruel and condescending manner toward her. Her anger gave her the courage to make her retort.

"I'm surprised you agreed to introduce me to any of your American friends since I had the gall to be born English."

"It gives me no pleasure, that's for damn sure,"

Donovan returned succinctly. "Perhaps you should use one of your many accents with which you lie so well and save me the embarrassment of having an English woman sharing my cabin. My sentiments toward your country are well known by the Atkinsons."

His words held such cold, arrogant sarcasm that Alysson's own anger built by degrees as he led her across the room, holding to her elbow in a painful grip. She was tired of him! Tired of taking his insults and suffering under his sneering contempt! She had signed his stupid annulment agreement, and still he treated her like dirt beneath his feet! Well, she was sick and tired of taking it! If he wanted an accent from her, he'd get one he would never forget! What could he do anyway? Throw her overboard?

When they reached the captain's table, Brace and the other man rose at once. Donovan released her arm and smiled warmly down at her as he spoke to his friends, while Alysson looked at him coldly, thinking that he should have been the actor instead of her.

"Miss Tyler, please allow me to introduce my good friend and business associate, Mr. Richard Atkinson, and his lovely sister, Miss Evelyn Atkinson. I told them you are a close friend of the family, and we were honored to give you our protection on the crossing."

He looked expectantly at Alysson, obviously waiting for her to verify his story, and Alysson gave him her most dazzling smile before she turned glowing green eyes to Richard Atkinson.

"Aye, 'at be the truth o' it, guvna," she trilled shrilly in her best rendition of Billy's cockney accent. "Donnie, 'ere, 'e be a real blue-blood gent the way 'e took me in 'is own cabin and gave me 'is bed and all. Me pappy, 'e insisted, if ye get me drift?" She winked broadly at Mr. Atkinson, who was staring at her with openmouthed shock, then she smiled brightly up at

Donovan. Donovan's jaw went rigid as Alysson began again, this time leaning down close to Miss Atkinson.

"I sure be glad to get to meet a fine colonial gull like yerself, missy." She reached down and pumped the astonished lady's hand, and Brace took one look at Donovan's blanched face, a muscle twitching furiously in his cheek, and decided he had better do something and quick. He laughed, clapping his hands as he stood.

"Bravo, Miss Tyler, we have all heard what an accomplished actress you are, but that accent was magnificent! Don't you agree, Richard?"

Richard's look of disbelief slowly settled into an amazed grin. He shook his head. "I swear I thought you really talked that way! You certainly had me fooled, Miss Tyler."

Brace's eyes held Alysson's for a second, and she took heed of his warning look.

"Why, thank you, Mr. Atkinson," she answered graciously in perfect English diction. "Mr. MacBride insisted that I display for you one of my accents, and I do like to please him. He's such a *charming* host."

Mr. Atkinson didn't appear to hear her mocking inflection, so intent was he on admiring her beautiful face, but Brace heard it, and so did Donovan. Donovan clenched his jaw harder, and Brace spoke quickly.

"Now, Miss Tyler, you promised me a turn around the deck before you retire, and I intend to hold you to it." He smiled at her. "If you'll excuse us, gentlemen, Miss Atkinson."

He guided Alysson off before anyone could object, and he did not slow his pace until they were out of the dining room and in the companionway that led to their stateroom. Then he stopped and looked down at her.

"I think perhaps my brother deserved what you just did," he said, shaking his head. "But I better warn you that he's going to be angry as hell about it."

Alysson sighed, already regretting that she had allowed her anger to get the better of her good sense. "I am sometimes quite impulsive, Captain MacBride, as you can probably tell, but do you think he'll be really angry?"

"He'll be furious," Brace returned without hesitation. "Not many dare to provoke him on purpose, except perhaps my brother and me, and he rarely lets us get by with it." He smiled as they neared the door of the stateroom. "My advice to you is to go straight to bed and stay there until morning. He'll have calmed down by then. But"—he paused, grinning—"if he's rubbing that scar on his eye when you get up, stay abed. That's a sure way to know when he's angry."

Alysson thanked him, watching as he strode off, wondering why he had helped her. He hardly knew her. She entered and gazed longingly at the bolt on the door. She shivered, not daring to slide it into place, although a barrier between her and Donovan MacBride sounded most tempting at the moment. What in heaven's name had possessed her to act in such a way? It had been a foolish thing to do!

Now that she was alone, she was very afraid of facing Donovan's wrath, and she hastily took Brace's advice. She undressed quickly and slipped into a soft white nightdress, then climbed into her bunk and pulled the curtains together, hoping he would stay a long time with the Atkinsons before he retired. Feeling a little more secure now that she was safely in her bed, she slowly unpinned her hair, releasing the braids and pulling long brush strokes through the heavy tresses. Brushing her hair usually calmed her nerves, but this night, that effect was not to be had as she vividly remembered the look in Donovan MacBride's eyes as she had left the dining hall on the arm of his brother. He wouldn't dare lay a hand on her, would he? A delicate shudder shook her frame at the mere thought, as she remembered the strength of his fingers around her arm. No, Brace wouldn't let him hit her, would he? And now that they were nearly out of the river channel and into open sea, it was unlikely that he would put her off the ship. If he did, what would he tell the other passengers? No, he couldn't do that without embarrassing himself.

She plumped the pillow behind her and, still holding the brush, her lips curved in a tiny smile as she remembered the stunned look on his handsome face when she had called him Donnie.

Her satisfied expression faded abruptly as the outer door opened and shut, and she froze in alarm, holding her breath as rapid footsteps crossed the cabin toward her. The curtains across her bed scraped back with a screech of metal, and Alysson cringed, staring with wide green eyes at the dark fury on Donovan's face. He was not rubbing the scar, but only because both his fists were clenched at his sides. Terrified by the dangerous look in his eyes, her first impulse was to get away from him. She lunged for the end of the bunk, intending to dart around him, but he had her before she could make her escape, jerking her up and giving her a brutal shake that sent her hair swirling over her shoulders and back again.

"You've made me look like a fool twice now, and I'll be damned if I'll let you do it again!"

Alysson struggled under his biting grip. "Leave me alone! You're a monster! I hate you!"

She sobbed it out, more out of fear than pain, and Donovan thrust her back on the bunk, his fingers going to the scar below his eye.

"Not as much as you will hate me, English, you can count on that, because I mean to have my revenge for your treacherous little trick and all the trouble it's causing me. Revenge is sweet, indeed, and you have only just begun to taste it."

Alysson stared up at him in mute fear, and Donovan kept hard eyes on her for one instant longer, then jerked the curtains together again. He paced across the room then, running both hands through his black hair. He moved with agitated strides to the liquor cabinet behind his desk and splashed a stiff shot of whisky into a glass. He took a drink, glancing again at the girl's bunk. Never had he been so angry at any one person, never since he could remember. He drank again, struggling to control his uncharacteristic rage. He wanted to go back and shake her again. He wanted to throw her down and make her sorry for ever having met him.

He took off his coat and loosened his black silk cravat, then sat down on the edge of his bed. He was still churning inside with a fury that he could barely believe. He, who had always found it easy to hide his real feelings from others, who rarely let his temper show, much less get the best of him. What was it about the bloody English girl that affected him so powerfully? One after another, she had wrung emotions out of him; first the thundering, shuddering desire that had gripped him body and soul from the first moment he had laid eyes on her, and now the unreasonable, simmering rage over her lies and attempts to make a fool out of him.

He lay back and put one hand over his eyes, trying to calm the riot in his mind. He froze as a low sound drifted from across the room. Weeping, carefully muffled in a pillow. An artful attempt to make him feel guilty, no doubt. A shade of that very response nibbled at his conscience, and he clenched his jaw harder. Damn her, how could she look so innocent, so incredibly young and sweet, and be such a conniving liar? He remembered the look in her eyes when he had threatened his revenge, huge and green and frightened, and the way she had pulled the blanket up to her chin in a childlike gesture, as if she had expected him to beat her senseless.

What in the devil was the matter with him? he thought suddenly. Here he was close to feeling sorry for her, when it had been she who had humiliated him in front of his friends! And intentionally!

He closed his eyes, consciously relaxing muscles that were rock-hard with tension. He tried then to close his ears to the pitiable sound of her tears. Probably another one of her specialties, after accents, he told himself firmly. What had she said that first night? "I can be anything I want. I am an actress." He would do well to remember those words flowing so sweetly from those soft, pink lips. She had smiled so enticingly, all the while knowing exactly who he was, what she meant to do, spreading herself out to tempt him, make him forget all caution, and he had, damn her! Her innocent expressions and pitiable tears were only tools of her craft, as false as everything else about her.

A defensive crust solidified around his heart, squeezing out any compassion he might have felt. Her tears were counterfeit. He should remember instead the real tears he had seen in his life. He squeezed his eyes tight as an ancient pain oozed from the blackest pits of his mind. Roaring orange flames against the black night sky, his mother kneeling on the cold ground, sobbing, her arms around her children as they watched their home torched by the redcoats. His heart constricted with a greater agony as another horrible image burned into his brain: another night, more tears, and the terrible sickness inside him as he watched the Hessian mercenaries cut his father's body from the gallows.

No, there was no room left in his heart for a lying English actress who used her tears and lips and beautiful body as weapons to achieve her own ends. Alysson

Tyler was cast in the same mold as her villainous father, and Donovan would never, ever let himself forget that.

The next morning Alysson awakened at dawn when she heard Brace stirring at the other end of the cabin. She rose as he left for his watch, then dressed quickly, vowing to be up and away before Donovan MacBride awoke. Even the thought of facing him after what had passed between them the night before sent her cold with dread. Tiptoeing, she made her way across the quiet cabin and out the door, breathing deeply as she came out on the deserted main deck. She moved to the port rail, looking out over a rolling gray sea, over which the sun was just beginning to burn away the morning mists.

They had left the coast of England behind sometime during the night, and as she looked out over endless miles of Atlantic Ocean stretching in every direction, as far as the eye could see, she felt a great diminishment of spirit, a depression that weighted her heart like a lead boulder. Her head ached from the hours of weeping despair, and she shuddered to think how her eyes must look. How could she bear the rest of the voyage being in such proximity to a man who hated her so much? He was so cruel, so totally unfeeling, and she swallowed convulsively as she remembered the look in his dark eyes when he had threatened revenge on her. Tears welled, and she wondered how she could have more after all she had shed through the night.

She was alone on the deck except for a handful of crewmen attending to the morning watch, and she avoided them as she walked forward to the carved figurehead. The *Halcyone* sailed with a brisk easterly at her stern, and Alysson closed her eyes as a fine seaspray blew upward from the plunging bow. It felt cold and salty and good against her hot face, and she raised her fingertips to push against her swollen eyelids, well aware she had to perform for Rosalie soon. The dreamed-of audition, her chance to become an actress, and she felt terrible and looked even worse.

For over an hour, she stood alone in the bow, welcoming the wind that whipped at her cloak. She knew that Billy Brock had come to the forecastle deck and was busy erecting a small dressing room with the help of the ship's carpenter, but she did not turn to greet him. It was only when Odette's cheerful voice hailed her that Alysson turned around.

Odette's happy smile faded at first sight of Alysson's face. "What is it, Alysson? You look terrible. Is it the *mal me mer?* Are you ill from the waves?"

"No, I just didn't sleep well."

Odette made sympathetic clucking sounds, then took Alysson's arm and led her toward the finished dressing room. "Do not fret, *mon amie.* I am very good with the *cosmétique.* Mademoiselle Rochet taught me herself. It will be easy to hide those circles under your eyes. You will be pretty before Rosalie comes for you, you will see."

Alysson ducked beneath the canvas flap that Odette held up for her. Billy Brock was arranging the dressing tables and costumes inside, and he smiled at them, although his eyes lingered on Alysson's red, puffy eyes.

"Billy, fetch me some powder and the pots of lip rouge. Poor Alysson is not well, and for her big day, poor *petite.* Hurry now!"

Alysson sat down in front of a mirror nailed to a crossboard and smiled wanly as Odette fussed with her hair, brushing out the tangles and braiding it. When Billy brought a small case to her, Odette set it on the table and picked out a small jar of theatrical makeup.

"You see, Alysson, we have everything we need to

make you look good again. Here is the lip rouge and black kohl for your eyes."

She knelt beside Alysson, applying makeup gently beneath Alysson's eyes, then blending it carefully over her cheekbone. "*Voilà*. You see, the shadow is gone, and now we will rouge your cheeks like so."

Alysson was amazed at how much better she did look, but even more, she felt grateful to have a friend who cared enough to help her. Donovan MacBride had made her feel worthless and despicable with his hostility and harsh words. She needed a friend.

"Thank you, Odette. Thank you for helping me."

Her words were heartfelt, and Odette squeezed her hand. "But, of course, I will help you. Did you not help me when I was *a éméchée* and could not act? But listen, I hear Rosalie outside."

Worry overtook Alysson's face, and Odette smiled encouragingly. "You will be wonderful, I know it!"

Outside, Rosalie examined the makeshift dressing room with a critical eye as Edgar and Milton wrestled a trunk of costumes inside. It was not the Park Theater in New York, but it would have to do, and actually, it mattered little. She had agreed to do a play on shipboard for the sole reason of giving her new players some much needed practice.

She sighed. Milton and Edgar were both good, of course, with years of experience on the stage, but the others were young and green, with hardly any experience at all, except for what Alysson Tyler had done in the countryside. Odette and Billy, however, were another story. She had seen talent in them, of course, but their accents were their biggest drawback. It would take time and constant coaching, and Odette's French accent would be easier for audiences to accept than Billy's atrocious cockney. He was already speaking better, though, and many of the bit parts he would play had few lines, if any. She had given him the role of Romeo so he would have to practice.

She saw Odette and Alysson come out of the dressing room together, and she moved to them, eager to see Alysson perform.

"Here is your script, my dear," she said to Alysson. "Would you like a moment to look over your lines? You may choose whichever scene you wish."

"I know the play well, Madame Handel," Alysson answered, already decided on which scene she would do. One which fit her melancholy mood. "I believe I'd like to do Juliet's death scene."

"As you wish, dear. I'll have Billy read with you."

Rosalie moved to the rail where Edgar had placed a chair for her. She looked around, glad that most passengers were not yet stirring abovedecks. They would do well to have all their rehearsals early, so they would be afforded some privacy, if privacy could be had on a ship at sea. She watched as Alysson and Billy spoke together, thinking they made a handsome pair, both so young and pretty. She settled back to watch as Alysson lay down on the deck, feigning Juliet's drugged sleep. She nodded approvingly as Alysson opened her eyes, placing her fingertips to her brow in a gesture of confusion. Rosalie was quite amazed by the range of emotions that flitted over Alysson's face, showing so well the return of memory. Alysson's voice came softly, yet held the drowsiness of one just awakening.

" 'O comfortable friar! Where is my lord? I do remember well where I should be, and there I am. Where is my Romeo?' "

Rosalie winced as Billy began the part of Friar Laurence.

" 'I 'ear some noise.' " Billy stumbled the words out

nervously, reading slowly from the script. " 'Laidie, come from 'at nest o' death...' "

Rosalie exchanged a look with Edgar, who grinned and shrugged, then both turned as Billy finished and made his exit, and Alysson's face reflected her sorrow at finding her lover dead.

Rosalie's lips parted as the girl crawled on her hands and knees to where an imaginary Romeo lay, her face ashen with grief as she reached out as if to touch his hair. Her expressions were extraordinary, revealing every nuance, every feeling, and Rosalie watched in awe as Alysson began again, real tears glittering in her eyes.

" 'What's here? a cup, closed in my true love's hand? Poison, I see, hath been his timeless end.' "

Rosalie watched a sudden anger slowly overtake Alysson's sorrowful face.

" 'O churl! drunk all, and left no friendly drop to help me after? I will kiss thy lips: haply some poison yet doth hang on them, to make me die with a restorative.' "

Alysson seemed to cup a man's face in her palms, her kiss gentle, and Rosalie sat spellbound as she raised a tear-stained face, her next lines uttered soft and brokenly.

" 'Thy lips are warm!' "

There was a pause, and it took Rosalie a moment to realize Alysson was waiting for someone to cue her line. She looked around to find the others caught in rapt fascination at Alysson's performance.

" 'Lead, boy: which way?' " Rosalie called out the watchman's lines herself, and Alysson finished the scene.

" 'Yea, noise? Then I'll be brief. O happy dagger!' "

Alysson snatched up an imaginary knife with both

hands and held it high in front of her with outstretched arms.

" 'This is thy sheath;' " she cried, plunging it down into her breast, " 'there rust, and let me die.' "

Her face contorted for a moment, then the expression faded slowly, and she fell forward and lay still.

No one said anything for the first moment, then the sound of sporadic applause sounded from behind them, and Rosalie turned to find several seamen showing their appreciation with a great deal of enthusiasm.

Alysson smiled at them as she got up, looking eagerly at Rosalie for her reaction. Rosalie looked at her a long moment, thinking she had never seen it done better. She nodded brusquely.

"Not bad for a beginner. It'll take some rehearsal, of course, but the role is yours."

# Chapter 5

For the next fortnight, Alysson lived and breathed for the morning sessions when she took on the life of Juliet, though a tragic life it was. She spent all her time with her new actor friends, totally avoiding any contact whatsoever with Donovan MacBride. She made it a point to leave before he rose for the day and to retire very early so she would be safely sleeping in her bunk when he returned from the evening repast. She hardly saw Brace MacBride either, since he apparently took his role as captain most seriously and was rarely in the stateroom at all, other than to sleep.

Her spirits gradually revived, and she began to enjoy herself more. Rosalie seemed well pleased with her acting, and she learned much about makeup and costumes and props, more than she had thought possible in so short a time. She spent a lot of time with Odette, but actually, more and more of her time seemed to be in the company of Billy Brock. She had begun to help him with his lines for the part of Romeo. He reminded her of her friend Freddie, and she found him to be very sweet, though not very talkative. They made much progress with his accent, and it was not nearly so pronounced now as it had been on the day of Alysson's audition.

On the second Sunday out, they held a dress rehearsal, though the day was dark and forbidding and the waves choppy enough to send Odette below, holding her belly and cursing the sea in vituperative French.

The rolling ship bothered Alysson not at all where she sat in the forecastle dressing room, removing her makeup. Billy entered behind her, dressed in the sumptuous velvet robes of Lord Capulet, one of the three roles he was playing. She half turned, smiling as he pulled off the heavy purple cape.

"You were very good today, Billy. I hardly had to prompt you at all."

"I surely do thank ye for helpin' me," Billy said shyly with lowered eyes. "'Tis easier when I do it with you. You know all the lines, even better than Rosalie or Edgar."

Alysson laughed. "I grew up in the country, and I had nothing else to do but read. Shakespeare was my favorite."

"Sometimes I forget that you are you and think that you really are Juliet," Billy said quietly, shrugging out of his tunic. Alysson hardly heard him; her eyes were focused in horror on his bare back. Scars covered it, crisscrossing each other in cruel white lines that covered nearly every inch of exposed flesh. She gasped aloud, and Billy whipped around, quickly slipping his shirt over his head. He seemed embarrassed that she had seen them, and they looked at each other without speaking.

"I'm sorry, I usually keep them covered."

"How did you get them?" Alysson breathed, still horrified.

Billy looked around uneasily, his fingers fidgeting with his sleeve, and Alysson spoke quickly.

"That's all right. You don't have to tell me." She paused, her eyes dark with empathy. "I'm just sorry you suffered like that." Her voice turned bitter. "I know what it's like to be under the hand of someone cruel, someone you hate, with no way to escape."

Billy sat down across from her, the compassion on

her face bringing up a raw surge of emotion inside his chest. He swallowed hard and licked dry lips.

"You 'ave suffered the whip too, 'aven't ye?" he whispered. "I can see it sometimes in your eyes."

Alysson looked down, remembering the bad times. "Yes, but not like you, not anything like you."

Billy stared at his lap. It had been over a year since he had been aboard the brig *Intrepid,* but the memories of those years at sea would never, never leave him. He had never told anybody all of it, not even Rosalie when she had found him in the streets of Paris and had taken pity on him. But Alysson was different. She seemed to understand, to really know how he felt. He was half surprised at his next words.

"I jumped ship. I'm a deserter."

Alysson laid her hand over his. "It looks like you had good reason."

She smiled at him, and to Billy's mortification, he felt tears burning in his eyes. He wiped them away, and Alysson's heart twisted.

"You're free now, Billy, and so am I. In America, we can both start all over, and now we have each other and Odette and the others, too."

Buried emotions struggled inside Billy, and he put anguished eyes on Alysson.

"The worst o' it was knowin' that I never did nothin' to deserve the floggings. 'Twas the sailing master who 'ated me and for no good reason, either. 'E just made up stories 'bout me and told the captin'. Said I stole things and said things, and I didn't, I didn't do none o' it." He stopped, surprised to find his heart pounding, his palms wet with sweat. His eyes found Alysson's again. "It was like 'e . . . like 'e liked to see me suffer. And 'e did other things too, things so awful that . . ."

His voice trailed away, and Alysson's brow creased

with remembered pain. "My father was like that, Billy. He used to hurt my mother for no reason at all."

"Was he the one who beat you?" Billy asked, looking almost fearful.

Alysson nodded. "Sometimes he did, but it was Mama he liked to hurt."

"I was a foundling and they put me in a home, but I ran away when I was nine and joined the navy. I never knew no father or mother."

"My mother was an angel," Alysson said after a moment. "She's dead now, but I know she's in heaven."

Billy nodded, and they sat in silent companionship for a time, each struggling with inner demons, until Milton stuck his head around the flap.

"Captain MacBride's ordering all the passengers below. A storm's brewing, and there's to be no supper this night. He's asking all the passengers to go down and tie themselves in. Come on, Billy, you can help me spread the word."

After Billy left, Alysson packed away the loose jars and costumes and made sure they were lashed securely before she made her way outside to the deck. The day was heavily overcast, the winds strong and gusty, and she watched for a moment as the seamen prepared for the coming storm, bringing in the sails, battening down the hatches and any loose barrels or crates on the decks.

As the weather gradually grew worse, heavy rope lines were strung about the deck for handholds during the worst of the storm. Alysson stood in an out-of-the-way spot, pulling the hood of her cloak over her hair as the first raindrops began to fall. The sky was ominously dark now, and she braced her hands firmly on the rail to combat the increasing pitch of the ship. She was the only passenger still abovedecks, and she looked out over the raging waters as a jagged bolt of lightning streaked the sky. Like Shakespeare's *Tempest*, she thought, then looked at the figure of Halcyone, thinking she did little now to calm the sea for Captain MacBride.

It began to rain harder, and still Alysson lingered, reluctant to return to her stateroom. Donovan MacBride would be there, and the thought of being alone with him was not something to which she looked forward. In truth, she preferred the elements of nature around her, despite their violence at the moment. She would rather stay here forever than go down to join him. A harsh bellow from the quarterdeck changed her mind.

"Miss Tyler! What the hell are you doing up here? One of you men down there get her below before she ends up washed over the bloody side!"

It was certainly the angriest she had ever seen Brace MacBride, or heard him speak to anyone, and she went docilely along with the sailor who took her arm and led her to the door under the quarterdeck. Once inside, she stumbled against one side and had to hold on to the wall rail as the ship dipped from beneath her feet. Then sighing in defeat, she headed for her cabin. She would go directly to bed, she decided, so she wouldn't have to endure *him.*

Donovan looked up from his paperwork as Alysson entered and made her way across the tilting cabin toward her bunk. She did not deign to give him a glance, but even that annoyed him, and he frowned after her. His eyes moved over her pink-flushed face and damp golden hair as she pulled down her hood. He resolutely returned his attention to his work. He cursed under his breath, when a moment later he read the same line for the third time, finding himself listening to the sounds Alysson was making behind her screen. He could almost see her stepping out of her skirts, could visualize with graphic detail the sight of her white silk stockings being rolled over her calf. Even more vivid came the mental picture of her in his arms in bed, soft and willing, pressing herself against him, her silky hair entwining around them. Damn her!

He forced himself to concentrate again on the document he held as the storm gradually worsened, rolling the *Halcyone* to and fro like a gigantic rocking chair. He felt the slow rise as the ship reached the first gigantic wave, then plunged abruptly into its deep trough. His chair was bolted to the floor, and he held to its arms, familiar enough with inclement weather at sea to have buckled himself tightly to the chair before the waves became too violent. Alysson was not so well prepared, having had no such prior experience, and she had to grab for dear life to the rail affixed to the wall of her bunk. Her privacy screen was not secured and went over with a crash to slide halfway down the cabin.

From across the room, Donovan watched without comment as she managed to straighten her nightgown while the ship righted itself again. She barely got the drapes closed when the ship again plummeted to bow, and Donovan shook his head in irritation as the screen went crashing back to the other side of the stateroom. When the ship reached an even keel, he unbuckled his restraining strap and retrieved it, thrusting it into a closet.

He sat down behind his desk again and strapped himself in, then took a silver flask from the breast pocket of his coat where it was draped over the back of his chair. He untied his cravat and released the top buttons of his shirt. He had a feeling it was going to be a very long and uncomfortable night. He drank deeply from the whisky, welcoming the slow burn in his throat, then screwed the cap back in place and put the flask inside his opened shirt for safekeeping.

Once again, he turned his attention to his papers. Despite all the work he had brought along for Lionel

Roam to handle, he knew there would be twice as much awaiting him at his office in Manhattan. He did not relish the thought of that, though he was looking forward to being home again. He had missed his sister, Olivia, and her daughter, Katie, and he didn't like leaving them alone for so long especially with Jeremy detailed at Fort Niagara. It had been even longer since he had seen his other brother, over a year now, and he made a mental note to send a letter to Jeremy as soon as they set anchor in New York. But even before that, he would push the bloody annulment through the courts and dispose of his unwanted liaison with Alysson Tyler.

Thunder cracked like cannonfire outside, and he could hear the howl of the wind and rain beating at the ports. The ship creaked and wallowed through the hostile seas, and he wondered how Brace fared on deck. All the candles in the stateroom had been doused for fear of fire except for two hanging lanterns, one near his desk and the other at mid-room, and they swung crazily from their ceiling chains, casting grotesque moving shadows up and down the walls. Brace had predicted a bad one, and Donovan had learned long ago to trust his brother's judgment when it came to the sea.

The ship suddenly lurched downward again, with more violence than before, and Donovan jerked his eyes from his reading at hearing a muffled squeal. He looked up just in time to see Alysson tumble headfirst through the curtains of her bed, rolling head over heels toward him in a great flurry of bare arms and legs and white silk. She landed in a tangled heap against the settee nearest to him. She did not move for a moment, and Donovan sat forward in alarm.

"Are you hurt?"

"No, no, I am quite fine" came her rather breathless reply, and Donovan had to smile as she scrambled up and held on to the settee as the ship righted itself. He watched as she tugged and pulled herself along the wall rail to her bunk again, without once asking for his assistance.

"If you'll tie yourself to the rail behind your bunk, that won't happen," he advised indifferently, but he received no answer as Alysson heaved herself unceremoniously into her bed.

Donovan stared at the closed curtains, scowling darkly as he resumed his task. He soon was engrossed with it, unconsciously bracing his foot against the desk each time the ship rolled in the battering storm. Ten minutes passed in this way, until a particularly violent plunge to bow again sent Alysson flying out of her bunk, despite her every effort to stop herself.

"Oh, for god's sake," Donovan muttered impatiently, unbuckling his strap again and heaving himself to his feet. He had to hang on for the space of an instant, and Alysson clung to a secured table leg with both hands as the room stayed completely upended for what seemed an extraordinarily long time.

Donovan reached her as the ship began to even out, and before Alysson could protest, he had swung her over one broad shoulder as if she were a ragdoll. She found herself in the ignominious position of hanging upside down, his strong muscles working beneath her cheek as he pulled his way up toward her bunk. He lowered her to it, not as gently as he could have, frowning blackly as he took the leather thong from its hook near the foot of her bed.

"Since you don't have enough sense to tie yourself in, then I guess I'll have to do it for you!"

He reached for her, holding to the wall rail with one hand as the ship careened to starboard, but Alysson desperately evaded his grasp.

"Please! Please don't tie me! I can't bear to be tied up!"

Donovan froze, the strap dangling from his hand, his eyes riveted on green ones, huge with terror. He almost fell as the floor dropped out from under him, but he caught himself, then somehow caught Alysson around the waist before she was thrown to the floor again.

He hesitated for a second longer, still holding her back against his side, then pushed her down on the bunk and sat down beside her, swinging one leg over her lap to brace his foot on the opposite wall. It effectively held her in place and braced himself at the same time, and Alysson gasped, gripping his trousered leg as the ship pitched again. She could feel the hard muscles of his thigh tighten beneath her touch, but she held on anyway, grateful that he had not tied her as he had first threatened.

His black eyes were on her, the look in them highly unsettling, and she looked everywhere but at him. Why had she blurted that out? Now he knew one of her secret fears, and she hated herself for telling him. But even the thought of being tied brought back terror that turned her insides to ice. She watched as he reached inside his shirt and brought out a small silver flask. He pushed his booted foot against the wall as the ship plummeted downward, and Alysson gasped, gripping his leg again. She was amazed at how unaffected he remained during such a raging storm.

Donovan dropped his eyes to where her fingers clutched desperately at his leg. This time, and maybe for the first time in her life, she was not lying. The fear he had seen in her eyes had been real. Someone had tied her up, and it had probably been her father. He looked at her pale face and heaving chest, realizing she was still very much afraid. Of the rope? The storm? Or him?

"Would you like a drink?" he asked, holding the flask out to her, and Alysson looked at him in surprise, then eyed the flask suspiciously.

"What is it?"

"Don't worry, it's only whisky, not poison," he answered dryly. "It'll bolster your courage a bit, if nothing else."

Alysson hesitated. "Is it really whisky?"

Donovan's face did not change. "I don't usually carry milk around with me."

Alysson stared at him blankly, then realized in amazement that he had meant it as a joke. She was more shocked by that than his offer of the whisky. She took the flask from him, and Donovan raised a brow expectantly as she tilted it back and took a tentative taste. Her eyes came up to his in surprise as the potent brew burned all the way down her gullet to the pit of her stomach. She handed it back to him, eyes watering.

"It's very good," she told him, her hand holding her throat.

Donovan gave a low laugh. "I take it you haven't had any before."

He took another drink, then offered it to her again. He was surprised when she took it readily and drank, deeply this time. She coughed as she gave the flask back.

The first drink had warmed her insides, and under the circumstances, Alysson decided, she needed all the bolstering she could get. It felt good to have something in her stomach, even if it was fire. She had seen her father drink whisky until he fell into a drunken stupor, and perhaps that would be the best way to ride out a storm at sea with Donovan MacBride's muscular leg pinning her to the bed. Donovan took it from her, surprised by the very pleasant smile she was bestowing on him, one that carved dimples in both soft cheeks.

"Have you had anything to eat today, English?" he asked suddenly, and Alysson shook her head.

"Not since breakfast. There wasn't any supper, you know, but your whisky is making me feel an awful lot better. I mean, really good."

"Yes, I should think so," Donovan returned with a shadow of a smile, taking a gulp before giving the flask to her again. If she was of a mind to get a trifle drunk, he was not about to stop her. Perhaps with liquor clouding her brain, she might be compelled to tell him the truth for a change. The ship rolled, and Alysson held the flask tightly in her hands for the duration of the towering wave, while Donovan's eyes stayed glued to the front of her nightgown. The ribbons between her breasts must have come loose when she had fallen, and he could not take his eyes from the glimpse of softly curving white flesh revealed to him. Sweet-smelling flesh that he had caressed with both his hands and his mouth, flesh as smooth as the finest satin.

A low giggle brought his attention reluctantly to her small, beautiful face. Her slanted eyes glinted like emeralds in the dusky light. She lifted a long silky lock as she watched him, twisting it idly around one slender forefinger, and Donovan felt the most overwhelming urge to do the same thing. Unable to resist the temptation, he reached out and picked up a soft silken strand, watching in fascination as it curled around his fingers.

"I do believe you have the most beautiful hair I've ever seen," he said quietly. "The color of the sun."

Alysson smiled with pleasure, raising her incredible eyes to him, her smile open and so exquisitely lovely that Donovan felt a curious sensation curl inside his chest. He wasn't sure what it was, but he knew it was dangerous, and he pulled his eyes from her face.

"I think I will try a bit more of your whisky, if you

don't mind overly much," she said with another winsome smile.

"And I think, come morning, you'll be the one who will mind," Donovan murmured, well aware she was already tipsy.

Alysson drank and kept the flask with her as she observed the man watching her so intently. He was acting most agreeably for a change. Silence reigned for a while, the howling of the wind eerie in the darkened cabin.

"Well, Mr. MacBride, why don't you tell me all about your courtesan lovers?" Alysson said after a time, bringing Donovan's eyes swiveling to her in stunned disbelief. She smiled with an utterly wicked sidelong glance from beneath her long black lashes.

Donovan grinned. She was not used to drinking, that was damned certain. "I'm surprised that you even know what a courtesan is, English. Most well-bred young ladies like you don't, and if they did, they wouldn't question a man about it."

"Who said I was well-bred?"

Donovan laughed then, but Alysson hardly noticed it. She felt good, very good, better than she had ever felt in her whole life.

"Of course I know what a courtesan is," she went on, her speech slightly slurred, and she was no longer aware of the severe rocking of the ship. "Do you think me naïve?"

Donovan's grin widened further as she hiccuped, then covered her mouth quickly with her hand. He remained silent, watching as she drank more whisky, then leaned her head back against the wall.

"As a matter of fact," she said dreamily, "I think I shall be a courtesan myself someday, after I become the most famous actress in New York."

Donovan smiled. "You'd be better off sticking to acting and leaving the other to those more suited for it."

Alysson's eyes flew open indignantly. "Such as your Countess Kinski?" she asked sarcastically.

Donovan frowned. "What do you know about Marina?"

"I know she is your lover and that you killed her husband in a duel and that you keep her in a house for your own pleasure."

Donovan gave a sardonic snort. "That just about covers it, I'd say."

"Then you admit it?"

"I don't admit anything."

Alysson drank again, watching him over the flask. "Odette and Milton said it was true, but despite what you say, I know I am as suited to it as your Russian lover."

"Indeed?"

"Yes, indeed, I do," she insisted defensively. She paused to smother a hiccup. "Odette has been with many men, and she says it is quite nice lying with them, and it must be true, because even though I hate you so much, when we lay in your bed together before my father came, I had the most incredible feelings inside here." She placed her hands on her stomach. "I cannot imagine how wonderful it must be with someone you don't hate."

Donovan stared at her, wondering if she were really so innocent. She talked and acted almost like a child at times, but after all, she was an actress. She could slip roles on and off as easily as a satin cape. He'd seen her do it. Nevertheless, he was intrigued by what she had said.

"What kind of feelings, English? Maybe it was something you ate."

He grinned, and Alysson found his remark funny.

She laughed. "Oh, no, they were wondrous indeed. Didn't you feel them?"

Donovan wanted to laugh. He'd only felt them every damn day and night since he had met her. She went on, saving him a reply.

"Do you really want to know how I felt? I felt like Shylock."

"The Jewish moneylender in *The Merchant of Venice?*"

Alysson giggled. "No, silly, the dog I named after him. He was a beautiful white spaniel I once had; Freddie found him on the moor. He loved it when I scratched him on his belly." She smiled at the memory. "He used to collapse on his back and stick his legs in the air and wait for me to do it, and that's how I felt when you were kissing me."

Donovan stared at her incredulously, then leaned back his head and laughed aloud. Alysson laughed with him, then drained the flask and gave it back to him.

"What happened to Shylock?" Donovan asked, and Alysson's face sobered.

"Papa shot him."

Donovan frowned, wondering what kind of childhood she had suffered. "Why would he do that, Alysson?" he asked gently.

"Because I set Shylock on him when he was hurting Mama."

"Is he the one who tied you?" Donovan asked then, wondering if she was drunk enough to tell him anything he wanted to know. She looked down and didn't answer, and he tried again. "You can tell me."

She still wouldn't look at him. "Yes."

"Why?"

"There wasn't any reason, only because he knew that I hated it." She shivered. "He left me there all day and

night until Mathilde and Freddie untied me." She
sighed deeply, closing sleepy eyes.

"Who are Mathilde and Freddie?"

"Why do you ask me so many questions?" she said,
suddenly querulous, then, to Donovan's utter astonishment, she squirmed out from beneath his leg and cud-
dled herself against his left side, her cheek on his
shoulder.

"I am so sleepy of a sudden," she murmured, sighing
again as her long lashes drifted together.

Donovan looked down at her as she settled into
sleep, her breathing gradually becoming even and regular. After a moment, he transferred the small red-gold
head gently into the crook of his arm where he could
see her face while holding her secure against the peri-
odic bucking of the ship. How innocent she looked
while she slept, like a small child. She was so very
young, certainly much younger than any woman with
whom he had been involved. But the feel of her soft
young body pressed so intimately against his side
brought anything to mind but childlike thoughts of her
and he was painfully aware of the devastating effect she
had on him.

He sat very still for a very long time, holding her,
wondering about her, wondering whether he could trust
her, wondering what else she had suffered with a cruel
tyrant of a father like Tyler. He looked down at her face
again, brushing a soft golden tendril from her cheek.
She was so fragile-looking, her skin so white and delicate and easily bruised. The idea of Daniel Tyler hurting her, tying her up, suddenly filled him with rage.
His muscles went tight with it, and he wished he had
been around then to protect her, and her mother too, by
the sound of it. Tyler was a rotten coward, gutless,
except around women and little children, and Donovan
would have made him sorry he had ever been born.

Amazed at his own feelings, he stared down at Alysson. Perhaps he had been wrong about her. He felt differently now where she was concerned, an odd protectiveness that surprised him as much as it would have her if she knew about it. Any kind of attachment between them would be the worst possible thing, he told himself firmly. Even if she was innocent, and he was beginning to think maybe she was, she was still Daniel Tyler's daughter.

If he was smart, he thought, he would tie her in now while she slept and go to his own bed where he belonged. He looked at her then, so very small and peaceful in his arms, her long hair wrapped around her shoulders. He picked up a lock, caressing it absently, remembering vividly the terrible look in her eyes when she had thought he was going to tie her to the rail. He sighed in defeat, settling her more comfortably in the circle of his arms, before he leaned his head against the wall and closed weary eyes, trying all the while to forget the feel of her body against his own. It would be a very long night, in more ways than one. Alysson Tyler had been born with everything it took to tempt the saints themselves, and Donovan MacBride was no saint.

# Chapter 6

"Are you feeling better now, Miss Tyler?"

Alysson nodded, giving Stephens a grateful smile. "Yes, thank you. The powders you brought stopped my headache."

"Mr. Donovan thought they might help you."

"Mr. MacBride sent them?"

"Yes, miss. Will you be wanting anything else? Your bath is ready now."

"No, thank you very much."

Alysson waited until he left the stateroom, then put her palm against her forehead. Never had she felt so ill, and never, ever would she touch another drop of whisky. Though she had slept well past noon, she had awakened with a pounding head and suffered the entire afternoon with a queasy stomach. Now, it was nearly dark outside, and she was just beginning to feel like herself again. A long soak did sound wonderful. Then she would go to the dining hall and try to eat something. Now that her stomach was settled, she was beginning to feel quite empty. Her stomach growled loudly as if to verify her thoughts, but she took time to carefully arrange the silk screen around the small brass hipbath. She didn't expect either Donovan or Brace to return any time soon, but she was not about to chance one of them walking in on her toilette.

She moved behind the screen to undress and found it very dark there since the screen blocked even the dusky light from the portholes. A candle was affixed to the wall beside the tub, and she took a moment to light it, then hurriedly unlaced her bodice and slipped out of her gown and the silk chemise she wore under it. Sighing with pleasure, she sank to her shoulders. It was salt water, but it still felt warm and heavenly.

All her life, she had taken exceptional pleasure in the luxury of bathing, one of the few ways she had been able to relax by herself. Even in Cornwall, Mathilde had heated water for her daily baths. Those days seemed very long ago now, and a pang of sorrow pierced her heart as her mother's long-suffering face rose wraithlike in her mind.

"Poor Mama," she murmured to herself. And Mathilde and Freddie. She missed them dreadfully. Not a day passed when she didn't think of them and wonder how they fared. She closed her eyes and leaned her head back against the padded tub. The water was very hot, raising steam around her until her face was beaded with perspiration, but it felt good. Whisky was indeed a wicked thing. "O God, that men should put an enemy in their mouths to steal away their brains!" she thought, quoting the lines from *Othello*. She understood them now as she had never understood them before.

An unsettling thought crept into her mind. She remembered little of her conversation with Donovan after she had begun to drink from his flask. Her brow furrowed in concentration. Had she asked him about his mistresses? She vaguely remembered something about that, but not his answer, which was most provoking. She wondered then if he had felt as bad as she had when he had awakened. Somehow she didn't think so, for she had roused enough at one point to hear him up early giving instructions to Stephens and then more to Lionel Roam.

She tried to remember what had passed between them while the storm had raged, finding herself very thankful that the day had dawned clear and the ship rode upon smooth seas. Just the thought of plunging and rolling made her stomach heave. And Donovan MacBride—he had been almost nice to her, at least she thought he had. She distinctly remembered him smiling at her, and could it be that he even laughed at one point? That was hard to believe, considering the somber, angry expression he always wore around her. She wished she could remember better. It was kind of him to sit with her as he had. Surprising, to be sure, but he had not tied her when she had asked him not to. And he hadn't looked at her with that terrible icy hatred in his black eyes.

Alysson's own eyes flew open as someone entered the door across the room. Dismayed, she sank deeper into the tub as masculine voices drifted to her. Donovan's deeply timbred voice was recognizable at once, and she did not move, realizing that Brace had entered with him. A moment later, she heard Lionel Roam and the voice of another man she could not place.

Her finely arched brows drew into a small frown. They had never entered when she was bathing before; Donovan was always busy with his business concerns in the small adjoining office, and Brace was usually on watch. Embarrassed, she sat still in the water, feeling like a fool. After a few tense moments during which they didn't appear to notice her presence, she continued with her bathing, careful not to splash the water. If she was very, very quiet, perhaps they would never even know she was in the room with them.

His mind on the business at hand, Donovan seated himself behind his desk while the other men took the velvet-cushioned chairs across from him.

"I believe we will be more comfortable in here since there are four of us," he said crisply. "Do you have the proper documents for us to sign, Mr. Roam?"

"Yes, sir. Each is prepared in triplicate as you requested."

Lionel Roam set his small leather case upon his knees as he answered, opening the lid to retrieve the requested documents. He ceremoniously placed a copy in front of each of the other men, then sat back to wait, his part in the transaction finished.

"My brother will be my witness to your signature, Mr. Creighton. I trust you do not have an objection to that."

"Of course not, Mr. MacBride. Captain MacBride's reputation for honesty and integrity is certainly as well known as your own," came Mr. Creighton's quick, flattering reply.

Lionel suppressed a smile. Creighton, along with every other merchant in New York, or any other American city, would agree to just about anything to enter into a partnership with MacBride Enterprises. Donovan MacBride was brilliant, a businessman and financier whose shrewd financial acumen in banking and real estate was well documented and respected. Why, even since Lionel himself had been in Donovan's employ, he had seen the MacBride wealth grow by the day, despite his employer's inclination to invest in any profit-promising deal, especially real estate on the island of Manhattan or the village of Brooklyn across the East River. He was by most estimates one of the wealthiest and most powerful men in New York, or the whole country for that matter.

And from what Lionel had been able to ascertain from gossip around the MacBride offices, the vast fortune had been built single-handedly from what little was left of the shattered MacBride merchant enterprises after the war. Fierce patriots, the MacBrides had lost nearly everything they owned when the British had occupied the city during the revolution. He was proud to work for Mr. MacBride, and despite his keen business-oriented mind, MacBride paid his help well, very well. Lionel himself had been able to put back a sizable nest egg for his future.

Despite his wandering thoughts, Lionel was careful to keep one ear trained on the business conversation flowing around him, in case he was asked to verify a detail later on. His attention faltered momentarily at the sound of a low splash across the room. Engrossed in their dealings, his colleagues seemed not to have heard, but Lionel glanced curiously in the direction from which it came. He started violently in his chair, then felt his cheeks grow hot as an embarrassed flush rose to the roots of his hair. Nonetheless, he could not look away as he beheld the shadowy form of a very shapely lady obviously in the act of bathing. She took her toilette behind a silk privacy screen, but a dim light from somewhere behind her created the most revealing silhouette of her every movement. After a long, throat-drying moment of watching, he forced himself to avert his gaze. He knew the lady must surely be the most beautiful Miss Tyler, who shared the MacBride stateroom. Although his employer had made it clear in no uncertain terms that there was no attachment between them, Lionel had seen Donovan MacBride's eyes on her often when she was unaware of him, and Lionel thought it best not to be caught watching her bathe.

A nonchalant glance assured him that Donovan had not noticed the lovely vision on the screen, since Donovan sat half turned away from that side of the room. Lionel turned his regard to Captain MacBride and found the younger MacBride brother watching the sight with the utmost enjoyment. A moment later, Mr. Creighton became aware of the same tantalizing view, and Lionel almost chuckled at the way the older man's mouth gaped for an instant before he caught himself and hastily looked away.

Lionel made a valiant effort not to look in that direction again, but despite his good intentions, his eyes strayed back to the shadowy form to find it now standing upright, one arm outstretched as Alysson toweled herself dry. His breath caught, and he wet dry lips as he envisioned Miss Tyler's beauteous features and lovely young figure. Donovan MacBride was not the only man aboard aware of her most charming presence; Lionel had heard many comments from fellow male passengers about her.

"That should do it then, gentlemen," Donovan murmured, laying aside his quill pen and sprinkling sand over his signature. He lifted his eyes to find his three companions looking elsewhere. All of them realized he watched them at approximately the same time, and all reacted quite differently. Mr. Creighton flushed a beet red, while Lionel Roam began a rather nervous clearing of his throat, of a sudden inordinately concerned with gathering together the signed documents and stowing them inside his case. Only Brace met Donovan's questioning eyes, his own quite openly amused as he tipped his head toward the far side of the cabin.

Donovan frowned, twisting in his chair, and had no trouble finding the object of the three men's fascination. Alysson now stood with one foot poised on the side of the tub as she languorously dried a shapely shadowed thigh, and Donovan felt his loins tighten in a quick, powerful reaction that both amazed and appalled him. He turned back, and only Brace felt secure enough to meet his gaze. He grinned knowingly.

"If you'll excuse me for a moment, gentlemen?"

There was an immediate nodding and muttered words of agreement all around amidst more throat-clearing. Donovan rose and strode across the cabin, smiling to himself as he stopped beside Alysson's screen, intentionally blocking the enticing view from those still sitting before his desk.

"Miss Tyler?"

A startled splash came from behind the screen as the shadow froze in the process of stepping from the hip-bath. Alysson's voice came, very low and uncertain.

"Yes?"

"I think it best if you extinguish that candle."

A short silence ensued, then came another tentative reply from her.

"But how will I see to dress?"

"Perhaps, Miss Tyler, you should be more concerned with how much the gentlemen with me can see."

He heard a shocked gasp, then the candle went out at once. Donovan smiled again as he rejoined his uneasy colleagues across the room.

Some time later, Alysson's face still burned with mortification as she sat motionlessly on the edge of her bed. She was fully dressed now in a high-waisted rose velvet gown, chosen intentionally for its modest cut and prim lace collar. It had never even occurred to her that they might be able to see her movements through the screen. Oh, how horribly humiliating! What if Donovan thought she had done it on purpose? She was sure that was exactly what he would think. Hadn't he accused her before of being wanton? He had even accused her of enticing the two men on the quay the day they had set sail!

She frowned, picking up her brush and drawing it through her hair. Just when he had begun to treat her a little better, that had to have happened! Well, she wouldn't be intimidated again, she vowed, twisting her thick hair into a heavy chignon at her nape. She would act as if nothing had happened, and if he mocked her or accused her, then she would totally ignore him.

Nevertheless, she listened intently for any movement across the room. The meeting had broken up soon after she had doused the candle, but she knew that Donovan had remained behind because she had heard him summon Stephens after the other three had retired from the room. Besides that, she could detect the aromatic aroma of the cigars he favored. Completely dressed now, she fidgeted restlessly with the brush in her hand, wishing he would leave the cabin so that she could escape without having to face him. Her stomach rumbled quite heartily, reminding her how hungry she was. She had not had a bite since the morning before the storm, but still she sat, thinking he would surely leave soon.

Moments later, she heard Stephens enter amidst unfamiliar clinking and rattling sounds, and when her curiosity got the better of her, she hazarded a cautious peek around the side of the screen. The rotund little valet had draped a small pushcart with white linen and was setting flame to a triple-branched silver candelabra upon it. Alysson next scanned the room for Donovan's presence and was startled when her search found him in one of the deep leather chairs nearby, calmly watching her furtive perusal of the cabin. Embarrassment assailed her again, and her first inclination was to duck back and pretend she hadn't seen him. Before she could accomplish it, Donovan stood and smiled.

"I have taken the liberty of ordering us a private supper tonight, in the hope that you will honor me with your company."

Alysson stared, doubted, then recovered from her shock and tried to regain her composure as she stepped from behind the screen. Donovan walked to her chair and held it, and Alysson sat down, more than suspicious of his motives. He moved to his own place across from her, and both remained silent as Stephens served them with his usual elegant demeanor.

"That will be all, Stephens. Thank you."

Stephens left silently, and Alysson took a deep breath, deciding to get it over with before he could mention it.

"I am very sorry about disrupting your meeting, but I was already in the bath when you arrived. You see, I persuaded Stephens to let me use the hipbath. I thought you would be busy in your office, and I really didn't mean—"

"I know. Stephens asked my permission about the bath before he brought it in for you. It slipped my mind, or I wouldn't have brought my associates here."

Alysson stared at him, especially astonished by the friendly smile he was giving her. He certainly didn't appear angry. But why not?

"Would you like some wine?"

"No," Alysson said quickly, covering the top of her goblet with her fingers.

Donovan smiled. "I was afraid you had too much last night. Are you feeling better?"

"Yes, thank you."

Alysson watched as he filled his own goblet with the ruby-red liquid, unreasonably uncomfortable with him. She couldn't remember all that had passed between them, but he, no doubt, could. Nevertheless, the poached sea trout on the platter between them smelled heavenly, and her stomach would not be still. She began to eat, trying to forget he sat so near. It was impossible, for he ate little himself, instead drinking occasionally, his eyes never leaving her. Finally she could stand no more of it and laid down the heavy silver fork. She met his gaze.

"Why are you staring at me?"

He remained unruffled by her abrupt question, his

eyes still searching her own. Those black eyes fascinated her, so dark and unreadable, yet piercing enough to always make her feel vulnerable and insecure.

"I was wondering if I could believe you. If you have been telling me the truth about yourself from the beginning."

Alysson was surprised. "I did tell you the truth. You chose not to believe me."

"You did very little to convince me," he countered, sipping his wine.

"What good would it have done? You tried and convicted me, and the truth sounded like a lie even to me. I knew I had done nothing wrong, so I could live with your unjust accusations. 'To thine own self be true,'" she added.

Donovan's mouth curved slightly at her dimpled smile. "And if I remember correctly, another line from *Hamlet* said, 'Smile, smile, and yet a villain be.' I suspect that holds for villainesses as well."

Alysson had to laugh. "You too are a follower of William Shakespeare? I would not have thought it."

"No? My education was quite extensive. It was more surprising that you have studied him so assiduously. Rosalie tells me you can recite *Romeo and Juliet* from memory. It surprised me the Italian nuns would teach English plays to their students, especially one about love and suicide."

Alysson looked nonplussed. "Italian nuns?"

"You were schooled in a convent near Rome, were you not?"

Alysson laughed at such a notion. "You were misinformed, sir. I grew up in Cornwall with my mother."

Donovan was startled but didn't show it. Was she lying again? His men had been most thorough.

"Your mother?" he asked slowly. "I thought she died when you were very young."

"She died recently."

Donovan read the pain in her green eyes before it was hidden by the thick veil of her lashes.

"Your father never mentioned he had a living wife," he began, but Alysson's eyes came up, hard with loathing.

"He hated her, and he hated me, but not as much as we hated him. He killed my mother before my eyes, only a month before I met you. He hit her with his fist, and she broke her neck when she fell down the steps of our farmhouse."

Donovan's face showed no horror, no sympathy, and Alysson breathed deeply. "I don't suppose you believe that either, do you? Another of my lies, you're probably thinking, but I don't really care. I am only glad to be away from him, and even the length of this ocean isn't far enough for me. I tried to get away from him the night we met, but unfortunately ended up with you."

Her face was now flushed high with angry color, her fists clenched on the tabletop, but Donovan reminded himself that she was an actress, a very good actress. The emotions could be part of her act to win his confidence, all planned in advance by her father and her. But what she said fit with the other things he knew about her, the mystery of her whereabouts in London, the lack of friends and acquaintances who had known her in her childhood, as well as her hatred of her father and fear of being tied. He was sure she hadn't lied about that.

"You had no formal schooling, then?" he asked, pouring her a glass of wine. She looked as if she needed one.

She took it and sipped it, leaning back again, and consciously relaxing her muscles. "No, not after my grandfather died and Father took us out to Cornwall."

"Then where did you study Shakespeare? Surely not in Cornwall."

"I found an old trunk full of books in the attic of the farmhouse. I read them all. There was little else to do."

Damn if he didn't believe her. But how could Lord Tyler deny a girl like Alysson the advantages of his wealth and prestige? With her intelligence and beauty, she could have been the toast of London society. She was his own daughter. Why would he stick her out in the wilds of the Cornish coast? There was much more to it than probably even Alysson knew, and he decided then that he would find out. He listened closely as Alysson went on.

"Besides, I learned everything I needed to know from my books. More than I would have in school. Odette says she went to a convent school and that she only learned sewing and how to walk properly with a book on her head. She has never even heard of Seneca or Plautus."

A vision of the flighty Odette and the other sophisticated whores of Mademoiselle Rochet's sitting around their red velvet sitting room reading the ancient Roman plays came into Donovan's mind. He laughed softly.

"No, I daresay she wouldn't know of those two. But she knows a good deal about life. I think you probably quote Shakespeare because you have experienced so little."

"It is true that I haven't done many things or been many places, but I know much of love and hate, and revenge and ambition, because Shakespeare wrote of all of it. I know the terrible consequences of jealousy from reading *Othello*. And ambition from *MacBeth*. Shakespeare was very wise, you know, and I need only remember his words to understand people. You, for instance"—she paused, her eyes on his face—"you are like *Hamlet* was, obsessed with revenge against me."

Donovan smiled. "And what about *The Merchant of Venice?* You mentioned Shylock just last night."

"We discussed Shakespeare last night?"

Alysson wondered at his strange smile, and when he didn't answer, she spoke.

*"The Merchant of Venice* taught me about greed and hatred."

"You do amaze me, English, but you seem obsessed with tragedies and villains. Don't you know anything about the happier side of life?"

"I have known little of that," she answered truthfully, "but I will, for I intend to have a wonderful new life in America."

"What do you intend to do with this new life of yours?"

"I intend to become a great actress, the greatest actress who ever lived." She smiled. "Would you like to hear more of my dreams?" He nodded, and she continued. "I'll have dozens and dozens of flowers in my dressing room on opening night, and as many men waiting at the stage door for me as Odette said awaited her in London. And I will choose the one who gives me a crown of white roses laced with silver ribbons."

She had obviously spent a good deal of time conjuring up such dreams, Donovan thought, watching her magnificent eyes glow brightly as she revealed to him what she wanted the future to hold for her. If what she had said last night were true, she had lived a very lonely life of hardship in a very lonely place with few friends or luxuries. Her dreams had been her escape. Tenderness rose in his chest, and he found himself wanting to help her achieve all her dreams and more. Stiffening, he caught himself up short, angry at himself. She had a way of getting beneath his guard, making him forget his usual cynicism.

"You think me silly, don't you?" she said suddenly, and Donovan shook his head.

"No, I think you just might reach your goals someday."

"Do you really?"

She was like a child again, pleased at his confidence in her. Donovan nodded. "You'll be an actress then, but what about the other things that most women want so much?"

Alysson leaned back again, smiling. "Do you mean a husband? That is something I will never have. After I am free of you, I will never marry and let some man hurt me and rule my life as my father did to my mother. And I will never become a man's mistress, even though no man will want me for a wife without a dowry."

Donovan wondered if she could actually believe that. Men would want her, all right, any way they could get her. She would be sought after by every man in New York from the time she stepped off the *Halcyone*. He looked toward the door at the sound of a knock, and Billy Brock appeared there, his hat in his hand.

"Pardon me, Mr. MacBride. I didn't know ye were suppin'." He looked eagerly at Alysson. "We was worried 'bout ye, Aly. Ye missed the rehearsals and all, and nobody's seen ye all day. Are ye all right?"

Donovan watched Alysson, who was obviously delighted to see the boy. She rose at once.

"I was ill this morning, but I am fine now. I should have had Mr. Stephens tell you. Here, I am finished now, and we can go for a walk around the deck if you want." Belatedly, she remembered she was dining with Donovan. She looked down at him as he rose politely. "You will excuse me, won't you?"

Donovan inclined his head. "By all means, Miss Tyler."

She smiled up at Billy and took his arm, and Donovan sat down again after she left. He took a cigar from his gold case and leaned forward to light it on the taper in the middle of the table. He puffed it to flame, then sat back, staring at the vacant chair across from him. Alysson had jumped up as if guilty when Billy came in and found them alone. Did she like the boy that much? he wondered, then was brought up short by another idea. Did she think herself in love with the young pup? They were certainly together every minute of every day. The thought did not sit well with him, and he frowned, realizing he was acting almost like a jealous beau. He dismissed the idea, laughing to himself. What an absurd thought. He had never been jealous a day in his life, especially over women.

# Chapter 7

Another full week of rehearsals brought the day of the play, and there was a good deal of excitement and anticipation among the passengers, who were in deep need of a pleasant diversion after long days at sea. It was late afternoon, the sky a clear lapis-blue with white cumulus clouds resting on the far horizon like mounds of whipping cream. Pleasant breezes propelled the proud *Halcyone* at a swift clip, sails billowing like proud flags to catch the favorable gales while the actors performed beneath them on the forecastle deck.

Most spectators had chosen seats on the main deck, where boards had been laid across barrels for makeshift benches, but Donovan stood by himself at starboard stern. His regard remained steadily on Alysson as she stepped out and leaned over the forecastle rail to gaze down at Romeo where he stood on the starboard stair. She was dressed in a flowing brown velvet gown of medieval cut, the bodice low and square-cut, the sleeves tight-fitting and ending in a point over the back of her hand. Her bright hair was loose and rippling down her back, while the sides were plaited into a crown of gold atop her head.

Donovan could not take his eyes off her, as fascinated with her loveliness and regal poise as was the rest of the audience. Although he knew it was her first real production, she showed no hint of nervousness, her words flowing with the poetic ease which William Shakespeare had no doubt envisioned when he penned them. She was perfect for the role of Juliet with her youthful beauty and endearing look of innocence.

His breath caught as Alysson leaned over farther, tentatively extending her hand toward her lover. She quickly withdrew it, her face reflecting the confusion and conflict that a Capulet would have suffered upon admitting her love for a Montague. It was intriguing the way she could display such convincing expressions, especially as young and inexperienced as she was. She was superb, he admitted to himself, experiencing his own conflicted emotions as he realized she would indeed achieve her dreams of fame and fortune that were so important to her.

A tolerant smile tugged at the corners of his mouth as he recalled her naïveté the night of the storm. "I have decided to become a great actress and courtesan in New York," she said matter-of-factly, and he well knew that she had the ability to excel in both professions. Her exquisite beauty would be enough to tempt any man, and she had talent and wit as well, and a sweet softness about her that muddied a man's mind, making him crazy to possess her.

Donovan glanced down at the benches below him. The male passengers were as enraptured by her as he was. One would have had to be blind during the last weeks to have missed the masculine gazes that followed her as she strolled along the decks or entered the dining parlor with her friends or stood at the figurehead with the wind in her hair as she was wont to do. Richard Atkinson had courted her openly since the night Donovan had introduced them.

He frowned, shifting his stance and clasping his hands tightly behind his back. He was certainly not immune from her charms, that was damn certain. It was those beguiling green eyes of hers. She could enchant anyone with them. She would be an overnight sensation in New York, and he had been troubled of late by the idea of her arriving there alone and vulnerable to the first man who decided he wanted her.

Gritting his teeth, Donovan chided himself. She was not his responsibility, blast it! She was not really his wife! And she never could be! She was pure poison to him with her kinship to Lord Tyler, but in addition, she was so very young, hardly more than a child, and he had become fond of her, despite his determination not to. Any relationship between them was completely impossible, totally out of the question, and he knew it only too well. For even if she was not involved with her father and his intrigues, she could easily be used by him against Donovan. Other memories came to him, the way her mouth had trembled beneath his lips, the way she had pressed her soft body eagerly against him, all effectively shaking his resolve to keep her at arm's length for the rest of the voyage. He clenched his jaw, fighting his own weakness concerning the girl.

"Sail ho, lee to starboard, Captain!"

Donovan jerked his head up at the sound of the lookout's cry, far above him on the mizzenmast, then shielded his eyes from the glittering glare of the sun off the gray-green waves. He scanned the distance for approaching ships, finally picking out several dark specks against the skyline. He looked around for Brace and found that most of the passengers were not aware of the call, their attention riveted on Alysson and Billy Brock in their balcony scene.

Donovan saw Brace pacing back and forth along the starboard rail, a silver-plated spyglass in his hand, and Donovan walked to his brother's side.

"Can you see their colors?"

"Three British warships at full sail," Brace muttered, lowering the glass and handing it to his brother.

"Damn," Donovan muttered as he brought the warships into his sights. "Are you going to outrun them?"

Brace hesitated, glancing down at the people congregated at midship. "That's what I'd like to do, but if they take chase and fire on us, some of the passengers could be killed or wounded. I can't take such a chance." Frustration erupted, and Brace rammed one fist into his open palm. "Dammit, Donovan, they have no right to intercept us! By god, I'm going to arm the *Halcyone* before she sails again. I'm sick of the way the British harass us!"

Donovan nodded grimly. "It'll end in war and soon. They still treat us like bumbling colonial inferiors, and President Madison and Congress are growing as tired of it as the merchantmen."

"I relish the thought of sinking a few ships of the pompous bastards," Brace said through gritted teeth. "Mark my words, someday they'll tremble at the mere mention of the *Halcyone.*"

For the duration of an hour, Donovan and Brace watched the English warships gradually devour the gap between them while the play continued uninterrupted, with few of the passengers aware of the interlopers. It was not until the British flagship let loose a warning shot that the unsuspecting playgoers became aware of their proximity, and though the cannonball fell harmlessly into the sea a good distance from the *Halcyone*'s bow, it served to start a near panic on the main deck.

"They intend to board us," Brace said in a growl. He barked angry orders to drop sail, and silence descended over the passengers as the heavily gunned British brig drew around to tie up at starboard. A hailing call came from the bridge of the brig, asking for identification.

"The *Halcyone* out of London and bound for New York, Captain Brace MacBride commanding her," Brace called tightly.

"Prepare to stand by and be searched."

"I protest under the tenets of international law!"

"Prepare to be boarded or considered enemy sympathizers" came the British response, and Donovan put a restraining hand on Brace's tensed arm.

"Do as they say, Brace. We have no choice now. All we can do is issue a protest with Washington when we reach New York. Our crewmen are Americans with papers to prove it. They can't impress them.

Alysson had listened to the angry exchange between the two ship captains from a spot at the corner of the forecastle rail. Billy stood with her, and they watched in silence as a party of blue-coated officers gathered on the other ship to board the *Halcyone*. Alysson turned quickly to Billy as he made an odd, strangled sound. She found his face blanched white, his eyes aghast as he stared at the boarding party. Alysson grabbed his arm.

"What is it, Billy? Tell me!"

Billy wet parched lips, his eyes dark with terror. "Oh, 'od, it be 'im," he groaned with quivering voice. "'E'll take me back. 'At's the only reason they board foreign ships, to look for deserters. I can't go back, I can't go back!"

His whole body began to shake, and Alysson tightened her grip on his arm as panic twisted his face.

"Who is it? The one who beat you?"

"No, it ain't 'Iggins, it be Lieutenant Tabert. I 'ad 'is watch!"

Alysson looked back at the British officers, then searched desperately for Donovan among the passengers on the maindeck. He would help Billy, she knew he would. He was an important American, and his brother was the captain! Surely he could do something! She finally picked him out near the gangport standing tall and rigid beside Brace. They waited for the British, and there was no way she could get to him before they were boarded.

"Come on, Billy, hurry! We've got to hide you somewhere before he recognizes you!"

"It ain't no use, it ain't no use," Billy cried, his voice rising shrilly. "Captain MacBride will give 'em the names of the passengers and crew. They'll question everyone and search the ship! They'll find me! They will!"

Alysson took him firmly by the arm. "Ssssh, they won't find you! Come on, hurry!"

Few of the passengers took notice of young Romeo and Juliet as they moved quickly across the stage to the tented dressing room. All eyes were on the MacBrides as they received the British commander with cold civility.

"Get your clothes off, Billy!" Alysson whispered as soon as they were inside. "Quickly, put on the costume you wore when you played the serving maid!"

"No, no, that won't work. 'E'll recognize me name off the passenger list, and they'll look for me! Oh, God..."

Alysson bit her lip and looked around frantically, her eyes alighting on the rack of costumes. One of Billy's outfits hung at the end, and she grabbed it, her heart pounding.

"Then I'll have to be you! I'll be a boy named Billy Brock, and he won't be looking for you anymore!"

"No, you can't, they'll know, they will!"

Alysson whirled around and grabbed Billy by the shoulders. She shook him as hard as she could, her face angry. "Stop it, Billy, and get hold of yourself! It's either that or go along with them without even trying! Is that what you want to do?"

Billy sobered at once at her harsh words, then hurriedly shrugged off the velvet tunic he wore. He left on his breeches, stepping quickly into the dress that Alysson thrust at him. She took a fringed shawl from the trunk and threw it at him.

"Put this on, too! I can hear them calling out names!"

Alysson pushed him down in front of the mirror as he pulled the shawl around his shoulders, then she colored his mouth with lip rouge. She applied more beneath his smooth cheekbones as Odette had taught her, then hastily put on him a black ringleted ladies' wig that Billy wore when he played his female roles.

"Here's Rosalie's bonnet, put it on!"

Billy obeyed, tying the red ribbon beneath his chin, his hope returning as he stared at his reflection in the mirror. He hardly recognized the pretty, raven-haired girl staring back at him, her face white and her eyes wide and afraid.

Alysson's heart hammered harder as she scrubbed the cosmetics off her face. She stripped off her gown and pantalettes, uncaring of Billy's presence as she donned the brown breeches and shirt of Billy's peasant costume. She pulled her hair back and stuck it into the cap, then leaned down to look in the mirror. She frowned in dismay. She looked nothing like a boy! Not one iota! And her hair bulged inside the cap, too long and thick to be thus confined! Now what would she do?

"What if they ask me questions?" Billy whispered fearfully. "What if they can tell I'm not a girl?"

"Shut up, Billy! Just step forward when they call my name and mumble if you have to, for heaven's sake!"

Her sharp anger stopped Billy's words, and he stared at Alysson as she tried desperately to stuff her long hair into a different cap. It would not be contained there either, and Alysson panicked as shouts came from outside. She would *not* let them have Billy again!

Her gaze settled on a jar of butternut dye where it sat

on the dressing table. She picked it up and, without hesitation, began to slather it over her face and hands, while Billy gasped in horror.

"What are ye doin'?"

"They won't suspect an Ethiop, and I can wear Milton's Othello wig!"

"But your eyes are green!"

"Then I'll squint! Go on out now in case they call my name! We can't be found in here! And remember to act like a girl!"

Billy's face paled, but he left as directed, and Alysson wiped the excess stain off her face and hands, pleased with the effect. She looked different now, like a light-skinned Negro, but her red-blond hair would not do. She grabbed the black woolly wig from its hook, but seconds later she knew her hair would not be hidden beneath it. Frantic again, she looked around, trying to think what to do as the sound of booted feet clomped up the forecastle steps.

A look of steadfast determination settled over her face, and she picked up the shears from the dressing table. An awful, sick feeling congealed in the pit of her stomach as she gathered her long blond tresses over one shoulder. She closed her eyes, then hacked haphazardly at her hair until it hung in ragged layers just below her shoulders. The deed done, she took no time to mourn its loss but stuffed her shortened hair into the wig. She hid the shorn golden locks inside her shirt and ducked out the tent flap. She had to find Jethro!

Donovan had no idea of Alysson's whereabouts, and in truth, he had given her very little thought since they had been accosted by the British man-of-war. He was barely able to contain his rage as he stood stiffly beside Brace. The British commander's name was Captain Hargrove, a short, stocky man with a complexion burnt a copper-red from sun and weather. He had peremptorily demanded the names and birthplaces of the *Halcyone* crew and officers, and Brace's face had been set in granite as he had handed them over. Each name was being called and the men questioned, then herded like cattle to the port rail.

Donovan watched in silent rage, infuriated at his helplessness. It was galling to be forcibly boarded by the British now that they were so close to American waters. They were being treated as if they were rebellious subjects instead of Americans who had won their independence through a long and costly war.

He stood stiffly as the passenger list was given up to the officer by Brace, and the civilians on board stepped forth docilely as their names were called. He frowned as several British seamen roughly pushed a handful of American crewmen from belowdecks where they had been sleeping after their midnight watch.

"Alysson Tyler," the British first lieutenant called sharply, and Donovan immediately searched among the crowd for her, hoping she wasn't frightened by the ordeal. To his utter astonishment, a very pretty, black-haired girl stepped hesitantly before them, a girl he had never seen before and who bore not the remotest resemblance to Alysson. Every muscle in his body went hard as the girl looked up at him for a brief moment, but long enough for Donovan to recognize Billy Brock. A guarded glance told him that Brace was also cognizant of the boy's disguise, and Donovan worriedly searched among the other passengers for Alysson. He stiffened in alarm when he found a very small mulatto boy standing at the front of the crowd beside his Negro driver, Jethro. Good God, he thought, comprehension dawning; for whatever reason, they were perpetrating a very dangerous charade. He put his attention back to the captain, who was looking at the disguised boy with narrowed eyes.

"Where are you from, Miss Tyler?"

Donovan's face bore no hint of anything amiss, but he cringed·as Billy mumbled something incoherent that was barely audible. Captain Hargrove frowned, and Donovan stepped forward.

"I beg your pardon, Captain, but the young lady is traveling with me." He put his arm protectively around Billy's waist and drew him closer. "I am sure you know Lady Alysson's father, Lord Daniel Tyler. He is an esteemed member of Parliament and well known in London." Hargrove's ruddy face registered first surprise, then a crafty interest, and his tone immediately took on a more respectful note. He bowed from the waist, smiling broadly at Billy.

"Forgive me, my lady. Your father is an old acquaintance of mine. I am sorry we have inconvenienced you."

His eyes wandered admiringly over the big blue eyes and black curls, and he grinned widely as a becoming blush rose in the fair lady's cheeks.

"Ah, she blushes prettily, does she not, Mr. MacBride? You are fortunate, indeed, to have the honor of traveling with such a lovely companion."

"Indeed I am," Donovan agreed amicably, "but perhaps you would allow her to return to our stateroom. She has not been well of late. Seasickness, you understand."

"Of course," Captain Hargrove said with a gallant bow, and Donovan gave Billy a gentle but firm push toward the door to the passenger quarters. Billy moved away, increasing his step as he received a long and appreciative whistle from one of the British seamen lounging against the rail.

Alysson heaved a relieved breath as Billy disappeared below, but Donovan's black eyes were fixed on her in warning as Edgar and Milton, then Rosalie and

Odette were questioned, all of them keeping their eyes firmly away from Alysson.

"Billy Brock" came the expected call a moment later, and a young officer standing just behind Captain Hargrove started visibly. He stepped forward at once.

"Your pardon, sir, but there was a boy by that name who served aboard the *Intrepid* a year past. He deserted ship, sir."

Alysson's motives became crystal clear to Donovan then, as did the very real peril into which she placed herself.

Alysson steeled her nerves, then put a suitably frightened expression on her face, all of which was not manufactured. She stepped forward, facing the sun with her eyes half-closed.

"You are Billy Brock?" the captain asked in surprise.

"Yassir," Alysson answered with voice atremble. "I be from Charlestown in de Carolinas."

"You're very light-skinned for an African, are you not?"

"Yassir, I is dat. Me pappy was de massa. But dis here is my cousin Jethro." She gestured to the big black man behind her, who nodded, eyes huge and white as he twisted his cap in his hands.

Donovan blinked at Alysson's very convincing rendition of Jethro's Southern drawl, then he stepped forward again, terrified she would say the wrong thing if she continued to chat so brazenly with the Englishman.

"Forgive the boy's impertinence, Captain Hargrove. He was sired by one of my distant relatives, the owner of Oak Briar Plantation in Charleston. I've been trying to teach him respect for authority, but as you can see, he is still in need of discipline." He gave Alysson a menacing frown. "Get along with you now, boy, and get back to work, before I put my boot to your backside."

Captain Hargrove looked at Donovan a moment, then at Alysson, then at his second lieutenant.

"Surely this is not the boy from the *Intrepid,* Mr. Tabert?"

The uniformed officer shook his head quickly. "No, sir, the boy I knew was blond and curly-headed, and he spoke with the tongue of a guttersnipe."

The captain looked down at his list again, dismissing Alysson with a wave of his hand, and she scooted away with Jethro in tow, in no need of further urging. Donovan watched her tensely until she disappeared into the door that led to the staterooms. He stood beside Brace as the British finished their search, then took their leave. The fact that Lord Tyler's daughter sailed on the *Halcyone* no doubt triggered their magnanimous attitude, for few American ships searched did not yield up at least one deserter, most of whom were Americans, innocent of the charge. Donovan waited until the brig had separated from the *Halcyone* and Brace called for full sail, then he went after Alysson. The little idiot could very easily have been hanged for an accomplice if Billy had been found out, and with each step he took to his cabin, he became angrier at her reckless behavior.

He jerked open the stateroom door, slamming it shut after him, and Alysson whirled around from where she stood beside her bunk.

"You little fool! Do you realize what could have happened to you out there?" he said in a growl, starting toward her. He stopped in his tracks at first sight of her cropped hair. "My God, what have you done to your hair?"

He sounded so horrified that Alysson averted her face, self-consciously putting her hand to the back of her hair. Hot tears threatened, but she fought them back.

"I had to help Billy. I had to cut—"

"Of all the stupid, irresponsible things to do! Blacken your face and pose as a boy! They could have hanged you both from the yardarm, and we would have had to stand by and watch! And cutting your hair off! How could you do such a—"

"Do you think I wanted to cut it!" Alysson cried furiously, interrupting his tirade as her own anger and regret exploded. "Do you? Do you think I want to look like this?" She held out a ragged strand of hair, then sobbed brokenly, burying her face in her hands.

Donovan stared at her, realizing in that moment what a sacrifice she had made. He moved to her, and to his surprise, she came into his arms. She clutched at him, crying into the starched front of his shirt, and Donovan's heart twisted with compassion. What a brave and unselfish thing for her to have done for Billy! Powerful emotions were set astir in his chest, emotions that were as frightening to him as they were unwelcome, and he sat down on her bunk, drawing her onto his lap and murmuring soothing words. She wept heartbrokenly against him, and he stroked her soft red-blond hair, feeling the loss of it himself as he crushed her slight weight into his chest. After long moments, the storm of tears subsided to a low sniffling, and he took his handkerchief from inside his coat and silently handed it to her. Alysson took it, weakly leaning her head against his broad shoulder, grateful for his strength, grateful that for once there was someone willing to hold and comfort her. After a time, she got up, suddenly embarrassed.

"You must think me very silly," she said, very low. "To cry over my hair when it will surely grow back, when Billy could have been taken away."

Donovan looked at her small brown-stained face as she raised her eyes to him, looked at the ragged locks hanging about her face, and a tenderness he had never known before welled up to pull at his heart. His voice was quiet.

"I think you did a very brave thing. Billy should be very grateful to you."

"Poor Billy. He was so scared," Alysson said. "I should go see if he is all right."

She started across the room, then stopped with her hand on the doorknob and looked back at him.

"Thank you for helping us." She hesitated. "And thank you for holding me a moment ago. It made me feel better."

She was gone then, leaving Donovan alone. He sighed, shaking his head. Never had he wanted a woman with such irrational, obsessed single-mindedness as he wanted Alysson Tyler. He was tired of fighting his own feelings. He wanted her, and he was going to have her. She needed someone to take care of her when they arrived in New York, and it might as well be him. His mind made up, he sat down at his desk, deciding just where and when he would tell her of his decision.

# Chapter 8

Though it was well past the midnight hour, Alysson stood alone at her favorite spot beside the carved figure of Halcyone. The moon was full and white, casting a glittery silver trail that seemed to beckon the ship to the very brink of the night sky. She looked upward to the stars, amazed at how very close they seemed when at sea. She felt the urge to reach up and try to touch them, smiling at her own fanciful thoughts.

It was very peaceful alone in the darkness, and she closed her eyes as spindrift flew on the wind to strike her face and hair, cold and wet. She brushed it off her cheeks with her fingertips, then her hands went on to touch the shortened locks at her nape. It had been just over a week since she had cut it, and it felt very strange without the heaviness of her long hair. She heaved a deep sigh, lowering her hands to the rail as she gazed at the silver disk hanging low over the horizon.

Tomorrow they would land in New York, and she would finally set foot upon American soil. Contemplation of that moment raised several markedly different emotions inside her heart. Anticipation, of course, but the quivery excitement was dulled by a fierce dread of the unknown. Despite her eagerness and dreams of the stage, she was starting anew, without her mother, without Mathilde and Freddie. She would be on her own with no one but herself on whom to depend. Would she like it there? Would life be good to her, or would she find the same suffering and unhappiness she had left behind in England?

She frowned, trying to shake off the burgeoning worries. She did have friends, she reminded herself. Both Odette and Billy were in much the same situation as she. They had never been to America before, but they seemed only happy about it, showing none of the fears that she felt. She would have them with her and a way to make a living, for Rosalie had already offered her a place in her company. What more could she ask?

A dark, bearded face rose in her mind to taunt her, and she squeezed her eyes shut, not wanting to see it. Donovan MacBride, her legal husband for weeks now, and nothing less than a stranger. Her feelings about him had been strong from the beginning. First, a strange, fearful attraction, then hatred, and now she could almost think that she liked him, though she found him impossible to understand. He could be so cruel—she had certainly seen that side of him—but he had had a legitimate right to be angry with her then. Lately, however, he had been nothing but kind, and he *had* stepped forward to protect Billy and her against the British officers.

Nevertheless, she couldn't really say she knew him. She wondered briefly if anyone did, even Brace and the rest of his family, if he had any. He had promised to wreak revenge on her, to make her suffer. Had he relented to her? Or was he only biding his time to see it done? His black eyes seemed to follow her constantly of late, inscrutable, but still able to raise gooseflesh upon her skin. What was he thinking when he looked at her? She had a feeling she would never know that, unless he wanted her to. She jumped as a low voice sounded just behind her.

"I thought you might need this."

Donovan's hands touched her, placing his warm woolen cloak around her shoulders, his fingers lingering there as Alysson turned to look up at him.

"Thank you. I'm sorry if I awoke you when I left the cabin."

"I wasn't asleep."

He leaned back against the rail beside her, the moonlight creating inky shadows around his eyes and mouth, making her wonder if he looked at her or out to sea. Uncomfortable not knowing, she transferred her own gaze elsewhere.

"The stain on your face is almost gone now."

Alysson glanced up at his unexpected comment.

"Only because I have nearly scrubbed my skin away, so I would not arrive in New York as a blackamoor."

Donovan laughed softly, amused by the old Shakespearean term she had used. "Are you anxious about landing?"

"A little."

He said nothing in answer, and as the silence between them drew out for an embarrassingly long interval, Alysson strove to end it.

"Will you tell me about your country? Is it really as wild and fierce as I have heard?"

Donovan braced his hands on the rail, and Alysson watched the wind whip his black hair.

"Yes, it is wild and huge, at least a hundred times the size of England, or more, now that Bonaparte has sold us the Louisiana Territory."

Alysson tried to comprehend such a vast land as he continued. "Most of it is still unexplored and untamed, with wild forests where no white man has ever set foot. It is said there are high mountains and wide, swift-flowing rivers that would dwarf your Thames."

Alysson listened with rapt attention. "And the red-skinned savages? Do they eat white babies as I have heard?"

Donovan twisted his head to look at her, then chuckled. "They are primitive people, but not as heathen as that. They are proud and fierce and fight for their lands, and there are many around New York State. But since the war, they are peaceful, unless incited by the British against us. You mustn't be afraid of them. They would never attack New York."

Alysson smiled. "I think you are very proud of your country."

"We are free there, and we will never tolerate the tyranny of England or any other country to compromise that freedom."

Alysson thought about his words for a moment, thought of the power her father had wielded so ruthlessly over his servants and his family, thought of Billy's scarred back at the hands of British seamen.

"I think I shall like it in America," she murmured.

Silence reigned for a time again, until Alysson reached out hesitantly to touch his sleeve. He looked down at her, and she took a deep breath, determined to set things right between them before they parted company on the morrow.

"Before we land and go our own ways, I want you to know that I am very sorry about all the trouble I have caused you. I know you didn't want to marry me, and I know you hate my father, and me as well, but I do want you to know that I appreciate your bringing me to America and giving me my freedom. And also for helping Billy as you did." She paused for breath, then held out her hand, smiling uncertainly. "I would like for us to part as friends, if you think we could."

Her smile faded when he did not answer or take her hand, and her first thought was that he was refusing her friendly overture. Then he gave a low laugh. His arms came around her with whipcord quickness, pulling her tightly against his hard chest. She was drawn to her toes, his mouth attacking hers with warm, relentless passion that sent her blood surging madly. Her knees weakened, and she slid her arms up his chest and around his neck as the kiss continued, long and breathless and devastating, until Alysson could no longer think.

"We'll be much more than friends, sweet," Donovan muttered hoarsely against her lips. "I want you, I've wanted you from the first, and I'm going to have you."

Pleasure that defied reason wafted over Alysson, caressing her like a slow warm wind. He wanted her! He didn't want an annulment! And she wanted him! She did! She wanted to be his wife! She gasped weakly as his mouth moved to the side of her throat, his long fingers tangling in her hair to pull her mouth back to his.

"I can give you anything you want, your own house, servants, jewels. As my mistress, you'll be safe from other men who might take advantage of you."

Alysson stiffened in his arms, then pushed her palms against the broad expanse of his chest. She breathed deeply, feeling slightly sick, and insulted. She controlled her voice, but could not eliminate the hurt threading through her words.

"You only want me for a mistress?"

Donovan's hands dropped away from her. He leaned against the rail, his voice quiet.

"No, I am offering you my protection and every earthly luxury and comfort that I can possibly give you. I want you with me, but I can't have strings binding us that would be hard to break. Your father has made any other kind of arrangement between us impossible, and you know it."

"I see," she said softly, trying not to show just how

humiliated she felt. "Then I am sorry, but I shall have to say no."

Donovan didn't say anything for a moment, then he reached out, lightly touching her bright hair.

"Perhaps you should think about it before you refuse me so quickly. You want me as much as I want you. The way you kissed me a moment ago told me that."

Alysson could not look at him. "Perhaps I do, Mr. MacBride, but not enough to be kept by you. I told you once that I would never become a man's mistress, not under any circumstances, not yours, or any other man's."

She left then, and Donovan shook his head as he watched her move away, her golden hair glinting in the moonlight. It was the height of irony. All the long weeks he had spent trying to argue himself out of wanting her, out of asking her to become his mistress, and she had turned him down flat, making the whole thing a ludicrous joke.

She had driven a wedge between them as he had not been able to bring himself to do. But it was for the best, he knew that. His brain had told him all along that he should stay far away from Alysson Tyler. Her father was an enemy; she could be an enemy. But even though he knew that and knew it well, the hot currents of desire that shook him every time he looked at her had won the battle with his common sense.

Rosalie would have to be the one to keep an eye on her in New York, for despite the independent pride Alysson Tyler had just thrown in his face, she *was* too young and too innocent and too damn beautiful to be left on her own. He was only the first man of many who would make the very same proposal that she had spurned so haughtily tonight, and one day she would probably accept. But it would never be him. He sighed heavily, bleak eyes on the moonlit sea stretching out before him.

It was late the following afternoon when the *Halcyone* sailed into the deep, dark blue water of New York harbor. Most of the passengers stood at the railings in anticipation of the landing while their servants and various crewmen carried heavy trunks and portmanteaus to the main deck in readiness for disembarkation.

Alysson stood at the midship railing with her friends, and a lump rose in her throat as she looked out over the waters to the southern tip of Manhattan Island. The sun was setting, gilding the distant city and glittering in the water stretching out between them.

"I can't believe it," she murmured to Odette, who stood beside her.

*"Oui,* it is most exciting to see it at last! Is it not, Billy?"

Billy took his eyes from a large U.S. Navy frigate anchored in the harbor, the stars and stripes of its flag fluttering in the brisk wind.

"Aye, 'tis good to be 'ere."

Milton stood close on the other side of Alysson, and as he leaned near and pointed across the water, she detected the ever-present odor of wine on his breath.

"There, that spot of green with the trees? That's the Battery."

The three newcomers looked with interest as he continued. "Over yonder is the Hudson River, but we'll be sailing up the other side of the island on the East River. The MacBrides have their warehouses near Beekman's Slip."

As they sailed onward to enter the great river channel, Milton continued to point out streets and landmarks, but the names meant little to Alysson. She looked at everything eagerly: the ships at anchor, sails furled and decks deserted, tall masts spiking the sky like drawn swords, and the shoreline of the city, with its wharves and slips, one after another in close succession. Even as late in the afternoon as it was, the bricked streets and buildings were bustling with people, while seagulls wheeled and screamed over the water and quays.

Alysson turned her attention back to Milton as he pointed out a distant steeple rising above red-tiled roofs and verdant treetops.

"There's St. Paul's Chapel, see, the tallest steeple there. It's just down Chatham Street from the Park Theater. Rosalie intends to go there to find work for us."

At the mention of Rosalie, Alysson glanced around and found the red-haired actress on the quarterdeck in conversation with Edgar and Donovan MacBride. Her brows drew down, and she looked quickly away, feeling the same hurt and humiliation that she had experienced the night before.

"What is wrong, *chérie?*" Odette followed Alysson's eyes, then smiled knowingly. "You do not wish to leave Monsieur MacBride's company, *oui?* He has been most attentive to you since the British stopped us."

Billy and Milton were talking together about the horseracing tracks so popular in the city, and Alysson lowered her voice.

"I think he is arrogant."

Odette smiled. "Perhaps he has reason to be, eh? But did you not say only a week ago that you thought you had misjudged him?"

Alysson looked out over the busy wharves, debating whether or not to confide Donovan MacBride's insulting proposal to Odette. Why shouldn't she? Odette could be trusted.

"That was before he asked me to become his mistress."

She heard Odette gasp, then looked at her to find the young French woman leaning against the rail, her hand held weakly to her breast.

*"Non? Mon Dieu,* what a lucky *femme* you are. Will you go with him tonight, then?"

Alysson frowned in annoyance. "Of course not. I turned him down."

Odette's eyes widened in disbelief. "But he is beautiful, so tall and dark, and he is so rich! It is a dream come true for one new to America!"

"Not for me. I never intend to be kept as a man's plaything."

Odette shook her head, her eyes going to the big handsome man that Alysson had so foolishly rejected. His black eyes were on Alysson in a way that made Odette feel quite giddy, even though she was not the object of his attention. She had no time to comment on his burning look, for Captain MacBride came striding down the deck toward them.

"Ladies." He greeted them with a smile, tipping his hat. "We will be landing soon, and I wish to take this opportunity to bid you farewell, for I will be employed elsewhere shortly."

Alysson smiled, truly regretful at having to say good-bye to Brace MacBride. Though she had seen little of him because of his duties, she had liked him from the beginning. "Perhaps we will meet again, Captain MacBride. We intend to find employment at the Park Theater, and I hope you will do us the honor of attending one of our performances."

"It will be my pleasure, indeed, if I am still in New York. As soon as my ship is armed and provisioned, I intend to sail for New Orleans. I have recently acquired a plantation there."

"Then I hope Halcyone will do her duty and calm the waves and make your voyage a safe one. If we do not meet again, I will remember your part in this crossing with fondness."

Brace glanced at his brother and found Donovan watching their discourse with the utmost interest. He grinned at Alysson. "I am quite sure, Miss Tyler, that we will meet again. Until that time, I bid you good-bye. And to you, Mademoiselle Larousse, a fond *adieu.*"

Odette smiled after him. "I have heard much of this New Orleans. It is very French, they say. Perhaps I should sail there with the handsome captain."

Alysson laughed. "Oh, no you don't! I need a friend here in New York!"

A short time later, they were joined by Rosalie and Edgar as the *Halcyone* was maneuvered into the docking slip.

"Girls, be ready to leave at once, for we must find lodgings for the night. We must stay together until we are settled in a boarding house."

Alysson and Odette nodded, and Rosalie moved away again with Edgar in tow to oversee the unloading of their theatrical trunks. The crew brought the bow of the ship into its berth with skillful ease. Eager to be off the MacBride ship at last, Alysson took Odette's arm and hurried her toward the gangport. Billy and Milton joined them, handing them across the wooden gangplank to the slip. Milton gallantly tucked Alysson's hand in the crook of his arm, then offered his other arm to Odette, as they made their way toward the brick quay, where longshoremen already waited to unload the cargo.

"Look there, Milty, who is that lady? Such *élégance!*" Odette asked, and both Alysson and Milton turned to look where she indicated.

An open landau drawn by two magnificent Arabian horses sat quayside, and inside, upon the plush gold squabs, sat a beautiful lady dressed completely in white. She wore a wide-brimmed white straw hat bedecked with yellow roses, and even from their position several yards away, Alysson could see she was quite lovely, with jet-black hair caught to one side in flowing ringlets,

Milton grinned, tipping his tophat appreciatively to the lady in white. She nodded slightly, then returned her regard to the newly arrived ship.

"That, my dears, is the Countess Marina Kinski. No doubt here to welcome her lover and benefactor home from the sea."

Odette looked quickly at Alysson, and Alysson looked away from the countess.

"White seems a bit inappropriate for the lady," Odette said, giggling.

"Ah, but that is the countess's trademark. She is rarely seen in any other color. Donovan MacBride gave her that matched pair in keeping with her penchant for white. He bred them himself, if I was told right, and they are worth a small fortune. I wonder if he expects to be met with such open enthusiasm? Rumor has it that he had cooled their relationship somewhat before he sailed for England."

Alysson put her attention on Billy, who was securing a hired carriage for them, intentionally not looking at the woman in the landau. She felt strangely betrayed, and she was glad when Rosalie hurried up in her usual brusque, businesslike manner.

"Edgar is staying here to see to the baggage, so come along now before it grows dark."

Alysson walked with them to the waiting conveyance, fighting an intense desire to look back at the *Halcyone* one last time. Her good intention was the loser, and just before she was to step into the carriage, she turned to find Donovan MacBride moving with his long, pantherish strides toward the wharf and the beautiful woman awaiting him there. He looked in Alysson's direction before she could look away, and their eyes locked for one brief instant before she resolutely turned her head away and allowed Milton to hand her into the carriage.

She settled back beside Billy in the seat facing away from the ship, as Milton joined them and closed the door. She did not look back as the driver called out to the horses and the wheels rattled over the cobblestones of Beekman Street. Donovan MacBride was part of her past now, she told herself firmly. She was starting anew in America, and she didn't need him. She would make her new life a wonderful one, and she would do it on her own. But nevertheless, she could not smile as her friends did, and she felt cheated and forlorn and unhappy as she rode away from the man she had vowed to forget.

# Chapter 9

In Alysson's dream, Donovan leaned over her, his black eyes softly searching her face, his fingers gentle upon her brow. He smiled in a tender way, and she raised her arms up to welcome him. She frowned as something tugged persistently at her shoulder, disappointed as his dark, handsome face began to dissolve from her mind. She opened her eyes reluctantly to find Odette's face instead. She groaned, pulling the lace-edged pillow over her head. Odette was not to be put off and the pillow was jerked away.

"Do not be such a lazy, Alysson! Everyone but you is at breakfast, dressed and ready for the celebration!"

The mention of breakfast brought Alysson up amid the crisp white bed linens, rubbing sleepy eyes as Odette shook her head, making her dark, beribboned curls dance.

"You must dress quickly, and you must wear something very cool. *Mon Dieu,* if this New York is not a terrible hot place! The streets, they are like fire beneath your feet!"

Odette left in a flutter of excitement, and Alysson looked around the homey room with clusters of pink roses on cream-colored wallpaper and ruffled white curtains. Above her, hand-crocheted ivory lace hung in a tasseled pattern off the curving rosewood canopy. She sighed, remembering the sweetness of her dream, as a soft chiming took her eyes to the porcelain clock atop the white mantel.

It was not the first time she had thought of Donovan during the two days they had been in New York, and she had already admitted to herself that she missed him. Even after his insulting proposal, she wanted to see him again. Angry at herself, she threw back the soft chenille spread and stepped on the embroidered bedstool, then down to the worn flowered carpet covering the floor. She crossed to the wing chair beside the open window, perching on its arm a moment to peer down into the narrow street two floors below.

It was a beautiful day, though already hot, despite the early hour, and nattily dressed gentlemen strolled along the paved walks with ladies carrying brightly colored parasols. The bright sunshine brought a smile to her face. Ever since they had left the *Halcyone* and settled into their rented rooms at Mrs. Thackeray's House for Boarders on Ann Street, the skies had been dark and gray. Hours of rain and drizzle had plagued the city. But although they had barely set foot out of the house, she had enjoyed her time with her friends, for they had taught her to dance, and to play several parlor card games that were quite enjoyable. But now, at last, she could explore New York!

The warm breeze caressed her face, enticing her to stay at the window, but it was already ten o'clock, and she moved to where a bright yellow pitcher and bowl sat on a high mirrored stand. She bathed her face, the water cool and refreshing, then patted it dry. Rosalie had insisted that she share a room with Odette, and Alysson had welcomed the idea. During the lonely years in Cornwall, she had often longed for a young female friend, and though Odette's constant chatter sometimes was wearying, she enjoyed the French woman's worldly tales of Paris and the life she had led there.

She sorted through the dresses hanging in the tall oak

armoire, selecting a cool gown of pastel lemon muslin, hoping the low rounded neckline would be comfortable in the heat. She had a feeling the summers in New York would be very much warmer than those of England. She donned the dress quickly, brushing her hair into a loose knot atop her head, with fine golden tendrils wisped around her temples and nape. Remembering her tendency to sunburn, she picked up a white straw hat with pink ribbons and the silk parasol that matched her dress. She hurried out into the upstairs hallway, feeling very hungry. Dark blue wallpaper sporting huge pink carnations led the way down the steep front stairs, proving the buxom Mrs. Thackeray's love for flowers, and the muted hum of conversation and clink of cutlery behind the dining room doors indicated that breakfast was still being served.

Alysson stopped in the doorway and searched among the tables until she found Odette and the others at a table overlooking the small walled garden behind the house. The mouth-watering aroma of the flaky biscuits for which Mrs. Thackeray was famous wafted enticingly in the air, and Alysson moved to the mahogany sideboard where a long mirror reflected large platters of breakfast fare kept warm by blue and white flowered china domes. Her friends bid her good morning as she sat down in her place beside Odette, and she smiled at Edgar as he filled her cup with the strong bitter coffee that Mrs. Thackeray served each morning. She sipped it, wishing it was the flavorful tea that Mathilde had brewed in the cottage.

"The parade is to begin at the north end of Broadway, near Catherine Street," Edgar said. "When it ends down at the Battery, the flotilla will sail in front of the viewing stands set up there. It should be a grand show."

"Oh, it will be great fun!" Odette cried, eyes shining. "I am sick of cards and parlor games and having Billy tromp on my toes!"

Billy blushed as the others laughed, for he well knew what a battering he had given Odette's feet when she had taught him the waltz.

"What is this celebration, Rosalie?" Alysson asked as she picked up a small pitcher of honey and poured a bit over her biscuit. "I have heard no one say, but I cannot remember a festival on the fourth day of July when I was little."

Her remark caused a short silence followed by an outbreak of amused laughter, leaving Alysson as well as Odette and Billy looking around in surprise.

"I daresay you British wouldn't consider it a day to rejoice over, my dear," Rosalie answered, still smiling. She patted Alysson's hand. "Today is our Independence Day, the day we severed all ties with England and your king."

"Oh, I see," Alysson said, feeling quite foolish not to have known.

Edgar smiled at her. "Nearly thirty years it's been since we became free, and every year we celebrate this day to show how proud we are to be Americans."

"I have thought of hiring a conveyance to take us down to the harborfront," Rosalie said, changing the subject. "But I am sure the streets will be crowded with carriages and such. Would any of you be averse to the walk? Broadway should be quite gaily decorated, and the girls and Billy really haven't seen much of the city yet."

"Oh, *oui,* madame, let us do that! Perhaps we will meet some rich and handsome American men who will want to come calling on us!"

Rosalie eyed the two smiling young girls across from her, one so blond and fair, the other dark, but both lovely to look upon. She would have trouble indeed keeping the men away from them—she had met her own late husband after he had seen her in a performance, God rest him—but Donovan had been most explicit about her keeping an eye on Alysson. "Let us be on our way," she said, "or it will be impossible to find a place in the stands."

Alysson paused on the brick stoop with its decorative yellow iron rails and pots of geraniums, letting the others move ahead of her to the sidewalk, where couples and family groups were making their way down Ann Street to the parade route. Billy stood at the bottom of the steps, and as he looked up at her, she admired the way he looked in his stylish brown frockcoat and matching waistcoat. He no longer looked like a young lad but like a dashing rake, and Alysson was proud to have him as an escort.

She snapped up the eyelet-edged yellow parasol and laid it against her shoulder, and Billy grinned widely as she tucked her hand in the crook of his arm. They followed along after Rosalie and Edgar, who led their little procession, with Odette and Milton in the middle.

"Isn't this a lovely street, Billy?" Alysson murmured as they strolled past the neatly kept buildings of red brick. Most of the front doors opened directly onto the street with small porches protecting the entrance, and on this day of patriotic celebration, brightly colored American flags abounded everywhere, vivid with their red and white stripes and stars. Great festoons of red, white, and blue bunting draped the upstairs balconies and windows, with paper streamers floating off lampposts and hitching rails.

"I wish I had been born here," Billy said suddenly, with enough wistfulness in his voice to bring Alysson's eyes to him.

"Don't you feel like an American right now,

though?" she returned gaily. "I do, and I intend to pretend I am, so no one will know."

The sparkle in her green eyes made Billy laugh, and Odette smiled back at them as they turned down Chatham Row toward Broadway. Just across from them, a three-cornered park with tall, beautiful trees and neatly planted flower beds surrounded a stately public building with an elegant cupola high atop the roof.

"That's City Hall across the way there. A Frenchman by the name of Mangin designed it. I met him once when he was working on the Park Theater," Edgar told them, then gestured with his ivory walking cane to the wide avenue stretching out before them, full of rattling wagons and every conceivable type of bunting-draped conveyance. "Odette, love, Broadway is where all the young men dally about when the weather is fine to flirt with the young ladies who use this walk as a promenade to show off their newest gowns and bonnets."

"What good fortune, then, that it is so close to our house," Odette returned, eagerly pulling on Milton's arm to lead him in that direction. The rest of their party followed them, crossing through the cool circles of shade from the trees lining the busy street. They were soon caught up in the hordes of pedestrians crowding the length of Broadway to await the start of the parade.

At the corner of Cortlandt Street and Broadway, Edgar bought each of them a small American flag from a grinning, curly-haired child, and Alysson and Billy waved theirs with pride as they pushed their way to a good viewing position just behind the long hitching rail of an apothecary shop.

The bustling excitement and noisy crowd reminded Alysson of the London fairs she had attended with her grandfather Laurence, and it was hard for her to believe that those days had been so long ago, and now, an ocean away. Thoughts of England brought the painful uncertainty of Mathilde and Freddie's fate, but the distant sound of drums and fifes sent all such memories fleeing from her mind, and those around her broke into a cheer as a military band came into sight several blocks up the street.

Alysson placed her gloved hands on the rail, leaning forward so she could see the approaching musicians better. Her smile faltered as she caught sight of a tall, lean man just across the street. His black hair blew in the wind as he leaned down to speak to the woman beside him, and Alysson's heart sped alarmingly. A moment later when he turned slightly, she realized it was not Donovan. She felt somehow relieved, yet deeply disappointed at the same time, and she frowned at her own perversity, annoyed with her weakness. Why did he haunt her the way he did? He had certainly made no attempt to see her again or to try to change her mind about becoming his mistress. She would probably never see him again, and she should be glad about it! But even as she harbored such thoughts, her eyes scanned the jostling, whistling crowds around her and she wondered where he was and with whom he was viewing the parade.

The throbbing drums came closer, and Milton leaned close to her and spoke loudly over the rousing tune of the marching band. "They're wearing the uniforms of the Continental Army! From the Revolution!" he shouted. "See that float behind them? That's General Washington. He was our first President!"

Alysson could vaguely remember hearing her grandfather speak of George Washington, and not in the most reverent of terms, but she looked with interest at the seven-foot-tall likeness of the famous American. A squad of uniformed honor guards marched in queues along each side of the float, and the handsome, tanned officer in charge saluted smartly to Alysson when she smiled and waved her tiny flag.

"Look there! Aly! Billy! The Americans honor *Français!*" Odette cried, excitedly pointing to the next bunting-covered wagon. Perhaps fifty French flags decorated a statue of General Lafayette, and Odette cheered and clapped with enough enthusiasm to gain her the smiling attention of those nearby.

Alysson laughed and applauded as well, until the next float sobered her. She stood silent amidst the cheering at the sight of the fallen British soldiers portrayed there, scarlet coats filthy and bloodstained, the proud Union Jack dragging behind the wagon. It was more than startling to see her country so defiled as a villainous enemy, and she glanced at Billy but found him clapping with wild enthusiasm. She looked back at the float, readily understanding why the people of New York applauded such a sight. They had fought and won their war for independence long before she was even born, but Edgar had told her much about the suffering and hardship the people of Manhattan had endured before the victory had been won.

The shrilling notes of a horse-drawn calliope followed, the calliope carried by a wagon fashioned after a Roman chariot. She was more impressed, however, and rather frightened, as a huge gray beast lumbered toward them, a man in flowing Arabian robes upon a scarlet-draped seat high atop the animal's back. She had never seen an elephant before, and both she and Odette stepped back fearfully as the tusked monster passed their spot. Acrobats and tumblers in beautiful costumes leapt and cavorted, and were followed by magnificent white horses with long flowing manes and arched tails. The beautiful animals pranced gracefully past them, hooves ringing on the bricks.

"Those Arabians are from the MacBride stables. See

the silver *M* on the saddles," Milton whispered in Alysson's ear, and Alysson hated herself for her eager search of the riders, who handled the spirited horses with expertise. The man she sought was not among them, and she watched several squads of war veterans march past before horse-drawn firewagons ended the parade.

The spectators turned en masse toward the Battery Park, and Alysson proceeded along with Billy, both of them eagerly digesting the sight and smells of their new country. The streets seemed very straight and wide after the twisting, narrow lanes of London, and as they came upon the older part of the city, Alysson could detect the Dutch influence in the narrow buildings with stepped gables. They passed shops of every description: a grocery, a printer's, a tailor's shop, a stationer's store, a shoemaker's shop, a cloth merchant's emporium, fish and oyster markets with their smell of the sea; but it was at the shop of Madame Bouvier, a famous couturière, that she and Odette lingered, exclaiming over the tiny fashion dolls displaying the latest rages of Europe. Above the streets, people hung out the windows, shutters thrown wide in the noonday sun.

When Alysson's party passed the neat verdant lawn of Bowling Green to cross the busy intersection of Market and State streets to the Battery, Alysson remembered that Milton had pointed out the park to them as the *Halcyone* had sailed up the East River.

It was much larger than it had seemed from the ship's rail. Tall trees dotted the grass with shady spots, and she noted that many young trees had been planted in orderly rows along a railed brick walk which overlooked the vast island-dotted harbor. Dozens of ships and smaller craft floated in the choppy gray waters in readiness for the naval parade, their masts and sails decorated with bunting and flags. As they moved along the walk where makeshift tents and awnings had been erected to shield spectators from the hot sun, Rosalie pointed to the huge Battery flagstaff, which Alysson thought resembled a gigantic brick butter churn.

"There, by the flag, we would have a splendid view of the flotilla. Come along, girls. Stay close so we won't become separated. In this throng, we would never find each other!"

The sea breeze touched their faces, invading their long skirts with welcome coolness as they walked along until the boom of a cannon from the newly constructed Castle Clinton caught their attention. Sails were hoisted one by one on the ships, and as wind filled the canvas, the first ship in line sailed past the Battery grandstands to enter the Hudson River.

"Rosalie? How very nice to see you again so soon!"

Alysson turned as the masculine voice came from behind her, just as the tall man who had spoken bowed from the waist to kiss Rosalie's hand. He was dressed richly in a dark green jacket, the buff-colored waistcoat cut fashionably short atop matching breeches and dark boots, the cuffs of which were turned back at the knee to reveal a buff lining. Alysson thought him most attractive with his white-blond hair and long curving sideburns, and she studied him surreptitiously, wondering who he was as he carried on a polite discussion about the parade with Rosalie. A moment later, he turned to her and smiled, his eyes brown and warm and friendly.

"And you, I suspect, must be the lovely Miss Tyler?"

Alysson was surprised that he knew her name but returned his very pleasant smile as Rosalie introduced them.

"Alysson, let me present Mr. Douglas Compton. You

remember my mentioning his name, I am sure. I went to see him yesterday at the Park Theater."

"How do you do, Mr. Compton," Alysson said, and the smiling brown eyes held her for an instant longer before Rosalie introduced him around her group. He greeted each person with equal politeness, but immediately after the introductions were complete, he turned back to Alysson.

"I would be pleased if you all would join me to view the flotilla in my tented pavilion. I am sure that you ladies would enjoy the spectacle much more there out of the sun."

Rosalie smiled gratefully. "How very kind, Mr. Compton. We would be delighted."

"It's just across the walkway there. May I have the pleasure of escorting you, Miss Tyler?"

He crooked his arm in invitation, and most impressed with his gallant manners, Alysson put her hand on his arm. It faintly surprised her when he familiarly covered her gloved fingers with his hand, but he gave her no time to withdraw it as he led her toward a blue and white striped awning held aloft by red poles.

A Negro manservant in spotless white livery awaited beneath the red-fringed canvas where velvet-cushioned chairs had been placed. Douglas Compton took Alysson's elbow and led her to the chair next to his own, and she sat down, just as salutes were fired from the ships passing the Battery. Alysson watched in fascination, awed by the huge naval frigates and merchantmen with sailors perched high on the yards above the decks. All the while, she remained very aware of the man beside her as he showed an acceptable degree of attention to her, at times pointing out the name of a ship or offering her refreshment from the table of lemonade and sweetcakes tended by a second servant.

"Look Alysson, the *Halcyone!*" Odette exclaimed,

and Alysson leaned forward with interest as the graceful ship with its carved figurehead sailed into sight.

"The *Halcyone?* Is that not one of the MacBride ships?" Douglas asked, and Alysson looked away from him, angry at the blush rising in her face.

"Yes, she is captained by Brace MacBride. We made the crossing on her."

"I see. I have a spyglass here. Would you like a better look at her? Perhaps you will spot someone you know in the crowd at her rails."

Alysson looked at the spyglass he held, wanting very much to scan the *Halcyone's* decks, but she hesitated, because she knew with self-contempt for whom she would look. At her hesitation, Odette leaned around, with a disarming smile to Douglas Compton.

"May I look through the glass, Monsieur Compton, if Alysson does not wish to? I would very much like to see the handsome captain once more." Douglas handed her the glass, and she smiled as she focused it on the swift-moving ship. "There he is at the quarterdeck rail! We have seen him there often, have we not, Alysson?"

Alysson nodded, but her muscles grew tense as Odette moved the instrument over the decks.

"There are many visitors aboard," Odette murmured. "And there is the other Monsieur MacBride with his Russian countess."

Alysson's heart sank in a way that appalled her, then fluttered to life again as Odette amended her first observation.

"But wait, she does not wear the white, but black, and she is much too tall for that one. And there is a child with them! Who can they be?"

Alysson gave up her intention not to look, taking the glass from Odette, but was too late to get a glimpse of Donovan and his companions as the ship canted to starboard to sail into the river channel.

"Most likely it was Donovan MacBride's sister, Olivia," Douglas commented. "As I understand it, she has a child, too. A daughter, I think."

"I didn't know he had a sister," Alysson said, unable to hide her surprised interest, and Douglas nodded.

"Yes, she's the oldest. The little girl has some sort of disability, I believe, and her mother has lived in seclusion with her on Donovan's estate in Brooklyn Heights since her husband died. Wildwood is the name of the place, but I have never met the lady myself."

He smiled again, and Alysson decided he had the warmest smile she had ever beheld. As the afternoon progressed, he spoke often to her in an affable way that made her quite comfortable with him. He made no secret that he enjoyed her company. As the last ship ended the water parade, Alysson was disappointed that the day had come to an end.

"I am hosting a party tonight at my home," he said to Alysson as she stood. "Please come."

The brown eyes and smile made it hard for her to refuse him, but Alysson glanced uncertainly at her friends.

"Thank you very much, Mr. Compton, but I have made plans to accompany my friends to view the fireworks display later tonight."

"Then they are all invited as well," he insisted, then included them in a louder voice. "You must all come to my house tonight. There will be dancing and entertainment, and Rosalie, perhaps if you could come, we could take a moment to further discuss the employment of your company at the Park."

Rosalie smiled. "How nice of you to invite us, Mr. Compton. Of course we will come."

"Around seven o'clock, then. My house is just next to the theater," Douglas said, and as Rosalie moved away he took Alysson's fingers and raised them to his lips. "Until then, Miss Tyler. I hope you will save me a dance."

"Of course," Alysson returned with a smile, and after they had taken their leave of Douglas Compton's pavilion, she decided that he was a very nice man. She would indeed save him a dance or two or three, and she would insist that as soon as they returned to Mrs. Thackeray's, Billy would practice the waltz with her so she wouldn't step on her host's toes!

# Chapter 10

Douglas Compton smiled at the pretty young woman, who blushed becomingly as she curtsied before him. He remained in his position near the front door as she moved away with her mother in a rustle of blue taffeta. She was the daughter of Daniel D. Tompkins, the governor himself, and a feeling of self-satisfaction welled inside Douglas as he surveyed with cynical eyes the social and political elite of New York. He kept his contempt for them well hidden beneath the friendly smile that came so easily to him.

During the rebellion, his family had remained loyal to the king, unlike the traitors surrounding him now. He had been a boy then, just reaching manhood, and his father had thrown his wealth and power behind the occupying British forces as any loyal subject would have done. They had lost everything after Cornwallis's defeat at Yorktown. They had been forced to flee with the British forces when they left New York in 1783, settling first in Canada, then later returning to England. But these people, these very people that he now entertained so lavishly, had taken everything they had owned. Damn them.

Douglas bowed as another couple arrived, and he greeted them with a warm welcome. John Tiedgemen was a judge, and Compton made sure he and his wife held a brimming goblet of fine champagne before he resumed his position at the door. Another party was entering the foyer, and he searched the ladies in their glittering turbans and elegant finery for a glimpse of Alysson Tyler.

He frowned when she wasn't among them, pulling a solid gold watch from the pocket of his white silk waistcoat and snapping it open. It was already half past eight; they were late. Their tardiness annoyed him, but at the same time made him all the more eager to see Alysson again. Never had he expected Lord Tyler's daughter to be so beautiful, though her father had mentioned in one of his letters that her beauty would work in their favor in her marriage to MacBride.

Douglas took a glass of wine from one of the maids, very curious as to what had gone amiss. It was unusual for Lord Tyler's plans to go awry—that was one of the things Douglas had most admired about his English benefactor. He revered the man, a real lord, descended from kings, and he had since the time his father had introduced them ten years ago. They had found then that they shared the same burning desire to bring the Americans to heel again, which was why Douglas became a British spy. It had been Lord Tyler's suggestion that Douglas return to New York and purchase the Park Theater. His idea and his money. And since then, the theater had been invaluable in their intelligence work. As Daniel Tyler had said, most of the Americans had short memories of the Compton family's loyalties in the war, and as the owner of the most prestigious theater in the city, he not only had contact with the *crème de la crème* of society but the actors he had recruited for his cause were perfect to transport secret information from city to city under the cover of their traveling troupes.

He nodded as a curvaceous widow he knew slightly sought him out to bore him with her fawning flirtation, but he disentangled himself quickly, glancing once more at the door. Only a week ago, he had received the comminiqué which Daniel Tyler had penned, revealing at length the amusing account of his daughter's forced marriage to Donovan MacBride. His Lordship had clearly been elated by his success and had instructed Douglas to make an effort to gain her friendship once she had arrived. But her arrival had fostered a very different set of circumstances, and though he had tried to find out more from her by mentioning Donovan MacBride and the *Halcyone,* it had done little good. She had acted mildly interested but not willing to say very much. The whole matter intrigued him, and he had already decided to find out exactly what had happened during her crossing on the MacBride ship. They had to be married; Lord Tyler had witnessed the ceremony himself.

A faint smile lifted his lips. Not that the unexpected development displeased him. Alysson was fair game to him if she really wasn't married, and there were many ways he could use her for his own purposes. She had found him attractive; he had seen it in those big green eyes of hers. And it was apparent that she was young and vulnerable; it should be easy to win her over. He had thought of little else since he had spent time with her that morning, but he would have to be very careful. Her father had mentioned her intelligence and willfulness, as well as her beauty, and Douglas would just have to make certain that she never had any reason to distrust him. If things went well, he might even marry her himself. The idea of being the son-in-law of an English lord rather appealed to him.

When Alysson did arrive not long after, Douglas had hardly greeted the others before he took her hand and smiled down into her eyes.

"I was afraid you weren't coming," he whispered, and Alysson smiled, thinking he looked most handsome in his black evening attire.

His eyes still held the friendly twinkle that she found

so disarming, and she willingly took his arm and let him lead her toward the ballroom. White tapers by the hundreds illuminated the huge room, casting a soft glow over the glossy floor. They passed beneath an immense crystal chandelier ablaze with more candles and white wall panels where huge murals of pastoral scenes were framed in red velvet and gold.

The dancing had not begun, and Alysson moved along at his side as he maneuvered her through the milling crowd, introducing her to different friends and acquaintances along the way. Belatedly, Alysson realized Odette and the others had not followed them.

"Mr. Compton, I'm afraid we have become separated from my friends."

"Exactly, my dear. I want us to be alone for a time."

Alysson had to laugh at his admission. "Alone? In here?"

Further conversation was made impossible as an elderly man came up to him. He was short and stocky with a perpetually flushed complexion and a long gray beard, and the woman with him was of similar height and build, her silver hair piled in an elaborate coiffure decorated with ostrich feathers and glittery black beads.

"Good evening, Doctor Whittingham. And Madam Whittingham. I hope you are enjoying yourselves this evening."

"Yes, indeed we are, my good fellow. Your gatherings are always worth the trouble of walking on this blasted leg of mine," the doctor returned in a good-humored, blustery explosion of speech.

Alysson smiled, and Douglas winked at her. "May I introduce Miss Alysson Tyler. She has recently arrived from London with Madame Rosalie Handel's theatrical company." He looked back at Alysson. "Alysson, Doctor Whittingham is my physician, as well as that of most of the other people in this room."

Rosalie Handel's reputation was well known to them, and Douglas's introduction brought many interested questions from the Whittinghams. As Alysson answered them, Douglas observed her, his eyes roving admiringly over her small, exquisite face. Her gown was pink silk, a very delicate shade decorated with satin roses of a darker hue. His regard lingered momentarily on the soft white flesh curving so temptingly beneath the lace of her neckline, though its cut was quite modest compared to most of the ladies in attendance.

He could tell the dress was expensive, fashionably high-waisted in the French style and draped gracefully around her legs. It was probably from the trousseau furnished by her father, and Douglas tried to visualize the naked limbs hidden beneath the smooth pink fabric. Her hair was pinned into a loose knot, surrounded by pink rosebuds, high atop her head, with fine red-gold tendrils curling tantalizing around her face. Her hair seemed rather short for the current fashion of New York, but it gave her a youthful, devastatingly disarming look of innocence. Suddenly eager to be away from the doddering old couple monopolizing her, he made an excuse and pulled Alysson away from them.

"I hope everyone doesn't find you as fascinating as they did, or I never will have a moment alone with you."

Alysson found him more charming with each passing moment, and Rosalie had seemed pleased that he had invited them to his home. After all, he did own the theater in which Rosalie wanted them to work, and Alysson reminded herself to do nothing to offend him.

"There is someone I want you to meet," Douglas said as he caught sight of a man standing by himself near the open terrace doors. He guided Alysson toward him, and as they neared, the stranger reached out and clasped Douglas's hand in a warm handshake. They were obviously quite good friends, and Alysson thought the other gentleman to be the most elegant-looking man she had ever seen. He looked to be a bit older than Douglas, in his late forties perhaps, and he stood very erect, making him appear taller than he really was. He was clean-shaven, with dark blue, penetrating eyes, but his hair was most striking—a great leonine mane, prematurely silvered, that created a marked contrast to his tanned and unlined face.

"Alysson, allow me to introduce one of the greatest actors in the country. Mr. Adam Sinclair. Adam, this lovely lady is Miss Alysson Tyler."

Alysson felt all color drain from her face, and the hand she had extended to him stilled in midair. She thought he looked as shocked as she felt, then he gave a puzzled smile, and she realized it must have been her own stunned reaction that had surprised him.

Douglas had noted it as well, and he leaned down to her, concerned. "What is it, my dear? Are you unwell?"

Alysson recovered herself quickly, but her mind raced with the idea that the man standing in front of her was Adam Sinclair. Could it really be him? Her mother's true love?

"I'm sorry, Mr. Sinclair," she said breathlessly, "but I was so shocked to hear your name. I've heard my mother speak of you so many times."

Douglas hid his own surprise at her revelation, then turned inquisitive eyes on Adam.

"Indeed?" Adam Sinclair was saying in a deep, sonorous baritone that Alysson knew would be magnificent upon a stage. "I do hope it was with kindness that she spoke of me, but you have me at a disadvantage, I'm afraid. What is your mother's name?"

He smiled then, a look of perplexed interest on his face, and Alysson was quick to tell him.

"It was nearly twenty years ago, but I am sure you will remember her, because I believe you became very good friends during your stay in London. Her name was Judith Hampstead then. She said she met you one day when the wind blew away her hat and you retrieved it for her."

"Judith Hampstead?" Perplexity brought Adam Sinclair's heavy black brows down into a frown. "I am afraid I have no recollection of such a lady." He glanced around the room. "Is she here with you tonight?"

Alysson shook her head, disbelieving that he did not remember her mother, when Judith had spent so many years mourning his loss. "No, she died several months ago, but when you met her you were performing at the Crownover Theater in Southwark. She said you gave this to her."

She pulled a long silver chain from where it had been hidden in her bodice, holding out the dainty silver filigree cross for him to see. "Surely you remember giving this to her."

Adam and Douglas both gazed down at the necklace in her palm, then Adam shook his head, looking truly regretful.

"I am very sorry, Miss Tyler, but I have never seen that cross before. Douglas here can tell you that I am quite fond of jewelry such as that, and I am sure I would have remembered such a beautiful piece of work. Perhaps your mother somehow confused my name with one of the other actors."

Alysson felt a curious hurt, an ache inside, as if Adam Sinclair had forgotten her instead of her mother, but she could not insist that he remember Judith. She tucked the cross back into its place.

"Perhaps you are right, Mr. Sinclair. My mother was forgetful at times."

"I am sure not having met her was my loss, especially if your mother was as beautiful as her daughter."

An image came to Alysson: a frail, broken body on the flagstones of the cottage.

"My mother was very beautiful, Mr. Sinclair. Everyone thought so."

She looked away from them, suddenly wanting to be away from Adam Sinclair. She scanned the room for her friends and found Rosalie and Odette near one of the crimson-draped buffet tables, then froze under her second shock of the night.

Donovan MacBride stood with them, looking very tall and arrogant in his dark jacket and trousers, his spotless white cravat a vivid contrast to his dark skin. He had shaved his beard since the last time she had seen him, and Alysson stared at the lean contours of his face, thinking he looked even more handsome than before. Waves of emotion shook her, and she hated herself for the heat rising in her face, for he was not alone. His Russian mistress stood between Brace MacBride and him, her white lace dress looking very much like a bridal gown. Suddenly horrified at even the thought of having to confront the two of them, Alysson turned to Douglas.

"Please excuse me, gentlemen, but I really must rejoin my friends now."

Both men bowed gallantly, and she moved away and out onto the balcony, certainly not willing to seek out Odette and Rosalie just yet. Not when they stood with Donovan. The cool night breeze felt good upon her hot face, and she was grateful for the cloak of darkness that hid her flushed and agitated appearance. Others were milling about the garden, awaiting the fireworks display, and Alysson walked down a path lit at intervals by glass-encased oil lamps on tall brass stands, every conceivable kind of feeling whirling in a boiling vortex inside her.

The introduction to Adam Sinclair had been a shock, and a disappointment, but it was Donovan's unexpected appearance that made her hands tremble. She had known he would go back to his mistress, but the sight of them together was more than she could bear. She hated herself for her own feelings.

The first fiery explosion suddenly brightened the starry skies above, and Alysson raised her eyes as the next appeared, a brilliant yellow starburst blossoming against the blackness like a gigantic sunflower. White and red pinwheels followed, with showers of sparks falling groundward to delight the spectators, and she could hear the crowd from the ballroom spilling into the gardens to ooh and aah as each new rocket burst into vivid splashes of color. She wanted to be by herself for a few moments longer, however, and she chose a small bench in the shadows. She watched silently until the grand finale ended the display with a glorious show of color and sound, engendering enthusiastic applause in the gardens around her.

The guests began to wander toward the house again in small, scattered groups, and it wasn't long before the lilting strains of a waltz floated from the open doors. Alysson remained where she was, calling herself a coward, but still hoping Donovan would be gone before she must return to the ballroom. Her thoughts returned to Adam Sinclair and her mother, and it made her feel very sad to think that Judith had been so lonely and unhappy in her marriage that she had created a fantasy about a young American actor. It broke her heart to think of it and brought back so many painful memories that a rush of tears burned her eyes. She suppressed them, then went rigid at the sound of Brace MacBride's deep voice nearby. A woman answered him, and Alysson came to her feet and fled her hiding place, heading for the terrace.

A waiter stood there holding a silver tray of crystal goblets of champagne, and though she had once vowed never to imbibe again, she took a glass and gulped from it as the servant moved away. She gasped then, spilling her wine as a strong arm encircled her waist. The next thing she knew her back was against a tree trunk and Donovan MacBride was staring down into her face, his arms braced on either side of her to prevent her escape.

"You made me spill my drink," she stuttered breathlessly, her eyes on his face, half-hidden by shadows.

"You shouldn't be drinking anyway, English. You do remember the night of the storm, don't you?"

She remembered it all right, and the shiver that coursed over her proved it.

"I've been looking for you. Why have you been hiding out here?" His lips brushed her earlobe as he spoke, raising gooseflesh to her toes, and Alysson swallowed hard, feeling weak.

"Please, please let me go. Someone will see us."

"It's too dark for anyone to see us. Have you missed me, sweet? Have you regretted saying no to me so quickly?"

"No," she lied, her whole body beginning to quiver from the way he was leaning his hard, muscular body into hers.

He laughed softly. "My offer still holds, you know. I want you. Now. Tonight. Come home with me."

More than anything, Alysson wanted to slide her arms around his neck and press against him, but she couldn't let herself do it. She would not, would not become another of his mistresses. Like the Russian. The thought of the Countess Kinski brought anger with it.

"How callous can you be?" she hissed softly. "To do this with me, here and now, when your lover is just steps away from us. Do you really think I want to take her place and be treated that way?"

She tried to pull away, but his fingers held her arms.

"Marina's with Brace tonight. There's nothing between us anymore, except friendship. I want you, and only you."

Alysson leaned her head against the tree, eyes wide, his words bringing an appalling pleasure to her.

"I won't be your mistress," she managed with shaky conviction. "I'll never be your—"

His lips cut off the words, hot, demanding, and a moan was forced from her as his hands slid down her body to clamp her slender hips tightly against his hard thighs.

"Yes you will, English. Someday I'll have you," he whispered huskily, and the underlying arrogance of his words did much to steel the weakness seeping over Alysson.

"Why should I settle for that?" she said, trying again to push him away from her. "I have already met another man, Douglas Compton. He finds me attractive. Perhaps he'll want me for his wife—"

Donovan grabbed her by the arms then, his face dark. "A word of warning, Alysson—stay away from him. Everybody in the city knows how he makes a game of seducing the actresses that work for him, only to discard them when the next one comes along."

"Then he sounds a lot like you, doesn't he?" Alysson retorted, finally able to twist away from him, only to find Douglas Compton and Adam Sinclair standing a few feet away.

"Alysson? We've been looking for you," Douglas said slowly, his eyes on Donovan MacBride, who stood just behind Alysson.

"I'm afraid I was ungentlemanly enough to cause her to spill champagne on her dress," Donovan explained smoothly. "But I believe it has dried now, hasn't it, Miss Tyler?"

"Yes," Alysson murmured, her face so hot that she knew they must suspect something more had happened between them. How much of their conversation had Douglas overheard?

"I see," Douglas said, glancing at Adam, then back to Donovan. "I don't believe you've met Adam Sinclair, have you, Mr. MacBride?"

"No, I haven't had the pleasure, but your reputation on stage precedes you. I understand you're a brilliant actor," Donovan replied, stretching out his hand.

"Thank you very much. It's nice to hear that."

Alysson was more than relieved when Douglas took her elbow.

"I was hoping for the first dance with you, my dear. May I have that honor?"

"Of course," she said too eagerly, but she felt much safer as she accompanied Douglas inside and went into his arms, far away from Donovan MacBride's more dangerous embrace. They whirled around the floor amid the other dancers, and Alysson began to discount Donovan's warning about Douglas Compton. It was Donovan who made her feel helpless and vulnerable and out of control, not Douglas.

It was much later that night when Alysson blew out the bedside candle and crawled beneath the soft, downy coverlet beside Odette.

"Did you see the young *officer* who danced with me so many times, Alysson?" came Odette's sleepy whisper. "He was fine to look upon, do you not think it? Big and blond and handsome in his blue uniform. He is an American lieutenant, Jonathan Wheeling, and he is quite taken with me, I can tell it. He has already asked Rosalie if he could call here upon me. Do you think he will?"

"Yes, I am sure he will."

*"Ooh la-la,* he is so divine. I cannot wait to see him again."

Odette's words dwindled into a yawn, and Alysson stared wide-eyed into the darkness, not sleepy at all.

"Odette?"

*"Oui?"*

"Mr. MacBride asked me to become his mistress again tonight."

"He wants you very much, *chérie.* I could see it in those black eyes of his."

Alysson turned her head on the pillow. "How can you tell?"

"He watched you when he first came when you were with Monsieur Compton. Poor Madame Kinski. She watched him as he watched you, and who can blame her for being so sad? Monsieur MacBride is *magnifique."*

Alysson smiled dreamily, remembering the way he had said he wanted her, the way his lips had felt against her skin. "Yes, he is magnificent, isn't he?"

A few moments passed with only the ticking of the clock, then Alysson stirred again.

"Odette?"

*"Oui?"*

"You have known a man, haven't you? You know, in that way. When you were back in France?"

*"Oui,* I have been with a man."

"Does it make you feel strange when they touch you? I mean, have you ever felt all shaky and hot, and really quite sick, almost?"

Odette giggled at her description. "You silly little

goose. You are in love with Monsieur MacBride. That is why you feel that way. Don't you even know it yet?"

Alysson didn't answer, and Odette eventually settled down to sleep. Was Odette right? Did she love him that much? She searched her heart for the answer, lying awake in the darkness, listening to Odette's soft snore. She did flame up to meet his every touch, like fire to a wick, and she swallowed hard to think of how hot his lips had felt, searing her skin and making her heart pound. He wanted her, she knew he wanted her, but he couldn't really love her or he would want to marry her. Would being his mistress be such a terrible thing? she wondered. Most men had mistresses, and Odette had said that gentlemen often spent more time with their mistresses than their wives.

No, she said firmly to herself, realizing she was beginning to waver in her resolve. She didn't want that. She wanted to be his wife.

As light misted the room, bringing looming shadows along the walls, she finally closed her eyes and sighed, drifting into troubled dreams.

# Chapter 11

At half past eleven the next morning, Douglas Compton sat behind the large mahogany desk in his study. He leaned back, folding his hands on his chest as he contemplated Adam Sinclair, who sat with crossed legs in a green velvet wing chair across from him.

"I thought it quite odd that Alysson Tyler seemed so sure you were acquainted with her mother," he said, watching Adam with narrowed eyes. "Were you telling her the truth?"

Adam lifted a shoulder in a careless shrug. "I was in England for a long time and knew a great many ladies, but I don't recall one named Judith Hampstead. As I told the girl, I would have remembered that cross. Usually it was the women who gave me expensive gifts."

He grinned, but Douglas remained silent as a heavy-set Negress in a white apron and red bandanna entered carrying a small gold tray. He took a snifter of brandy from it, swirling it absently as Henrietta presented the tray to his guest. As the maid left, he watched Adam take a drink.

"It's a shame you weren't involved with her mother," he commented. "It would have presented you with a perfect way to gain her confidence, but I suppose it's too late now to change your story."

"I think I could gain her confidence, if you'll let me try. She's a lovely creature."

Compton smiled. "Yes, she's quite beautiful, and

young and naïve enough to influence rather easily, I should think. But I'll be the one to do it. Once we get her working at the Park, I should have no trouble winning her over." He sipped his brandy, thoughtfully surveying the actor across from him. "There's something going on between MacBride and her. I can feel it, and I think we interrupted something between them in the garden last night. Do you get that impression?"

Adam shrugged again. "He was probably trying to seduce her. You know how he is with women." He shifted in his chair, leaning forward to take a cigar from the enameled box atop Douglas's desk. He clipped it, holding it to his nose to sniff its aroma. "Maybe MacBride recruited her to work against us," he suggested as he lit it. "And if that is the case, you should be cautious about forming any kind of relationship with her. According to Rosalie Handel, she's one hell of a good actress, and more than one man has been undone by a woman like her. I don't relish the thought of facing an American hangman because of her."

Douglas stiffened visibly, then hunched forward, both his palms flat on the desk. His brown eyes became hard, dissolving his usual amicable expression.

"Don't ever take me for a fool, Adam. I will use the girl as I see fit. She can be very useful to me."

Adam smiled. *"If* you can get her to work for us."

Compton's face relaxed again. "Let me worry about that. I expect you to help me with her. They should be here soon, and we can get started."

When the grandfather clock in Douglas Compton's vestibule struck the noonday hour, Alysson and Rosalie were led past it into the elaborate front receiving parlor to await the master of the house.

"Isn't Mr. Compton's house beautifully done?" Rosalie remarked, and Alysson looked around at the rich wall covering of cream brocade flocked with pale blue fleur-de-lis. The furnishings were elegantly crafted, and polished to a glossy shine. Alysson picked up a fragile porcelain shepherdess with crook and lamb, examining the exquisite detail. She turned as Douglas entered the room behind her.

"Ladies! I am so glad you could join me on such short notice. You have both met Mr. Sinclair, I believe."

Alysson nodded; she was inwardly dismayed to find that Adam Sinclair was to join them, but she shook it off quickly. Perhaps he might remember her mother yet. She watched as Douglas came toward her, finding it impossible not to respond to his charm as he squeezed both her hands affectionately.

"Thank you so much for coming. We have some exciting things to discuss."

He opened a set of sliding wooden doors, revealing a small, intimate dining parlor decorated in shades of lavender and green. Two maids waited in unobtrusive positions at either end of a long sideboard. Douglas seated Alysson at the table to his right while Adam held Rosalie's chair for her. The men took their places at the ends of the table, and Douglas gestured to the maids, then kept a light and entertaining repartee going as they were served the first course, a cold salad of shrimp and savory rice. It wasn't until they were nearly finished with the sweet course of pound cake and glazed cherries that Douglas leaned back to gaze down the table at Rosalie.

"Besides my fondness for entertaining beautiful ladies," he began, smiling, "I'm afraid I have an ulterior motive for inviting the two of you here today."

"Indeed?" Rosalie cocked an elegant curved eyebrow. "That sounds quite ominous, coming from a man so renowned for charming the ladies."

Alysson looked quickly at the redheaded woman, well aware that Rosalie's remark was aimed at her. During their entire carriage ride from the boarding house, she had endured Rosalie's lengthy accounts of Douglas Compton's reputation for seducing the young actresses at the Park, many such affairs having ended in duels. But even so, Alysson still found such a notorious reputation at odds with her impression of her quiet-spoken, smiling host.

"Not ominous, I assure you." Douglas gave his easy laugh. "But very exciting. You see, I have had a wonderful idea which concerns the two of you, and Adam as well. That's why I asked him to join us."

Alysson glanced at Adam and found him looking at her. The expression in his eyes was as distinctly unsettling as it was fleeting. She lowered her own gaze, disturbed by the look he had hidden so quickly beneath a friendly smile. It had been so intense, so intimate, that it was almost chilling. But what had it been? Hunger? Or perhaps longing? The idea frightened her, and she decided in that moment that it was Adam Sinclair of whom she should be wary. She kept her eyes away from him after that, watching Douglas instead.

"I don't know if you are aware of it, since you arrived from England so recently, but Adam's been working with me at the Park. We're in preparation for a production of *King Lear* at the moment."

"I have heard much of your talent," Rosalie said to Adam with genuine admiration. "I assume you will play the title role?"

Adam nodded, and Douglas went on. "He will be superb as Lear, but I have need of a supporting cast for him. After having met all of your company yesterday at the Battery, I realized they would fit my needs splendidly. Your talent is as well proclaimed as Adam's,

Madame Handel, and you told me last night yourself that Alysson is very good."

Alysson raised her eyes to Rosalie, unable to hide the excitement in them, but Rosalie appeared only mildly interested. She raised her glass and drank, now the businesswoman.

"We have been offered a play at the Macon Theater, but if your offer is substantially better, I'll be happy to consider it."

Douglas did not hesitate. "I'll double whatever it is," he offered, shocking Alysson. His eyes came to her, warm and friendly, before he looked back at Rosalie. "You see, Adam and I both think you would be wonderful as Goneril, and we thought Alysson would be good as Cordelia."

Cordelia, Alysson thought in wonderment. A marvelous part, and she knew the role of Lear's youngest daughter well. She put eager attention on Rosalie.

"You have hired yourself a cast, Mr. Compton," Rosalie said. "Providing, of course, that we can come to mutually satisfying financial terms. But I only have three men and one other girl, as you are aware."

"That will be no problem at all, madame, and I thought perhaps you and Adam might sit down for a few minutes now to discuss the various role assignments. You see, I want the rehearsals to start immediately. The opening performance is already scheduled for August eighth, when the current play ends."

"We are finished now, aren't we?" Adam said, taking his cue. "Perhaps Madame Handel and I could use your study for our discussion."

"Of course, and while you are busy there, I would be delighted to show Miss Tyler around my gardens. They are quite pleasant in the daytime."

He was up, drawing back Alysson's chair before any of them could protest. Though Rosalie watched with displeasure as he escorted her charge out of the tall French doors into the garden, she had no choice but to follow Adam Sinclair into the adjoining study.

Outside, Douglas held Alysson's arm as he guided her along the graveled garden paths.

"Are you pleased about playing Cordelia?" he asked, "or would you rather have one of the other parts?"

"I have always wanted to play her," Alysson admitted, "but I am most willing to take any role Rosalie decides upon. I love to act, but I am very new at it. I hope I won't disappoint you."

Douglas looked down into the slanted green eyes raised to him. "I think it would be very hard for you to disappoint me, Alysson."

It was the first time he had used her given name, and the softness of his tone was almost like a caress.

"You're very kind," she murmured, stepping away to look at the red roses twining around a nearby trellis.

Douglas broke the stem of one of the largest blossoms. "This will, no doubt, be the first of dozens of roses thrown at your feet. I can foresee it already."

"I have often dreamed of such a thing," she admitted with a small smile, then sobered as she remembered a different night when she had confided all her dreams and aspirations to Donovan. She couldn't make herself so vulnerable to a man again, she vowed, and she sat down on a nearby iron bench.

The shade there was deep and cool, and as Douglas sat down beside her, Alysson listened to the sounds of the city filtering over the high brick wall surrounding the garden. Somewhere down the street a vendor hawked hot corn, and closer to her a horse and wagon clopped and rattled its way past the Compton house.

"I am afraid I have a confession to make, Alysson," Douglas said, and surprised, Alysson looked up to find his brown eyes riveted on her in abject apology. "There is something I haven't told you about myself, and now that I have gotten to know you a bit, I feel rather guilty about it."

"I don't understand."

Douglas hesitated, hoping he wasn't making a mistake with what he was about to say.

"You see, I knew you were coming to New York, even before you arrived. I learned of it in a letter from your father."

It took every ounce of Alysson's willpower to meet his searching look. "You are a friend of my father's?"

Although she was trying hard to hide it, Douglas was perceptive enough to realize she was distressed by his revelation. Not about to destroy the fragile tenet of their budding friendship, he was hasty to reassure her.

"Not really. Actually, I don't know his Lordship well at all; we're only occasional business associates. But he did mention in his last correspondence to me just a few weeks ago that you would be arriving on the *Halcyone*. He suggested that I call on you sometime to make you feel welcome."

"Oh, I see," Alysson murmured, not able to imagine her father being that solicitous to her welfare. She nervously fingered the soft petals of the rose in her hands, glad Douglas was not a good friend of her father's. "You have certainly done that by offering me employment. I am very grateful to you for that."

Douglas still watched her, and Alysson was totally unprepared for his next words.

"I realize that I surely must be mistaken, but I understood him to say you were married to Donovan MacBride before you sailed from London."

Alysson froze, then her face flamed with embarrassment. She inwardly cursed her father as she had done so many times in her life. She stared at the rose, unable to look at her companion. She had to tell him. What else could she do? She finally looked up, presenting him with a rueful smile.

"I can understand why you are confused, Douglas, but there's really a very simple explanation." She stopped, knowing it was not the least bit simple. Her relationship with Donovan was so complex and bizarre. "I fear you will think me a willful and disobedient daughter after I tell you this."

"I am sure I will not," he answered, but nonetheless he watched her with a great deal of interest.

"I was betrothed to Donovan MacBride when I was a child, just seven years old, and Father was most determined to carry out the match. My father and I often quarreled, so I suppose he wanted to get rid of me. I found out later that Mr. MacBride wanted the marriage even less than I, so even though we were married while in London, we agreed to have a legal annulment once we arrived here. It has worked out very well for both of us, but I am sure my father will be furious once he learns of it."

So that is it, Douglas thought, exulted to have wormed so much out of her so easily. It obviously embarrassed her to speak of it, and it was a very good sign that she would confide it to him as she had. He patted her arm.

"I won't say a word about it to him," he assured her. "But is does surprise me that Mr. MacBride would give you up. I can only feel indebted to him, however, because if you were still married to him, I wouldn't have the pleasure of your company at this moment."

Alysson wondered why he didn't appear the least bit scandalized at the way she had disobeyed her father and annulled an arranged marriage. It was an outrageous thing to have done. It surprised her when Douglas suddenly leaned forward, and she felt a moment's panic when she realized he meant to kiss her. To her relief, his lips only grazed her forehead.

"I do so want to be your friend, Alysson," he said. "And if you will only let me make you my protégée, I think you could become a very famous actress."

Alysson smiled with pleasure at that prospect, but some moments later as they walked back toward the house, the warnings given to her by Donovan and Rosalie rose in her mind, making her a trifle wary of Douglas Compton's motives. He was taking a very big interest in her, after having only just met her the day before, and he'd not even seen her act yet! So far he had been nothing but a gentleman, but she would just have to make sure he was never in a position to be anything else.

# Chapter 12

Nearly a fortnight after New York's gala Fourth of July celebration, Donovan MacBride stood on the deck of a slow-moving ferryboat, his eyes intent on the shore of Manhattan and the Catherine Slip. He had spent the night in Brooklyn at his estate there, but he had risen early to return to the city. It was barely past dawn, the rising sun slowly gilding the water, the morning quiet except for the screaming calls of gulls gracefully riding the wind currents over the harbor. Behind him, the plodding footsteps of the ferry horse beat a rhythmic path around its treadmill, propelling them to the far shore.

When the boat nudged into the Catherine Street Ferryhouse with the clattering ring of pawls and ratchets, he waited impatiently for the mooring lines to be fastened, then led his great stallion down the gangplank. He mounted, touching his heels lightly to the bay's flanks, then inhaled the salty air of the riverfront, feeling relaxed and comfortable in his worn leather riding breeches and plain linen shirt.

Warlock was eager to run, hooves clattering loudly as the huge horse pranced sideways on the cobblestones, but Donovan held him with a firm hand, cantering north on Cherry Street past a cluster of stores and warehouses, all shuttered and sleeping in the quiet of the morning. He turned east on Clinton, riding up Arundel to where Grand Street turned into a country lane lined with neat fencerows separating grassy fields and small farms. He could see the rooftop of the Rutgers Mansion, the sights and smells around him bringing back memories of his youth, of the war. He had not returned to his birthplace in a very long time, not wanted to see it, though he had worked for years to buy it back after his family had lost it during the war. He would rebuild it someday; he had vowed that when he was barely more than a child.

A mile farther along, he caught sight of a white square of paper nailed to the base of a tall elm tree that stood along the roadside, and he drew Warlock up beside it. He stared at it for a long moment, then reached out with one gloved hand and tore it from the tree.

Alysson stared back at him out of her glorious green eyes, looking young and innocent and unbelievably beautiful. The artist's etching had caught the sweet, childlike essence of her with uncanny ability. Her likeness on the playbill had caused an immediate stir of interest among the populace of the city since Compton had ordered it plastered to every lamppost, tree, and public billboard in New York. Adam Sinclair and Rosalie Handel had been given top billing, as was their due, but it was the words beneath the picture that made his fist clench where it lay upon his knee. "Introducing Miss Alysson Tyler," he read, "the most beautiful and charming English protégée of Mr. Douglas Compton, esteemed owner of the Park Theater."

He grimaced, and with jaw clenched tight, he folded the stiff parchment into fourths and tucked it into the inside pocket of his brown leather vest. He spurred Warlock into a gallop, hugging his thighs to the sleek powerful muscles moving beneath him. Unwanted visions of Alysson came drifting across his mind with extreme clarity, especially the way she had looked dancing in Douglas Compton's arms the last time Don-

ovan had seen her. All pink and white and soft, and too
damn desirable for any man to resist.

He cursed beneath his breath, remembering the way
she had trembled in his arms, how sweet and smooth
her skin had tasted. He had thought to forget her once
he was away from her, but he hadn't. He couldn't drive
her from his mind no matter how hard he tried. Never
had a woman ruled his thoughts in such a way. But she
refused to come to him. She wanted him as much as he
wanted her, although she was too young and stubborn
to know it. Instead, she preferred to let Compton pro-
claim her as his new possession for the whole bloody
city to see. The rumors about them were already flying
high and low in the coffeehouses, especially the Tontine, which he frequented. Some already said they were
lovers. He didn't believe that, and he'd be damned if he
would ever let it happen.

He gritted his teeth, his mood black as he turned the
stallion into a weed-choked road that wound between
twin rows of tall silver-leaf maples. The wind set them
aflutter as he rode along glinting their silvery lights
high above his head. He slowed his horse to a walk on
first sight of the burned-out shell of his childhood
home. Charred red bricks blackened the wall behind the
crumbling portico balcony above the front doors. He
and Olivia had eavesdropped on their parents there,
laughing behind their hands as his father had kissed his
mother good-bye when he left to join the army. His
eyes went to the ancient white oak that leaned close to
the side porch where they had pushed Jeremy in a
wooden swing before he could walk. The swing was
gone now, except for a frayed end still dangling from
the high limb. Bitterness boiled up inside him, leaving
a foul taste in his mouth.

He dismounted and tied his reins over a broken slat
of the picket gate, then looked around as he tugged off

his riding gloves. Somewhere nearby a bird trilled a happy song despite his presence, but there was no indication that anyone else was about the place or had been for a long time. His eyes wandered over the dilapidated facade of the great manor house as he climbed the steps to the stone porch, its stately white pillars still intact, though covered with encroaching ivy. The windows were securely boarded as he had ordered, and the sign prohibiting trespass was nailed to the front door. He took the heavy iron key from his pocket and turned it in the lock, opening the door into his dark, haunting past.

The vestibule was dark and cool, golden motes of dust dancing in a slanted ray of smoky light entering the fanlight above his head. He looked around the fire-gutted interior, remembering that night, remembering it all, then moved across the hall, his boots clomping loud and hollow on the wooden floor. A door stood ajar beneath the charred front staircase, and he passed through it to the kitchen hall. He stopped on the threshold, staring at the large kitchen with its cooking fireplace and brick walls. It was there they had lived afterward. For three long years he had lived in that one room with his mother and sister and two brothers. Never enough food, never enough wood to stay warm in the frigid months of winter. It was a miracle they had survived at all.

A board creaked behind him, and Donovan whirled, pistol in hand, but he relaxed as he recognized the man in the doorway.

"It's good to see you," he said, clasping a man's hand as he slid the small gun back into his holster. "Were you followed?"

Adam Sinclair shook his head. "No. I doubled back twice, then came through the back wooded lots. There's an overgrown carriage road behind the spring-house."

He sat down at a dusty trestle table, looking up at Donovan. "I know it's dangerous for us to meet like this, but we had to talk."

"Does Compton suspect that you're working for me?"

"No. He's a cautious man about revealing information, but he's trusted me ever since I passed him that communiqué the President let you release to me. He tells me just about everything his agents pass along to him."

Donovan leaned back against a wooden support pillar, watching his old friend. They had met years ago when they served a stint at Fort Niagara together. He knew something serious must be bothering Adam for him to chance such a meeting.

"Do you have something for me?" he asked, and Adam nodded.

"Yes, I learned two days ago that there's a new British agent operating in Washington. Compton calls him Agent Z. I don't know his real name, but I do know he's courting the daughter of a congressman from South Carolina. That should help you pin him down for surveillance."

"Good. I'll send that along in my next dispatch. Anything else?"

Adam hesitated, then raised eyes full of worry. "I'm very concerned about Alysson Tyler."

Donovan sat down across from Adam, dark eyes watchful. "Why?"

"Compton wants her. He's doing everything he can to seduce her."

"And has he?" Donovan's voice was low and hard.

Adam looked at him strangely, then shook his head. "Not yet, but I think he'll try to make her his mistress."

"She'll never agree to that."

"How do you know?"

"I know."

Donovan watched Adam stand, obviously uneasy. He paced a few steps away from the table, then looked back, his hands on his hips.

"I want her out of the theater and away from him. You know what kind of bastard he is."

The anger in Adam's voice betrayed his strong feelings, and Donovan frowned.

"Why are you so interested in Alysson's welfare? Does she pose a threat to your cover?"

A tense silence followed; the two men stared at each other.

"She's mine, Donovan," Adam said finally. He sighed heavily, running both hands through his thick silver hair. "She's my daughter."

Donovan didn't move. "She's what?"

"I swear it's true. That's why we've got to get her away from him. I can't bear having him around her, seeing him touch her."

Donovan stiffened, a quiet rage filling him at the thought of Compton's hands on her. He stifled it, wanting to know more. "How can she be your daughter?"

Adam sank down on the bench again, his face stricken. "It's a long story. God, I can hardly believe it has turned out this way myself."

"Tell me."

"Twenty years ago, I went to London to appear in a play, and during that time I met Judith, Alysson's mother." He swallowed hard. "She was so lovely then, so very young, and she enchanted me. I think I fell in love with her the very first time I looked at her." He stopped, remembering, and Donovan remembered too, the first time he had seen Alysson in the black nightgown, her long golden hair spread over her shoulders.

"She was from a wealthy family," Adam went on, "and already betrothed to Lord Tyler. He was titled and important, and I had nothing to offer her. Her father wanted the match between them, so we eloped. We only had a month together before her father's men found us and dragged her back for the wedding."

"Couldn't you have stopped them?"

Adam made a derisive sound. "He made certain I couldn't. Hampstead's men beat me within an inch of my life and threw me on a ship to New South Wales. The bloody bastard sold me into slavery."

Donovan stared at him, trying to digest all he was being told. If Alysson really wasn't Tyler's daughter, it would change a great many things between them.

"If she married Daniel Tyler after she was taken back, how can you be sure that Alysson is your child?"

Adam met his eyes with steadfast confidence. "She is mine. I have no doubt whatsoever. Judith was already pregnant when we eloped. Alysson told me herself that she would be nineteen on May fifteenth and that makes it all fit."

Donovan began to rub at the scar on his eye, trying to think. "Do you mean you never knew about her or tried to see her until now?"

"I was in New South Wales for ten years before they let me buy my freedom. When I was able to return to England and made inquiries, I was told Judith was dead. I heard that Tyler had a daughter somewhere, but I could never find out where she was."

"That's because he had them both out in Cornwall at some peasant cottage."

"Cornwall? Why?"

Donovan looked at Adam's face, already tortured with regret, his dark blue eyes full of anguish. It would do little good to tell him the suffering his wife and daughter had endured during those years. Adam looked ready to break apart as it was.

"Does Alysson have any idea about any of this?"

"The first time we met, she asked me if I knew her mother. God, she even showed me the cross I gave Judith as a wedding present." Adam's voice cracked. "It took everything I had to deny knowing her; I had to because Compton was standing right there." He brought down one fist hard, the loud bang sending dust swirling up from the table. "I'm telling you, Donovan, Compton is fascinated with her. He's had plenty of women, and I've seen how easy it is for him to manipulate them, but it's different with Alysson. I can see it in the way he looks at her. If it wasn't for Rosalie's influence on her, he'd probably already have had her. And lately he's even considered marriage! He's intrigued with the idea of being the son-in-law of a titled Englishman."

Donovan thrust back his chair, his face dark with anger. Adam watched a muscle flex and relax in Donovan's cheek.

"She won't do that, Adam."

"You underestimate the man's charm, then. He's promised her everything but the moon, everything she has always wanted, turning her head with offers of fame and fortune on the stage. She's so young and eager to succeed. I'm telling you, we've got to get her away from him."

"She can't marry him. She's married to me."

Adam's mouth dropped, and he could only stare at Donovan.

"Married to you!"

"That's right."

"How can that be? How can you stand to have Compton courting her the way he is if you are—"

"I can't explain it all, but you can rest assured she'll never marry Compton."

"How can you stop it? No one knows you're married, do they? Alysson doesn't act as if she's married. I can't believe you are."

"Believe it. We were supposed to have an annulment, but I never saw to it. We're married, and we're going to stay that way."

Adam kept shaking his head. "But you've always said you would never marry. Are you willing to make such a sacrifice?"

"It's not a sacrifice. I wouldn't do it if I didn't want it that way."

Adam's surprise turned into heartfelt relief. "You love her, then?"

"I want her away from Compton before she gets hurt, and I want her with me. *Lear* opens in two weeks; I'll take her then."

"Two weeks! Are you mad?"

"I'm not taking her opening night away from her, dammit. She's dreamed about it too long," Donovan said firmly, and Adam stood in protest.

"But what if Compton manages to seduce her first? She's your wife, man."

"You'll just have to make damn sure that he doesn't," Donovan said through clenched teeth. "Do what you have to do. Just keep him away from her. Do what you can to turn her against Compton without endangering yourself, and I'll tell Rosalie to do the same."

The deadliness in Donovan's tone silenced Adam, and neither man spoke for the next few minutes.

"How is she?" Donovan asked at length.

"She's fine," Adam said, then grinned proudly. "And she has extraordinary talent. You should see her in the role of Cordelia."

"I've seen her."

Adam hesitated. "Are you sure you can get her to

leave the theater? She loves it so, and Compton can give it to her on a silver platter."

"She won't have a choice in the matter," Donovan returned abruptly. "Now listen closely because I have some information I want you to pass along to Compton. The outlook for war is building, and I want them to think our troops along the Canadian frontier are being strengthened. Doesn't Compton have close contacts with the commanding officer at Fort Erie, near Niagara Falls?"

"Yes, he lived in York for a time. He has a lot of friends up there. Indians, too."

"All right, then we can assume he'll send it there."

Adam listened carefully as Donovan related the false data, but it was Alysson's danger that controlled his thoughts. Even later, after Donovan had gone, and Adam walked to the springhouse at the back of the old mansion where he had left his horse, he worried that Donovan was waiting too long. Alysson was growing fond of Compton, he could see it. But by god, he thought, swinging up into the saddle, he would strangle Compton himself before he let him lay a finger on his daughter.

# Chapter 13

On the opening night of *King Lear*, Alysson stood alone in her dressing room at the Park Theater. Baskets of flowers sat on the tables and chairs around her, with more vases on the floor—roses, lilies, daisies, all lovely, their sweet perfume filling the small room. Nearly all of them had been sent to her by Douglas, but there was a large bouquet of sweet-smelling peonies from Adam Sinclair. She smiled as she brushed her hair, grateful for the kindness of both men during the past month of rehearsals. In truth, Douglas had grown a trifle annoyed during the last few weeks at the determined way Adam had paid her court.

She wound her hair into a neat chignon and pinned it low against her nape, then laid down the brush. She inhaled deeply and put her hands on her stomach, which seemed filled with dozens of hummingbirds, all beating their wings in a desperate attempt to escape. Suddenly overcome by nerves, she moved to the full-length mirror for a last-minute inspection of her costume.

As Cordelia, she wore a high-necked, high-waisted silk gown the deep rich red of burgundy wine. Golden ropes crisscrossed between her breasts, and she bent to straighten the folds of the skirt, arranging the wide panel of gold brocade at the front to best advantage. Voices chattered and called to one another in the outside corridor where all the confusion of preperformance jitters reigned.

As she sat there, listening to them, unbidden thoughts of Donovan writhed in her mind. She had learned weeks ago that she could not force him out of her mind, so she no longer even tried. Would he come to see her perform tonight? Was he already outside, in one of the private boxes, perhaps? She had not heard from him or seen him since the night of the ball at Douglas's house, but her mind had dwelled on what Odette had said that night in bed. Was she in love with him? Was that the reason she longed to see him so much? Was that the reason she wanted to share with him her happiness at being on stage for the first time? Sometimes—no, often—she had wondered if she had made the wrong decision when she had turned him down.

"Alysson?"

She whirled, not having heard Douglas enter, and he laughed at her edgy reaction.

"I'm sorry if I startled you. Are you that nervous?"

Alysson smiled. "I never thought I could be so nervous."

Douglas came forward to take her hands reassuringly. "You'll be wonderful, I have no doubt of it, and after tonight, you'll be surrounded by admirers."

Alysson looked at him, thinking how very much he had done for her. "I care nothing for that. I only hope to do well so you'll be proud of me. You have been a good friend since I came to America."

Her words had been sincere, but it surprised her when Compton suddenly held her close. His lips found hers, and Alysson closed her eyes and let him kiss her. He was only the second man to ever do so, only Donovan before him, and though his mouth was eager and not unpleasant, she felt none of the fire in her blood that left her trembling when Donovan touched her. He released her as Odette thrust open the door without knocking.

"We're on in five minutes, *chérie,*" she chimed, her face flushed with excitement. "And the house is full, how do you say, to the rafters?"

Alysson and Douglas laughed, and Douglas bowed low over Alysson's hand. "I wish you luck this night, but I know you have little need of it. Later we will celebrate your success at the party at my house. I think the two of us will celebrate this night for a long time, for more than one reason."

He smiled and touched her cheek, and Alysson watched as he bid Odette good luck. He was going to ask her to marry him tonight, she thought. He had hinted at it more than once in the past weeks, but she did not know how to answer him. She liked him a great deal; he had been good to her. But did she really want to be his wife? As he left, Alysson looked at her best friend.

"Are you as nervous as I?"

"It feels as if I again have the *mal de mer!*" Odette exclaimed, weaving back and forth in time to imaginary ocean waves. "But you will forget all about it once the curtain goes up. It is that way with all of us."

They walked arm and arm to the cavernous backstage area where the painted backdrop for King Lear's palace had been set in place. It was a magnificent creation of pillars and arched stone windows with real brass torches glowing with flames which encircled a carved oak throne with scarlet cushions. Alysson had only a line or two to speak during the first scene, and she was glad of it as she listened to the loud buzz of the audience on the other side of the heavy velvet curtains.

"It *is* sold out! See!" Odette whispered next to her ear, and Alysson put her eyes to the parted curtains to look out over the gilded elegance of the Park Theater. It was huge, with hundreds of velvet padded seats on the main floor behind the glowing orchestra lights, but Alysson's eyes went to the upper levels where the private boxes stretched with curving grace from each side of the stage into the darkness at the rear of the theater. By the light of the gigantic crystal chandelier she could see that nearly every seat was taken.

She drew back as the oil lamps on the lower levels were extinguished and an expectant hush came over the crowd. A soft whoosh of velvet brought the curtain slowly back, and she stood off to one side with Odette as Billy, playing Edmund, the illegitimate son to Gloucester, and two other American actors portraying the Earl of Kent and the Earl of Gloucester entered from the far side of the stage.

The play began, and moments later, she was cued to take her place behind Adam as Lear, with Rosalie and Odette, who would play her older sisters, and the lesser actors playing the attendants. She smiled at Adam as he stepped back to speak to her.

"This will be your night," he whispered with a warm smile. "You'll steal the show from all of us."

"You are much too good as Lear for that to happen," she insisted.

"But I am an old man, and you are a beautiful ingénue. This will be your night."

Alysson watched him move back into place, thinking it little wonder that her mother had embroidered such a fantasy concerning Adam Sinclair. She had found him kind and gentle in the last days of rehearsals and parties, and she knew she must have imagined that strange look in his eyes that day in Douglas's dining room.

Their cue was given by Gloucester, and Alysson took a deep breath and followed Adam and the others to center stage. Oil lamps burned in a row, illuminating their faces, covered with heavy theatrical makeup, but all else lay in darkness in front of them. Her heart hammered with terror, her stomach rolled, her palms grew wet, and she was appalled at herself for feeling faint as Adam began his lines concerning the division of Lear's kingdom into thirds for his daughters.

It had certainly not been this way when she had played Juliet aboard the *Halcyone,* and she forced herself to concentrate on the dialogue. She listened as Rosalie spoke Goneril's tribute to Lear, ready to speak her own first line, and as Rosalie finished, she did so, in the way it had been written, aside to the audience as if she spoke to herself.

" 'What shall Cordelia do? Love, and be silent.' "

After those words from her, Adam said more lines, and to Alysson's relief, most of the terrible fear and trepidation inside her melted away and she began to grow calm. She had another short line after Odette's speech to Lear, then her lines came faster. She settled into her role, finding it elating to be part of the play, forgetting the crowd. She became Cordelia.

Her part allowed her to leave the stage near the end of Scene One, and since she had no more lines until the Fourth Scene of the Fourth Act, she returned to her dressing room to change into her next costume. It was a tight-fitting blue satin gown this time, with long flowing sleeves and a matching veil worn over her hair beneath a crown of gold. She sat down at her dressing table, smiling at her reflection. She had done her lines the best she could, and she was satisfied with them. And she was eager for the play to progress, because she had more lines in the last half. She had known from the beginning that Rosalie's and Odette's parts were more extensive in their roles of the ungrateful daughters, but it was the beloved youngest daughter that she had always wanted to play. And despite what Adam Sinclair had said, this was his play, for he was truly magnificent as Lear. He was superb with the language of Shakespeare, the staccato words of rage and incredulity or the short, bitter bursts of cursing. Alysson admired him very much, and she had learned much from watching his technique.

A tap on the door arrested her thoughts, and she rose and went to answer it, expecting it to be the stagehand who cued her. She opened it, shocked momentarily at the sight of the tall Negro standing just outside.

"Jethro? What are you doing here?"

Jethro grinned at her, his teeth looking white and enormous against his wide ebony face. He twisted his hat in his hand as he spoke, his eyes admiringly on the elegant costume she wore.

"De captain, he sent me, Miz Alysson, wid dis."

He held out a small nosegay of violets, and Alysson looked down at it. "Captain Brace."

"Yassum. For good luck, he say."

"How nice of him to remember," she said, hiding her disappointment. "Is he here?"

"Yassum, and Massa Donovan. He sent dis."

Alysson's heart leapt as he held out a small shiny white box.

"I sorry I late wid dem, but I had a pack of trouble wid de carriage. Thar a whole passel of white folk outside dis place."

Alysson smiled as Jethro handed the gift to her and began to back away from the door. "I gots ta get back now, fore a body can bodder with Massa Donovan's rig."

"Good-bye, Jethro, and thank you."

Alysson shut the door, holding the box to her breast. He *had* come. Pleasure flooded her with such joyful waves that she felt giddy. She had secretly hoped for weeks that Donovan would come. Smiling, she slowly lifted the lid, wondering what he had sent, and at the sight of the contents of the box, a rush of emotion rose up to close her throat. Tears welled, and she bit her lower lip as she lifted the small crown of white rose-buds from a bed of glossy green leaves. Ribbons of silver lace entwined the tiny roses. The memories came rushing back, especially the way he had smiled when she had told him about her dreams. "I will choose the one who gives me a crown of white roses laced with silver ribbons," she had said to him, and he had re-membered. His gesture touched her heart more than anything else he could ever have done.

A small white card lay atop the leaves, and she lifted it, recognizing Donovan's small and precise hand. *I'll await you in the Mews* was all it said, and Alysson stared at it for a long moment. She shouldn't go, she thought firmly, she really shouldn't. She had promised Douglas to join him for his party, and she was sure he was going to ask her to marry him. No, she wouldn't go.

She walked to the mirror and took off the gold crown she wore, carefully pinning the white roses in its place. She tilted her head to admire them, then smiled. Yes she would. She would go with him. She wanted to see him, and after all, she had always said she would choose the man who gave her white roses and silver ribbons.

The rest of the play went smoothly, and the applause as the final curtain lowered was deafening. The cast received ten curtain calls, and Alysson was thrilled as Adam led her out to the front of the stage when the crowd insistently called for Cordelia. She smiled, stooping to pick up the roses being tossed to her, but even in her moment of triumph, she thought of Dono-van.

After much mutual congratulating among the cast members, she returned to her dressing room to don the new dress made especially for the opening-night party. It was beautiful, but rather daring, scarlet satin that bared her shoulders and most of her back, but she put it on quickly, anxious to see Donovan again. He most likely wanted to tell her that their annulment had become final, she told herself, but at least he had come to see her performance. She looked up as Odette entered behind her, all aflutter in jade-green silk with a large white dahlia pinned behind one ear.

"Hurry, *mon amie,* the party is beginning even now, and we will make our grand entrance together!"

"I'm afraid you will make it alone this time, Odette."

"What? You are not going? But you were the sensation, and Douglas is waiting for you there!"

A streak of guilt shot through Alysson, but she didn't change her mind. "Mr. MacBride has asked me to join him tonight."

Odette paused in the process of freshening her lip rouge, turning slowly to stare at her friend. They smiled at each other.

"So you have given in to him at last?"

Alysson dropped her eyes. "I don't know about that. But I do know I want to see him. Perhaps it will be the last time, I do not know. Will you explain where I am to Rosalie? And to Douglas? I feel very bad about not going to his party."

"Pooh! You are doing the right thing at last!"

Alysson was not so sure of that as she made her way to the rear entrance of the theater. The Mews was a narrow street just behind the Park, and on this night a long line of carriages waited there. She was momentarily shocked by the outcry when she stepped out of the stage door into the warm night air. Immediately, she was surrounded by fans who recognized her as Cordelia, and she stood in their midst, overwhelmed by their attentions.

Countless cards and sealed notes were thrust into her hands, but she hardly had time to look at them before strong fingers closed possessively over her arm. She looked up to find Donovan towering over her, and she went with him willingly as he shouldered a path through the crowded sidewalk to where Jethro awaited high upon the outside driver's seat of the MacBride carriage. Donovan assisted her inside and had barely climbed aboard himself when Jethro called to the horses and the carriage moved forward.

"This feels almost like an abduction," Alysson told him, as he settled into a seat across from her. "Is it?"

"Maybe it is," he answered. "Would that frighten you?"

Black eyes held her for a long, uncomfortable moment, the expression in them reminiscent of their first meeting in London when he had hired her to play his lover, and Alysson felt a ridiculous chill undulate up her spine.

"Should I be?"

He smiled. "No."

It was rare indeed for Alysson to see such a smile from him, and one so warm at that, but it made him look even more handsome in his dark evening cape, and she found herself very glad to be with him again. It had been such a long time.

"May I ask where you're taking me?"

"I have ordered us a late supper. A celebration of your debut."

"You saw the play?"

"Yes, and you were wonderful. But you already know that." His eyes dropped to the cards in her hands. "You do know what those are, don't you?"

"I suppose they are congratulatory notes," Alysson

replied, then looked at him in surprise when he laughed.

"They're offers from gentleman admirers who are quite as eager as I to sample your considerable charms."

Alysson smiled at that, sure he was quite wrong, as she opened one and read it, but the deep blush that followed revealed that Donovan had been right.

She lowered her long lashes from his amused smile, feeling very foolish and inexperienced but even more embarrassed that he had been the one to witness her naïveté.

# Chapter 14

Only moments later, the carriage stopped at Donovan's town house on Wall Street, and he assisted her down to the dark, cobbled stableyard, then led her up through a pair of tall doors into some sort of foyer. The house was quite dark, with black hulking shadows cloaking the walls, but Donovan led her to where a single lamp burned at the base of a carved staircase. Alysson looked around curiously as they climbed the steps, and Donovan stood back before a door on the second floor. Alysson preceded him into a large masculine bedchamber, where a table had been prepared for them in the sitting room section at the far end, the flames from the tall white candles reflecting on a glittering array of silver and crystal atop a lace tablecloth.

Donovan seated her there and sat across from her, taking a chilled bottle of champagne from a silver bucket beside him. He opened it, carefully pouring them both a glass. He handed one to her, then smiled, eyes glittering like obsidian disks.

"To your success tonight and the achievement of all your dreams."

Alysson smiled, feeling very relaxed and comfortable with him for a change. She let down her guard somewhat, feeling that he was her friend instead of a man of whom she must constantly be wary.

"Thank you for sending me the roses," she said earnestly, touching them in her hair. "It meant a lot to me."

"I wanted to send them. Are you hungry?"

Alysson realized that she was, and she nodded. "I have had nothing today at all. I was much too nervous to eat."

He said little, watching as she helped herself to the fresh strawberries and thick rich cream. Flaky biscuits were kept warm in a covered silver dish, but as she tasted one, she was more aware of his dark eyes moving with slow and thorough appreciation over her bare shoulders. The way he looked at her was almost like the caressing warmth of his fingers upon her flesh, and the sensation it initiated soon robbed her of appetite. She leaned back finally and met those unsettling black eyes.

"Why did you bring me here, Mr. MacBride?"

Donovan smiled. "Why do you think?"

Alysson looked at the champagne and fruit, the soft candlelight, then across the room to the draped bed already turned back for the night.

"Perhaps to seduce me?"

Strong white teeth flashed against his dark skin. "And is that the reason you came, English?" he countered, raising his goblet as if to toast her.

Alysson stood then and moved away. She stopped beside the fireplace, fingering the gold fringe on the servant's bellpull.

"Perhaps I only came to inquire about our annulment. I believe Douglas Compton is ready to ask me to marry him."

Donovan's muscles tightened, and he looked at her delicate profile silhouetted against the orange glow of the fire.

"Is that the only reason you came here?" he asked softly. "To find out if you're free of me?"

Alysson was silent for a moment, and he held his

breath as she looked over at him, her lovely face tinted gold in the candlelight. Her reply was very low.

"I came here, I think, because I would rather be your mistress than his wife."

Their eyes locked, and Donovan stood, moving until he was so close that Alysson was forced to tip her head back to look into his face. His black eyes were intense as he ran a finger down the elegant curve of her cheek. Alysson drew in a startled breath as the caress moved lower to the upper curve of her breast.

"I'm going to make love to you now, English," he said very low. "Don't try to stop me."

Stopping him hadn't even occurred to her, and she closed her eyes in breathless anticipation as his hands came up to close gently around her throat before sliding ever so slowly down to her shoulders and beyond, taking her gown with them. Long quivering shivers chased his fingers as his other hand went to the buttons of her bodice, and the gown fell with heavy rustle of satin. Another deft twist sent her petticoats to the floor after the gown until she stood him in only the delicate silk of her chemise.

Her eyes fluttered open to find him smiling down at her, then his mouth came down on hers, strangely gentle and undemanding, but she could only feel the closeness of him, the heat and strength of his muscular body. She pressed herself against him, wanting his arms around her again, and Donovan made an indistinct sound of pleasure at the feel of her soft body. He had wanted to possess her like this, to touch her and hold her, for so very long.

Alysson was hardly aware when he lifted her, carrying her to the bed, then he lay half atop her, his weight pinning her into the softness of the pillows. The smell of her perfume filled Donovan's head, made his blood race in surging, boiling currents, and he stared into her slanted eyes, seeing both the fear and arousal in them. He slid his fingers into the soft mass of her golden hair, tracing the contours of her face with his thumbs, disbelieving the silky softness of her skin.

Alysson's eyes closed as his thumb touched her trembling bottom lip, but her lashes opened again as he raised himself away from her and moved about the room, snuffing candles with his fingers, her body captured in a shivering, shuddering state, lying in trembling wait for his next touch. She looked away in a sweet fearfulness as he removed his clothes in the shadowy light. Then he was beside her again, pulling her against his naked chest. Alysson moaned at the feel of the hard, molded muscles, felt his hands in her hair again, his lips on hers, hot, moist, devastating. Her heart beat wildly, then stopped as he pulled loose the ribbons of her chemise to sweep away the last thin barrier between them. Alysson tensed, suddenly terrified as she felt the crisp fur of his chest against her breasts.

"Please, I have not known a man before."

Donovan grew still atop her, and Alysson's heart thundered as he rolled to his back, his arms tight around her.

"That pleases me more than anything else, my love," he whispered, and Alysson relaxed in his embrace, shutting her eyes as his palms slid down her back to her naked hip. "Don't ever be afraid of me, Alysson. I won't hurt you, I swear."

His quiet words did calm her, but she soon forgot her fears as he began to kiss her, his hands sliding over her body, exploring the silken hollows and curves, and she gave an inarticulate sound as his mouth found hers again, moving over her cheeks and lips, tasting gently, insistently, knowingly, her passion growing with each touch. His dark head moved lower, and Alysson sighed with pleasure as he reached the peak of her breast, his hair soft under her hands. Her body came alive, pulsating as his palm moved up her bare leg, over her thigh to the deep curve of her waist.

When he moved atop her, she could feel the thudding of his heart as he pressed his hips into hers, and she tensed as a sharp hurt tingled in her loins. She muffled her cry in his shoulder, and he held her tenderly, kissing her cheeks and eyelids and lips until she no longer felt anything but the heat of his body. When he began to move again, she slid her hands over the smooth brown skin of his wide shoulders, feeling the strength of his powerful muscles moving beneath her fingertips, and as she held tightly to him, her sense of reality began to fade. She felt as if they were one person, their limbs entwined, their breaths mingled, lips, tongues, hearts. She heard only her heart's wild beating and his low words of love until the sweet ecstasy they sought was reached at last in a shuddering, quivering explosion of swirling stars and rocketing colors as their love was fulfilled.

Donovan held her tightly afterward, but tenderly, for he had realized just what it meant to him to have her, to have her as his wife as he should have long ago. Alysson lay in contented wonder in his arms, sated, fulfilled, at peace with herself and with him. After a long time, she felt his mouth nibbling upon her ear, and she smiled.

"If I had known about this, I think I should have become your mistress aboard the *Halcyone* when first you asked me," she murmured, snuggling closer to his long hard length.

Donovan laughed, low and pleased. "And I would have kept you as my wife that first night instead of waiting until now."

Alysson's heart stilled, and she turned her face to look into his eyes.

"You want to marry me?" she asked doubtfully and he smiled, lifting a lock of silky red-gold hair to idly caress it between his fingers.

"I am already married to you, and have been for quite a long time."

"But the annulment . . ."

"I tore it up."

Joy swelled in Alysson's heart, joy such as she had never known before, and she met his mouth eagerly as he lowered his lips to hers in warm possession. She was his wife. He wanted her for his wife, she thought over and over, until his mouth left hers, and she could think again. She traced her finger along his chin, still disbelieving that they could really be man and wife.

"I do not feel like your wife. I feel as if we've just done something wicked and wanton and deliciously exciting."

Her breath caught as Donovan's hand moved up over her ribs to her breast.

"You are definitely my wife, my love, even though our wedding was a long time ago, and not exactly worth remembering."

Alysson did remember, vividly, and for the first time, such memories brought a smile to her face.

"It wasn't really so bad," she said, giving him a wicked sidelong glance. "They only held one gun on you."

Donovan laughed, then rolled until he was on top of her again. He looked down into her eyes, his hands holding her face.

"You should have had a wedding worthy of you, in a great cathedral," he murmured, his eyes serious. "In a gown of white silk and fine lace." His hand moved to the slender column of her throat, his thumbs resting lightly upon the rapid pulse he found there. "With five strands of pearls around your neck."

Alysson smiled. "I need none of that. I only wanted you to want me."

"Oh, I want you, love, you can believe that?"

His lips ended all thoughts of conversation, and Alysson met his passion, her heart bursting with her newfound love.

When light again misted their bedchamber, Donovan sat motionlessly in an armchair close to the bed. Alysson still lay in peaceful repose, but he had risen quietly an hour before to bathe and dress. Now he looked at his wife, asleep in his bed where she should have been since her arrival in New York. She lay on her side, one slender shoulder bare above the quilted comforter, her hand lying palm up beside her face, making her look very young and vulnerable.

Donovan shut his eyes, dreading the moment when she would awaken and he would have to tell her. He opened his eyes as she stirred, sleepily murmuring his name before she grew still again, and a surge of emotion rocked him where he sat. He had wanted her from the first moment he had ever seen her, the night they had been forced to marry. Then he had fought his desire throughout the voyage home when she had been so near yet so unattainable—the night of the storm, the day she had bathed so innocently behind the screen, the night she had turned him down. Every single night since he had set foot in New York he had dreamed of possessing her. He had thought himself caught in her spell, one that would be broken once he had made love to her. But now he knew it would never be broken. He loved her. He loved her as he had never loved another woman. It half amazed him still, though now he could admit it. It had grown slowly, steadily, inside him, and the depth and intensity of his feelings for her were almost frightening. He needed her, needed her love, her smile, her presence in his life. And as soon as she awakened, he would have to hurt her.

Upset by his own thoughts, he rose to sit on the edge of the bed, looking down at her. She had been hurt so much already—by her father, by Donovan himself when they had first met. It shamed him now to think of the cruel way he had treated her. A curling lock lay over her cheek, soft, with the gleam of spun gold, and as he gently smoothed it behind her ear, her long black lashes lifted to reveal sleepy emerald eyes.

"Good morning, my love," he murmured, and Alysson immediately raised her arms toward him.

Donovan pulled her up and against him, savoring the softness of her slender body.

"Did you sleep well?" he asked against the top of her head.

She laughed softly. "We barely thought of sleeping. Don't you remember?"

"I remember all too well," he answered, stroking her silky blond hair with his hand, then smiled as she snuggled closer. He had been astounded at the passion with which she had met his caresses through the night. It had been so good between them, fulfilling in a way he had never thought possible. "I shall have to take better care of you then and let you get your rest."

"I do not think you could take better care of me than you did last night."

She raised her face with a smile so adoring, yet so seductive, that Donovan had to laugh.

"I believe I have married an insatiable woman," he said, but Alysson only smiled, contentedly resting her head upon his broad shoulder.

"But that is your own fault, because you are too wonderful for me to resist."

Her words came shyly, and Donovan's expression softened. He laid her back, leaning down to kiss her, and Alysson met him eagerly, wrapping her arms around his neck and pressing her soft nakedness up against his chest until he groaned with the need for her. After a long moment, he forced himself to let her go.

"I have business I must attend to this morning, my love, and you are making it very difficult for me to leave you."

"Must you go?"

"I have a meeting at the Tontine, but I will be back this afternoon."

"But wait," Alysson said, glancing at the clock on the mantel. "It is nearly nine, and I want to go to the theater at noon for my after-opening rehearsal. If I dress quickly, will you take me there? Then perhaps you could come back early and watch us for a while."

Donovan's eyes dropped away from her, and Alysson watched as he rose and moved away. She waited uncertainly as he leaned an elbow against the mantelpiece, staring down into the cold grate. When he turned, the look on his face sent a chill of foreboding rippling up her back.

"What is it?" she asked fearfully, clutching the bedcovers against her breasts.

His voice was very quiet. "I'm sorry, Alysson, but you won't be playing Cordelia anymore."

Alysson stared at him in confusion. "I don't understand. What do you mean?"

"I mean I don't want you performing at the Park anymore."

Their eyes met, and to Donovan's shock, Alysson's silvery laughter tinkled into the air.

"You are teasing me, of course," she said, but when his face remained solemn, her own smile faded.

"I'm not joking, Alysson. Now that we are married, I don't want you performing there anymore."

Alysson sat up in rigid alarm now. "But you can't

mean it," she managed at last, her eyes wide with stunned disbelief. "You know how much it means to me, and I have only just had one performance. Please, I am committed—"

"I'm sorry, truly I am, but it has to be this way," Donovan said to cut off her entreaty, unable to bear the shattered expression in her eyes. If only he could tell her the whole truth, tell her Adam was an American agent, that he was her father, that Compton was a dangerous traitor, then perhaps she might understand. But he couldn't, he couldn't tell her anything. He looked back at her and found her eyes full of hurt tears, and unable to stand her suffering, he went to her, taking her hands and pressing them to his lips.

"Please try to understand, my sweet. You are a Mac-Bride now, my wife. My family is well known and respected here in New York. It wouldn't be seemly for you to be on the stage, especially in Compton's theater. I've told you of his reputation for seducing his actresses. He's notorious for it, and there's already gossip about you and him. Half the people in the city think you are his lover. I don't want you anywhere near him."

He was jealous, Alysson thought, letting out a relieved breath. That was why he was saying such things to her. "Nothing happened between Douglas and me, you know that now, after last night, and nothing ever will, I swear it. But if it concerns you, I will make sure I am never alone with him, not for a minute, and you can come with me and watch us the whole time, if you wish. I'd like that very much, truly I would."

Donovan swallowed hard, wavering beneath her beseeching plea and imploring green eyes, wanting to give in to her, wanting to give her anything she ever wanted. But he couldn't, he couldn't allow it. It was too dangerous, for her, for Adam, for all of them.

"No," he said firmly. "It's out of the question, and it's too late now to change anything, because I sent a note to Rosalie and the others last night telling them we were married and you were giving up your role in the play."

Alysson looked as if he had slapped her hard across the face, and Donovan winced as she backed away from him. Her face went pale as if some kind of realization had dawned on her.

"This is your revenge, isn't it? You promised me once that you'd make me suffer, and now you've found a way to do it!"

Donovan shook his head impatiently. "That's ridiculous, Alysson."

"How long have you been planning this?" she demanded then, anger taking hold. "And will it be worth it? Having to marry me like this? Or did you? Was that a lie, too?"

Donovan stared at her. Her accusations made no sense; her words were those of despair. She would come to realize that after she calmed down and had time to think, but he doubted very much if she would believe him until then.

"You are very definitely married to me, and if you want to see the annulment agreement for yourself, you'll find it in that desk drawer, torn in two as I told you. If I hadn't wanted you as my wife, you would not be in my bed now."

Alysson hardly listened to him, the full, devastating impact of his decree hitting her, crumbling all her happiness. He meant it, all of it, and Alysson had never felt so cold inside. Last night when she had fallen asleep, curled in his arms, she had thought everything was wonderful, that she had everything she had ever wanted, but now he had taken it all away from her, everything. She felt betrayed, weak, sick to her stomach.

"Why are you doing this to me?" she cried, her voice breaking. "How can you say you love me yet do this to me?"

Tears she could not stop welled and rolled down her cheeks, and as she turned away from him to sob into her pillow, Donovan gritted his teeth in frustration. He forced down his own feelings of helplessness and tried to soothe her.

"I know you're disappointed now, sweetheart, but after you have time to think about it, you'll understand my reasons." He hesitated, the sound of her weeping like talons puncturing his heart. He stood and looked around, his fists on his hips, not knowing what else to do. It would take her time to adjust to the idea, and he would just have to wait until she did.

"We'll talk about it again when I come home," he said finally, then paused at the door, looking at her huddled form upon the bed. "I'll send Stephens to Mrs. Thackeray's for your things."

Alysson didn't answer, and he sighed, closing the door quietly behind him.

The moment he was gone, Alysson came upright in the bed, wiping at her tears, fury boiling over. He couldn't do this to her! She'd leave him! She'd divorce him! Her friends would help her! Or Douglas! She'd go to Douglas, and he would help her get a divorce and Donovan could be damned! If indeed they were married at all, she thought bitterly. She was not at all sure he was telling her the truth about the annulment.

She turned her eyes to the desk, then crossed the floor to it, pulling open the first drawer. Lying on top was the legal document that she had signed aboard the *Halcyone,* torn in half, but her gaze went to what lay beneath it. She picked up one long, golden lock, her eyes filling with tears again. Her hair. He had kept it from the day when she'd cut it, the day the British had stopped them at sea. He had cared about her even then. She sobbed, unfolding the other paper in the drawer to find a playbill with her picture upon it. He did love her, he really did. She sank to the floor and wept into her hands, her feelings about him all mixed up and confused.

After a time, she got up and sat down in the desk chair. She would not cry anymore, she told herself firmly; she was tired of crying. It didn't do any good anyway. Now it was time to decide what she should do. She tried to think, to understand why Donovan was insisting that she quit acting. The reasons he had given her still did not ring true, but the accusations she had made to him seemed less reasonable now that she was calmer. Donovan was a rich and powerful man, and if he had wanted revenge upon her, there were ways he could have done it without marrying her. And though she knew Donovan was domineering, and even cruel at times, she couldn't believe he would take her career away from her for no other reason than just to hurt her. She remembered the way he had touched her during the night, remembered the way he had called her his love, and the way he had smiled as if pleased when she had said she was willing to become his mistress. There had to be some other reason, some good reason that he wasn't telling her.

He had not been vindictive or cruel when he had forbidden her to go back to the theater, but almost regretful, now that she thought of it. Hope rose inside her. Perhaps she could persuade him to change his mind. She loved him; she wanted to be his wife, but she also wanted to be an actress. More than anyone else, Donovan knew that. She had confided more to him about her dreams than she ever had to anyone else. She thought of the way he had sent the note to Rosalie without even discussing it with her, before he even knew if she would agree to remain his wife. She grew furious to think of such arrogant self-confidence, but her rage faded quickly. How could she be angry with him for that? All along, she had wanted him to want her for his wife, and she had come to his house with the intention of becoming his mistress. She loved him, she loved him!

Douglas Compton's face rose in her mind along with an overwhelming sense of guilt. Despite all the gossip about his reputation, he had been ready to offer her marriage. He had given her a job when Donovan had not wanted her. He had given her a wonderful debut in his theater, and she had rewarded his friendship by running away with Donovan without a thought to Douglas's feelings. What must he think of her? He would be so hurt, and he would probably lose a small fortune if he had to cancel *Lear*.

It was a terrible thing for her to have done to him when he had been so kind to all of them, giving them plum roles, even star billing. He didn't deserve such treatment.

Her chin rose with resolve. No matter what Donovan thought of him, she owed Douglas an explanation. In person, not through some impersonal note sent to Rosalie by Donovan. She would dress and go to the theater. Rosalie would be there, and she would explain everything to both of them. It was the least she could do. After that, she would come home and do everything in her power to persuade Donovan to change his mind. Her course decided, she sat back to channel her thoughts, determined to formulate the best argument

possible with which to win Donovan to her way of
thinking. She pondered for a long time, decided it
would be best to wait until they were in bed together,
then discuss it with him. Yes, she determined with a
confident smile, that was exactly where she would beg
him to reconsider.

# Chapter 15

Douglas Compton crumpled the note from Rosalie Handel and flung it from him. Damn MacBride! Just when he was ready to ask Alysson to marry him, just when she was ready to accept, MacBride decided he wanted her after all. No wonder Lord Tyler detested the man enough to want him dead. Not only was he a formidable adversary in their secret war; he was a personal enemy as well.

Agitated, he moved to the windows and stared out into the rainy morning, trying to think of a way to do away with MacBride once and for all. Assassination seemed plausible; Douglas had several good men who could do it and make it look like an accident. Mac-Bride's death seemed the only way to wed Alysson now, since she had gone freely to MacBride. The idea of her running off as she had rankled, and his jaw clamped into a hard, tight line.

A cloaked figure hurrying down the block past his house caught his eye and he pushed back the lace drapery for a better view, starting in shock as he recognized Alysson. When she reached the theater doors and found them locked, she looked around as if undecided what to do, and Douglas ran into the hall to fling open his doors. A fine rain was beginning to fall, and he hurried down the steps and across the street before she could leave.

"Alysson! I saw you from my windows! What you you doing here?"

He looked down into puffy, red-rimmed green eyes, and, elated, took her hand.

"What is it? You've been crying, haven't you?"

Drops pelted them as the rain came harder, and Alysson pulled up the hood of her cloak.

"I came to talk to you and Rosalie, but the theater's closed."

"I canceled the rehearsals, but come, you're getting all wet. We'll talk about it in the house."

Alysson allowed him to hurry her across the street and inside, dreading the conversation they were about to have. She waited while he gave her cloak to Henrietta, then walked with him into the parlor.

"Are you all right, my dear? I've been very worried about you."

His solicitous concern did not help Alysson's guilt over what she had done to him, and she looked down, unable to meet his eyes.

"I only hope that you can forgive me for last night. It was unforgivable for me to go off with Donovan without telling you first."

Douglas's anger rose like a cornered snake, but he did not allow it to show. "I was more hurt than angry, and I was worried because I thought your marriage to MacBride had been annulled."

Alysson took a deep breath. "I love him, Douglas. I can't help it. I've loved him all along, but I wasn't sure he really loved me until last night. I never meant to hurt you, please believe that."

Douglas kept his face in iron restraint, but inside, he cursed MacBride to the deepest pits of hell.

"I can't say that I like it, but you know that your happiness is the most important thing to me."

She should have known that Douglas would be understanding, Alysson thought, but somehow his kindness made her feel even worse. She let him pull her down beside him on the sofa.

"Alysson, I can understand what you've just told me about you and MacBride, but I cannot understand your decision to quit the play. You were a sensation last night." He gestured toward several newspapers scattered over a low table near them. "All accounts are giving you rave reviews for your performance. It's mad for you to even think of giving it up."

Regret took hold of Alysson and wouldn't let go. Tears welled, and angry at herself, she dashed them away.

"I don't want to give it up, but Donovan insists upon it. He says now that I'm his wife, it would be improper for me to continue on the stage."

So that was the reason for her tears, Compton thought, hardly able to contain his satisfaction. MacBride was a fool after all. His refusal to let her perform was exactly what Douglas needed to drive a wedge between them.

"But that's absurd. Many fine actresses continue their careers after they marry. Rosalie Handel, for example. She was on the stage for years before her husband died. It makes no sense."

"I know. I feel the same way, and I intend to try to make him change his mind. He is really a very reasonable man, Douglas, and I'm hoping perhaps Rosalie will help me persuade him. That's why I was looking for her. Really, I should be going to Mrs. Thackeray's now to speak to her."

She began to rise, but Douglas caught her arm and held her beside him, an idea forming in the back of his mind that might very well be the answer to all his problems.

"But there's no need for you to go out into this storm again. Rosalie's coming here for lunch, before the hour is out. And so are Edgar and Adam, so you would probably miss them if you left now. You see, I called a meeting this morning so we could discuss what should be done about *Lear,* now that you have dropped out."

"I really am very sorry for causing all this trouble for you, Douglas. You've done so much for me, for all of us—"

"Don't please, there's no need for apologies. It's not your fault, now is it? Everything is going to be all right, don't you worry. As you said, Mr. MacBride is a reasonable man."

"I appreciate your understanding, Douglas. You are very kind."

Douglas smiled down at the genuine gratitude in her face, thinking things couldn't go any better for him if he had planned them himself. "You will stay and talk to Rosalie, won't you? Or is MacBride waiting somewhere for you?"

"No, he had some business at the Tontine."

"Good, but I'm afraid I have an important errand that I have to take care of before Rosalie and the others arrive. It won't take long, so please make yourself comfortable. They should be here any time now, and you can tell them I'll be back shortly."

Alysson stared at the rain spattering the windows for a time after he left, then as lightning flashed outside, she grew uneasy and moved to the window in time to see Douglas descend the front steps to where his coach waited at the curb, the gusting wind billowing his dark cape out behind him. Thunder rumbled as he departed. Alysson turned as Henrietta brought a tea tray for her. She took a cup of the hot brew gratefully, then moved restlessly around the room, wishing Rosalie would come. She wanted to be at home when Donovan arrived there; she was anxious to try to reason with him again.

It was still hard to believe they were really married, that he really wanted her for his wife. Vivid pictures of the night they had shared in his big carved bed brought tinglings through her body and a deep rosy color into her high cheekbones, and though she stood alone, she was embarrassed by the intense longing she felt to be entwined in Donovan's arms again. She picked up one of the newspapers, wanting to get her mind off such unsettling thoughts.

It was folded to the review of the play, and she read it eagerly, smiling at some of the kind remarks, not only about her but about her friends as well. One remark about Billy delighted her particularly, and she hoped he would come along with Rosalie so she could show it to him. She read another account, also quite complimentary, and she wondered whether Donovan would relent and let her continue as Cordelia if she showed them to him.

The rattle of a carriage outside caught her attention, and relieved that Rosalie had arrived, she hurried to the window. She gasped at the sight of a shiny black coach, a silver *M* upon the door. Shocked to a standstill, she put her hand to her mouth as the door opened, and Donovan stepped down into the rain. How had he known she was here? she thought in dismay, as Brace descended after his brother. Both men looked back as Douglas's carriage rolled to a stop just behind them. Worms of foreboding writhed in the pit of her stomach as Adam and Douglas joined the MacBride men. Her fears intensified as the four men moved up the steps, and a moment later, when the parlor door opened, she stood paralyzed as Donovan's black eyes found her. She flinched, for never in her life had she been subject to a look so full of icy contempt and cold loathing. He looked away without a word, and the other three men stared at her, their faces somber. Donovan spoke to Brace, his voice low and totally devoid of emotion.

"Take her down to the coach while we complete the arrangements."

"Wait," Alysson began as Brace took her arm.

"You had better come along before there's any more trouble," he murmured under his breath, and Alysson looked at Douglas in confusion as she was led past him.

"Don't worry, my dear, everything will be all right. I'll see to it."

Alysson saw Donovan stiffen at Douglas's soft reassurance, and cold tension lay over the room like a clammy glaze. She was glad when she could leave.

"What has happened? How did you know I was here?" she asked Brace as soon as they reached the front steps, and he glanced down at her, his eyes as cold as Donovan's had been. He opened the door of the carriage without answering her questions, then walked away.

Alysson was surprised to find another woman already in the coach. As Jethro slapped the reins and the carriage lurched forward, knocking Alysson back into the cushions, she cried out to the woman with her.

"Where are we going? What about Donovan and Brace?"

The woman eyed her with pure malice. "As distasteful as I find it, my brother has asked me to escort you back to his house."

It was then that Alysson realized the woman was Olivia, the sister Odette had seen with Donovan on the *Halcyone* during the flotilla. The woman continued to stare silently at her, looking very much like Donovan when he was the most angry. Her dark wavy hair was pulled back in smooth wings at the temples, lightly sprinkled with silver, but her eyes were light blue, the color of ice, as she held them with unblinking hostility on Alysson's face.

"I don't see how you can ever look yourself in the mirror again if Donovan is killed today," she intoned bitterly.

Alysson's face went white. "Killed! What do you mean?"

Olivia shook her head, her anger coming at Alysson like pointed steel spikes. "Don't play the innocent victim with me. I see through your young and vulnerable act, as my brothers could not. You know perfectly well that Douglas Compton challenged Donovan to a duel."

Alysson sat frozen, but Olivia continued, her eyes narrowed. "In front of everyone at the Tontine, just as the two of you planned it, so Donovan had no recourse but to accept the challenge."

Alysson could only stare at her, stunned. "No, I don't believe it. Douglas would never do that. Why would he do such a thing?"

"You *are* quite a little actress, aren't you? Donovan must have been insane to have married you. That's why we were at the Tontine with him, so he could tell us the *good news.*"

Her sarcastic insults had no effect on Alysson, who thought only of Donovan's danger. "We must go back and stop them! It's all a terrible mistake! It's got to be!"

"The only terrible mistake was the one Donovan made by marrying you. And you couldn't stop anything now, even if you tried. Donovan has too much honor and too much pride to back down after all the things Douglas Compton said in public. You've shamed us all, the whole family. You've ruined our good name."

"What did Douglas say? Please, you must tell me!"

Olivia leaned forward, her fists clenching in fury against the black silk of her skirt. "He said Donovan took you by force last night, then made you give up your career. He said you had come to him, begging for his help, seeking refuge in his house. Do you really have the gall to deny your part in all of this, when we found you waiting there for him?"

Alysson's teeth caught at her lower lip as she realized how guilty she must appear to all of them, especially Donovan. She had been so angry at him when he had left that morning that he might really believe she had done what Douglas had told him. But why would Douglas tell him such things? How could he have misunderstood her? He couldn't have misunderstood her, he couldn't have! He had wanted to challenge Donovan, she realized suddenly, trying to control the fear burgeoning inside her. Her voice quavered alarmingly when she tried to talk to Olivia.

"None if it happened that way, I swear it, I swear it on my mother's grave. You must have Jethro turn around so I can explain to Donovan. I *have* to explain it to him!"

"Even if you were telling the truth, and I don't believe a word you say, it's too late now. And frankly, I don't think Donovan will ever want to see you again."

Olivia turned her gaze to the rain-blurred afternoon outside, and Alysson stared at the angry lines of her profile, horrified, unable to believe that the terrible nightmare was really happening. Olivia was right. It was her fault for going to Compton's house. What had she done? she asked herself again and again as the coach rattled over the rain-slicked cobblestones, a helpless, hopeless, freezing fear descending over her until she could not breathe.

A wet, clinging mist hung low over the Hudson River early the next morning, giving the water an eery appearance as the long boat from the *Halcyone* was rowed toward the dueling fields of Weehawken

Heights, New Jersey. Donovan sat in the bow with Brace just behind him, and no one spoke as the four crewmen with them leaned their backs into their task. When the keel of the boat scraped to a stop on the sand, Donovan stepped out first, looking up to a steep, rocky elevation covered with small trees and tangled bushes. The grassy fields stretching out above the water had seen the blood of countless men who had come there to defend their honor or that of a friend or lover, and one of the finest men Donovan had ever known, Alexander Hamilton, had been mortally wounded in this very spot seven years earlier. Donovan had sworn on the day that great patriot and statesman had died so needlessly from Aaron Burr's bullet never to duel again, and his face hardened to think he had been forced by Compton to break his vow.

Douglas Compton was known for taking pride in the duels he fought, and Donovan was overcome by an intense desire to kill the bloody bastard now that he had the chance. But he couldn't do that. Not with Adam firmly entrenched in the Compton camp. They had been able to pass along valuable British information to Washington, and Compton's death would destroy Adam's years of infiltration in the English spy network. As much as he wanted to aim his pistol for Compton's heart, Donovan wouldn't.

He turned as Brace stepped from the boat, the gold-hinged ebony box which held their father's dueling pistols in his hands. He tried not to think as they climbed the short distance to the field. Compton had chosen Adam Sinclair for his second, and Adam had had no choice but to accept. Donovan stood silently waiting as Adam and Brace met a short distance away to examine and load the pistols, with Dr. Whittingham standing by as a neutral party and surgeon, should one be needed. He tried not to think of the other times he had stood waiting in such a way—in Venice when Marina's cruel and sadistic husband had fallen beneath his bullet. Donovan had aimed to kill that time, to free her from the constant, senseless batterings that she had endured, and the memory gave him nothing but disgust. Alysson's latest treachery came to him then, and he felt lethal rage rising in his chest, slowly, steadily, like steam in a kettle. He forced himself not to think of her, of the way he had felt when he saw her in Compton's house, waiting for him. He slowly emptied his mind, pouring it all out, all thoughts, all emotions.

"Adam says Compton plans to turn a fraction early and fire before you get all the way around," Brace said softly, handing Donovan a loaded pistol. "He's out to kill, so he'll aim for your chest. Take a long step to the left when you turn."

A few yards away, Douglas smiled to himself as Donovan removed his coat and vest, handing them to Brace MacBride, before he turned to face Douglas. He wore a white shirt with ruffled cuffs and dark breeches, and he had a relaxed, coiled quality about him, like a stalking panther. When Douglas met those black eyes, he found them unreadable, deadly, frightening. He found himself slightly unnerved as he hadn't been before when facing an opponent. He had always prided himself on his marksmanship; he had killed nine men on this very field, and he meant for Donovan MacBride to be the tenth and most satisfying.

Most of the others had been old men with whose wives he'd had a dalliance, or young hotheads angry with him over their sister's seduction, but MacBride was deadly with a pistol and had emerged the victor each time he had dueled. Douglas had challenged MacBride in order to have a legitimate excuse to kill him, and he wasn't about to let him walk away alive. In a very short time, Alysson would be a widow, and Donovan MacBride would cause him no more trouble.

Donovan said nothing as they moved to face each other, and Doctor Whittingham instructed them on the rules. As the old man finished, Douglas spoke, very low, so only Donovan could hear him.

"Make your peace with God, MacBride, for I intend to kill you. Alysson came to me once, and she will again. I don't intend to give her up."

He felt triumphant as a muscle flexed and held in MacBride's cheek, the first sign of emotion from him. Jealous rage had been the doom of more than one man facing Douglas in a duel. Perhaps it would be again.

"I will call out twenty paces, then you will turn and fire. If after the first discharge, honor has been attained, the challenge will be at an end. If not, your seconds will reload, and you will step off the distance again. Are there questions?"

No one answered, and Donovan and Douglas turned back-to-back.

"One," Doctor Whittingham called, stepping back from them. "Two ... Three ..."

Douglas moved with measured footsteps, his finger tight against the trigger as the count reached eighteen. He would turn just after the count reached twenty, and he would kill Donovan MacBride.

"Nineteen ... Twenty."

He whirled and fired just as Donovan began to turn. The crack of Compton's pistol broke the heavy silence, sending a flock of crows cawing and fluttering from their roosts in the trees. Donovan's gun was up but not yet aimed when it felt as if his upper arm were hit by a drawn-back fist. His pistol discharged with the impact, and he clutched his wounded arm. Simultaneously, Compton screamed as Donovan's bullet hit him in the leg.

Donovan watched dispassionately as Compton writhed in agony upon the ground, then slowly he lowered his smoking pistol to hang at his side. Doctor Whittingham ran to kneel beside Compton, opening his black leather bag as Brace came forward to examine Donovan's arm.

"Adam was right, the bastard turned early," Brace said. "It's a good thing he told us."

He ripped Donovan's blood-soaked linen sleeve as he spoke, pulling it back to examine the raw bullet wound. "It's not too bad, but you sure as hell won't be using this arm for a while."

Donovan said nothing. He gripped his arm tightly as the doctor worked on Compton's shattered kneecap, sickened by the sight of it, sickened by his participation in the duel. He turned and started toward the riverbank with Brace behind him. As they took their places in the boat, and it was pushed into the water, Brace looked at Donovan.

"What about Alysson?"

"Tell Olivia to take her to Wildwood where I won't have to look at her," Donovan said bitterly, then turned his gaze to the far shoreline of Manhattan.

# Chapter 16

For the next two weeks, Alysson lived in virtual seclusion at Wildwood. She did not see or hear from
Donovan or anyone else, other than Olivia, who treated
her with cold dislike. Olivia had told her that both
Donovan and Douglas Compton had survived the duel,
but nothing else, and Alysson longed to know more.

She had overheard Olivia telling one of the servants
that Brace had sailed to Philadelphia for some kind of
special cannon for the *Halcyone,* but she had no idea of
the date of his departure or his return. And she was not
sure he would treat her with any more cordiality than
his sister did. He blamed her for the challenge, just like
everyone else.

She sighed, guilt racking her again as she sat alone
under a latticed grape arbor on the sweeping, verdant
lawns of the MacBride estate. Thick entwined vines
shaded her place on the long white rattan swing affixed
by chains to the ceiling beams. She looked down
through the giant oak and maple trees dotting the
lawns, where sheep had been let loose to crop the
grass. Far down the hill, the East River glittered in
the sun like a rippled silver mirror.

Wildwood had been built atop the rolling hills in the
heights of Brooklyn, a beautiful wooded setting for the
enormous white brick mansion. The house was impressive with its long porches supported by stone pillars
and a balustraded roof. The house was every bit as elegant and expensively furnished as her father's London

house. But a warm atmosphere pervaded Wildwood's wide halls, fragrant with the scent of lemon oil and beeswax, and filled with smiling servants. Lord Tyler's house had been cold and austere with no joy and no laughter.

Alysson looked up at the round tower rising from the center of the front wing, high above the red-tiled roof. Several days after her arrival, she had found a library there, with tall windows overlooking the rooftops and church spires of the distant Manhattan Island. She had spent a good deal of time there, reading or peering at the wharves and slips with a spyglass.

On this day, however, the insufferable heat of late August had driven her outside, and she fanned her flushed face with her lace handkerchief. Even her place in the deep shade was nearly unbearable, and never had she suffered so in England's cooler climate. For a fortnight the heat wave had plagued them, and though she wore her coolest dress of lavender muslin, without a single petticoat, rivulets of perspiration trickled down her back and between her breasts.

Even the usual wind from the river had settled into a heavy stillness, and she stood up restlessly, lifting out her bodice where it clung to her sticky skin. The heat had been making her ill, and she was often quite sick to her stomach. A wave of nausea swept her, and she began to walk, not wanting to think of the grueling weather, not allowing herself to think of Donovan.

She strolled toward the house on a path of white bricks that curved eventually to the back lawns. Several Negro servants tended beds of begonias and brilliantly hued and beautifully arranged in splashes of red and white and pink beneath the lofty trees shading the porches. She paused there to admire them. There were so many different varieties of flowers: neat, orderly beds of marigolds and peonies, scarlet salvia and climbing roses on star-shaped trellises. Clay pots filled with green ferns and glossy ivy hung suspended beneath the colonnaded verandas.

Hedges perhaps a foot high lined the carriage drive that wound in front of the house, as well as the neat bricked walkways. She wandered down one of the walkways she had not taken before. It led through a high brick wall where laundry maids were hanging freshly washed linen upon long lines suspended between poles. When they saw her, they looked away, whispering among themselves and stealing glances at her. Alysson was used to such ostracism from the household staff. She really couldn't blame them. They were obviously very loyal to their master, and she had caused him trouble and embarrassment.

Pain and loneliness pierced her, for she missed him, missed what they had shared. They had been so happy. But she wouldn't think about that night when she had lain so contentedly in his arms. It hurt too much.

The path forked just ahead of her, and she knew one branch led through a deer park to the famous MacBride stables, but she turned toward a dense forest at the edge of the grounds.

The trees there were choked with undergrowth and vines, and she thought it strange that they had been left in such a wild state when the rest of the grounds were kept so meticulously. When she came upon a narrow dirt path meandering back through the dark leafy trees, she took it without hesitation, welcoming the cool respite from the glaring sun.

Trilling birdsong echoed in the silent woods, and she stopped, lifting her face as a gentle breeze rose to whisper through the boughs above her head. Her thoughts went back to Donovan, as they always did, and deep, cutting regret slashed her heart. For one night, he had held her tenderly the way she had always dreamed he would. Was that all they were destined to share? She was at fault, she knew. She should never have gone to Douglas, yet how could she have known he would be compelled to challenge Donovan the way he had? Still, Donovan had not even given her a chance to explain. He had tried and convicted her on the word of others, like the Moor of *Othello* with the innocent Desdemona. She had nothing now. Her acting profession was denied her, her husband was gone, and even her friends could not reach out to comfort her.

Tears of self-pity welled, and she suppressed them. She had cried enough in her bed at night. She was tired of crying, weary of feeling sick and miserable. She bent and picked up a stick, then threw it from her in a sudden burst of anger.

"Damn you, Donovan! Why won't you listen to me!"

Her voice resounded through the empty woods, and she stood very still, closing her eyes. More than anything, she wanted Donovan to come to her, to let her tell him why she had gone to Douglas's house. But she knew he would not come. He believed everything Douglas had told him. She had seen it in his eyes. She shivered. She would never, ever, in her entire life, forget the way he had looked at her that day.

She walked on, dispirited, until she came upon a swift-flowing stream next to an old stone millhouse. She sat down heavily in the dappled shade of a mossy bank, staring across the rippling green currents to where the water gushed in a torrent over a series of smooth, flat rocks sloping gradually into a deeper pool below them. It looked like a wide, curving slide, she thought, remembering how she and Freddie had played and splashed in a similar stream in Cornwall.

Her troubles of late had made thoughts of her old friends less frequent, but she wondered about them now as she tossed small stones, listening as they *kerplunked* into the water. She wiped perspiration from her brow, reaching down to dip her handkerchief into the water. She pressed the cloth to her forehead and cheeks, then looked around as an idea came to her. No one was about. In truth, the overgrown appearance of the place, suggested no one ever came near.

She removed her shoes and stockings quickly, gasping as she put her bare toes into the cold water. It felt so good, though, that she could not resist the temptation of a swim. She stood, quickly removing her dress, then waded out in her chemise, submerging to her shoulders. It felt wonderful, took away some of the queasiness in her stomach, and she felt better than she had in days. She swam a few strokes, then floated on her back in the deeper water.

A small cluster of hickory trees stood on the edge of the bank, their thick branches overhanging the water, and the angry chatter of a squirrel caught her attention. She watched it as it hopped about the limb with its tail held upright, then scolded her soundly before circling underneath the branch to stare upside down at her out of bright beady eyes.

A different movement took her eyes along a nearby limb, and Alysson was startled to discern a small elfin face peering through the thick green foliage. It took her a moment to realize that the spying child was Olivia's daughter, Katie. She had seen the child several times since she had come to Wildwood, but always at a distance, for Olivia had, no doubt, forbidden the little girl to associate with her.

The squirrel chattered again, hopping along the limb as if showing off. As it came very close to the child's hiding place, Alysson remembered a game she had played with Freddie.

"Hello, Mr. Squirrel," Alysson called out suddenly. "What on earth are you doing up there?"

The playful young squirrel froze at the unexpected sound of Alysson's voice in the quiet glade, cocking his head to one side as if contemplating her. Smiling, Alysson threw her voice, using her best Irish brogue.

"I am looking for nuts if it is any of your concern, miss! Must you stare at me!"

It seemed very much indeed as if her words had come from the preening squirrel above her, and a startled rustling came from the branch where young Katie hid. The leaves parted slightly to reveal an incredulous little face, eyes wide upon the talking squirrel.

"Did you know a little girl followed you here?" the squirrel said then. "She's right there above you. See her?"

The squirrel had remained very still as Alysson had spoken for him, making the charade seem all the more real, and Alysson answered in her own voice.

"Don't be afraid, Mr. Squirrel. She won't hurt you. Will you, Katie?"

There was a long silence, then a tiny voice came from the leaves. "No."

The squirrel scampered away at a voice so close to him, and Alysson called up to Katie.

"I guess he doesn't want to talk anymore, but I'll talk to you if you'll come down and swim with me."

There was no answer, and somehow Alysson knew she should not insist. She closed her eyes and floated on her back, but when she opened them again, the child was on the bank, sitting on her heels as she watched Alysson. She was very small and looked to be around seven or eight with dark red hair swinging in long braids over her thin shoulders. Her small, heart-shaped face was covered with freckles. Alysson smiled at her but did not speak, afraid Katie would scamper away as the squirrel had done. A few minutes passed before Katie broke the silence.

"I happen to know that squirrels can't talk."

Alysson paddled closer. "Did you not hear that one speak?"

"Squirrels can't talk," Katie repeated with a stubborn slant to her small jaw that Alysson was sure she must have inherited from Donovan.

"All right, I guess you are just too clever for me. And you are right. It was I who spoke for Mr. Squirrel."

Katie looked inordinately pleased with herself, but it took a few more minutes for her curiosity to prompt another question.

"How did you do it? It sounded as if he said those things, but I know he didn't," she added quickly.

"It's just something that I learned to do when I was little like you, but some people can't do it at all. Do you think you could?"

The child nodded, and Alysson smiled. "Then you must try it, but you cannot move your lips. Your voice must come from the very back of your throat. Listen."

Alysson demonstrated, and Katie jumped in surprise as Alysson's squirrel voice sounded again from the limb above them. Her eyes grew rounder, but she tried herself. To Alysson's delight, her first attempt was not bad at all.

"That's very good, Katie, much better than most people can do at first."

Alysson's praise gave the child the confidence to try again, and with each ensuing attempt, Katie lost a bit of her reserve. Alysson listened and complimented her, not wanting to frighten her away. It would be very nice to have a friend at Wildwood with whom she could talk, and Katie had shown more willingness to be her friend than anyone else she had met there. Perhaps Katie was lonely, too.

When Katie grew tired of trying to throw her voice, she pulled off her stockings and shoes to dip her feet into the stream.

"It's too cold," she said at once, lifting them back out.

"Only at first, then it feels good." Eager to talk to the child, Alysson asked her a question. "How did you get here without me seeing you? I didn't know you were anywhere around until I saw you near the squirrel."

"Macomi taught me to walk in the forest without even snapping a twig or rustling a leaf. I followed you all the way from the grape arbor," Katie told her with pride, and Alysson wondered who Macomi was and why Katie was left to run loose in the woods. She wondered if Olivia knew her daughter was so far from the house.

"Who is Macomi?"

"She is my nursemaid."

"Does she know you are here with me?"

To Alysson's surprise, Katie's face crinkled into a smile. "Of course," she said. "She is right there, behind you."

She pointed one small finger to the other side of Alysson, and Alysson gasped as she turned and found an old Indian woman squatting on her haunches not five yards away, her broad face impassive.

"How long has she been there?" Alysson cried in alarm, and Katie shrugged.

"Since I came down from the tree."

Alysson looked again at the Indian dressed in fringed brown garments that blended with the forest colors, afraid she and the child had heard her curse Donovan in the woods. Thank goodness she had left on her chemise when she had decided to swim.

"Is it true a man shot my uncle Donovan because of you?" Katie asked with unexpected bluntness, staring at Alysson out of wide blue eyes. "Mama says you caused him to be hurt and that's why he doesn't come home to see us anymore. I miss him. He always brings me a special sweet from the city called ice cream, even though it's very expensive."

Remorse gripped Alysson, but she tried to explain. "I'm sorry about that, Katie, but I'm sure he'll come to see you again soon. He's very angry at me for something I did, but it has nothing to do with you."

"What did you do? He never gets mad at me."

"I left his house and went to see a man he doesn't like. I'm very sorry now that I did it, because I love your uncle Donovan very much."

Apparently the answer was quite enough for Katie, because she stood, changing the subject.

"I swim, Macomi," she said aside to the Indian, then added something else in a rapid guttural language that Alysson could not understand.

Macomi nodded, and Katie immediately squirmed out of her flower-sprigged white dress and executed a perfect dive off a log. Alysson watched her for a moment, then turned halfway around to look at the Indian.

"Do you speak English, Macomi?"

"I speak."

Alysson smiled with pleasure. "Good. Perhaps you will teach me your language someday."

She looked admiringly at the Indian's attire, especially the wide belt that seemed to be made of some kind of purple shells.

"That's a lovely belt. Did you make it yourself?"

"Wampum. For dead daughter."

Alysson was immediately sorry that she had asked about it, hoping she hadn't said the wrong thing. Macomi turned her dark eyes to Katie where she swam in the deep water.

"I would like very much to be Katie's friend, Macomi. Do you think she'll let me?"

"You her friend now."

Alysson smiled at the answer, but during the next hour, Alysson still found the little girl to be very shy and a trifle wary about becoming too intimate with Alysson, though it didn't stop the child from asking Alysson plenty of questions about herself. After a time, they dressed and started home upon the trail. Alysson felt refreshed and hungrier than she had in a very long time.

They had hardly passed the brick wall at the back of the gardens when Olivia hurried across the grass toward them. As soon as she was close enough, she hugged Katie to her. She turned hostile eyes on Alysson as she knelt, holding her daughter at arm's length.

"Katie, I was so worried about you! No one could find you! Where in the world have you been? You're all wet!"

"I have been swimming with Alysson, and I do not think she is terrible. She says she loves Uncle Donovan and is sorry about what she did."

Olivia looked quite startled by that. She turned to Macomi. "Please take Katie in to dress for dinner. I have need to talk to Alysson alone."

The child went obediently, and after they had gone, Alysson and Olivia looked silently at each other.

"I must tell you that I am very surprised to find Katie with you," Olivia began, frowning, and Alysson interrupted, not wanting the child to be scolded because of her.

"I know you don't want me here, and I know you believe I am to blame for the duel, but I swear to you that it was the last thing I wanted to happen. As far as Katie is concerned, it's not her fault that we were together. I talked to her first, and I found her to be a very sweet little girl. But if you don't want us to become friends, I'll stay away from her."

Olivia looked at her strangely, then back to the rear gallery where Katie and Macomi were just disappearing into the kitchen wing. She gestured to a nearby bench.

"Will you sit with me for a moment and let me tell you about my daughter?"

"Of course," Alysson said, surprised but pleased by the invitation. She had hoped for an opportunity to get to know Donovan's sister better. She waited as Olivia looked down, obviously reluctant to begin.

"I was very surprised to find Katie with you because she rarely speaks to anyone other than Macomi and me, and her uncles, of course. It's really quite odd that she has taken to you as she has. With most people she doesn't know, she runs and hides and refuses to come out to meet them at all."

Alysson thought that very strange behavior for an obviously well brought-up child. "Is that because she lives out here alone and is not used to having other people nearby?"

Olivia hesitated, then gazed out over the lawns, a faraway look coming into her blue eyes.

"No. She had a very bad experience when she was little, only four years old. She's never completely recovered from it. Nor have I."

Alysson could see the pain in her face. "I'm sorry. Please, don't speak of it if it's painful for you."

Olivia met her eyes. "Yes, it is still very painful for

me as well, but I have learned to live with it. Katie has not."

She stopped, sighing deeply before she continued. "You see, Katie witnessed her father's death." She paused, the next words coming harder. "He was murdered by a Mohawk raiding party, and he was ... scalped."

Alysson gave a horrified gasp, but Olivia didn't look at her, remembering that day six long years ago with a vividness that she had prayed would dim in time.

"We were traveling on business to Montreal with a large party, several wagons and a detail of armed men. We didn't worry about the Indians, because there hadn't been much trouble since the war. When we stopped at a stream near the Canadian border for the night, Katie managed to wander off. We never understood why she did that because she knew better, but Jason went to look for her, and later, when we found them, he was already dead. Thank god, we found Katie hiding nearby in some bushes. She was unharmed, and we think maybe he hid her there when he heard the Indians. No one knows for sure. Katie has never spoken of that day to anyone, and she's never been the same child since."

"How horrible for all of you," Alysson murmured with sincere compassion. "It must have been terrible to lose your husband like that."

"Yes. Even after all these years I still miss him." Olivia smiled slightly. "Katie is the very image of him, all that red hair and freckles. I think I would have lost my mind after his death if Donovan hadn't brought us here to live at Wildwood. Katie still suffers from nightmares, and Donovan's taken her to a dozen different doctors. None of them has helped her, and we have found that she does better here at Wildwood with just the family around her. She usually refuses to come out whenever we have visitors, so I just stopped inviting anyone here." She met Alysson's eyes. "It was quite a shock to hear her talking to you as she did. She even defended you to me."

"I had no idea of her past, of course, but I thought she must be very shy. I think it was a squirrel who helped me befriend her."

"A squirrel?"

Alysson explained, and Olivia smiled. "Well, for whatever reason, I think she has decided that she likes you. And that is a very good sign. I hope you will become friends."

In the following weeks, they did become friends. Alysson spent many hours in the company of Katie and Macomi. She was amazed at the quiet maturity of the little child, and she found Macomi fascinating. Alysson asked the old Indian woman many questions about her tribe and its customs, and all were answered in Macomi's laconic way. Alysson was able to very quickly pick up some of her Indian dialect, which she learned was Seneca, one of the six nations of the Iroquois tribe. Soon she could understand much of Macomi's conversations with Katie, and the days became easier to bear as Olivia's guarded acceptance of her began to melt into the beginning of a friendship.

It was only at night, in her luxurious damask-draped bed with her windows open to the night sounds of crickets and tree frogs, that Alysson would relive the feel of Donovan's hands moving over her body with such exquisite gentleness, would again feel his warm lips upon her naked flesh, until she moaned with frustration and growing anger at her helplessness. He was not suffering the same longing and unhappiness, she told herself. He was most probably back in his countess's bed, holding her and touching her. The mental images of such a scene tormented her, but it was only in her dreams that her husband held and kissed her, making her even more sick and miserable upon awakening each morning, alone and forsaken in her empty bed.

# Chapter 17

Donovan sat in his open carriage across from Odette and Billy Brock, but he had said not one word to them during the length of time it took to be ferried across the East River to the base of Front Street in Brooklyn. As they rode along the road to Wildwood, they remained quiet, well aware of his anger with them. He shifted the black silk sling on his arm into a more comfortable position as they passed through the arched iron entrance gate of Wildwood. The bullet wound was still painful at times, though Doctor Whittingham had said it was healing well. He had been bridled with the bloody sling for nearly a month now, and it was a damned nuisance. He frowned blackly at the two across from him. Odette looked down at once, but Billy Brock stared defiantly at Donovan as if he would like very much to have his hands around Donovan's neck.

Donovan looked away from Billy, annoyed. Neither of them would be here at all if they hadn't threatened to bring in the authorities if he did not prove to them that Alysson was safe and well. That was all he would have needed, more scandal over the duel, so he had agreed to allow them a visit with Alysson to prove he hadn't beaten her senseless or locked her in some dungeon, as they no doubt believed with their overactive, theatrical imaginations.

His face hardened. There had been moments in the past month when inner devils had driven him to contemplate such punishments with relish. Each time he thought of how she had lain in his arms that night, so soft and innocent with her sweet smile and warm green eyes, only to betray him on the morrow with another man, he would feel sick inside, as he did now, wanting to see her, wanting to hold her again, despite her treachery. He hated himself for that weakness. She had run away from him, damn her, had run to Compton and waited at his house for him to make the challenge which would free her from her marriage.

Halfway down the hedge-lined road, the house loomed into sight, and he could see Olivia where she stood on the side porch waiting for them. A footman ran to open the doors as the carriage came to a lurching stop, and Donovan stepped down and moved up the steps toward her as Billy helped Odette to the ground.

"I'm sorry I couldn't give you much advance warning, Olivia, but Alysson's friends over there were bloody insistent about coming today."

Olivia glanced down at the two young people below them, who were looking around the porch and lawns with a great deal of interest. "I had plenty of time to prepare for tea, and supper later if they decide to stay. Now that you've arrived, I'll send someone for Alysson and Katie."

Donovan jerked his head toward her. "Where are they?"

"Macomi says they went to the old mill. They left early this morning before I got your message."

"Just the two of them?"

Donovan's surprise was evident, and Olivia's smile was pleased.

"You would not believe how Katie has taken to Alysson. It is really quite miraculous how Katie liked her from the very first time they met."

"Alysson finds it easy to charm people," Donovan

muttered sourly, glancing at her two loyal friends below. "Until she decides to knife them in the back."

Olivia hesitated. "I've talked to her, Donovan, and I don't believe she meant for any of this to happen. She feels dreadful about it. She sincerely does."

"So now she has you fooled, too," Donovan said harshly, angered that his own sister was defending her. "She is quite a good little actress; you'll find that out when you get to know her better." His black eyes grew harder. "And I don't intend standing around here waiting for her to show up. I'll take them out to the mill myself, so they can see her and then get the hell off my land."

Olivia shook her head at the terrible controlled rage her brother was displaying as he hurried down the steps and led their two guests away. She knew Alysson was hoping his anger had cooled during the past weeks, but it still burned inside him. She could not help but pity poor Alysson. She sighed, hurrying toward the kitchens to see about having tea served, if Donovan let Alysson's friends stay long enough.

The walk through the woods was not a long one, and Donovan led the way with Billy and Odette close behind him. He had not been to the mill spring for years, had nearly forgotten it even existed. He rarely came to Wildwood at all, except for Sunday visits to see Katie and Olivia. His business affairs made it necessary for him to reside in the city.

The path was more overgrown and wild now than he remembered, and he made a mental note to have it cleared, especially if Katie liked to play there. When they came out into the clearing beside the millhouse, no one was in sight.

Donovan saw a pile of clothing lying in the shadow of the mill's wall, and he left Billy and Odette at the edge of the stream to walk over and pick up Alysson's gown. He frowned, then jerked around as a shrill scream shattered the peaceful afternoon. His jaw dropped, when at midstream Alysson came sliding into sight from the top of the curving rocks, Katie held firmly between her knees. Neither saw the three people watching them from the riverbank, and Katie squealed with unqualified glee as they went airborne off the smooth slide to plunge with a loud splash into the deep pool below.

Seconds later, both came up laughing and splashing, and it was not until Odette called Alysson's name that the two in the water became aware of their presence. Alysson saw them first, her face mirroring a shock that went quickly into pure delight.

"Odette! Billy!" she cried, paddling to waist-deep water where she could stand. She sloshed toward them, smiling, still unaware of Donovan, who stood in the shadow of the crumbling wall. But he saw her, and his eyes riveted like iron on a magnet to her firm young body, the thin silk chemise plastered provocatively to every lush curve. His mouth went dry; his loins reacted with so powerful a surge that he was appalled. It was then that he remembered the presence of another male, and Donovan's muscles went rigid when he found Billy staring with openmouthed appreciation at Alysson's scantily clad body.

Before Alysson could reach her friends, Donovan waded into the water, fully dressed. She stopped in her tracks as he loomed before her, his face black with fury. His dark eyes swept her body, and her delight at seeing her friends diminished a bit as she realized what she wore. She crossed her arms over her breasts, unaware such an action made them even more enticing. Her eyes were drawn to the silk sling holding Donovan's injured left arm. It was the first time she had seen with her own eyes the consequences of the duel, and the color drained from her face.

"For god's sake, put your clothes on," Donovan ground out the words between tightly clenched teeth, thrusting her gown toward her. Alysson took it, red-faced with embarrassment and humiliation.

Donovan turned his back on her, then glared at Billy until the boy turned his eyes elsewhere. Odette met Alysson at the bank to help her pull the gown over her head.

Odette laughed softly as she watched Donovan wade out to Katie and swing the child up with his good arm to ride on his hip as he stalked out of the water.

"So, *mon amie,* he is still possessive of you. Billy and I feared he was treating you badly, so we made him bring us here. But I see you are having a good time with the little one, there."

"Oh, Odette, I am so glad to see you!" Alysson whispered, hugging her close. "And you too, Billy!"

The young man came to her, and Alysson hugged him with equal enthusiasm, despite a disapproving frown from her husband.

"Are you all right, Aly?" Billy asked, his eyes narrowing on Donovan. "Has he done anything to you?"

"No, of course not. I'm fine!" She laughed and shook her wet hair. "Can't you tell?"

"I'm taking Katie back to the house," Donovan said tightly. "I trust you can find your own way."

Long, angry strides took him away from them, and Alysson put her arms around her friends' waists as they followed, happy to be with them, but even happier that Donovan had come home, even if he was furious with her.

When they reached the house, Odette accompanied Alysson to her bedchamber to change into a dry gown, leaving the unfortunate Billy downstairs alone with a very unfriendly host. Once in Alysson's room, Odette smiled as she helped unfasten the back of Alysson's damp gown.

"Are you truly all right?" she asked, holding the dress as Alysson stepped out of it. "You look a little pale, and thinner too, I think. We have all been very worried about you."

"Yes, I'm fine, really. At first I was lonely here, but now Katie and I are together often, and Donovan's sister, Olivia, treats me with kindness."

They sat on the bed together, and Odette searched Alysson's face.

"What on earth happened? When you left with Monsieur MacBride the night of the opening performance, I never expected such terrible things to come of it. Everyone in New York is still talking about it."

"Nor did I. It all just happened. Douglas said things that weren't true, and Donovan believed him. I never meant for there to be a duel or for Donovan to get hurt. I felt awful today when I saw his arm."

"You mean you haven't seen him since the duel? That's been weeks ago!"

Alysson looked away. "No, he blames me for everything." She met Odette's eyes again. "And he is right in a way. I should never have gone to Douglas, but I wanted to explain to him why I was giving up the play. I don't know why he challenged Donovan."

"Because he wants you too, of course. Donovan will forgive you soon. He is your husband, is he not? It is just all the scandal and newspaper accounts that have wounded his pride. Soon he will come to you. I saw it in his eyes when he saw you in the stream today."

Alysson sighed. "I am afraid to hope. He won't even talk to me."

"That is because he is a man, and men have such stupid and stubborn pride. Do not despair. He will not

last long, now that he is near you again. He will fight it
for a time, then he will grab you up and make love to
you."

Alysson smiled, hoping her friend was right. She
looked at Odette, realizing that she had missed her best
friend very much.

"What did the newspapers say? Were they very un-
kind?"

Odette's lips curved as she lifted the small velvet
purse dangling from her wrist. She opened the draw-
string and pulled out a folded scrap of newspaper.

"I brought these in case you had not seen them.
Much of it is speculation and much is simply lies, I am
sure."

Alysson slowly unfolded the paper, not sure she
wanted to see what was written there. "TWO PROMI-
NENT CITIZENS WOUNDED IN DUEL OVER ACTRESS,"
she read with dismay, then looked at the next clipping
with equal horror. DUEL OVER ACTRESS RUINS POLITI-
CAL ASPIRATIONS OF MACBRIDE. COMPTON RECOVERS
WOUND WHILE ALYSSON TYLER HIDES IN SECLUSION."

Alysson didn't want to see any more, and she gave
the clippings back to Odette, her face stricken.

"They are horrible," she said, feeling for the first
time the very real humiliation Donovan had suffered
because of her. "Has Donovan answered any of these
accusations?" she asked, afraid of another duel.

Odette shook her curls. "No, it is said he has carried
on his business as usual, and even frequented the Tontine Coffeehouse and the Belvedere Gentlemen's Club
as if nothing had happened. No one dares to confront
him about you, of course, except for Billy and me. We
threatened to get the constable if he did not let us see
you."

"You didn't!"

"Oh, oui, we did! We were very worried about you."

Alysson's smile faded. "What about the countess? Have you seen them together?"

"He has not been with any woman, I am sure. At least not in public, for everyone would be talking about it if he escorted anyone. I have seen the countess only once, with Captain MacBride."

That relieved Alysson a great deal, but there was another question she had to ask. "And Douglas? How is he faring?"

Odette looked uncomfortable for the first time, and a barb of fear snagged Alysson's heart.

"Odette! He isn't dead, is he?"

"No," Odette answered slowly, "but the doctor says he will not walk again without a cane."

Alysson stared at her. Her anger with Douglas had begun to fade long ago, and now she only felt sorry for him. His lies had cost him a great deal. She smiled slightly as Odette put her arm around her, giving her an encouraging squeeze.

"Come, let's go down. Billy will be squirming under those terrible black eyes that Monsieur MacBride always puts upon him. Billy's been beside himself since you've been gone. You should have seen the way he stood up to Monsieur MacBride this morning. He is becoming very brave."

Downstairs again, they found the others on the side terrace, and Alysson looked first to Donovan, who sat at a table with Katie and Olivia. Alysson hoped he would want to speak with her, but he looked coldly away. She walked with Odette to join Billy at the other table, but watched her husband as inconspicuously as she could, aching inside each time he moved his arm and winced with pain.

"If you are very unhappy here, I will find a way to take you away."

Billy's soft words brought Alysson's attention back to him. She smiled, laying one hand over his.

"You are a very good friend, Billy, and I am so grateful that you cared enough to come here and see about me. But I cannot leave."

"If he is cruel to you, I will . . ."

Alysson stopped him. "He is not cruel to me. He is angry with me right now, but he is my husband." She looked at Donovan again, who looked away when their eyes met. "And I love him. I want to stay here with him."

Billy looked unconvinced, but Odette smiled knowingly.

"If you should ever need me, Aly," Billy said earnestly, "just send word. I mean it. You know I would do anything for you. You saved my life, and I won't ever forget it."

"I know." Wanting to change the subject, she entreated, "Tell me about the play. Who took my place?"

She listened as they told her about the new actress that Rosalie had found, but even with their assurances that she was not nearly as good in the role of Cordelia as Alysson had been, Alysson's spirits fell as the afternoon grew into dusk and it was time for them to leave.

Donovan waited silently on the veranda above them as they said their good-byes. As Alysson stood in the drive watching their carriage until it was out of sight, she was suddenly quite terrified at the prospect of facing Donovan alone. Hands atremble, heart fluttering, she took a deep breath, then turned to confront him, only to find the porch empty. She felt both relieved and hurt. Her biggest fear was that he would never forgive her, that he would treat her with terrible icy contempt forever. Resolve hardened inside her. If he would not come to her, she would go to him. She would make him realize how much she loved him. She would not give up until she erased the hatred from his eyes.

Much later that same night Donovan sat behind the desk in his study. He rested his head on the back of the chair, shutting his eyes. His arm throbbed, his head ached, and all he could think about was Alysson. Despite everything, despite all that she had put him through, he couldn't keep his eyes off her, couldn't forget she was close by with her silky soft hair and smooth white skin and trembling lips.

"Damn her," he cursed listlessly beneath his breath, pouring more whisky into his glass. He downed it quickly and refilled it. Suddenly every muscle in his body turned to stone as he saw her in the doorway.

"May I please come in?"

She was all soft and uncertain, with a tentative smile meant to disarm him. He clenched his jaw, and her smile faded a bit before she moved toward him. She looked beautiful, her green eyes like huge glowing emeralds in the flickering flame of the candle. Her hair had grown some and lay over her shoulders in a golden shimmer. Donovan's hand trembled with the need to reach out and touch her until he had to double his fists to prevent doing so. Furious at himself, furious at her, he dragged his gaze from her face. He stroked the scar on his eye, staring into the fire as she came slowly around the desk until the sweetness of her perfume filled his brain.

"I want to tell you how terribly sorry I am about what happened. I never meant for you to get hurt, you must believe me."

She stopped, startled by his cold, mirthless laugh.

"You should have thought of that before you went running to Compton."

Alysson grew bolder as her hope ballooned. He was

talking to her. "I only went there to explain why I quit the play. I said I was quitting to be with you."

"Brace and I are leaving for Washington tomorrow, but I intend to have a divorcement from you no matter what it takes," he said bluntly.

"No, please, Donovan, don't do that," she whispered, sinking to her knees beside him. "I love you so much. I've missed you so much."

When her fingertips touched his cheek, it was as if he had been touched by a heated brand. He looked at her, looked into pleading green eyes that seemed to swallow him body and soul. He hardly knew he groaned, and Alysson gasped as his unharmed arm came around her, crushing her against him, his mouth on hers, hard, hurting, punishing her, but she didn't care. He was holding her, kissing her, and her arms went around his neck as she met his passion eagerly, moaning with pleasure.

The tight embrace lasted only a moment before he thrust her from him and stood. Alysson sat back on her heels as he left the room as if pursued by a legion of Satan's demons. She raised trembling fingers to her lips, still hot and swollen from his relentless kisses. Joy swelled in her heart, because even though he had left her again, he had shed his icy self-control. Now she knew he still wanted her. The way he had kissed her had proved it. For the first time, she felt sure he would forgive her in time, and she shivered with happiness, determined to do everything she could to make him forgive her sooner.

# Chapter 18

The month of September ended with cooler weather and a blaze of crimson and gold over the forested hills of Brooklyn Heights. Alysson spent her time with Katie and Macomi, waiting for Donovan to return from Washington. Often the three of them strolled to the banks of the East River where several white gazebos had been built to face the water. It was pleasant to sit there in the crisp autumn air and watch small sailboats and sleek military frigates or merchantmen sail past them to port.

Katie had become very interested in acting since Alysson had told her about her short-lived career, and one afternoon, they sat together in the largest gazebo while Katie sorted through a box of her mother's discarded clothing in search of costumes. Since Alysson had lent her the old copy of Shakespeare that she had brought with her from Cornwall, Katie had fallen in love with the fanciful fairies in *A Midsummer Night's Dream,* especially with the antics of the mischievous Puck.

Macomi sat cross-legged on the floor nearby as she was wont to do, and Alysson rocked in a large wicker chair, deep in her own thoughts. She smiled at Katie, having become very fond of the little girl. She was such an unusual child, and it saddened Alysson that Katie was still deeply troubled by the death of her father. More times than she could count, Alysson had been awakened by the child's shrill screams of terror.

She lifted her eyes to gaze across the choppy gray waters to the distant shore of Manhattan Island, feeling an intense longing to see Odette and Billy and all the others. She missed them far more than she did the actual acting, and in the past weeks at Wildwood, she had found that it no longer seemed quite so important for her to be on the stage. It was Donovan she missed. Every day she thought of him, wondering where he was and what he was doing.

The first tingling of pain began in the lower reaches of her abdomen, and she tensed all over, holding her breath as sweat broke out upon her brow. She grimaced as a jagged thrust of pain knifed through her, then she gave a muffled moan as it began to subside. She breathed deeply then, wiping her brow, well used to it by now.

Macomi's dark eyes questioned her, but the Seneca woman did not speak, and Alysson turned her gaze back on the flowing river. She hadn't felt completely well in over a month now. At first, she had blamed it on the weather, but the dizzy spells plaguing her continued even though the days were cool. There was something dreadfully wrong with her, because, though the stomach pains were not constant, they were frequent. Macomi was still watching her, and Alysson found herself wondering about the old woman. Macomi rarely spoke about herself, though she told many stories of her youth in the Bear Clan of the Senecas.

"You know, Macomi, you have never told me anything about yourself. How did you come to be here at Wildwood with Katie?"

"Long Knife bring me here."

Alysson had learned early in her stay that Macomi referred to the Americans in that way, but she also knew Macomi used the term to signify Donovan. Her curiosity was piqued.

"Donovan brought you here, then? Were you a captive?"

Macomi shook her head. "No, I wife of white man. Name Gilly. He buy me from father for blankets and guns."

Alysson's first reaction was revulsion at such a barbarous custom. Then she thought of her own circumstances. She had felt bought and sold in the same way when her father had told her she had to marry an American named Donovan MacBride. That day seemed very long ago now, but she could still remember how afraid she had been to meet Donovan.

"Was it hard for you to leave your tribe and go with a white man like that?" she asked.

"Gilly good. I gave him child."

"A little girl, wasn't it?" Alysson said, remembering that Macomi had mentioned a daughter to her at one time.

"My people war with Gilly. Burn house and barn and kill him. I hide in trees, but baby die in snow before I could reach white man's fort at the Great Falls of Niagara."

Her words were uttered softly, calmly, but Alysson could read shadows of pain in the old Indian's eyes. Her heart went out to her.

"I am sorry, Macomi."

Macomi's expression did not change. "Long Knife at fort. He bring me here to be nurse for Katie. I been here many year. I be nurse for your baby."

Alysson smiled. "I would very much like to have a baby." If Donovan would ever come home and want her again, she thought sadly. He would, she told herself firmly. She would make him want her again.

"Your baby come after maple flows, when leaves are born," Macomi said.

"What?" Alysson said blankly.

Macomi put her hand against her midriff, then gestured to Alysson's stomach in sign language that Alysson could not misinterpret.

"Oh no, Macomi, I am not going to have . . ." Alysson began, but as Macomi nodded again, she paused, her mind standing still at the idea. She had spent only one night with Donovan. Could it be true? A baby, his baby? She put her hand to her abdomen, trying to think. How could she be so blind? Never had it even occurred to her that she might be with child. She knew nothing of the signs or symptoms. Was that the way of it? Was a baby the cause of her nausea and pain? Eyes wide with wonder, she looked to Macomi, who watched her silently.

"Are you sure? How can you know such a thing?"

"I know. Baby come in spring."

A multitude of feelings surged inside Alysson, obliterating the first shock she had felt. She was going to have a baby! Joy bloomed, making her smile, then fear gripped her. Would he want a child of hers? Would it make a difference in the way he felt about her? He would have to be pleased; any man would want a son. It was wonderful! A miracle! She looked at Macomi again, realizing that there was so much she didn't know.

"Is there always an ill feeling, Macomi?"

"Sickness go as baby get bigger."

Alysson welcomed that bit of news with a great deal of relief, but there was so much more she wanted to know. She knew nothing about having babies; she had never even held a baby.

"And the pain?" she asked hesitantly, searching Macomi's coppery face. "Is it sharp and sudden? And"— she paused in embarrassment, lowering her voice to a whisper—"is there blood at times?"

Macomi frowned. "No blood. Bad sign."

Fear coursed through Alysson's veins. "It will be all right, won't it, Macomi?"

"Only spirits know. You must be careful not to displease spirits."

"You mustn't tell anybody yet, Macomi, please," Alysson begged, glancing at the little girl still playing happily with the old clothes. "Not even Katie, not yet."

The Indian nodded, then stood and moved away to help Katie button up the back of a velvet evening gown, leaving Alysson alone to contemplate the joys and terrors of knowing another person lived inside her. A child created from an act of love between Donovan and her. Surely it was a good sign, she thought, a sign that everything was meant to be all right.

In the next few weeks, as autumn grew older, bringing cold air and falling leaves, Alysson held the knowledge of her child close to her heart. The nausea abated somewhat, but the pain and other symptoms persisted, frightening her. She began to take better care of herself, avoiding anything she thought might hurt the baby.

During the long days, she grew to regard Katie as a precious little sister, and even Olivia became a dear friend. It was as if she finally belonged to a real family, a normal family. If only Donovan would come back, she would be happy.

He had sent one letter addressed to Olivia, but he had not mentioned Alysson. It hurt that he didn't care enough to ask about her, and on cold nights as she lay in her warm bed, she listened to the crackling of the fire and took turns being furious with Donovan for his stubborn pride and for being away so long, and smiling dreamily as she thought of the day she would tell him about their baby. The latter were the dreams that gave her pleasure, for she would imagine his glad smile at her news and the way he would hold her tenderly and stroke her hair. Why couldn't he just come home!

On the chilly afternoon of November 17, such thoughts circled in her head as she shuffled through the fallen leaves in search of a hiding place. It was Katie's tenth birthday, and the excited little girl had cajoled Alysson into their daily game of hide-and-seek. Katie was on the front steps, well on her way to the count of one hundred, and Alysson looked around, drawing her soft blue woolen shawl closer around her shoulders. She could smell the acrid odor of burning leaves as servants raked dead leaves into piles to be burned.

A haze of smoke hung over the lawn from the fires burning at sporadic intervals beneath the trees, and Alysson gave only a glance to the grape arbor as a potential hiding place, knowing Katie would look there first. As Katie's shout sounded from far up the lawn, Alysson's eyes alighted on the nearest pile of raked leaves, and smiling with a new idea, she knelt quickly, burrowing a hole in the middle of it. She covered herself with the brown leaves, chuckling as she crouched there to wait. Katie would never think of looking for her there. It was not long before she heard Katie calling from somewhere closeby.

"Aly! Come on out and see my surprise!"

Alysson did not fall for that, well used to Katie's attempts to trick her out of hiding. She could hear the little girl coming closer by the crackling and shuffling of the leaves, and as the footsteps passed beside her, Alysson snaked out a hand to catch Katie's foot. Her smile faded when she heard not a girlish squeal, but instead a muffled expletive no child would dare say.

"What the hell?" Donovan muttered, managing to catch himself before he went all the way down. He turned, frowning, then stared in amazement as Alysson rose to her knees from the middle of the pile of dead leaves, looking absolutely horrified at the sight of him. The expression in her eyes caused his irritation at being tripped to fade, and when Katie ran up, laughing delightedly at what Alysson had done, he grinned too, very glad to see Alysson again though he had told himself he wouldn't be.

"I didn't mean to trip you," Alysson began nervously, self-consciously pulling twigs and leaves out of her hair. "I thought you were Katie."

"So I gathered," Donovan said on a wry note, but he held out a hand to help her up, and Alysson took it eagerly. His long brown fingers closed around hers, and even that touch shook her, making her even more shy and self-conscious. It had been a long time since she had seen him, and he seemed even bigger and more masculine than she remembered. His face was deeply tanned from the ocean voyage, and as she met his dark gaze, her breath caught, for there was no hatred or contempt in his eyes this time, only a very serious look. She smiled up at him, and for one shivery instant she was sure he was about to pull her into his arms.

"Isn't it wonderful, Aly!" Katie exclaimed, effectively breaking off anything Donovan might be contemplating. "Uncle Donovan and Uncle Brace have come home in time for my birthday party! And they've brought me lots of presents from Washington!"

"Yes, I am very glad they have come home," Alysson said, looking at Donovan again.

"Then come with me quickly, because Uncle Brace is waiting on the porch for us," Katie went on, pulling on her hand. Alysson went along reluctantly. She would have much rather stayed behind to admire her handsome husband. He was even smiling now, probably at Katie's exuberance, and his smile did not vanish when he looked at Alysson. He was ready to forgive her, she knew it. She could finally tell him about the baby, and she could not wait!

* * *

"Are you really glad my uncle Donovan came home for the party?" Katie asked Alysson later that afternoon in Alysson's bedchamber as they readied themselves for her birthday supper. "Is that why you are brushing your hair so long and fussing so much with what you wear?"

Alysson turned sideways on her bench and looked at Katie. She sat in a chair just behind Alysson, her feet curled up beneath her, looking like a little doll in her fancy, ruffle-trimmed birthday dress tied with a wide ribbon sash. The bright yellow color of her gown made her red hair look even more fiery. Alysson smiled at her question.

"Yes, that is exactly what I am doing. I am glad he has come home again," she told her, then lowered her voice. "And I'll tell you a secret if you promise not to tell anyone."

Katie nodded eagerly, loving secrets, and Alysson went on in a hushed voice. "I intend to make him love me again so he won't leave us anymore."

"Mama says he does love you," Katie said, twirling one of the yellow ribbons holding back her long ringlets.

Alysson had turned back to the mirror, but at Katie's remark, her hand stilled where she fashioned a curl at her nape.

"Did she really say that?"

"Yes, she says he's just being stubborn and prideful."

Alysson resumed her brushing. "I hope she is right, but now that he's here I intend to *make* him notice me again."

"I know how you can do it," Katie said seriously. "You can do your squirrel voice or your horse voice, like you did down at the stables when we fed carrots to the mares. He'd like that."

A mental picture arose in Alysson's mind of her doing her squirrel imitation the next time she was alone with her big, angry husband, and her amused laugh tinkled into the air.

"I don't think he's ready for that yet, sweetheart. Maybe someday, though."

"But he likes to play games with me," Katie insisted. "Maybe we can get him to play hide-and-seek with us after the party. Remember, you promised me you would, and I get to hide first this time."

"I will. After all, it is your birthday. Come over here now and let me tie your ribbons. You've pulled them loose."

Katie came obediently, and Alysson quickly retied the bow, then stood to scrutinize her own reflection in the standing mirror beside the bed. Donovan was home at last, and he had been glad to see her. She had seen it in his eyes, and that fleeting look filled her with joy. She would win him over to her again, she would seduce him if she had to, but he would not leave her again without knowing about the baby.

"And that should put an end to any talk of divorcement," she murmured under her breath, putting a hand upon her stomach.

Katie looked up. "What did you say?"

"Nothing important," Alysson answered brightly, her heavy satin underskirts rustling as she turned slightly to check the draping of the emerald-green velvet. She arranged her mother's silver cross upon her breasts to best advantage, having chosen the daring décolletage to attract Donovan's attention. The high waist completely disguised her condition, though in truth, her body had changed very little thus far.

But it would soon, and she was suddenly all nerves at the thought of telling Donovan. She patted her hair, having taken Katie's advice and pulled it back at the

crown with a pearl-studded clip, leaving the rest to
flow unhampered down her back. It had grown much in
the past months, and she hoped Donovan would notice
it.

Taking Katie's hand, she lifted her heavy skirt, and
they walked together down the sweeping staircase to
join the rest of the family. They found them in the immense dining room, with its crimson velvet draperies
and rose-stenciled walls, for they were to dine formally
in honor of Katie's birthday. Olivia sat beside the fireplace with Brace, while Donovan stood with one elbow
propped upon the white molded mantelpiece. Katie ran
forward to be swung up into Brace's arms, but Alysson's eyes stayed solely on her husband. He looked
superb standing there, so dark and handsome in his
wine-colored velvet jacket and dark trousers, and his
black eyes moved over her for a long, lingering moment that made her knees turn to water.

"Katie gets the seat of honor tonight," Olivia was
saying, and Katie took the chair at the head of the table
where Donovan was accustomed to sitting. A dozen
gaily wrapped presents sat about her place, and Katie
shook one after another, smiling in excitement.

Brace smiled at Alysson as he led her to her place,
and she looked up at him in surprise as he seated her
across from Donovan's chair.

"I thought my big brother ought to get the pleasure
of ogling you in that dress," he whispered close to her
ear. "Wasn't that the idea?"

Alysson's eyes darted to him, and he winked. She
gave him a grateful smile as she sat, knowing then that
Brace was an ally as well as Olivia and Katie. They
would all help her.

"May I open my presents first, Mother?" Katie
begged. Olivia nodded with a smile.

Katie tackled that task with enthusiasm, unwrapping

first a box of candy and a beautiful doll that Brace had brought from Washington. Donovan had given her a tea set for the doll, made of delicate white china hand-painted with violets. Alysson had to smile at Katie's delighted exclamations at seeing the tiny cups and saucers. When she opened the package from Alysson and found the old book of Shakespeare that Alysson had lent to her, she laughed with pleasure.

"But, Aly, this is your very own book. You and Freddie used it in Cornwall!"

Alysson felt Donovan's gaze on her, and she smiled. "I have no need of it anymore, and now you can practice Puck's lines anytime you wish."

"'Up and down, up and down, I will lead them up and down: I am feared in field and town: Goblin, lead them up and down,'" Katie quoted from *A Midsummer Night's Dream,* causing them all to laugh.

"So we are raising another little actress, are we?" Brace commented, and Alysson looked up to find Donovan smiling affectionately at his niece.

After three courses of Katie's favorite foods, followed by silver dishes filled with ice cream, Katie bundled all her gifts into the lace-draped doll carriage that her mother had given her.

"May I go out and show everything to Macomi?" she asked politely. When her mother nodded, Katie turned to smile at Alysson. "Then we will play hide-and-seek. Remember, you said you would!"

"I'll be out soon," Alysson promised. After the child had left, Olivia turned the conversation to the trip to Washington.

"It was uneventful aboard ship. In Washington, Dolley was a beautiful hostess, as she always is," Brace told them. "She said she would love to have you come with Katie for a visit."

"We speak of Dolley Madison, the President's wife,"

Olivia explained to Alysson. "I met her years ago when she lived in Philadelphia with her first husband, John Todd. Before he died, they were great friends to Jason and me. I haven't seen her in a very long time now that she has moved to Washington."

Alysson was impressed to think that the MacBrides had such influential connections, for she knew the President was like the king of the United States.

"Dolley was certainly interested in hearing all about you, Alysson," Brace said. "She loves to go to plays and such, and she was curious to know something about the lady who finally ended Donovan's bachelor days. Dolley's been playing matchmaker for him for years."

Alysson looked at Donovan, who was frowning as if he didn't like the turn of the conversation, and she was suddenly quite sure that similar talk around Dolley Madison's table had been an embarrassment to him, especially if the duel had been mentioned. He said nothing, however, and Alysson waited patiently for a time, anxious to request a moment alone with him. She listened silently as they discussed other friends of theirs who served in the American Congress, most of whom she did not know. She grew very attentive, however, when Brace mentioned a possible war with England.

"The war hawks are screaming for it," he was saying. "And the western states are rallying behind them one hundred percent. The President's still trying to contain the war fervor, but Henry Clay and the others are hell-bent to annex Canada, and Florida, too. I can't say I don't agree with them. As soon as war is declared, I intend to turn my guns on every bloody British ship I can find."

"We are not prepared to fight another war with England," Donovan replied calmly. "And you know it, Brace. Our regular army has about eleven thousand men, and our navy is even more depleted than that. How many ships do we have with enough guns to put up a good fight? Five or six? It would be disastrous to initiate a fight with the British Navy. We need time to build up our defense first."

"And by the time we do that, their fight with Bonaparte will be over, and all the ships blockading the coast of France will be down our throats. We need to declare now, while most of their troops are fighting on the Continent."

Brace was becoming incensed, but Donovan remained unruffled as he took a sip of his wine. "War would be as big a mistake as the embargo was, and it would do you well to remember that the MacBride merchant ships are a big part of our business. We have as much to lose as the rest of the New England merchants, and I can tell you right now that they'll be opposed to a declaration of war."

Brace disagreed, too eager to get into the fight to worry about the opinions of the New Englanders.

"Our agents in England say Parliament doesn't believe we'll have the guts to declare on them, and the data from our sources here—"

"I think it would be better if we continued this discussion in private," Donovan cut in tersely, glancing pointedly at Alysson.

Alysson stiffened at the implication that she could not be trusted, but when Brace and Olivia both looked distinctly embarrassed, she smiled, trying to eliminate their discomfiture with a jest.

"Indeed you should, because I have been memorizing every word said here today to send to England. Perhaps to my father, since we are so close," she said sarcastically for Donovan's benefit. "Or perhaps I will even post it to the Regent himself."

Her green eyes sparkled, for the idea of writing the

Regent amused her. Brace and Olivia laughed, and Donovan's face grew hard.

"Or perhaps to Douglas Compton," he said with such ice-coated derision that silence dropped over the table like a heavy glass dome. There was little anyone could say, and Alysson's smile left her. With that one utterance, Donovan had revealed that he was still very angry with her.

Before she could respond, Katie rushed in the far doorway. "Come on, Alysson, let's finish our game before it grows too dark."

"All right, you go ahead and hide," Alysson said, rising. "I will come find you in a moment."

She looked back at Donovan as Katie departed, determined to talk to him alone.

"I would like to speak to you in private, if I may," she said.

"I'm quite sure there is nothing we need to discuss that Brace and Olivia cannot hear."

Alysson stared at him, not having expected him to deny her request.

"It really is a private matter," she said, lifting her chin stubbornly. "Perhaps tomorrow you could spare me a moment or two."

"I won't be here tomorrow."

He was angry again, and intentionally humiliating her in front of the others. Trembling with embarrassment and anger, she looked him in the eyes.

"Now that I think of it, I have nothing to say to you after all."

No one said a word as she walked out, her head held high. Then Olivia rose, giving Donovan a scathing look before departing in the same direction. Donovan clenched his jaw grimly as Brace leaned back, turning a disgusted gaze on his brother.

"Tell me, Donovan, are you going to divorce the girl

and get it over with, or are you getting too much pleasure out of making her miserable?"

Donovan didn't answer, and Brace shook his head,
then strode angrily out of the room, leaving Donovan
alone at the table. He drained his wineglass, already
ashamed of the way he had treated Alysson. It was the
mention of Compton that had brought all the simmering
anger roiling up to overwhelm him. His teeth came together hard as he thought of the hurt look in her eyes
and the way her bright smile had melted.

She had only wanted to talk to him, and he had humiliated her in front of everyone. He had been wrong to
do it; he had been wrong about a lot of things. Both
Brace and Olivia had told him why Alysson had been at
Compton's house that day, and he had had plenty of
time to think about it in Washington and on the voyage
home. Why couldn't he forgive her and forget it had
happened? Why did he try to hurt her, then feel worse
about it than she did?

"Damnation," he muttered under his breath, then left
the room in search of Alysson as the maids entered to
clear away the dishes.

Alysson ran down the front lawn, not stopping when
she heard Olivia calling her name behind her. Not
wanting to talk to anyone, she hurried toward the river,
past the servants still burning leaves. She walked all the
way to the gazebos, then pressed her back against the
trunk of a gnarled old oak tree where no one could see
her. She squeezed her eyes shut, stifling a sob.

Would he never stop punishing her? Would he be the
same kind of unloving, unforgiving father to her child?
Righteous anger flooded her, making her clench her
fists and clamp her jaw. She was tired of the way he
was treating her! She was tired of trying to make him
listen to her! She would leave Wildwood! She would
steal away the way she had left her father's house in

London, and Donovan would never know he even had a son! She would go tomorrow after he had gone back to the city, quietly without telling anyone. The hard resolve softened as she thought of Katie. How could she sneak away without saying good-bye to Katie?

It was then that she remembered Katie was hiding from her somewhere, and she wiped away her tears. Turning, she moved through the trees, wondering if Katie had grown tired of waiting and had returned to the house. She looked around, watching as a young servant boy lit a nearby pile of leaves with a torch, then she froze a moment later as a shrill scream shattered the quiet air.

To Alysson's stark horror, Katie scrambled from the blazing leaves, her yellow skirt a mass of flames. She screamed and screamed, and Alysson ran to her, trying to beat out the fire with her hands. The boy ran for help in terrified panic. Sobbing, Alysson managed to get Katie down, tearing frantically at the flaming skirts and petticoats as more leaves caught fire on the ground around them.

She finally managed to rip the dress from the struggling child, and she picked up Katie and began to run toward the house. Katie was hysterical, kicking and screaming until Alysson could barely hold her. She began to scream herself, for help, feeling as if she lived in a terrible, ghastly nightmare. Halfway to the house she saw Donovan running toward her, Olivia and Brace behind him.

"Katie's been burned! Help me!" Alysson cried. Donovan took the panic-stricken child from her and turned toward the house.

"Go for Doctor Whittingham, Brace, and hurry!" he yelled. Alysson leaned weakly against a tree as Brace ran for the tables. Donovan and Olivia hurried on toward the house with Katie's screams echoing back through the trees.

Feeling sick and weak, Alysson looked down at her burned palms, feeling the throbbing ache for the first time. It was then that the first ripping pain hit her, like a red-hot iron in her loins, and she groaned in agony, her legs buckling beneath her. She slid to the ground, clutching her stomach. She tried to call for help, but another savage pain hit her. Her body felt as if it were being ripped apart, and she cried out as she doubled over. It was her baby, she knew it was her baby, and terrified, she tried to push herself up. She didn't have the strength to do it, and she lay on her side, racked over and over by never-ending pains, each worse than the one before it.

It seemed an eternity before she heard Donovan's voice calling to her. Then at last he was there, kneeling beside her, turning her over. Vaguely, she knew that he had lifted her, that he was carrying her, but the pain became more than she could bear. She felt herself being sucked into a spinning, whirling vortex, spiraling downward into an inky black pit that finally, blessedly, took the agony from her.

# Chapter 19

Donovan paced back and forth outside Alysson's bedchamber, the thick Persian carpet muffling his anxious footsteps. He stopped at the balustrade, bracing his hands there to look down to the entry foyer where two maids were whispering together. As one of them started up the steps with a bowl of steaming water, he shut his eyes, feeling helpless and sick at heart. The doctor had been with her for over an hour now, and he could not bear the waiting. He saw it all again in his mind, seared there never to leave him, the way he had found her beneath the tree, all alone, moaning in agony, and the blood——the blood had been everywhere.

His fingers tightened around the carved railing, and he turned as the maid passed him, her eyes sorrowful. God, he hadn't even known about the baby. That was what she had wanted to tell him earlier. The realization devastated him, and he felt as if a giant hand had taken hold of his soul, twisting, twisting, until he dropped his face into his hands, grappling with fear that turned his heart to ice. He had never been a fearful man. He did what had to be done, allowing destiny to decree the outcome of his actions. But he could not bend to fate now. Not with Alysson. She was so young, so beautiful, so innocent. He thought of the way he had been treating her, the way he had hurt her, feeling sick shame all over again.

He whirled around as the door opened behind him, tensing with dread as Dr. Whittingham stepped out. He looked tired, his shirtsleeves rolled to the elbow, his spectacles pushed atop his head. He was wiping his hands on a linen towel, and he shook his head as he met Donovan's worried eyes.

"I'm sorry, Donovan. I tried but I couldn't save the baby."

Donovan's whole body went rigid, and Dr. Whittingham looked at his white face. "You didn't know either, did you? Neither did Olivia, but the old Indian nurse said Alysson's been having trouble with it for weeks now. Even if I had known sooner, I doubt if the baby could have been saved. I believe the strain of carrying Katie to the house brought on the miscarriage."

"What about Alysson?"

Donovan's voice was hoarse, his eyes bleak with loss, and Dr. Whittingham put a consoling hand on his shoulder.

"We finally got the hemorrhaging stopped, and I think she'll be all right in time, if she stays in bed and takes care of herself. She's very weak now and heartbroken about the baby, so it'll take a long time for her to recover, both physically and emotionally."

"Thank god she's going to be all right," Donovan managed, rubbing both palms down over his face. He felt weak himself, and shaky.

"I thought you could use a drink, Donovan," Brace said from behind him, pouring him a stiff shot of whisky from the bottle in his hand. Donovan took it gratefully and downed it in one deep draught as Brace poured one for the doctor.

"I heard what John said," Brace said to Donovan. "I'm sorry."

Donovan nodded dully, and the doctor took the glass offered to him, meeting Brace's eyes as Donovan poured another and downed it as quickly as the first. Dr. Whittingham drank with more caution. When he

had finished, he picked up his coat where it lay on a
chair beside the door.

"I guess I'll go now. Katie's sleeping under a dose of
laudanum, but she'll be fine. Her legs might be a bit
painful in the morning, but there won't be scars or any
lasting damage. I suppose we owe that to Alysson."

"Thank God for that," Brace returned, but Donovan
was no longer listening to them as he turned the doorknob of his wife's room.

The sick room was draped in shadows, for only one
dim candle burned on the bedside table. Macomi was
near the bed, gathering together the soiled linens and
bowls that the doctor had used, and Olivia stood at the
foot of the bed. As Donovan came forward, she moved
to intercept him. Her voice was a bare whisper.

"I don't think she needs to see you right now. She's
very weak and upset."

"I'm going to see her."

"I think you'd better wait—"

"I'm going to see her."

There was no hint of harshness or anger in his voice,
but Olivia knew the tone very well. Nothing would stop
him, and she gave up, motioning for Macomi to follow
her outside. Donovan waited until they had gone, then
crossed to his wife's bed.

Alysson lay facing him in the middle of the bed, her
eyes closed, one arm outside the covers. She seemed
very small, childlike, and pale, and Donovan closed his
eyes, his fingers biting into his palms. He hated himself
for all he had put her through in the past few months.
He had been the worst kind of fool; he was no better
than her abusive father. He sat down on the edge of the
bed and lifted her bandaged hand. He pressed his lips
against her fingertips.

"Alysson? Love? Can you hear me?"

She stirred at his low whisper, and Donovan smiled

tenderly as her eyes fluttered open. He held his breath as she tried to focus on him, afraid she would hate him, afraid she would blame him for everything. He could not suppress his groan of relief as she raised her arms to him, wanting him to hold her. He pulled her gently against his chest, smoothing her hair as she began to cry against his shoulder.

"I wanted to tell you about the baby. I wanted you to love me again."

She sobbed, her words slurred by laudanum. Donovan's own devastating sense of loss and regret pervaded his next words.

"I do love you," he muttered hoarsely. "I always have."

Alysson continued to weep, cradled in his arms, but not long afterward she lapsed into a drugged and peaceful sleep.

Donovan laid her back against the pillows, tenderly pushing her golden hair away from her temples. The strands were damp, darkened by her tears, and in that moment, he was gripped by such heart-wrenching pain that he felt he could not bear it. He paced a step or two away, restless, agitated, angry, helpless. He had almost lost Alysson. He had lost the child he had always wanted. He dropped his face into his hands, a sob catching in his throat as he grieved at her bedside, alone and with a mental agony he had never experienced before.

For the next few weeks, Alysson lay without the strength to sit up. Though her tears were frequent and profuse at first, they were spent in time as reluctant, sorrowful resignation settled over her. She felt an emptiness inside herself, a void that she was sure would never, ever leave her. Her heart ached with each thought of the tiny life lost before it had a chance to live. She had envisioned it all along to be a boy, black-haired, black-eyed like his father, but now she would never see him, never hold him.

Gradually she settled into the lowest depths of depression, despite the kind attention of Olivia and Brace, and the gentle nursing of Macomi. Even Donovan's presence could not cheer her, though he sat beside her for hours, holding her hand. She wondered vaguely at times if he really did care about her, or if guilt prodded his conscience. But most of the time she found it too wearying to think at all. She really didn't care anymore.

A fortnight after her miscarriage, as the first of December loomed, Donovan came to her after the supper hour, as was his custom. Macomi was moving about the chamber in her quiet way, lighting the night tapers set in the gold wall sconces. Alysson watched Donovan from her bed as he waited impatiently for the old woman to leave. When Macomi finally departed, he looked down at Alysson, smiling in his new and gentle way.

"How are you feeling?"

"I am better, I think" was Alysson's listless response, and Donovan absently stroked the scar upon his eye.

She watched him pace like a restless tiger over to the crackling fire, then back toward her again. He looked around as if unsure what to do, and Alysson waited, at a loss to understand his uncharacteristic behavior.

"I want to hold you," he said finally, looking down at her. "If you don't object."

He had certainly never asked her permission to do that before, or to do anything else, and it surprised Alysson so much that it took her a moment to nod. She was unprepared for the quickness with which she was gathered up into his strong arms, coverlets and all. He carried her to the hearth where a large wing chair faced the fire. He sat down, settling her comfortably across his lap, and Alysson rested her cheek against his shoulder, feeling very secure with his arms around her. Donovan laid his head back against the chair and stared into the flames, his fingers threaded through her loosened hair.

"I hate myself for what happened."

His words were so low and vulnerable and full of anguish that Alysson's heart twisted, for she knew what he was feeling. It was the first time he had mentioned the baby to her. She lifted her head and put a gentle palm against his cheek.

"It wasn't your fault. I should have been more careful."

He looked at her then, anger in his voice. "Don't blame yourself, don't ever blame yourself. I've acted like a fool about you from the day we met."

She didn't reply, but she knew it was time to set things right between them. She knew he would listen now.

"I only went to Douglas to tell him . . ." She stopped as she felt his muscles tighten beneath her, but he didn't speak, so she went on softly. "To tell him that I couldn't act anymore. The things he said were lies, I swear it. He told me Rosalie was coming to his house. That's the only reason I waited there."

Donovan was quiet. She had been innocent all along, and that made his own actions that much worse. He wouldn't blame her if she never forgave him.

"I'm sorry, sweet, I'm so sorry for all that you've suffered. I'll never do anything to hurt you again, I promise you that. I'll make it up to you, if you'll let me."

Great tenderness crept over Alysson, spreading a warm glow over her heart. She laid her head back upon his chest, closing her eyes, soothed by the steady thud of his heartbeat. Everything was going to be all right, she thought in quiet contentment. Everything was going to be all right at long last.

"Please, Olivia, tell me, I really want to know," Alysson insisted as she climbed back into her freshly changed bed.

Olivia handed the soiled bed linens to a young maid. "Katie is fine. Why won't you believe me? She's in her room right now, playing with her dolls."

"Then why hasn't she come to see me? It's been a month now, and I haven't seen her at all."

"She will someday soon, I'm sure. You know how shy she can be at times. You shouldn't fret so about it. You haven't needed children around bothering you. You're still recovering."

"But I miss her."

Olivia smiled. "She misses you, too. Now take your nap before Donovan comes in from the city."

Alysson watched the door close behind them, not at all satisfied with Olivia's explanation. Each family member, including Donovan, used the same excuse about Katie disturbing her, but something was wrong, she knew it. Since Donovan had assured her that Katie's burns had healed long ago, she could not understand it. But she was going to find out, and she was going to find out now.

She threw back the covers and stepped carefully down to the embroidered bedstool beside the bed. She had felt just fine for a week now, but the doctor had ordered more bed rest, and Donovan made sure she abided by it. She smiled, thinking about him. He had become a complete tyrant over her health, but he held her every night by the fire, tenderly, affectionately, with absolutely no passion. She was quite well enough now to miss the latter, and she wanted him to stay with her at night instead of going off to his own room. Apparently, however, Dr. Whittingham had said otherwise, and she grimaced as she drew on her silk dressing gown and moved toward the door. She rested several times en route, finding that she was much weaker when she stood upon her feet than she had expected to be.

She peeked out into the hall, feeling like a thief in the house, though her only crime was getting out of bed. Donovan's strict orders concerning her were enforced by the staff, as well as by Olivia and Macomi, but no one was in sight to stop her. She walked as fast as she could to Katie's door near the servant's back stairway. She eased open the door, smiling when she saw little Katie playing in the corner beside her five-foot-high dollhouse.

"Katie? Look, I've come to see you!"

Katie jerked around, and Alysson gasped at the expression on the child's face. She looked terrified, as if she were trapped, and before Alysson could say another word, the little girl fled past her into the hall.

"Katie! Wait!" Alysson cried, following her to the back stairs. Halfway down them, she stopped, gripping the handrail. "Please don't run from me, Katie! I'm too weak to run. I'll fall!"

Katie stopped and looked back from her place several steps below. Alysson sank weakly down where she was, leaning her back against the wall for support.

"I don't understand, Katie," she said, trying to regain her breath. "I thought we were friends. Why don't you like me anymore?"

"Because you hate me," Katie said, stunning Alysson

"Hate you? Katie, I love you, surely you know that. You're just like a little sister to me."

Katie wouldn't look at her as she twisted the long

ribbon sash of her dress. "It was my fault that your baby died. It was because you picked me up and carried me. I heard the maids whispering about it."

Alysson sat very still as Katie's face contorted with an ancient agony, and her words came, low and tortured.

"I did it to Papa, too. I made him die. He told me to stay in the wagon, but I wanted to play hide-and-seek with him, so I ran away and hid. Then all those men came in their paint and feathers, and I was so scared I couldn't even scream when Papa came running after me, and they, and they—"

Alysson went quickly to her, gathering the trembling child close.

"Hush now, darling, don't say those things. None of it was your fault. My baby was already sick. You had nothing to do with it. No one could ever blame you. And you did not cause your father to die. The Indians did it, not you."

"But don't you see," Katie said, her voice aquiver. "He wouldn't have been out there all alone if I hadn't gone there. He was looking for me."

Alysson bit her lip, compassion for the child filling her. How much she must have suffered in her little mind, blaming herself for so long. No wonder she relived it in her nightmares.

"Now listen to me, Katie," she said firmly, taking Katie's small face between her palms. "You were only four years old then, just a baby. How could you have known? Tell me that. Your mother told me about it once, and she said the Mohawks attacked the wagons too, isn't that right? Other people died then. Your father loved you. He wouldn't want you to think this way." She hesitated, looking into Katie's eyes. "I know how you feel, though. I saw my mother die, and it was horrible, just horrible." She stopped, remembering that day. "I thought it was my fault too, for a while, because I thought I had allowed it to happen. But now I know it wasn't my fault, and you must try to realize that, too."

Katie had listened to every word, her freckled face young and solemn, but the expression in her eyes seemed very old at that moment.

"I'm not sure I can, Alysson, but I will try very hard."

Alysson hugged her again, but they both drew back and looked at each other as Donovan's angry voice bellowed from the hallway above them.

"Olivia! Where in the bloody hell is Alysson?"

They began to laugh then, and Alysson called her husband's name before he could descend on her poor sister-in-law. Moments later, he appeared at the top of the steps to stare incredulously down at them.

"What in the blazes are you doing down there?"

"Talking," Alysson said, smiling and hugging Katie as he came down the steps toward them.

"Talking? You're not supposed to be out of bed yet, and you know it," he scolded, scooping Alysson up with his easy strength. "Go see cook, Katie. I brought you some ice cream from the city."

Katie scampered down to the kitchen, and Alysson rode back to her room in smiling silence. Far be it for her to complain when her handsome husband showed such loving consideration for her.

# Chapter 20

Olivia moved through the house, surveying with satisfaction the holiday cheer all around her. For the first time in years, the great staircase and mantelpieces were hung with ropes of evergreen and mistletoe. This would be a very special Christmas indeed, even though Brace and Jeremy could not be there. Alysson was up and around at last, if only for the last few days, and Katie —Katie was a totally different child than she had been a year ago at Christmastide. Alysson had done much to make Katie into the happy, smiling child she was of late, and Olivia would never be able to show her gratitude for such a miracle.

Yes, things were better than they had been in many a year what with Donovan home at Wildwood nearly all the time now. Alysson had been good for him too, making him less obsessed with his business and responsibilities. He was happy now, smiling often. He had needed to settle down with a woman like Alysson for a long time. He had had too many women, too many mistresses, and not enough love.

She stopped at one of the frosty dining room windows to straighten a long white candle decorating a fragrant, ribbon-decorated cedar wreath. She paused there a moment, watching the snow. Flakes drifted downward from the gray skies, blanketing the vast lawns in a patina of white, all the way to the river. It was a beautiful picture, but a nostalgic sadness pierced her spirit as she looked at it, bringing the timeless pain back to haunt her.

How Jason had loved Christmas and all the festive excitement that came with the holiday season! When they had first married and lived in their Philadelphia house, most of their Christmases had been snowy ones, with laughing sleigh rides and caroling with Dolley and their other friends. It had all ended so abruptly for them. Olivia sighed wistfully. She must remember to have the sleigh brought out, she thought, then turned, not wanting to dwell on the past, not when the future seemed so bright. She knew Katie and Alysson were in the private family parlor, laboring over their surprise for Donovan, and she smiled as she slid back the doors to join them.

Alysson stood at a round pedestal table where a small fir tree had been set. Katie was on a stepstool beside her, helping to tie small gifts and candles on its bough. It was she who saw Olivia first.

"Mama! Isn't it grand? And look, Alysson made cookies shaped like little angels! Her friend Mathilde taught her how back in Cornwall."

"Have one, Olivia, they're really very good," Alysson said, pushing a white ribbon through the hole she had made on one of the cookies. She tied it carefully to the tree, then smiled. "We always had a little tree like this. Mathilde said that in Germany, it is the custom to have one in every house. It does look pretty, doesn't it, Olivia? Do you think Donovan will like it?"

"Yes, I'm sure he will," Olivia said, coming closer to admire it. She had never seen such a thing done. It did seem strange to have a tree in the house, but the excited delight in her daughter's eyes made it worthwhile.

"Tell me more about Cornwall and Freddie," Katie

begged. "I think I'd like him very much. Did he really climb the ocean cliffs to rescue your dog?"

"Yes, but Mathilde was quite angry because it was a very dangerous part of the cliffs where the rocks often crumbled and fell into the sea. She punished him soundly for it, but he did save Shylock."

"He must be very brave."

Alysson thought of a day when Freddie had helped hide her mother and hadn't told her father where they were, even when Daniel Tyler beat him on the back with his riding crop.

"Yes, he is very brave. I miss him, and his mother, too." Emotion caught in her throat, but no one had time to notice as Macomi appeared on the threshold.

"Long Knife come."

"But the candles aren't lit!" Katie cried in a curious mixture of terror and anticipation. Alysson laughed at her panic as she lifted a candlestick and quickly lit the others, one by one. But she couldn't deny the excitement in her own heart, for Donovan had been required to spend the last few days in the city, and she had feared the snow would strand him there. He had promised to come home for Christmas Eve, though, and he had. They all gathered behind the tiny tree to wait, and Alysson smiled happily, thinking they had done a fine job decorating it until she noticed that something was missing.

"Uh-oh, we forgot the angel Gabriel! Where is he?"

They all scurried to find the paper figure. Katie saw it first on the sofa by the fireplace. Alysson barely had time to affix it to the tree before the door opened and Donovan stood there, still wearing his great black cloak. His wide shoulders were powdered with snowflakes, and he held his tall beaver hat in one hand. They all held their breaths in eager expectancy.

Alysson was so glad to see him at first that she didn't notice the expression on his face slowly changing as he stared at the glowing tree. Her own smile faltered as his brows came down, a warning sign that she knew well. She tensed.

"I want that thing out of here, Olivia," he said tersely, then turned on his heel to move away with long, angry strides.

A stunned silence followed in the parlor as Alysson and Olivia looked at each other in confusion. Katie looked up first at her mother, then at Alysson.

"Why doesn't he like it, Mama? We don't really have to take it down, do we?"

Olivia hesitated as Katie's blue eyes filled with tears, still shocked by Donovan's behavior. Never before had he denied Katie anything reasonable, and this was such a little thing. But Donovan was the master of Wildwood, and she could not ignore his wishes.

"Let's put it in Katie's room, then," Alysson suggested, when Olivia looked torn between taking it down and letting Katie have it. "He won't see it there." She took Katie's hand in hers. "Just think, you can have it all to yourself then. Even when you are in bed you can look at it. Won't that be nice?"

"Oh, yes," Katie said, wiping her tears with her fists. But Olivia was still very reluctant to defy Donovan's orders.

"I don't know, Alysson. He seemed very emphatic about taking it outside."

"Then I'll talk to him about it. Maybe I can.persuade him to change his mind."

Olivia was not completely convinced, but she tugged on the bellpull to summon a manservant to remove the tree to Katie's room, knowing that if anyone could persuade Donovan to reconsider, it would be Alysson.

\* \* \*

Twelve slow, hollow gongs marked the hour of midnight, but Donovan hardly heard them. He sat alone in his study, where he had been since he had arrived earlier in the afternoon. He stared at the fire, fingering the silver inkwell before him as he thought of Alysson. She was probably angry with him. He shut his eyes, listening to sleet beat against the windowpanes. He had ruined Christmas Eve for all of them; he had ruined it for himself. How could Alysson understand? How could Olivia or Katie? He had never told anyone about what had happened.

Anger shook him, deep, bitter, savage. He stood, frustrated, and paced to the windows. He had come home filled with eagerness to see Alysson again, determined to make love to her as he had hungered to do for weeks during her illness. Now he stood alone in the dark, wrestling with old demons.

He pushed back the heavy velvet drape and watched the sleet bounce off the glass. The chill of winter permeated the panes, but he already felt cold inside. Would those days of the war never leave him? Would he never forget?

Tired of his own thoughts, he let the curtain fall and walked through the darkened rooms and up the curving main staircase. He stopped outside Alysson's door, feeling compelled to open it, go to her, and try to explain. But he couldn't bring himself to do so. He strode on to his own bedchamber, slamming the door with every ounce of frustration that filled him.

Alysson started up from where she dozed in a fireside chair to watch Donovan move past her to stoke the logs with jerky, impatient jabs. He was still angry about the tree, she thought, pulling the soft coverlet up to her chin. A faint shiver coursed through her at the thought of facing his wrath; she was still a coward when he looked at her with those blazing black eyes.

Had she done wrong by waiting in his room for him? She had spent hours thinking about what had happened, and she had come to the conclusion that something was dreadfully amiss with him. It had taken her some time to realize it, but now she knew there had been more than anger in his eyes. There had been pain, as if he had seen something awful.

She jumped as Donovan suddenly flung the poker from him, emitting a curse that she had never heard him voice before. She tensed as he turned and saw her, but the initial astonishment on his face dwindled quickly. To her surprise, he came to her, dropping to his knees before her chair and pulling her into his arms.

"Alysson, Alysson," he muttered huskily, and she put her arms around his neck, instinctively knowing that he needed her; he needed her understanding.

"I love you," she whispered, and Donovan groaned, his lips seeking hers hungrily. It was a long moment before he let her go again, and she sank back into her chair breathlessly as he moved away to lean against the mantel. Still weak from what his mouth had done to her, she waited as he slumped down in the chair facing her, his eyes intent on the blazing fire.

"I was born the year the war started, Alysson, and it didn't end until I was eight years old," he said, then stopped as if he found it hard to continue. She waited silently until he began again. "When the redcoats took New York, my father was serving in the army as an officer. Mother was left with the three of us to care for. When I was six, they looted and burned our house."

Alysson's heart went out to him. Wearily he reached up to massage his temple, his chiseled profile in silhouette against the flames.

"The kitchen didn't burn completely, so we lived

there, all four of us, crowded into that one room. Olivia was ten, and she helped a lot because Mother was carrying Jeremy then. I was seven, and the oldest boy, so when our food ran out that winter, I was the one who had to go out and try to get handouts from the bloody Tories."

Donovan's hands gripped the arms of his chair, humiliation gripping him even after so many years had passed. Of all the things he had been forced to do during the war, begging for food had been the worst.

"My father managed to get into the city to see us after Jeremy was born, and somehow the British found out. They captured him, then a couple of months later they hanged him."

Alysson could hear the pain in his voice now, and a deep empathy stirred inside her. Never had she dreamed he had endured such suffering as a child, as much suffering as she.

"Mother died that same winter, of pneumonia, and after that Olivia and I took care of the little ones. I worked for people, cleaning stables and running errands, doing whatever I could. One night, just before Christmas, I was passing the place where the Hessians were quartered. They were the German mercenaries who came over to fight against us. It was snowing, but I saw something in their camp, glowing in the darkness, and I went toward it. I had never before seen a tree with candles on it."

Alysson finally began to understand, and her heart wrenched for that little boy standing in the snow.

"They didn't notice me at first because they were drinking. I guess they were homesick. Finally one of them saw me standing there and grabbed the food I was taking home. When I fought for it, he hit me with his fist." He touched the scar on his eye. "That's where I got this, from his ring. Every time I look at it in a mirror, I see that man again, with his long black beard, pointed cap, and angry blue eyes. I hate him now as much as I did then."

Alysson could not bear it, and she went to him, kneeling between his legs, cupping his cheeks with her palms. Her eyes were dark green pools of compassion, her voice as tortured as his.

"I am so sorry that you had to suffer like that," she whispered. "You were so little and alone."

Donovan looked at her, then drew her slender body close, holding her tightly, needing her in that moment as he had never needed anyone before.

"Love me," he whispered against her temple. "Forget all that I've done to you, and love me."

She answered with her lips, eagerly seeking his mouth, wanting to show him how very much she did love him. Their lips melded together, and she felt the urgency in him. His need for her filled her with pleasure. She pushed against him, and when he released her, she backed away, taking his hand to draw him to the rug before the fire.

The glimmer of the flames bathed them in a warm golden light, and Alysson smiled, her eyes shining with desire and love and her growing need to feel his strong arms around her. She held him in the spell of her eyes, slowly untying the sash of her robe. The soft silk slid away from her with the barest whisper of sound, and her fingers went to the silken frogs at her shoulders. Her gown slipped away from her body, and Donovan's eyes fell upon the vision revealed to him, the smooth perfumed white skin that he had ached to touch for so long.

His hands went to the buttons of his shirt, but Alysson swept them away, releasing his buttons one by one, then pushing the linen shirt off his wide brown shoulders. She leaned forward, tasting the smooth, tanned flesh of his shoulder, then tracing her lips downward over the molded contours of his chest.

He groaned, and Alysson sat back, watching as he removed the rest of his clothes, thinking he was the most magnificent specimen of manliness ever created. Then he was on his knees before her, one sinewy arm encircling her slender waist, pulling her tightly to him, crushing her soft breasts against the crisp black hair on his chest as he lowered her backward to the soft carpet.

She gasped in pleasure as he came down on her, the strong, muscular, manly heat of him taking her breath.

His eyes delved into hers, then his gaze moved to wander over the flawless, satiny skin of her brow and cheeks, then to the softness of her lips before he dipped his dark head to touch her mouth with infinite tenderness.

"You are everything to me," he murmured hoarsely. "Everything."

Alysson moaned with pleasure at his words, arching her neck as he pressed warm lips along the graceful, slender curve. His hands left her hair to lace with her slender fingers, holding them in gentle captivity on either side of her head. She closed her eyes, moistening dry lips as his mouth wandered lower over the soft curve of her breast to tease the deep curve of her waist. She writhed against his hold, and he released her hands so that she could encircle his neck as he came back to take her lips again.

She pressed up against him, her palms sliding down the broad, rippling muscles of his back to pull his lean hips into the softness of her body, crying out as they came together. His arms tightened as they began to move together, the thudding tempo of his heart against her breasts, his ragged, hoarse breathing next to her ear. No longer able to think of anything but the blood racing in her veins and the joy in her heart, she aban-

doned herself to the exquisite sensations he brought
to her. She shivered beneath him, climbing with him
to the moment they sought, the moment of blinding
brilliance, crying out in love and joy and exquisite
rapture as they became one person, one entity, one all-
encompassing love, now and always.

Alysson left the bedchamber the next morning feeling deliriously happy. She had awakened to find Donovan already gone, and she was eager to see him again.
They had made love early that morning when she had
awakened the first time to find his warm lips nuzzling a
path along her bare shoulder. They had snuggled together beneath the covers, entwined against the chill
morning air. More than anything, she hoped she had
conceived again from the closeness they had shared. So
much understanding, so much intimacy had been
shared that a child would be a lasting, precious re-
minder of the night she would never stop cherishing.

She moved quickly along the upper hall, peering
over the gleaming banister to the hall below. Voices and
laughter drifted up to her, and she shivered all over
with good feelings as she inhaled the mouth-watering
aroma of roast turkey mingled with the holiday fra-
grances of pine and cedar. She lifted her skirt and hurried down the steps with joy in her heart, but as she
rounded the curve of the banister, she drew up in surprise at the scene below.

Donovan stood near the tall front doors, overseeing
the raising of a twenty-foot Christmas tree in the middle of the hall. He saw her at once, for he had been
watching for her, and as he gave a sheepish grin, Alysson's heart swelled to bursting. She was deeply touched
by the gesture he was making to all of them. She
basked in the warmth of his black eyes as he left the
half dozen menservants laboring with the huge tree and

came to the base of the steps to wait for her. Katie, however, who was watching with Olivia on the bottom step, arrived at Alysson's side first.

"Uncle Donovan's changed his mind, Aly! I knew he would! I knew it! And he told me he would help us decorate it, too! Isn't it grand!"

"Yes, sweetheart, it's more than grand, it's wonderful!" Alysson returned, but her smiling eyes were on the tall dark man awaiting her below. It was he who she really thought was wonderful.

As she reached the third step from the floor, he took both her hands and pulled her close giving her a kiss that instantly created a shocked silence throughout the large hall. As the kiss stretched out for an embarrassing length of time, a chorus of giggles and whispers erupted from a group of girlish maids stringing ribbons through cookies.

When Donovan finally decided to release his wife, a hot flush had crept up her neck, and worse than that, she found herself most assuredly aroused from his tight embrace and searching lips. Even so, it was with extreme reluctance that she allowed Katie to pull her away to inspect the finished ornaments. She met Olivia's pleased smile with one of her own, knowing this would be a Christmas none of them would ever, ever forget.

The air of excitement permeating the house intensified as short white tapers were tied to the spreading branches, transforming the gigantic fir tree into an enchanting vision reflected four times over in the gold mirrors adorning the hall. Alysson reveled in Donovan's affectionate attention, pressing herself eagerly to his side when he put his arm around her waist and drew her close. She grew trembly and breathless when he lifted her hand to his lips to kiss her palm, the look in his dark eyes so intense that delicious tinglings jolted through her body, making her long for the hour when they would retire alone to their dark, draped bed upstairs.

As night fell and the candles sent out a golden glow in all the windows, they feasted around the glowing tree at tables set up for the MacBride servants and their families. Alysson acted as mistress of Wildwood for the first time, beneath her husband's attentive eyes. She was amazed by the staggering amount of food served by smiling maids to everyone present.

The meal began with a large tureen of plum potage placed at one end of each table and another of creamy oyster soup at the other. This course was accompanied by dishes of catfish curry and broiled eels. When they were removed and the first lace tablecloth lifted from the table, the maids brought platters filled with roast turkey, duck, and beef, as well as a large mincemeat pie, surrounded by smaller serving dishes of potatoes mashed with onions, turnip purée flavored with veal glazing, and countless other delicious foods.

Alysson could eat little of the bountiful fare, her appetite still poor from her illness, but those around her sampled each dish with unabashed fervor. When the last course was finished, all the platters were removed, as well as another tablecloth of fine white linen, and the fine wines that had been served throughout the meal were replaced by a selection of properly aged port and Madeira.

As two elegant, multitiered epergnes laden with sweetmeats, jellies, and preserved fruits were placed on the sideboard, all eyes were drawn to the hall where Stephens carried the blazing Christmas pudding, wreathed in mistletoe and held high in all its brandy-blazing glory.

After everyone had tasted their fill of the delicious sweets, baskets of holiday food and special gifts chosen by Olivia were given to each servant. Alysson watched silently, never so proud as when she raised her heavy crystal goblet to toast her handsome husband as master of the house.

Afterward, the servants cleared the tables, then drifted away to spend Christmas night in their own fashion. Alysson sat on a small settee with Katie as the family gathered in the parlor. Alysson was smiling at Donovan as he came over to her.

"I suppose Katie's waited long enough for her present," he said, his statement eliciting a hearty nod of agreement from the excited little girl. "All right then, close your eyes. You too, English."

"Me?" Alysson said in surprise, then obeyed, wondering what on earth he had in mind as she clasped Katie's hand. A few moments later, they were given permission to look, and did so eagerly, to find two large wicker hampers in front of them. They both looked at Donovan expectantly, then at Olivia, who stood just behind him. Donovan grinned.

"Well, what are you waiting for? Open them."

Alysson leaned forward and lifted the hinged lid to find a tiny white spaniel puppy curled in the bottom, fast asleep.

"Shylock," she murmured, unexpected tears burning her eyes. Katie, on the other hand, squealed with delight as her own spaniel puppy, as black as night, wriggled out of the hamper and onto her lap. She hugged the furry warmth to her, laughing as the puppy licked her nose with its wet pink tongue.

"Oh, thank you, thank you, Uncle Donovan, I love him!"

The look in Alysson's glorious green eyes was nothing less than dazzling, and all that Donovan needed. Other gifts were exchanged, but both Donovan and Alysson were glad when the hour grew late. They left the parlor hand in hand, and it was not long after that Alysson sat upon their bed, waiting as Donovan moved around the room, extinguishing the candles.

The little puppy was curled in her lap, and Alysson looked down as his rough little tongue licked her fingers. The sight of him brought back a bittersweet pang as she remembered the night she and Freddie had begged Mathilde to let them keep the first Shylock after they had found him wandering half-starved upon the cliffs.

"What is it, love?" Donovan said, his weight dipping the bed as he sat down beside her. Alysson smiled as he lifted her chin with one finger. "You looked so sad for a moment."

"I was thinking of Freddie and Mathilde."

Donovan looked at her a moment, then picked up the puppy and lowered him into the basket beside the bed. He took Alysson in his arms then, holding her close as he drew the covers over them.

"Tell me about them. You never have."

"They helped me take care of my mother. They were the only good thing in my life until I met you."

Donovan lifted her hand and kissed it. "What happened to them?"

"My father cast them out when he took me to London to meet you."

"Where did they go?" he asked gently, lifting a silky golden lock and caressing it between his thumb and forefinger.

"To their relatives in Standington, I think, but I worry that they may not be well and safe."

"I am sure they are, sweet, but would you feel better if we were to send a letter there inquiring after them?"

Alysson's eyes lit up with eagerness. "Oh, yes, could we, Donovan?"

Donovan smiled. "I'll see to it tomorrow."

Alysson smiled, reaching up to touch his chin, her eyes revealing all she felt in her heart.

"I'll never forget today," she whispered. "It was the best day of my life, and you gave it to me." Her eyes searched his. "Especially the tree for Katie, because I know it must have hurt you to do it."

Donovan propped his head on his palm, looking down into her face, framed by the satin pillows. He fingered a thick curl lying across her naked collarbone, his dark eyes at peace.

"You helped rid me of that memory last night, my love. Forever, I think. Now such trees as that one downstairs will only bring to mind last night, when I felt you willing and eager in my arms. I will think of the look in your eyes on the staircase this morning and Katie's happy laugh when she first saw the tree in the hall."

Alysson put her arms around his neck and pulled his head down to hers. As soon as his lips touched hers, so warm and seeking and gentle, she forgot about trees and puppies, and even Freddie and Mathilde. The snow continued to fall silently in drifts against the window-panes, while she soared to shuddering heights with her beloved husband, experiencing once again a sweet ecstasy that left her weak and sated and totally, endlessly, wonderfully content.

# Chapter 21

Lieutenant Jeremy MacBride arrived in New York in late January for a month's furlough, and it was with a good deal of anticipation that he crunched a path up the snow-packed walk of his eldest brother's town house at the corner of Wall and William streets. He kicked the bricked stoop to rid his knee-high black boots of snow, then entered the foyer without pulling the bell. He grinned when he saw his sister passing through to the parlor.

"Hello there, beautiful," he called. Olivia looked quickly around as he swept off his military hat with a flourish and bowed low before her. Her first surprise turned into pure delight.

"Jeremy!" she exclaimed, running to hug the youngest of her tall brothers. "I thought you'd never come home again!"

Jeremy laughed, holding her back to look at her. "I just arrived from Fort Niagara, and let me tell you, you're a sight for sore eyes! But what are you doing in town in the dead of winter? Katie's not sick, is she?"

There was no need for an answer to that question, because the little girl in question came sliding down the staircase banister, two spaniel puppies romping behind her. Her feet hit the floor, and she was three steps toward the kitchen before she caught sight of her long-absent uncle near the front door. She changed her course and came toward him at a run, squealing his name, the dogs yipping at her heels.

Jeremy laughed with delight and swung her up into his arms, eliciting more screams of pleasure. But as he hugged the child close, his brown eyes questioned her mother.

Olivia smiled. "There have been quite a few changes around here since your last leave."

"So I see," Jeremy replied, placing Katie on her feet, then tugging playfully on one of her fiery pigtails. "Could Donovan's new wife have anything to do with it?"

Olivia nodded. "Yes, indeed, she does. She and Katie are the best of friends, aren't you, Katie?" Katie nodded, examining with interest the long sword hanging from Jeremy's belt, and Olivia went on. "As a matter of fact, Alysson's the one who insisted that we spend the winter here when Donovan insisted that she stay in town with him instead of over at Wildwood."

"I see," Jeremy said, already liking his new sister-in-law for her kindness to his sister and his niece. "Is she around now? I'd certainly like to meet the girl who got old Donovan to give up all his fun with the ladies."

"She's gone for a walk, I think," Olivia said, looking at her daughter. "Katie, why don't you run into the kitchen and have Carla bring tea for us, then bundle up and see if you can find Alysson."

"Yes, ma'am," Katie cried and was gone at a galloping run, the puppies skidding on the polished floor in an attempt to turn the corner at the end of the hall. Olivia and Jeremy smiled after her, Jeremy shaking his head.

"I can't believe that's the same little girl who bade me good-bye two years ago. I could barely get her to look at me then."

"I know, isn't it wonderful? And I truly do credit Alysson for most of the change in her. But come, let's go into the parlor where it's warmer."

She took his heavy army cape of dark blue wool, hanging it upon the brass coat tree beside the door, then followed him into the parlor. She watched fondly as he moved to the fire and held his palms out to the warmth, thinking he looked more like their father with each passing year. He had the same black hair and brown eyes, but it was especially his wide dimpled smile and easy laugh that endeared him to her. He was certainly the most fun-loving of her brothers, and she had missed him very much.

"Tell me about this wondrous woman named Alysson, if you will," he demanded with a grin. "Very strange rumors have made their way to me all the way out to Niagara. And it's a good thing too, since Donovan, blast him, never even thought to tell me that he was married. I wouldn't know anything if it hadn't been for your letter. Except for one courier who said Donovan had been in a duel over her, but I found that hard to believe, knowing the way Donovan feels about dueling."

Olivia met his eyes. "It is true, I'm afraid. He had no choice, really. Douglas Compton forced him into it."

"And was it Donovan's wife's fault?"

Jeremy frowned with disapproval as he asked, and Olivia was quick to defend her sister-in-law from the same censure she herself had felt toward Alysson when she had first arrived at Wildwood.

"It's a long story. I blamed her at first too, until I got to know her better. I know you'll like her as much as the rest of the family does."

She paused as tea was carried in by one of the maids. Jeremy moved to the window as Olivia sat down before the silver tea set, carefully pouring the fragrant brew into two white porcelain cups.

"Donovan has changed a lot too, Jeremy. And for the

better, I think. He's not quite so . . . well, he's not quite so sober anymore."

Jeremy laughed at the word she had settled on and took the cup she offered him. "His wife has driven him to drink, has she?"

"No, of course not," Olivia answered quickly, smiling. "He's just become more domestic, is all."

Jeremy laughed again. "Domestic? Donovan? I'll have to see that to believe it." He took a sip of his tea, then lowered it with a grin as he saw Donovan's tall, erect figure moving briskly up the walk, the ever-efficient Lionel Roam hurrying to keep apace with his long strides.

"It doesn't look to me as if he's changed very much. Look, there he is now, his secretary following him around like a trained puppy."

A different movement caught Jeremy's eyes then, and he watched with interest as a small figure in a bright scarlet cloak ran around the tall hedge behind Donovan and Lionel Roam. His mouth dropped a degree as the newcomer let loose a snowball with enough accuracy to topple Donovan's tall beaver hat from his head.

"Good god, Olivia, is that her? Donovan will kill her!"

"Oh, no he won't," Olivia said, watching with a knowing smile.

Jeremy wasn't nearly so sure, his own experience reminding him that Donovan wasn't one to indulge in such lighthearted play. He watched Donovan whip around as Alysson turned and fled in the opposite direction. To Jeremy's astonishment, Donovan handed his walking cane to Lionel Roam and took off after the fleeing girl.

"I don't believe it," Jeremy said incredulously. "I just don't believe it. Donovan? In a snowball fight? He wouldn't even take time to do that when we were boys!"

"I told you," Olivia said, laughing at his expression.

Lionel Roam disappeared around the side of the house, but those watching from the window were more interested in Donovan as he caught up with his scarlet-clad attacker and tackled her with enough force to send them both tumbling headlong into a snowdrift. Jeremy laughed aloud.

"I'll be damned," he said. His grin widened, for Donovan was holding her down now, obviously exacting a penalty for her audacity. From the way it looked, Jeremy had little doubt about what Donovan wanted from her. He chuckled again as Donovan helped his wife to her feet, gently brushing snow off her hair and cloak. When they started for the front door together, Jeremy moved to meet them, more eager than ever to see his brother again.

Just inside the front door, Alysson found herself held tightly in Donovan's arms again, and she laughed softly as he pressed her back against the wall with his hard body, his lips warm and dry against her cold face.

"Since no one's around, I'll take part of my revenge now," he threatened in a husky voice. Alysson pressed herself against him, rather enjoying his brand of punishment. Perhaps she should meet him every day with snowball in hand, she thought happily, as his embrace tightened and one hand found its way beneath her skirts.

"Ahem," came the exaggerated sound of a throat being cleared. Alysson's face flamed with embarrassment when she realized a tall man, a complete stranger, had been observing them from the parlor door. Donovan's face broke into a welcoming grin, and he released her, striding forward to greet the man.

"Jeremy! Damn, but it's good to see you! Welcome

home!" he said, pumping his brother's hand, then pounding him hard on the shoulder.

While they were engaged with their greetings, Alysson took the opportunity to straighten her cloak and rebutton her bodice, her cheeks still hot from being caught in such a wanton display by the brother-in-law she had not yet met. She had no more time to make herself presentable, for almost at once Donovan was beside her, drawing her toward his brother.

"Alysson, this is my youngest brother, Jeremy. The one detailed at Fort Niagara. You've heard us speak of him."

She could see the resemblance now, of course—the well-turned, even features and curly dark hair—and she thought he looked very handsome in his army uniform with its gold epaulettes and brass buttons.

"Yes, I've wanted to meet you for a long time," she began, surprised when he took her fingers and bent low to kiss them. Jeremy looked at her then, amazed at how young she was, younger than any other woman his sophisticated oldest brother had ever been known to court. He smiled.

"And I have heard much more about you. I only wish the men in my command could aim their muskets with as much accuracy as you wield a ball of snow."

Alysson blushed to think he had seen that too, but Donovan laughed heartily.

"You will have to take lessons from her yourself, if I remember your aim from the last time we went shooting together!"

A moment later, Alysson excused herself to dress for the evening meal, pausing on the stairs to watch them go into Donovan's study together. She was still rather humiliated over the things Jeremy had seen, but when suppertime arrived, and Brace joined them as well, she felt very comfortable in the family circle. As she looked around the elegant, candlelit table with its imported porcelain and stemmed glassware where Olivia sat with her three handsome brothers, Alysson was very proud to be a MacBride. She grew warm with pleasure each time Donovan took her hand or included her in the conversation. Mostly they spoke of Brace's plans to sail to New Orleans to view the plantation he had acquired there, and of Jeremy's news from the Great Lakes and Fort Niagara.

It was much later after Alysson and Olivia had retired to their respective bedchambers, that the three men sat around the desk in Donovan's study, enjoying their cigars and a bottle of fine French brandy.

Brace's blue eyes gleamed with devilment as he sipped his potent drink. "From what I hear, Jeremy, this is the latest old Donovan has stayed up since Christmas Day, and I suppose it's your arrival that's kept him up past his very early bedtime hour. I believe he wouldn't be above retiring at noon if propriety would sanction it."

Jeremy laughed, and Donovan gave a good-natured shrug as he leaned forward to light a narrow cheroot on the candle before him.

"You're just jealous of my good fortune," he murmured, puffing the cigar into flame. His brothers smiled.

"She's a beautiful lady, big brother," Jeremy agreed. "There's not a man with red blood in his veins who would deny that."

Brace laughed to himself at Donovan's smug, self-satisfied look, remembering the way it had been between Alysson and Donovan aboard the *Halcyone*. A black widow, he had called her, but he did not remind his brother of those less happy days. Instead, he spoke of the war.

"Was there much talk of war at Niagara?" he asked Jeremy.

Jeremy nodded. "They want it, all up and down the Ohio Valley especially. They want the land north of the border, and they want to end the Indian trouble down there. Tecumseh and his Shawnees are in league with General Brock in Canada, now that Harrison beat them at Tippecanoe last fall."

Silence prevailed for a moment, then Donovan looked at Brace. "You just returned from Boston. What's the political climate up there?"

"They're threatening to hold back their militias if Madison declares war against Britain, but we expected that. They say Bonaparte's behind it anyway, and they fear him a lot more than they do England."

"The Corsican doesn't have designs on us," Donovan said. "But I agree that we're not prepared for a war, with either one of them."

"War is inevitable," Brace replied fervently. "The British treat us like a bastard orphan brother and always have. I, for one, am sick of being pushed around. You were too when they stopped the *Halcyone.*"

"They stopped the *Halcyone?* When?" Jeremy inquired, frowning. Brace told him, anger tightening his jaw even in the retelling of it.

"But it won't happen again," he finished. "I have her armed and ready now, and the day war is declared, I'll be the first privateer out of port."

"Our last intelligence set the British Navy at six-hundred-men-of-war, and more than a hundred of those are ships of the line, first-class fighting machines," Donovan reminded him again. "We have next to none, and you can take my word for it that Congress won't be enthusiastic about building more, even if they could afford to."

Jeremy nodded. "If we are to win a war, it will have

to be a land war, an invasion of Canada. If we can take Lower Canada, it would cut off the supply routes to Upper Canada, but we'll need more regulars for that, especially if the Indians ally themselves with Brock. I hate to say it, but we're sadly lacking in leaders, too. Most of our generals are old men who fought in the Revolution."

Donovan agreed. "Adam's been feeding the British exaggerated troop strengths as well as other false military information, just in case Madison is forced to declare. And if Henry Clay's support continues to grow, he won't have much choice."

"Does Compton have any suspicions about Adam?" Brace asked, and Jeremy noted how Donovan went tense at the mere mention of the man's name.

"No, and as long as he trusts Adam, we have a chance to feed him information that will help us if we do invade Canada. Adam says the Park Theater is a veritable nest of British spies, and both he and Rosalie have picked up all kinds of valuable information there in the past few months."

"Who is this Adam?" Jeremy asked, not familiar with the name.

"I met him when I served my time at Niagara. He hated the British even then, and for good reason, I found out later. They sold him into indenture in New South Wales, and he spent nearly a decade trying to buy his freedom. I trust him without question. That's why I recruited him to help us."

They talked a bit longer about the coming war, then reminisced about some of their past escapades together. But as the evening lengthened, Jeremy and Brace began to notice Donovan's frequent glances at the pendulum clock in the corner. To their amusement, it wasn't overly long before he stood and stretched.

"It grows late, so I'll bid you both good night. We'll talk again tomorrow."

After he had left with eager tread to join his lovely young wife, Brace and Jeremy exchanged a smile.

"You can't blame him," Jeremy commented, draining his brandy.

"No, Alysson would make any man eager for bed."

Their eyes met, and Jeremy grinned.

"Does Madame Bartholomew still have her house down on Pearl Street?"

Brace smiled, remembering with vivid detail the many times he and his brothers had visited that high-class establishment and sampled the considerable charms of its ladies.

"I believe she does, little brother," he said, crushing out his cheroot. "And since you've just spent a long, lonely winter at a fort full of ugly-faced recruits, I should think those lovely ladies would be a welcome change for you."

"Welcome, indeed," Jeremy said, standing. "Welcome, indeed."

# Chapter 22

Spring arrived, bringing the earliest flowers to cheer the walled gardens of New York. Crocus, trumpet-shaped daffodils, and scarlet tulips heralded warm weather and the awakening of the sleeping earth. Donovan thought not of such things, nor of the brisk traffic of pedestrians moving along the sidewalks of Broad Street as he held Warlock to a walk along the cobble-stoned thoroughfare. He had left the Stock Exchange early to spend the afternoon at home with Alysson.

He smiled to himself. The mere thought of her was like a healing balm smoothed gently over his restless mind. At times when she slept so peacefully in his arms, he would lie awake, taking account of his life, his successes and failures. Of all the memories that came to him at those times, the one he regretted the most was his behavior the night he had met Alysson. He had tried with cold-blooded calculation to seduce her, then later threatened her with rape. My god, how could she ever have fallen in love with him?

Even on the *Halcyone*, the things he had said and done were inexcusable. He remembered telling her he couldn't ever marry her, couldn't be bound by strings that were hard to break, he had said. He gave an inward mocking laugh. She had certainly made him eat those words. She held him to her, not with strings, but with velvet ropes that he never wanted to break. He had always prided himself on his independence, his ability to walk away from women with no regrets, but Alysson had been the change of that. He intended to make her forget all the unhappy times he had put her through. She would have anything and everything that was within his power to give her.

He turned Warlock upon Wall Street. Far down the road near the end of the block, he could see a small chaise as it left the gateroad of his house. He recognized the rig as that of Rosalie Handel, and he tipped his hat politely to Odette and Rosalie as they were driven past him. Alysson had invited them to tea often since he had brought her to the city, and Donovan was glad she had good friends to entertain when he was involved with his business affairs. Unfortunately, Alysson was still a bit of a scandal with the society matrons of New York, but that would change. He had the power and wealth to stifle such gossip about his wife, and he intended to do it.

A young groom ran to meet him when he reached his stables, and Donovan dismounted, walking with a quick step through the walled garden to the house. He pulled off his leather riding gloves as he strode through the downstairs rooms in search of his wife. He paused unseen at the door of the small sitting room that overlooked the rose garden. It had become Alysson's favorite place, with its pink and yellow chintz-covered window seat, and he smiled when he found her sitting there. The afternoon sun spun her hair into a shining golden halo. Her head was bent over a paper in her hands. Her fine-boned, delicate beauty rivaled any woman, anywhere.

"Hello, sweet."

He stepped forward, and Alysson looked up at once with a smile, but Donovan noted the way she quickly hid the paper in the pocket of her skirt. Jealous thoughts he didn't like crept into his mind, but were quickly dispelled by the way Alysson hurried across the room, welcoming him on tiptoe. She slid her arms around his neck to pull his head closer to her mouth, and he accommodated her in that intent, one arm lifting her from the floor. Several breathless moments passed before he spoke gruffly against the graceful curve of her throat.

"I missed you today."

Alysson smiled, very glad he had decided to come home early. "And I thought of you, my husband, the whole time I listened to Odette chatter about her latest beau. You only just missed seeing Odette and Rosalie."

"Good," said Donovan. "If they were here, I wouldn't be able to do this."

Alysson gasped as his fingers moved to the small pearl buttons between her breasts, deftly unfastening several of them as he sat down with her atop his lap. She closed her eyes as his hand slid beneath the soft chemise, his fingertips caressing the satiny curves until her blood pounded in her ears. He was pushing the gown down one shoulder now, tracing the bare flesh there with his tongue. Hot and aroused, Alysson barely managed her protest.

"Stephens will be coming for the tea things. I rang for him just before you came. He'll see us."

"Let him," Donovan replied carelessly, capturing her lips. But, not wanting to embarrass her, he reluctantly released her.

Pleased by her look of disappointment, he smiled as he helped her refasten her gown, for she fumbled nervously with the tiny buttons, glancing repeatedly at the door. The strong brown fingers working so close to her breasts did little to alleviate her fevered state, however, and it was not until the rotund valet did enter the room and Donovan removed his hands from her that Alysson began to breathe normally again.

Stephens arched a brow at the sight of his mistress

atop his master's lap, but went about his business of gathering the tea things upon his silver tray. He left quietly then, not in the least surprised about what was going on in the sitting room. Mr. Donovan's affection for his young wife was well known and well discussed by all the members of the household staff, so much so that the servants often tasted his scolding on the matter.

"What were you reading when I came in?" Donovan asked a moment later, his black eyes intent on her face. When Alysson stiffened guiltily in his arms, the shadow of a frown appeared between his eyes.

"Nothing, really, just something Odette gave to me."

"What is it?"

Alysson gave a nervous little laugh and sought to move away, but he held her in place.

"It's just an advertisement, is all," she said then. "You wouldn't be interested, really."

"May I see it?"

His polite request was more like a polite demand, and Donovan thought that Alysson didn't look as though she wanted to give it to him, but she reluctantly retrieved it from her pocket.

Donovan unfolded it, discovering it was a playbill for the Park Theater. Odette's name was at the top, leading the cast for the upcoming production of *The School for Scandal* by the English playwright Sheridan. Donovan looked at his wife, astute enough to realize what she must have been feeling as she read it. It could have been her name there; it *should* have been her name there.

"See, it is only a playbill," Alysson teased, but her bright smile did not hide the wistful look in her eyes.

"Would it please you to attend the opening performance?" he asked suddenly, and Alysson turned her head abruptly towards him, her initial surprise dwindling into pure pleasure, only to succumb a moment later into doubt.

"But didn't you see?" she asked uncertainly. "It's at the Park."

Both knew they would very likely see Douglas Compton if they attended. Although Donovan didn't exactly welcome that prospect, he realized it might do much to squelch the gossip about the duel if they appeared there together as if nothing had happened.

"If you want to go, we'll go. And we'll make it a family affair. Olivia and Katie will go with us."

"Oh, that would be wonderful!" Alysson exclaimed in excitement. "Oh, thank you, thank you! Odette will be so pleased because she so wanted me to come. I'll write her a note now and tell her we're coming!"

She started to rise, but Donovan's arm tightened around her waist.

"Write it later," he murmured, and Alysson settled back into his lap with no further urging, his kisses only adding to her happiness of the moment.

The performance was held on a Saturday night in late April, almost a fortnight later. Alysson dressed with care, wanting Donovan to be proud of her. She selected an apple-green silk gown with a low, square neckline and a matching satin cape, so she could wear the exquisite strand of emeralds and pearls that Donovan had given her for the occasion.

He awaited her downstairs, his tall, commanding frame resplendent in an elegantly tailored black jacket and white silk waistcoat, his long muscular legs encased in black trousers. Alysson basked in the sensual gleam in his black eyes as she met him at the bottom of the stairs. He smiled down at her his fingers lingering caressingly on her shoulders as he placed the cape around her.

"You're beautiful, my angel," he whispered close to her ear. "So beautiful that I think the evening will last much too long before I can have you to myself again."

Alysson lifted a hand to his cheek. "Thank you, Donovan, for doing this for me. It makes me very happy."

He bent for a tender kiss that could easily have exploded into much more as his small wife pressed her slender, voluptuous body against his legs. But Katie chose that very moment to arrive, skidding to a stop when she saw them. She placed her hands on her hips and shook her braids in disgust.

"Every time I come to visit, all you do is kiss Uncle Donovan," she complained to Alysson. The entwined couple broke apart, laughing.

Katie's mother, having arrived on the threshold just in time to hear her daughter's remark, was quick to reprimand her. "You had better see to your manners, young lady, or you may not be invited here so often."

Katie did not seem overly worried by that eventuality, as Alysson took her hand and led her outside, where Jethro waited with the carriage. Katie's enthused chatter dominated the short ride to the theater, where, at the hour of seven, elegantly attired theater patrons were gathering. Shiny, well-sprung carriages lined Chatham Row and the Mews behind the theater just as they had on the opening night of *King Lear,* now nearly nine months ago.

As Alysson walked alongside her husband, his fingers holding her bare arm with possessive pride, memories crowded her mind. That one night she had been the star, her name whispered in the darkness of the velvet-draped gilded boxes, and it was a memory she kept in a special compartment of her mind to take out at times to handle and cherish.

Her bittersweet feelings were transparent enough for

Donovan to read, and when they were seated high above the vast theater behind Olivia and Katie in the private box he had purchased for Alysson's first performance, he laced his long fingers with her slender ones.

"Are you very sad to be here again, love?"

Alysson looked into his soul-searching ebony eyes, full of concern and love and compassion for her feelings. How much he had changed since they had met. She had called those splendid eyes "devil eyes" once, she remembered, and thought him a devil through and through, but now it was hard to believe she could ever have felt such things about her beloved husband.

"A little," she admitted with honesty. "But I am content to sit here by your side."

Her answer pleased him, she could tell, but just then the lights dimmed, and she leaned forward eagerly. In truth, she had seen few productions herself, and it was rather fun just to sit back and watch the people on stage perform for her. The play was a comedy of manners, with outrageous jokes about the crust of London society, quite risqué in content. Most of the fast-paced, suggestive dialogue passed over Katie's understanding, as the child raptly watched the stage, drinking in beautiful costumes and amazing scenery changes. Odette was wonderful as the young and extravagant wife of the great-suffering but witty old man played by Adam Sinclair.

When intermission came and the lamps were slowly lit along the walls below, a muted buzz of conversation rose as the performance was discussed with much twisting and turning to see who was in attendance. The MacBride box received more than its share of attention and whispered conjectures, but Alysson ignored them, looking around with a great deal of interest.

When Donovan nodded and smiled slightly at someone in a nearby box, she followed his gaze. The Countess Kinski sat there in her usual white lace and feathers, two handsome, uniformed escorts vying with each other for her attention. Alysson looked quickly away. A suffocating streak of raw, agonizing jealously raced through her. He had known that gorgeous, raven-haired noblewoman, had known her well, had known and wanted her long before he had met Alysson. It hurt deeply to think of them having been together, even if it had been in the past.

"There is caviar and champagne being served in the restaurant on the third level," Donovan was saying. "Shall we?"

He rose, standing back to let the ladies precede him from their draped alcove, but a backward glance told Alysson that Marina Kinski was also ready to leave for the refreshment tables. As Alysson had feared, they met the Russian countess and her suitors in the wide, crimson-carpeted hallway just outside.

She steeled herself, trying not to show the jealousy knotting her stomach as her husband's former mistress smiled up at Donovan.

"Good evening, Mr. MacBride," she murmured in a husky, deeply accented voice. Alysson was chagrined to find that Marina Kinski was even more beautiful at closer range, with high aristocratic cheekbones, glossy black hair cascading over one shoulder, and eyes as black as Donovan's.

"Good evening, Countess," Donovan replied, nodding briefly to the officers with her. Alysson was instantly gratified by the way he put his hand upon her waist and drew her close beside him. "I don't believe you have met my family. This is my wife, Alysson, and my sister, Olivia. Katie, here, is my niece."

"How do you do," Marina said, her eyes dropping to

Donovan's proprietary hold on his beautiful young wife.

"How do you do," Alysson returned with as much graciousness as she could muster under the circumstances.

"Are you enjoying the play?" Donovan asked then. Marina smiled.

"Oh, yes, and it is a fitting way for me to end my stay in your country. I shall set sail for my home in Venice within the fortnight. I have found myself very lonely and homesick in the past few months."

Alysson read all kinds of things into her statements, but Donovan's expression did not change.

"Then we must wish you a safe voyage and all the best when you start anew in your native land," he said.

Marina inclined her head gracefully, and Alysson was distinctly relieved when Donovan led her away toward the gilded staircase, very pleased to be finished with the uncomfortable meeting and even more pleased to know that the lovely Countess Kinski was leaving the country.

"Take me backstage so I can see Odette and Billy in their costumes, please, Aly!" Katie begged once they were in the restaurant area, and Donovan was presenting goblets of champagne to Alysson and Olivia. "They could autograph my program, couldn't they? Like you told me you did when you played Cordelia."

Alysson looked at Donovan, and he nodded. "Go ahead, if you like. I'll take the time to enjoy a cigar. I see Doctor Whittingham near the doors."

Olivia decided to go as well, and Alysson led them through the lobby filled with milling people to the door that led backstage. The doorman there remembered Alysson well, greeting her with warm regard. When he allowed them to pass, Alysson moved through yelling prop men and costumed actors and actresses toward

Odette's dressing room, familiar with the hustle and bustle of opening night. She tapped upon the door with her knuckle, and when Odette's voice bid them to enter, she turned the knob. On seeing her visitors, Odette jumped up from her seat before her candle-ringed dressing table.

"Alysson! *Entree!* How *splendide* that you are here this night! And Katie and Olivia, too! Have you ever seen so many flowers? But, oh, of course you have! You received so many for *Lear!* Tell me, *mon amie,* did I do so terrible? Did you see when I missed my cue in the beginning of Act Two?"

"Did you? No one noticed, I'm sure. You were simply marvelous!" Alysson complimented her, hugging her friend. "And Billy! I could not believe how much he has improved since *Lear.* "

"*Oui,* he is quite the handsome roué now, and all the young ladies send him notes begging him to join them at their homes! And he is beginning to accept some of them!"

"We want to see him too, if we can. Katie would like both of you to sign her program for a memento of this evening. This is her first play."

"Of course I will, *mon* sweet bébé!" Odette crooned to Katie, most pleased by the child's request. "Come close, and let me see it!"

A knock sounded as Odette signed her name to the program, and Alysson's face paled when she saw Douglas Compton in the doorway. A moment of tension ensued as he stared openly at Alysson. Alysson finally spoke, wanting to alleviate the awkward silence.

"Hello, Douglas. We came backstage for a moment to wish Odette good luck. I hope you don't mind our being here."

He started toward them at her words, and Alysson's eyes dropped down to his legs, horrified at the way he dragged one foot slightly as he supported himself with a silver-handled cane.

"Of course not," he answered. "I am so glad you have come. I was just surprised at first to find you here." He took her hand as he reached her, holding it tightly for a moment. When he looked straight at Olivia with questioning eyes, Alysson was prompted to introduce them.

"This is my sister-in-law, Olivia Jenkins, and this is her daughter, Katie."

"How do you do, Mr. Compton," Olivia said politely, praying fervently all the while that Donovan didn't decide to join them backstage. Katie gave a small curtsy.

"It is my sincere pleasure to meet you both," Douglas said with smooth charm. "I do hope you are enjoying our production, Mrs. Jenkins."

Olivia moved her eyes to him from her vigilant watch on the door.

"Oh, yes," she answered. "Miss Larousse is delightful as Lady Teazle, and I thought Adam Sinclair magnificent as Sir Peter."

"Yes, Adam never fails to please the ladies. Perhaps you would like to meet him before you return to your seats?"

Anxious to get Alysson out of his company, Olivia was quick to decline his offer.

"I have already had the pleasure of meeting Mr. Sinclair," she said, smiling. Alysson was speaking to Odette again and didn't hear, but Douglas looked at her in surprise.

"Indeed? Do you know him well?"

"No, I met him only briefly a number of years ago in Philadelphia when he came to our hotel to meet with Donovan. They served a time at Fort Niagara together,

I believe, but at that time I had no idea he was such a good actor."

Douglas's whole body went rock-hard at Olivia's innocent revelation, but he held his face in strict control. His mind raced with dawning comprehension as the ladies chatted with Odette, who was changing her costume behind a screen. He grew cold as winter, lethal rage rising in an inferno inside him as he contemplated the implications of an old friendship between Donovan MacBride and Adam Sinclair. On the night of his Independence Day Ball, in his own presence, both had denied ever having met.

His fingers tightening around his cane until his knuckles showed white he watched Odette emerge from behind the screen. Alysson bent to straighten Odette's hem, looking so beautiful in the green gown that Douglas felt the loss of her all over again. Loathing fury took hold of him, burning hotter as he thought of MacBride having her instead of him, touching her, enjoying her. The bastard had crippled him and taken the only woman he had ever loved. And now, he knew Adam had betrayed him as well. God, he had trusted Adam, trusted him with everything, made him privy to every scrap of information he received. The bastard! The bloody bastard!

"We really should be going now," Olivia Jenkins was saying. "Before the candles are doused again."

He watched her thank Odette, then bid him good-bye before moving out the door with her daughter, seeming quite anxious to be away. Alysson stayed a moment to hug Odette again. But then, as a stagehand called for Odette and the actress rushed out the door, Douglas stepped in front of Alysson to block her passage.

"I've missed you, Alysson," he said softly so that Olivia could not hear him where she was hovering near the open door. "I've worried endlessly about you."

Alysson looked up at him, wondering how he could have done the things he had done to all of them. He had hurt everyone with his lies, but he had hurt himself more than anyone else. She pitied him.

"I am truly sorry about your leg, Douglas," she said, looking into his eyes. "I've wanted to tell you that for a long time. I don't understand why you challenged Donovan or told him the things you did, but I blame myself for coming to your house. I never wanted you to get hurt."

Her slanted green eyes were earnest, full of regret and sorrow, and though anger ruled him, Douglas could not be unaffected. Before she could move away, he reached out to run a finger down the curve of her soft cheek.

"I did it because I love you. I still love you. You should be mine instead of MacBride's, and someday you will be."

She looked visibly startled by his words, and she hastily turned and hurried out of the room. Douglas watched her go. Damn MacBride to hell, he thought. He would make him pay, pay for taking Alysson, pay for crippling his leg, pay for Adam's treachery, pay for everything.

The need for revenge was an acid eating away at his soul. If it took him forever, if it took him to the brink of hell and back, Donovan MacBride and Adam Sinclair would suffer for all they had done to him. Douglas would never rest until they did.

# Chapter 23

On the fifteenth day of May in 1812, Alysson celebrated her nineteeth birthday and, at Donovan's insistence, spent most of that afternoon in the luxurious shop of New York's most renowned couturière being fitted for a complete new wardrobe. It was his birthday present to her. By the time Madame Bouvier was finished showing her a vast array of satins, foulards, and brocades, as well as feathers, reticules, gloves, and slippers, all in compliance with her husband's orders that no expense be spared, dusk had descended over the city streets.

Eager to be away from the tedious hours of selecting day dresses and evening gowns, Alysson settled back into the gold velvet squabs to relax. Jethro slapped the reins, and she heaved a heavy sigh, feeling very tired from the ordeal at the overzealous French dressmaker's. But it had been exciting too, for she now wore a dress that Donovan had chosen personally for her. She examined the white satin gown with its yoke of fine Venetian lace, glistening with tiny pearls. Her fingers went to her throat where a five-strand pearl necklace with a diamond clasp was fastened. Donovan had described this very dress to her the first night he had made love to her, and Alysson treasured it as yet another token of his love, just as he had meant it to be.

She glanced out the window, anxious to arrive home. Olivia and Katie had returned to Wildwood the day before after a long stay, and though she felt a moment's guilt about it, she rather looked forward to a time alone with her most deliciously virile husband. At the moment, she would like nothing more for her birthday than to spend a long evening in bed with Donovan.

She laughed to herself at what a wanton hussy she had become, but nevertheless shivered to think of the feel of Donovan's well-practiced hands playing over her body. He was such an exciting man, sometimes so gentle with her, taking hours to caress her into a fevered state of sensation. But at other times, he would appear at the door at midday, pulling her off to their bedchamber to take her eagerly, hungrily, as if he could not wait another moment.

Chillbumps formed, undulating over her flesh as the carriage turned into the curving road in front of the house. She was surprised but pleased to see Donovan awaiting her on the front porch. He came upright from where he lounged one shoulder against the pillar, running down the steps, and she smiled eagerly at him as he pulled open the door.

"Where have you been so long?" he demanded, lifting her out and holding her close for a bare moment before he put her on her feet.

"Letting Madame Bouvier prick me all day with her sharpest pins and needles," she answered in mock vexation. Donovan laughed.

To her surprise and Jethro's amusement, he swept her off her feet and ran lightly up the steps with her in his arms. Inside, the lamps had not been lit against the encroaching night, and he carried her into the front parlor where the maids had drawn the drapes, making it very dark and private. He put her down, but kept his hands on her small waist, holding her close in front of him.

"Happy Birthday, my love," he said very softly, his

lips barely grazing her forehead. He straightened, smiling down at her.

"Tell me, sweet. If you could have anything this night from me, any birthday present in the world, what would you ask for?"

Alysson looked up at him, his chiseled face swathed in shadows, making his curly black hair even blacker, and she smiled sensuously, remembering her arousing thoughts during the ride home. She slid her palms slowly up the front of his gray jacket, her voice low, husky, and seductive.

"I would have you take me upstairs and undress me very slowly, like you did last night, kissing every—"

She gasped in surprise as Donovan's palm came up to muffle anything else she might have to say. He pulled her against him, and she heard the low rumble of suppressed laughter deep in his chest.

"Surprise! Happy Birthday, Alysson!"

Alysson froze as the loud chorus of voices sounded from all around them. Candles were lit one by one, revealing all the people who had been hiding behind furniture and in the shadowy recesses of the room—Odette, Billy, Rosalie, Olivia, and Katie. Alysson's face went from shock to dismay to scarlet. She hid her face in Donovan's fine linen shirt in utter mind-numbing mortification as they all gathered around them. She wouldn't look up, couldn't look at any of them, not ever again. The way Donovan was rocking with silent laughter didn't help in the least.

"Don't be so embarrassed, love, they all know how happily married we are," he whispered, leaning down close. But it was only when Stephens rolled in a huge cart with a three-tiered cake and candles that Alysson could face anyone. Her face still hot with a blush that would not go away, she sat down behind a small round table laden with birthday presents. Odette and Katie helped her unwrap them as the others were served warm plum cake and champagne. Donovan stood back, his eyes never leaving his wife as she finally got over her embarrassment and began to laugh and exclaim over her gifts.

The surprise party had turned out well after a month of planning, and he was still amazed that neither Katie nor Odette had let the surprise slip to Alysson. Neither were known for their trustworthiness when it came to keeping secrets, but Alysson had been more than surprised. He chuckled inside again to think of what she had requested of him in front of everyone. Her quick passion never failed to please and excite him, and it was so like Alysson to say such a thing, but always in private. In front of others, she was so shy and reserved concerning the intimate part of their marriage. She was embarrassed even when he kissed her in front of others, which was often. What she had said amused him still, but the time was at hand now for his real surprise, and he was very eager to reveal it to her.

"Come along, English, it's time for my special gift to you."

Everyone sat down and quieted as he went to her. Alysson put her hand in the one he extended to her, looking around curiously at her friends as he led her to the closed doors of the adjoining dining room. What more he could possibly do? He had done so much already. Love warmed her eyes to a smoky emerald glow as she looked up at him. He squeezed her hand, then slid open the doors.

Two people stood on the other side, and Alysson's expectant smile dropped away. She blanched white, then, to Donovan's startled dismay, burst into tears.

"Mathilde, Freddie," she managed brokenly. Even the unsentimental Rosalie Handel dabbed at her eyes with her hanky as Alysson went into the sturdy arms of the beloved old German woman, sobbing on her broad shoulder as she pulled Freddie close into their embrace with her other arm.

Donovan's initial concern disappeared as Alysson released them and went to him, hugging him tightly.

"Oh, thank you," she whispered. "You are the kindest, most wonderful man in the entire world."

Then she was gone again, wiping at her joyful tears as she drew her dear friends forward to meet her new American friends. Freddie and Mathilde smiled shyly at everyone, all the while trying to answer the countless questions Alysson was putting to them about their past year in England.

Donovan stayed in the background and enjoyed Alysson's happiness, having never quite realized the pleasure he would give his young wife, by bringing her friends to New York. When he had posted Alysson's letter to them just after Christmas, he had sent along one of his agents with orders to bring them back or not return himself. Though it had taken some time and expense to track them down, it was worth any amount to him. He hoped that now the sad, wistful look that had sometimes darkened Alysson's green eyes would be banished forever.

In the happy days that followed, Mathilde and Freddie settled into the MacBride town house with Alysson pampering their every need and desire, until they were quite bewildered by the unaccustomed luxury. Amused by young Freddie's discomfort in the company of the women day after day, Donovan finally took him to his offices with him. Once he learned of the lad's interest in the sea, he promised him a position as cabin boy on one of the MacBride ships as soon as Freddie was old enough. After that, Freddie spent most of his time at the harborfront and the MacBride Shipping Offices, while Alysson was pleased to have Mathilde remain at home with her.

On a warm June afternoon when the yellow cinnamon roses were blooming full and fragrant along the trellises, the two of them strolled leisurely through the gardens. Alysson stopped to cut a rose for her basket. She felt wonderful and carefree and happier than she had ever been in her life. She sat down on a low stone wall beside Mathilde, giving the old woman a spontaneous hug and kiss on the cheek.

"I am so glad you are here with me. Do you really like it here in America? Will you stay?"

"Ja, 'tis fine here. Your house is grand, so different from our wee cottage. But dis idleness is not goot. I need sometink ta do. Da cook, she need help wid these huge meals the master orders."

"Don't call him the master, Mathilde. He wants you to call him Donovan. He said so himself. You're our guest here. You don't have to cook or do anything."

"Ja, I work. I have always work," Mathilde answered stubbornly, then frowned as a familiar, mischievous smile turned up the corners of Alysson's mouth.

"What? You grin like a crocodile."

"I was only thinking that I may have the perfect job for you, if you absolutely must work."

"What is it then? Be assayin' what you mean."

Alysson's smiled widened.

"You can be the nursemaid for my babe," she said softly, putting her hand on her stomach. Mathilde stared at her, her ruddy old face slowly giving over to beaming delight.

"You are with child? Does the master know?"

"Not yet," Alysson said, her eyes dancing. "I only just found out this morning. That's where I went after breakfast. To Doctor Whittingham's office. I have suspected it for nearly two months now. I intend to tell Donovan as soon as he returns from his ride."

"He vill be pleased. It is almost sinful the way he dotes on you." Mathilde observed, but with an indulgent smile, for she had worried very much about Alysson in the months they had been separated.

"I rather like it," Alysson said with a grin, but the clopping of a single horse arriving in the cobbled stableyard sent her to her feet.

"There he is!" she cried, and ran without even a good-bye to Mathilde, down the path toward the gate.

"Do not run! Remember *der Kind!*" Mathilde cried after her, and Alysson did slow a trifle, climbing atop a low wall to await her husband's arrival.

He appeared a moment later astride Warlock, dressed casually for the morning's ride, his muscular thighs adorned in doeskin breeches, his high black boots caught in the stirrups. He looked so big and tanned in the white silk shirt he wore, and when he saw Alysson, his teeth flashed white in a wide smile. He guided the great stallion toward her, bending down to lift her easily with one arm to sit across the saddle in front of him.

"Hello, my love," he said huskily after giving her a thorough kiss.

"Hello, I've got a surprise for you," she began, but Donovan didn't give her time to say more.

"And I have one for you, but you'll have to come along with me to see it. Hold tight."

Alysson leaned back against his broad chest, feeling very secure in the circle of his strong arms as he spurred the horse down the carriage road to Wall Street. Ignoring the curious stares of passersby, he trotted down the length of William Street with her to Bowery Road. When they reached the dirt roads leading into the less populated northern part of the island, he broke into a gallop.

Alysson held on to the saddle tightly. The fast ride was exhilarating and wonderful, even though she had no idea where he was taking her. When he finally slowed the horse, they turned into an overgrown path that meandered through shady maple trees to a large manor house. Despite its burned and dilapidated exterior, Alysson could tell that it had been a beautiful home at one time.

"Where are we?" she asked as Donovan slid off the horse and reached up for her.

"This was my father's house." He set her down, looking up at the second story. "I was born up there, in the room with the iron balcony."

Alysson followed his pointing finger, looking at the house with new interest. As she walked along the weed-choked brick wall with him, his hand caught hers, and she remembered the haunting pain in his eyes the night he had told her about the British soldiers torching his home. She could see it so clearly in her mind, a little black-haired boy, trying to be brave for his mother, trying not to cry. She looked up at him, but he didn't seem to be reliving such memories as he led her around the side to the backyard. A short distance down the black lawn, a stone springhouse sat nestled among a grove of hickory trees, and while Donovan pumped her a cup of cold water, Alysson sat on the wall, looking around. For the first time, she saw the pile of freshly cut lumber stacked against the back of the mansion.

"You're going to rebuild it, aren't you?" she said, pleased by the thought of restoring the stately old house.

Donovan leaned one hip against the wall beside her and looked up at the house. "Yes, I am."

"And we are going to live here, aren't we?"

"No."

Alysson had been so sure that was his intention that she looked at him in surprise. "No? Then who will?"

Donovan smiled, his eyes intent on her face. "No one. I intend to make it into a theater for you. The interior has already been gutted, and if the weather stays good, it should be open by the end of the summer." Alysson's mouth gaped, and she stared wordlessly at him.

"Truly?" she said finally. "Do you mean it?"

"Of course I mean it."

She still could not believe he was really considering such a thing. "But you said it wouldn't be seemly for me to be on the stage. You said that—"

"That was then," he interjected, pulling her close and resting his chin on top of her soft hair. "I'll own this theater, so you can be completely in charge. You can choose the actors you want, and the plays as well, if you wish. I thought Rosalie and the others might be interested in playing here part of the time."

Overcome by emotion, Alysson could only lean against him. She could not speak, could not tell him what this last kindness meant to her. As tears sprang, she stifled a sob, and Donovan's arms tightened around her.

"You're going to have to stop crying every time I give you a gift," he chided gently, "or I'll think you don't like them."

"I like them all," she said, her words catching in her throat, and Donovan held her to him until she wiped her tears and pushed away from him, the magnitude of having her own theater and being able to pick any production she wished finally sinking in.

"Come and show me everything!"

She pulled him by the hand like an eager child, and Donovan followed her up the repaired back entrance into the kitchen. Inside the vast, gutted interior, he pointed out the newly built stage, taking great pleasure in each delighted exclamation from her, in each happy smile, for he had suffered much remorse for having been forced to take acting away from her.

"What will you choose for the opening performance?"

He leaned against the wall as he asked his question, hands in his pockets, watching as she walked back and forth along the edge of the stage. "*Lear* again?"

"Oh, no, I am tired of the tragedies. I am much too happy now to ever act in a tragedy again! I will put on a comedy, perhaps *A Midsummer Night's Dream,* since that is Katie's favorite." She looked down at him then, and he could see the beginning of something in those expressive green eyes of hers. "Could she play the part of Puck, Donovan? I know she could do it! She memorizes lines so well! And she would be so thrilled!"

"That's a decision Olivia will have to make, but I can't really imagine little Katie getting up on a stage in front of an audience."

"Oh, but she has a natural gift for it!" Alysson exclaimed, and Donovan grinned as she began pacing again, one forefinger tapping her chin as she decided who would play what and when the rehearsals would begin.

It was later when they rode homeward that he remembered the surprise she had mentioned to him.

"Tell me your surprise," he said against the top of her head. "We forgot all about it."

"Now?" Alysson asked, turning her face slightly to look back at him as they cantered along. When he nodded, her eyes took on a devilish glint.

"I just thought I would tell you that I am going to have a baby," she said nonchalantly and felt his whole body go rigid behind her. The reins were drawn back, skidding the stallion to a sudden halt, causing the spirited beast to prance sideways.

"What did you say?"

Alysson was enjoying his reaction, thinking it was rare indeed for Donovan to reveal any kind of shock.

"I said that I was—"

Before she could finish, he was off the horse and so was she. He held her at arm's length, black eyes searching her face.

"Are you sure?"

She nodded, smiling.

"When?"

"Before Christmas, I think."

He folded her in his arms then, holding her tightly. "My god, why didn't you tell me sooner? I've been galloping around with you like a complete idiot. That can't be good for you in your condition!"

"You didn't hurt me. The doctor said everything looked fine, and I'm having none of the symptoms I had last time. In fact," she exclaimed, twirling away from him and laughing, "I feel wonderful!"

"Nevertheless, I don't want you doing anything strenuous, do you understand? The servants can help you. And you ran to meet me, Alysson," he said, remembering, "and you climbed up on the blasted wall. You're going to have to be more careful with yourself!"

"I will, I promise," she said contritely. "Don't worry so much."

Despite her admonition, she felt a wonderful sense of well-being as he held her tenderly in his arms for the rest of the ride home. A journey which took twice as long because Donovan held his steed to a snail's pace, the likes of which Warlock had never experienced before.

# Chapter 24

Alysson walked down the center aisle to the stage, pausing a moment to watch Odette and Billy rehearse. A thrill shot through her to think that they were all working together again. She looked up as loud hammering sounded far above her head, where several plasterers were putting final touches on winged cherubs holding garlands of fruit and flowers. Velvet flocked crimson wall covering had been hung on the walls. It was still hard for her to believe that in the short space of a month the burned-out shell of the mansion had been transformed into the MacBride House Theater.

The only development to mar their plans had been the outbreak of the war between the United States and England. President Madison had declared war on the eighteenth day of June, and since they had received the news, Donovan had been preoccupied and very busy, often spending long hours organizing a committee called the Coast and Harbor Defense Association, to strengthen the defense of New York harbor. The occupation of the city when he was a boy was his blackest memory, and he was determined never to let it happen again. She rarely saw him through the day while she worked at the theater, and at times, he was even required to spend the evening hours with his committee work. Otherwise, the war had affected the city little thus far. But she often worried about Jeremy's safety way out on the Canadian frontier, as well as Brace's well-being down in New Orleans on the *Halcyone*.

Alysson looked around the front rows for Katie, then remembered that she had gone with Mathilde to the springhouse for a drink of cold water. She headed there in search of the child, passing the area where carpenters were finishing the dressing rooms, greeting with a smile those standing in the hallway before she stepped out into the backyard.

Katie was turning out to be wonderful as Puck; the mischievous fairy was very much like the little girl's own personality. But now it was time for them to run through their scene together, and Alysson hurried down the path to the spring, frowning when she found it deserted.

"Katie? Mathilde? Where are you?"

Almost at once, Mathilde stepped from the corner of the stone springhouse wall, and Alysson went toward her. The German woman and Katie had taken to each other from the beginning, and she wondered what they were up to now. As Alysson drew closer, she could see that Mathilde wore a very strange expression on her face.

"What's the matter, Mathilde? Where is Katie?"

At that moment she caught sight of Douglas Compton behind the springhouse. She gasped in horror when she saw that he held Katie tightly against him, a small pistol pointed at her temple.

"I don't want to hurt her, Alysson, I really don't, but I will if you don't do what I tell you. Both of you."

Katie whimpered and squeezed her eyes shut, and Alysson stood very still, her eyes riveted on the gun at the child's head.

"Please don't hurt her, Douglas. I'll do whatever you want."

"There's a path just behind you. Walk down it. You first, old woman."

Mathilde obeyed, and Alysson followed, trying to

think what she should do. If she screamed, the workers at the house would come running, but she was afraid to do that, afraid Douglas's gun would go off.

"Why are you doing this?" she asked, looking back at him as she walked. "She's just a child, a baby. Douglas, please—"

"Shut up," he snapped, and Alysson said nothing else as they came out of the trees to an overgrown, rutted road. The black Compton carriage waited there for them, and Douglas dragged the child to the door.

"Get in, and hurry up," he ordered harshly, looking around nervously. After Alysson and Mathilde had climbed inside, he pushed Katie up behind them. Alysson quickly gathered the little girl protectively in her arms, holding her close while Douglas clumsily maneuvered his maimed leg into the coach. He sat in the seat across from them, then tapped the barrel of the gun on the roof. He smiled as the carriage started to move. No one spoke, and Alysson tried to soothe Katie, whose muffled weeping was the only sound.

"Douglas, please, tell me why you're doing this. Where are you taking us?"

"You'll know that soon enough," he answered, leaning back with his gun resting on his bad knee.

Alysson looked at Mathilde, who sat beside her in wide-eyed terror, then back at Douglas, disbelieving that he really meant to harm them. He was not a cruel man; he was not a killer. He would never get away with such a kidnapping. Donovan would kill him for what he was doing.

They rode in silence, north, as far as Alysson could tell. A slow-rising panic crept up to curl around her heart as the coach was driven onto a ferryboat. He was taking them out of the city. But where? And why? She watched him closely, wishing he would look away so she could grab for his gun, but she gave up on that notion after a moment, afraid the gun might discharge and hit Katie or Mathilde.

After nearly an hour of bouncing and jouncing over rutted post roads, they rolled to a stop. Douglas got out first, then motioned them down. Alysson looked around, her gaze latching onto the large sailboat tied up on the wide river that stretched out before them . . . the Hudson River.

"Get aboard," Douglas said to Alysson, waiting as she stepped down on the deck. She reached up for Katie's hand to help her aboard, but Douglas pulled the child back.

"Not them. They're going back."

Relieved that they were to be released, she listened as Douglas spoke to Mathilde, who held Katie clutched against her skirts.

"Listen well, old woman. Take her home and tell MacBride I'm taking his wife on a little trip. Give him this with my compliments."

He handed her a letter, then Alysson watched Mathilde help Katie back into the coach. Katie calling out Alysson's name as they were driven away. Douglas limped to the railing and stepped aboard, and as three burly sailors pushed the small craft away from the dock, he gestured her toward a cabin in the stern. She bent and entered the low passageway, backing away in the large cabin as he followed her inside.

"Sit down, my dear, and get comfortable. We have a long trip before us."

Alysson obeyed, taking a seat on a small cushioned bench, watching warily as Douglas put his gun into a holster on his belt. He retrieved a bottle of wine from a cabinet, smiling at her as if she had just joined him for tea.

"Would you care for a glass of wine, Alysson? Please don't look so frightened. I would never hurt you, never. You know that. I've done everything possible to make sure you'll be comfortable on our journey. You see," he said, gesturing to the luxurious surroundings. "I've had every convenience brought aboard for you. There, in the trunk, you'll find all the clothes you will need. I had them made for you at Madame Bouvier's."

"Why are you doing this to me, Douglas? What do you possibly hope to gain?"

"Gain? I'll gain revenge on your dear husband and Adam Sinclair, and I'll have you with me again. I've loved you from the beginning, and I intend to marry you when we reach England."

Douglas was mad, Alysson thought with icy fear. He was really insane. She chose her words carefully, afraid now to anger him.

"Please, Douglas, let me go. I know you and Donovan are enemies, but I am legally married to him. You can't get away with kidnapping me like this."

Douglas lowered himself carefully into a chair across from her, arranging his leg in a comfortable position. He took a sip of his wine before he answered, watching her over the rim. He smiled slightly.

"Poor little Alysson," he murmured, half to himself. "You are so naïve. You don't have the slightest idea what's been going on all around you all these months, do you? You don't know about me, or about your precious Donovan's secret life, and you don't even know who Adam really is, do you?"

Alysson's brow furrowed, not understanding what he was talking about. "I thought Adam was your friend. What has he done? Why do you want revenge against him?"

"Because he's a bloody traitor!" Douglas flung at her harshly, and Alysson pulled back from the cold mad light that had come into his eyes. "He made a fool out

of me! For months! Pretending to work with me against
the Americans, and all the time he was reporting everything we did back to MacBride!"

"Against the Americans?" she repeated slowly. "But
you're an American!"

"Oh, no, I consider myself as English as you are.
England is the mother country, and she always will be.
You would be astounded at how many Americans still
feel that way. England should rule the United States
just as she does Canada, and she will again. This war
will bring them back to heel, just as your father and I
planned all along."

"My father?" Alysson said, sickness congealing in a
hard lump in the pit of her stomach once she began to
understand. Douglas was a British spy; he worked for
her father.

Douglas's smile was lazy, self-satisfied. "No, Daniel
isn't your real father, but you don't know about that
either, do you? Adam Sinclair fathered you, and that's
why he'll be only too glad to do exactly what I tell him
to do."

All color drained from Alysson's face. "Adam? My
father? I don't believe you."

"You can believe it, my love. Lord Tyler told me
himself in a letter, after I wrote and told him all about
your little silver cross and all the interesting things you
told me about your mother. His Lordship's been trying
for years to find out the name of Judith's lover, and it
rather raised me in his esteem when I told him about
Adam Sinclair. He is most eager to get Adam back in
England where he can exact his own revenge on him.
Revenge is the sweetest nectar life has to offer, Alysson, and I'll soon be enjoying it myself."

Still stunned by his revelations, Alysson could only
stare at him. But slowly his words began to sink into
her mind, and everything began to make a terrible

sense. It was true, all of it was true, and she thought back over the weeks when she had been so close to Adam Sinclair. He had treated her with such kindness. He had known all along, she realized instinctively. He had known from the beginning. But if he spied for Donovan, as Douglas had said, he couldn't have told her. So many things she had not understood began to fall into place, like pieces of a jigsaw puzzle.

No wonder Donovan had insisted that she quit the Park Theater. No wonder he had been so angry when she had gone back to Douglas's house.

"They'll come after us, and they'll kill you," she said softly, thinking that if she only had a weapon, she would do it herself.

"But that's the idea, my dear. And when they come to rescue you, I'll be ready for them. I've had a long time to make my plans, ever since the night I found out about Adam's treachery. I have your lovely sister-in-law to thank for that. Just one slip of her tongue, and all the deceptions of MacBride and Adam came crumbling down around them."

Fear slithered alive to crawl up Alysson's throat at his self-confident smile. Douglas was a clever man, and he knew as well as she did that Donovan would come after her. Donovan would walk into whatever trap Douglas had in store for him.

"Sleep well, Alysson, my dear," Douglas said, rising to limp toward the door. "And as I said, don't be afraid of me. I don't intend to hurt your in any way. After I settle my score with MacBride, I intend to take you to Daniel Tyler, whole and sound. Eventually we'll marry with Daniel's blessing. I've planned it all with great care and someday you'll agree that I'm doing the best thing for you."

Alysson stared at the door as it closed behind him, the bolt sliding into place with a metallic clank. She looked around her desperately, knowing she had to escape. Somehow, some way, she had to escape before Donovan and Adam came after her. She searched the cabin methodically for a way out, a window or door, but there was nothing, not even a loose board that she could pry up. She sank down on the bed built against the wall, dispirited and afraid, because she knew Douglas would never be so careless as to let her escape. Never.

# Chapter 25

Shrouding, early-morning fog hovered just above the ground, rising in patches to flit like restless wraiths among the dark trunks of gigantic white oaks and big-boled chestnut trees. Donovan knelt on one knee in the silent gray depths of the woods, Warlock's reins held loosely in one hand. He pressed his fingers into an impression dug by a hoof in the damp leaf mold covering the forest floor.

"We're getting closer," he muttered, glancing at Adam Sinclair, who sat astride his horse just behind him. "We should overtake them soon."

Adam nodded, his face drawn, as eager as Donovan to press on. Donovan remounted, touching his heels to spur his stallion. His own jaw was set, hard, inflexible. He was enraged with a fury that had not left him since Mathilde and Katie had burst into his study sixteen long days ago, weeping and hysterical.

His fingers curled into hard fists as he thought of Alysson in the hands of a madman like Compton for so long. If he hurt her or their child, if he touched her, Donovan would kill him with his bare hands. He should have done it when he'd had the chance. Each day that Alysson had been gone from him, a strip of his heart had been jerked away, bleeding inside his chest with a wound that would not heal until he had her safely in his arms again.

He pressed onward, along the trail of the riders he followed. They had bypassed the road to Buffalo, no

doubt afraid to show themselves there, and if Donovan's guess was right, they were headed toward Cattaraugus Creek, which entered Lake Erie about thirty
miles south of Buffalo. Compton probably had boats
awaiting them there to row his party across the east end
of the lake to Canada, where the British held Fort Erie
near the mouth of the Niagara River. He had to overtake them before they left American soil, before Compton was safe in the sanctuary of the fortified British
stronghold.

Compton's letter had demanded that they turn themselves over to him at Fort Erie in exchange for Alysson.
It was a stroke of good luck that Compton had lived in
the area and chosen it for the exchange site, because
both Donovan and Adam knew it as well, from their
stint at the American Fort Niagara. It lay on the other
end of the Niagara River on Lake Ontario, but their
missions had often taken them upriver past the Great
Falls.

They were so close now. They had made very good
time since they had left, within only hours of the abduction, riding all day with only an hour's sleep at
night. Even with good winds, Compton had not been
able to outdistance them by far, not at the grueling pace
they had set for themselves. The trail had been easy to
follow, even after Compton had left his boat and started
the overland trek on horseback. The ferryman on the
Mohawk River where Compton had acquired his provi-
sions had remembered them well, especially Compton's
pretty blond-haired wife.

A muscle flexed and held in the lean contours of
Donovan's cheek, his black eyes as hard as flint as he
continually searched the silent thickets around him.
They were in the middle of the wilderness now, and
though most of the Iroquois had been forced out of
western New York during and after the Revolution, to

resettle in Canada, small war parties often paddled back across the lakes to raid outlying homesteads and to murder American settlers. They hated the Americans, who had taken their sacred lands from them, hated them with unyielding, unrelenting loathing.

Donovan picked his way carefully along for nearly an hour, every muscle tense and ready. He continually fought down the stark, raw fear curling like icy ropes in his belly, fear of what Alysson had suffered as Compton's captive, fear for the baby she carried. He remembered her anguish over the loss of their first child, remembered his own anguish, and new waves of fury passed over him.

The faint acrid odor of burning wood drifted to him, and he pulled back on Warlock's reins.

"Smell it?" Adam whispered, and Donovan nodded, his heart beginning to hammer as he dismounted, peering through the dim gray light. He tied his reins to a bush as Adam swung off his horse, both men taking time to muzzle their mounts. A neigh or whinny would betray their presence.

Measuring each footfall with stealthy care in the way the swift-footed Oneida army scouts had taught them, they proceeded in total silence, using the cover of trees until they could see a narrow plume of smoke ahead of them. They crouched down, then Donovan inched forward on his stomach, gun in hand, while Adam crept quietly behind him. Thick bushes and brambles ringed the clearing where Compton and his party were camped on the bank of the Cattaraugus, and Donovan wriggled his way soundlessly to where he could peer down through the tangled undergrowth.

The remnants of a fire smoldered in a ring of stones where a tripod was suspended over the coals. Donovan first saw Compton where he sat with his back against a tree, his head nodding as he dozed in the early morning

light. Donovan moved his gaze to where half a dozen
or so men lay sleeping, wrapped in dark woolen blankets, looking for Alysson. He didn't see her at first, but
as he scanned the site again, he saw her a short distance
away from the men, and a surge of pure rage boiled
through his heart.

She was tied to a tree; the bloody bastard had her
bound and gagged. All he could think about was how
she hated that, how frightened she had been aboard the
*Halcyone* when he had started to tie her to the bunk. He
squeezed his eyes shut, wanting to yell and curse,
wanting to jump up and kill every one of them. But he
couldn't get her out if he did that, and he suppressed
the mind-splintering anger he felt, methodically forcing
it all back inside himself.

She was awake, he realized, as he turned his gaze on
her again. Awake, and struggling desperately with the
cords binding her hands. He knew they didn't have
much time to get to her. A gunshot would awaken the
other men, and he and Adam would be outnumbered
and outgunned. He turned to Adam, who lay beside
him, tense with the same kind of fury that Donovan
felt.

"Can you get Compton?"

"With pleasure," Adam whispered tightly.

Donovan looked back at the sleeping camp.

"I'll get Alysson, and once I do, you make your
move on him. Then try to scatter their horses, if you
can."

Adam backed away without the snap of a twig, and
Donovan lay still, waiting another moment before he
made his move. He had lived and fought and killed
with Adam when they had been in the army; he had no
doubt about Adam's ability to overpower Compton. He
moved himself, crawling on his belly, his eyes alert on
the men sleeping in their bedrolls. When he reached a

point just behind Alysson, he moved up close, hugging the ground, and cut the ropes holding her to the trunk.

"It's me, Alysson, don't make a sound," he whispered softly, and Alysson struggled, pulling her hands free, jerking away from her gag.

"It's a trap, it's a trap, run," she cried desperately. Donovan brought up his pistol as blankets were flung off the waiting ambushers, every gun barrel sighted upon his chest. His eyes darted to the other side of the clearing, his only hope that Adam would be able to pick them off. He saw Adam then, rising from his cover, gun pointed at the men around Donovan. But before he could fire, an arrow whistled from the trees behind him, piercing the meat of his shoulder. Adam fell sideways, screaming in agony, and Donovan let his own gun drop as Alysson sobbed and clutched him as if she would never let go. Donovan held her against his chest, his eyes on Compton, who now stood a short distance away.

"You made good time, MacBride, better than I expected you to. But my friends there in the trees kept me apprised of your every movement."

Donovan looked around as ten lean Mohawk warriors melted out of the surrounding woods. Their faces were savage, adorned with ominous slashes of war paint, their scalp locks long and decorated with feathers and shells.

"I tried to warn you," Alysson sobbed brokenly against his chest. Donovan's grip tightened, but his eyes did not leave Compton's face.

Douglas frowned at Alysson's display toward her husband, his voice sharp.

"Come here, Alysson, now! Or you'll make it worse for him!"

Afraid for Donovan, Alysson immediately pulled away, her face white with fear as she went to Compton's side. Compton pulled her against him with one arm, so tight that Alysson struggled to free herself.

"You bastard," Donovan said fiercely, lunging for him, but he got no farther than a step as a scar-faced Indian behind him sent his tomahawk down in a glancing blow off the base of Donovan's skull.

Alysson screamed as Donovan fell to his knees. As the Mohawk warrior grabbed his hair and jerked his head back, Alysson pulled away from Douglas, throwing herself over Donovan's half-conscious body.

"No, no," she cried, holding his head against her breast. Compton stepped forward before the Indian could thrust her away.

"Get him in the canoe," he ordered sharply, pulling Alysson up and away from Donovan.

She sobbed as two of the savages took his arms, dragging him toward the riverbank. She sought to follow, pulling against Compton's grip, and his fingers tightened, his voice coming low with warning.

"Don't be a fool! Blue Jacket's my friend, but I can't tell him what to do. I can't protect you if you anger him!"

"Please, Douglas, don't let them hurt them any more. You've got them now. Take them to the fort and give them up. Please, I beg you. Both of them are hurt. They need a doctor."

"Shut up," he said, pulling her by the arm, and Alysson stumbled along with him, her heart breaking as they passed Adam, who lay groaning on the ground. One of the Mohawks bent over him, pulling him up roughly with one hand. He broke off the feathered end of the arrow protruding from the back of his coat, pulling it out of his shoulder with one sharp jerk. Adam blacked out with the pain and was pulled by the Indians to where Donovan lay near the water.

Alysson watched helplessly as they stripped off the

coats and shirts of both prisoners, and tied their wrists together in front of them, making no effort to bind the bloody wound on Adam's shoulder. When they began to spread the black, oozing mud of the river bottom on their faces and chests, Alysson grabbed Douglas's sleeve.

"What are they doing to them?"

"They always paint their prisoners before they take them back to their village. Get in the boat, quickly!"

Alysson looked back again, but Douglas shoved her toward one of the long canoes of thin elm bark that the Indians had dragged from hiding along the bank. She looked back as Donovan and Adam were dumped unconscious into the bottom of another boat, terrified at what the Indians might do to them. She had been frightened of the fierce warriors since the tall, English-speaking one brought his war party to meet Douglas. As the Indian moved agilely into the canoe behind her, her gaze fell on the dark blue jacket he wore. It was the uniform of an American officer, very similar to the one Jeremy wore, but the gold epaulettes some American soldier had worn so proudly were now hung with scalps, of every color and length.

Alysson shuddered, numb with renewed fear as the canoe was pushed into the current. The Indians dipped their paddles into the river with deep, sure strokes, breaking the smooth surface of the water in long ripples that spread out behind them in expanding V's to break gently upon the bank.

Donovan strained to open his eyes, but he couldn't quite garner the strength to do it, and he stopped trying, feeling disoriented and confused. Something had happened, he thought dazedly, something he had to remember, something to do with Alysson. She was in danger! He forced open his eyes to a wavery, underwaterlike world, then shut them tightly as a pounding pain erupted in the back of his head, a deep, hollow clanging as if someone beat insistently upon an iron door.

After a moment, he tried again and focused upon a smooth expanse the color of copper. It seemed to wave and ripple, and when he finally recognized it for what it was, everything came flooding back to him. He continued to watch the Indian's bare back, where muscles moved fluidly with each paddlestroke, feigning unconsciousness as he tried to think. A moment later he realized that Adam lay in the bottom of the boat, slumped near Donovan's feet. At first, Donovan thought he was dead, and then he saw the slight rising and falling of his chest. Dried blood covered his shoulder and chest over some kind of blackish-gray paint, and Donovan saw then that he was covered with the mud himself. It had dried in the sun, making his flesh tight and uncomfortable.

He moved his eyes slightly, aware by the sounds behind him that at least two other Indians paddled in the stern. From what he could tell, they were already on Lake Erie, and he tried to estimate how long he had been unconscious. By the position of the sun, it appeared to be well past noon. They were heading northwest, probably toward the Niagara River.

Easing up his head just enough to see the boat in front of him, he saw Alysson in the lead canoe, the sun glinting off her bright hair. She was all right. He licked parched lips. He had to think what to do. He had to regain his strength enough to find a way to escape with her.

The journey continued, the sun burning down on the calm surface of Lake Erie, the Mohawks tireless in their paddling. As the afternoon lengthened, the pounding in Donovan's head gradually became a dull ache, and Adam began to show feeble signs of life, with muffled moans or gasps of pain.

The sun was low in the western sky when they paddled through the shadow of Fort Erie, close enough for Donovan to make out the scarlet coats of the British soldiers high atop the walls. There was no attempt made to land there, and the party of canoes passed unmolested into the channel of the Niagara River. Since they had bypassed the fort, Donovan did not know their destination, but he did know the American stronghold of Black Rock lay ahead on the United States side of the river. If they did manage an escape, that would be their only chance. Fort Niagara and Jeremy lay too far away, miles past the Great Falls. Donovan knew that Compton would have to land soon, because the Niagara River was unnavigable after it forked around a large piece of wooded land. Goat Island sat at midpoint in the river just before the waters plummeted hundreds of feet over a horseshoe-shaped fall on the Canadian side and a similar drop near the American side.

When they passed Black Rock, the Indians kept their craft very close to the Canadian shoreline, far out of the reach of the American guns. Donovan began to frown as they proceeded farther downriver in the current of the river. They were getting very close to the falls now; he could see the trees looming up on one end of Goat Island, could hear the distant thunder of millions of tons of falling water.

When the rippling white rapids that slanted across the river a mile or so from the falls came into sight, Donovan was able to see the cloud of white mist rising where the river poured in its rushing, boiling torrent to the lower river channel. He breathed easier as the Mohawks shifted their course before the prows of their canoes could enter the rapids, angling toward a small island near the Canadian bank. The Dufferin Islands, he remembered, and as they came closer to the banks, he could see where an Indian village of longhouses and crude log huts was clustered on one shore. As they glided closer, one of the Indians behind Donovan gave a shrill cry like the staccato barking of a fox. Women and children spilled from the village to greet the returning war party. Donovan slowly pushed himself into a sitting position as the canoes were beached upon a sandy stretch of the bank.

Donovan was pulled roughly out of the canoe, and Adam groaned pitiably as he was jerked out of the boat to be ducked beneath the water several times to revive him. The warriors dragged him to Donovan's side, and Adam slumped forward, barely able to stand.

Donovan's eyes were on Compton as he led Alysson toward a wide clearing in the middle of the lodges, all the while working to free his wrists from the cords that were binding him. During the last hour he had managed to work them loose, and he continued to twist at them, down low where no one could notice. The Indian women and children gathered around the newly arrived prisoners, pelting them with rocks and dog dung, while they shouted curses and insults at the hated Long Knives.

A call from the blue-coated chief stopped the harassment, and the tormentors ran to arm themselves with sticks and rocks, then formed into two long lines facing each other. Donovan knew then what fate was planned for Adam and him. A gauntlet, he thought, a chill passing over him. They were going to have to run the gauntlet.

# Chapter 26

Alysson stood next to Douglas, trying to understand what was being said as excited Indians surrounded them. Many of the Mohawk words were similar enough to Macomi's Seneca tongue that she could pick up snatches, but they were speaking very fast and she understood little other than that it was the prisoners about whom they spoke.

Trembling all over, she stared at the three tall stakes driven into the ground in the middle of the ceremonial grounds, charred black, and it was then she remembered Macomi's tales of the barbarous Iroquois custom of burning prisoners alive. She felt faint as she tried to see Donovan and Adam down near the river. All the villagers were lined up now in front of Adam, and she jerked her eyes around as Douglas took hold of her arm.

"I don't think you should watch the gauntlet. It's not a pretty sight," he said.

Alysson's heart stood still at his words. Macomi had explained the gauntlet in gory detail back at Wildwood. Alysson started to run down toward Donovan. Douglas caught her fast, holding both her arms as she tried to twist away.

"No, let me go, I won't let them do it, please, we've got to stop it!"

"You can't stop it and neither can I. Let me take you inside the lodge before they start."

"No!" she cried, but her words were drowned out by the beginning of the drums and turtle-shell rattles.

Alysson turned her terrified gaze on the shouting women and children. Each one held a weapon of some kind, a few older youths at the far end holding thick cudgels the size of Alysson's wrist. She covered her mouth with her hands, tasting the bitterness of bile rising in the back of her throat as Adam was given a hard shove by the Indian beside him. He stumbled blindly into the far end of the deadly corridor, and Alysson groaned in pure horror as the women there raised their sticks and clubs, raining blows on his back and wounded shoulder.

"No, no, stop," she cried, sobbing as Adam tried to move forward, making a weak attempt to cover his head with his tied hands. He fell once, somehow managing to get up, despite the blows landing viciously all over his bare back. He staggered forward again, but did not make it a yard when he was again driven to his knees.

"Stop it, stop it!" Alysson screamed, but no one could hear her for a great cheer went up as Adam finally fell to the ground and lay still.

A commotion at the far end of the gauntlet sent her tear-blurred eyes back to Donovan, and she saw him jerk away from his captor, snapping the ropes that held his wrists as he spun toward the unsuspecting warrior. One iron-knuckled fist into the Indian's jaw sent the Mohawk flying backward, but Donovan ran for the queue of stick-wielding women and boys. He rammed a young warrior at the end of the line with his shoulder, knocking him to his back, and Alysson cried out with joy as Donovan wrested the heavy club from the boy's hand.

With a great cry of rage he swung it in a wide arc around him, sending terrified Mohawks scattering in every direction away from the big white man. As he reached Adam, he jerked him up bodily and slung him over one shoulder, his eyes on Alysson's place where Compton still held her.

"Damn him!" Compton shouted, releasing his grip on her to jerk his pistol out of his belt.

"No!" Alysson cried as he aimed it at Donovan's chest. She knocked his arm upward, and when the gun fired harmlessly into the air, she lunged away toward Donovan. Douglas caught her again, and she struggled impotently as a swarm of armed Mohawk warriors surrounded Donovan. Adam was jerked from his grip, and then there was a great deal of confusion and shouting everywhere as Donovan was pulled off in the midst of the angry Indians.

Douglas cursed, pushing Alysson into the nearest lodge.

"Keep her inside," he yelled to a young warrior near them, and headed at a limping run toward the crowd around Donovan.

The young Mohawk sat down at the entrance, watching her, and Alysson looked around the long narrow house, helpless to do anything. She paced back and forth, upset, terrified for Donovan. It had grown very quiet outside now, and she stopped, trying to see out the flap. What were they doing to him? She thought in agonizing desperation. Where had they taken him?

It seemed a hundred years passed while she waited there. Twilight descended over the quiet camp; the only sounds detectable were the rush of the river and the distant roar of the falls. When it was very dark, the Indian youth made a fire in the center of the lodge. Alysson moved to it, then whirled as two warriors entered, carrying Adam between them. They laid him on a racklike bed covered with deerskins that was built against the wall, then left again, taking the younger guard with them.

Alysson ran to her father and gently turned his face toward her. He groaned in agony, and she leaned down close to him.

"Adam? It's Alysson. Can you hear me?"

Even in the dim light, she could see that his face was so bruised and swollen that it was hardly recognizable. Tears rolled down her cheeks as he tried to speak.

"Alysson?" he managed through cracked, dry lips.

"Yes, I'm here," she whispered, blotting gently at some of the deep cuts on his face and chest with the end of her skirt.

"I'm sorry, so sorry . . . I tried to find you . . . find your mother, I loved her," he mumbled, his labored words sliding into an incoherent slur.

"I know, please don't try to talk, try to rest."

He slipped back into unconsciousness almost at once, and Alysson tore strips of fabric from her skirt, trying to bind his bleeding shoulder as best she could. He had lost so much blood, so much. He couldn't die, she thought, he couldn't die. Not before they could talk. Not before they had gotten to know one another as a father and daughter. Please, she prayed, please let him live.

The sound of faraway drums and chanting suddenly came to her, and she jumped up in alarm, running to the flap. The boy still sat outside, blocking her escape, but she could see the glow of a fire against the dark night sky. She put one hand over her mouth as nausea engulfed her. What if Donovan was there, tied to a stake? The idea was too painful to bear, and she paced anxiously, checking on Adam who breathed in rapid, shallow gasps.

"Come," a voice said from the door, and Alysson turned to see two old women standing there.

She hesitated, looking at Adam, but each of them took her by the arm and pulled her outside.

"Where are you taking me?" she whispered in Seneca, but they said nothing, pulling her through the darkness of the village. The moon was very full and bright, glittering on the river as they stopped in front of a small hut on the bank of the cove. She slapped at them as they began to pull off her ragged skirt and petticoats, but they persevered with their task until she was thrust naked and trembling into the hut.

Terrified, she went to her knees, covering herself with her arms, but there was no one inside. It was hot, stifling hot, and perspiration broke out all over her skin as she huddled in one corner, afraid of what was going to happen to her. Not long after, the same two women came for her, pulling her outside and into the cold water of the river, without a word spoken.

The water was frigid, a shock to her overheated body, and she came up sputtering and shivering, only to be pulled out and dried with a soft cloth. She was given a long fringed tunic of some soft animal skin, then taken to a lodge nearby.

It was pitch-black inside, and she could feel some kind of soft fur beneath her feet. She backed into the farthest corner away from the door, sure now that she had been prepared for one of the Indians, perhaps the blue-jacketed chief. She knew it instinctively, and she quivered all over, holding her stomach, thinking of the baby she carried, terrified for it, terrified for Donovan.

She tensed as a tall figure appeared in the door of the lodge, pressing herself farther away as he moved into silhouette and she saw the feathers of his scalp lock. She inched down the wall away from him as he stepped into the darkness of the lodge.

"Alysson? Where are you?"

It was Donovan's voice, Donovan's beloved voice,

and she sobbed out his name in joy. He came to her, his strong arms bringing her tight against his chest, and she clutched him desperately, afraid that he was a dream, that she would awaken and he would be gone.

"Are you all right?" he asked softly, holding her trembling body close.

"Yes, but I was so scared for you," she mumbled against his chest. "I thought they would kill you, burn you . . ."

"Sssh, sweet, we are safe now, both of us. I am one of them."

"One of them? What do you mean?"

"They were impressed that I destroyed their gauntlet. They said I had the soul of a Mohawk and adopted me into the tribe. That's what the singing and chanting was about."

"But they were going to kill you. They were going to make you run the gauntlet!"

"Their ways are hard to understand, but we've got to leave here now while they're having the feast. Compton's trying to get the chief to turn me over to the English, but when I told them you carried my child, they let me come to you."

"Yes, we must go quickly, but what about Adam? We can't move him. He's hurt too badly."

Donovan pressed her head against his chest, his voice low and sorrowful.

"He's gone, Alysson. I just saw him. The beating was just too much for him."

Alysson went rigid in his arms, then wept against his chest. Donovan held her, but his eyes were on the door, afraid Compton would do something to prevent their leaving.

"I'm sorry, my love, but Adam's gone now and there's nothing we can do for him. I've got to get you out of here. If the British take me, Compton will take you with him. We've got to get to the other side of the river where we'll be safe."

Alysson tried to stop crying as he helped her up, but the tears continued as they stepped outside. No one was in sight, and Donovan led her quickly between the lodges to the beach. The river stretched down to the falls in a silvery ribbon, the full moon hanging low in the sky. Donovan hurriedly helped Alysson into one of the canoes.

"Hold it, MacBride. You aren't going anywhere."

Donovan whipped around to find Douglas a few yards away, moonlight glinting on the pistol in his hand. He wasted no more time, shoving the canoe into the water as he leapt into the stern. Douglas pulled the trigger, but the bullet missed Donovan where he hunched low, paddling as hard as he could.

"He's coming after us," Alysson cried, able to see Douglas pushing a boat into the water. Donovan thrust his paddle deeper, angling the lightweight craft upriver against the current toward the opposite bank. He had to go wide, keeping upriver from the rapids that led to the falls, but the current was strong, pushing the boat back toward Goat Island. He could not risk getting any closer to the island, and he leaned lower, using every ounce of his strength. They were past the midpoint of the fork that wound along the American bank when the crack of Compton's gun came from behind them. Donovan leaned forward, protecting Alysson with his body, but the moment he stopped paddling, his momentum was lost. The canoe turned dangerously, sliding sideways and backward, sending them farther down the narrow channel that led to the American falls. Before Donovan could right the boat and begin to paddle again, Compton came alongside, grabbing at the side of their canoe.

Alysson clung to the sides of the rocking craft as

Donovan cursed, swinging his fist to backhand Douglas. The blow knocked Douglas away from them, but to Donovan's stark horror, the other canoe upended, flinging Compton into the water and ramming the paper-thin side of their own boat.

Alysson screamed as the flimsy canoe began to sink, but her cry was ended abruptly as the boat went over, dumping both Donovan and her into the water. She came up choking and gasping as she tried to swim in the perilous current.

"Donovan!" she cried, her words flung away by rushing water and wind. Donovan fought desperately toward her as they were swept on toward the falls. He finally managed to reach her, clutching one hand to the back of her tunic. They had already bypassed the small island that lay between Goat Island and the shore, and he fought his way toward an uprooted tree that had been jammed sideways from the shore. It was the only chance they had, and with superhuman effort, he lunged at its branches as they were swept past it. Somehow he managed to grab hold of a submerged branch. He held Alysson tightly, getting her body between his arms, hearing her screams of fear. But even as he held her there, safe for a moment, he could feel the tree swaying from their combined weight as the steady current pounded at its anchoring. They had little time before it gave way. He saw Compton then, flailing his arms in the water, trying to reach them.

"Hold on to the tree, Alysson! Hold on!" Donovan yelled over the roar of the river.

Alysson clutched it, her cheek against the rough wet bark, water gurgling and splashing over her head. Donovan held her securely there, reaching out his hand toward Compton. When Douglas was an arm's length away, the tree shifted, breaking Donovan's grip. Compton was swept past them. Donovan held Alysson with one arm and the tree limb with the other, helpless-now to help Compton as he was taken with increasing velocity toward the Great Falls.

Donovan shut his eyes as the other man disappeared into the white mist at the edge of the thundering water. He wasted no more time, knowing their fragile lifeline could snap at any moment.

"Lock your arms around my neck," he said, pulling hand over hand down the limb toward the bank. Alysson obeyed, resting her head on his shoulder, coughing and sputtering each time another wave of water crashed over their heads.

Donovan inched along as fast as he could, and when his feet touched the muddy bottom, he still could not stand against the pull of the water. He dragged himself along the roots until he was able to push Alysson out of the water onto the rocky bank. With his last remaining strength, he pulled himself up to safety to lie beside her, holding her quivering wet body against him, her tears of fright and grief drowned out by the endless roaring of the falls and the thundering of his heart.

# Epilogue

*Wildwood*
*Christmas, 1812*

The fire crackled cheerfully on the hearth in the small family parlor, and Alysson sat on the floor before it. She smiled contentedly as she gazed down at her sturdy black-haired son, suckling contentedly at her breast. Bright emerald-green eyes looked up at her, and as she murmured an endearment, he stopped his nursing long enough to present her with a wide toothless grin.

She laughed softly, quite sure he was the most beautiful baby who had ever lived, then looked up as Donovan rose from his chair across from them. He eased down beside her, his smile tender as he put one large palm atop little Adam's head.

"You looked so beautiful just then when you smiled at him," he whispered, and Alysson laid her head against her husband's wide shoulder, feeling content and safe.

A chill rose as she remembered how close they had come to perishing over the falls as Douglas had. It had been months ago now, but she would never forget the terror, the helplessness, she had felt being swept downstream. She barely remembered the aftermath—she supposed she had been in shock for a time—but she knew Donovan had carried her up the riverbank to Black Rock. They had recuperated there for a week before they had returned to New York. And poor

Adam, the man she had not known as a father until it was too late to really love him as such. Why did he have to die? And in such a cruel way?

She shivered, hating that memory, having seen him fall beneath the clubs and sticks a thousand times in her dreams. Donovan's arm tightened around her shoulder, and she leaned close to him. She was safe and happy now, despite the war that still raged, and very glad that Donovan worked in the defense of New York instead of at Fort Niagara or on the seas, as Brace was doing with the *Halcyone*. She looked at Olivia then, who sat reading the letter that had just arrived from the *Halcyone*, while Katie helped Mathilde and Freddie string decorations for the huge fir tree in the hall.

"My word," Olivia said suddenly, sitting straighter in her chair. Everyone looked at her.

"What is it?" Donovan asked, taking his son from Alysson to prop him against his bent knees. Adam gurgled with pleasure and held fast to his father's long brown fingers with both his chubby fists.

"Brace says he's been accused of kidnapping some French heiress who stowed away in his sea chest while the *Halcyone* was docked in New Orleans."

Alysson turned alarmed eyes to her husband, and Donovan frowned.

"What else does he say? Has he been arrested?"

Olivia read further, then raised her eyes to them in wonder. She shook her head.

"Why, he says nothing else about it at all. There is a long description of this girl, Chalice, and her eyes are a strange silvery color, but he says little else about the charges against him."

Donovan stared at her, then threw back his head and laughed.

"Well, then, I don't really think we need to worry about him overly much." He smiled at Alysson. "It sounds to me as if this Chalice might have picked the right place to hide."

Alysson returned his smile, hoping he was right. It was time for her handsome blond brother-in-law to settle down and find the same happiness with his silver-eyed lady that Alysson had found here in America with his brother. Or almost as much, she thought with a smile as Donovan lifted their son playfully into the air. For, indeed, no one could be as happy as she.